CUPID

A FORGOTTEN GODS NOVEL

Book Three

MELISSA SILVA

DEDICATION

For everyone that hopes for something more. Something better. A way out of the darkness when you feel like there is no light left within you. For all the souls that keep running and want to give up...

There is someone out there that sees you for you. That sees the fading ember trying to burn bright again.

You are important.

You are amazing in your own way.

You are *loved.*

TRIGGER WARNINGS

Sexually Explicit Scenes

Explicit Language

Breath Play

Mental Health

Torture

Suicidal Ideations

Attempted Suicide

Violence

Murder

Depression

Death

Bondage Play

Fear of Intimacy

PLAYLIST

Love into a Weapon- Madalen Duke

Running For Your Life- UNSECRET, Butterfly Boucher

Drip Off- Austin Giorgio

Eye of the Storm- Ivy & Gold

abuse me- Ex Habit

I'm Proud You Stayed- Isaac Mather

Love It All- Isaac Mather

Drinking with Cupid- VOILÁ

Sin- Ash to Eden

GIVE ME YOUR LOVE- Chris Grey

Fatal Attraction- Reed Wonder, Aurora Olivas

Who Do You Want- Ex Habit

Secrets- Omido, Ordell, Rick Jansen

Off The Edge- VOILÁ, LUNA AURA

Kiss Me Slow- VANÉS

Losing Faith- Nevertel

Bad Girls Do It Well- Ex Habit

Whispers- Halsey

Put It on Me- Matt Maeson

Fallout- UNSECRET, Neoni

Stay on the Edge- SHUNÉ

Carry You- Blindlove

UNETHICAL- Faouzia

Redemption- Besomorph, Coopex, RIELL

Right Here- Chase Atlantic

COPYRIGHT

ISBN: 978-1-998500-23-9

CHAPTER ONE

EROS

THREE MONTHS AGO

"There's someone fucking in the bathrooms." I sigh, turning to my flustered assistant at the comment, and setting my drink down on the bar top. "This is getting ridiculous, Sir."

"What would you like me to do? The point of this building is for people to have a good time, and if that involves sexual desires, then so be it."

"I didn't sign up for this. They're doing it basically out in the open."

"Which pairing was it?"

"What?"

"Was it one of the couples involved in the speed dating event we held on the second floor?"

He frowns and gnaws on his lip. "I think so? I don't know, I didn't exactly get a good look at their faces since they were practically eating

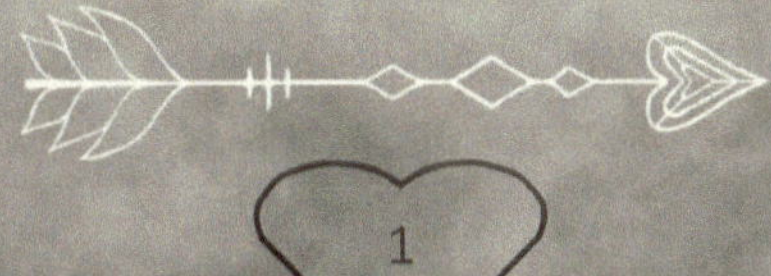

each other and naked...so fucking naked." He shudders, closing his eyes.

"Do you have a problem with sex, Kevin?"

"No!" he squeaks, a little bit too quickly. I lift a brow, turning in my stool to lean my back against the bar. "I just...I didn't expect to be *seeing* it."

"Have you ever *had* sex?" He crinkles his nose, and I chuckle. "You knew when you applied for this job what would come of these unions."

"I didn't sign up to be watching people fuck in a bathroom," he grumbles. "I thought this would just be assisting you. The idea of helping people fall in love was intriguing, but I—"

"You don't like women, do you?"

"Excuse me?"

"Kevin, there's nothing wrong with not liking the opposite sex...in a sexual manner. I can tell it's not the thought of sex being an issue, but walking in on a couple that way—"

"I'm not gay!"

This poor soul. I can smell the lie—sense the beat of his heart quickening in panic at being called out—but hiding his true-self is just going to make him miserable in the end.

"Who are you trying to convince?" I ask, tilting me head curiously.

"I—" His throat bobs, his neck reddening as he mulls over his words. His shoulders slump and he sighs, dragging his fingers through his hair. "No one knows," he whispers, his tone sounding defeated. "My family doesn't approve of...*that*."

"You want to know what I think?" He glances up, his eyes filled with an internal pain that makes my heart clench with pity. "I think that the only thing that matters is your own happiness. You will not be happy here until you are happy with yourself. If your family truly loves you, they will accept you as you are. If they don't, you will find those who do."

"I'm scared," he chokes out, blinking rapidly.

I reach over and take the tablet from him, setting it down on the bar. "Come here." I motion him towards me, and he slowly moves to stand in front of me. Gripping his wrist, I pull him into my arms, hugging him tightly. He hesitates for a moment before gripping into my back through a small sob. "You're welcome in my club whenever you wish, but I feel that it's best for you to not work for me, at least, at the moment. Go out there and have some fun."

He pulls back and wipes at his eyes, giving me a sad smile. "I'm sorry."

"Don't apologize. I don't want any of my staff feeling uncomfortable and feeling like they're forced to do things or see things they don't wish to witness." I nod towards the dance floor. "That one there has been watching you since you came over to see me."

He glances behind him, catching sight of the man that has in fact been watching him. He's good looking, dark blonde hair pushed back from his face and deep blue eyes that settle on Kevin in front of me. The interest is definitely there; they just need a little *push*. Subtly pointing my finger at him, I let my power out, the golden light of my arrow piercing through his heart. The man's eyes widen and he stops dancing, taking a small step towards us.

"Go dance with him," I say to Kevin, drawing his attention back to me.

"You have a good thing going here, but I think it could be something more."

I quirk a brow. "As in?"

He shrugs. "You have the space, so why not use it? People obviously want somewhere to be intimate, and I'm sure there are plenty that have some desires they wish to explore. I think you could turn this club into more than just a club with dating events."

I mull over his words, the idea forming in my mind as he gives me a wide grin. "I think you're right," I chuckle.

"Excuse me?" Kevin turns at the voice, his mouth dropping open comically. "Uh, I saw you and I was wondering..." The blonde man smiles awkwardly, rubbing the back of his head and dropping his eyes to the floor. "Do you want to dance with me?"

Kevin quickly looks back at me, and I nod, motioning for him to go with him. "Sure!" He says happily. The man freezes, his eyes wide, like he can't believe he actually agreed. "I'm Kevin," he says holding out his hand.

"Luke," he responds, sliding his hand into Kevin's to pull him back out onto the dance floor.

I smile as I watch them, happy with this turn of events, and committing myself to the connection blooming between them. Pointing my finger to Kevin's back, I let another pulse out, watching as it spears him through the back. My grin widens when he takes the reins, pulling Luke in closer to kiss him.

"Rex!" I call out, turning in my stool to grip my empty glass. "Another."

I grab the tablet as he runs off to grab me another drink, pulling up the search engine. I need help with the idea I have, someone with a vision and an ability to turn my thoughts into reality.

"Here you go, Sir."

"Thank you, Rex."

"What are you searching for?"

I glance up at him, taking in his curious gaze. "I think the club needs some improvements and renovations, so I'm just trying to find someone that can help with that."

"Hmm, an interior designer might be your best bet. They can help bring a vision to life. Most actually have contacts with contractors as well, so it's all packaged together."

"An interior designer," I murmur, punching it out into the search engine. I scroll down a bit, pausing on one of the site links.

Beyond Dreams Design catches my eye instantly, and I click it, scrolling through the information. The site is presented beautifully, with previous work examples, mock designs, and a catch phrase that has me smirking. *Where the dream world becomes your reality.*

I have my own personal experience with the dream world, Morpheus being well known, and the news of his brother Ikelos defecting to the mortal plane. The rumors of his misadventures have been circulating amongst the other gods, the most interesting being he fell for a mortal and has been able to hold a physical mortal body in this world.

Mckenna Black. She's been working in the industry for quite a few years now, and her resume is extensive, with clients ranging from homeowners to business moguls. She travels quite a bit by the sound of it, so she would be within my picks for companies. I narrow my eyes on one of the construction photos, swiping my fingers on the screen to zoom in.

I can't stop the laugh that bubbles up my throat when the image comes into full focus, showing me a very familiar face with arms covered in tattoos. "Well, would you look at that," I muse. "Looks like there's no question on who I'll be contracting for this project, Mckenna Black."

CHAPTER TWO

EROS

PRESENT DAY

"Impressive," I muse, following Mckenna around the building as she and her sister, Addison, show me what has been done. "This turned out better than I could have imagined."

"Thank you," Mckenna beams. "I'm sorry that you had to close the club for some of it, but I think you'll be happy with how that turned out as well."

"I'm sure it's everything you promised me. Did the rooms on the fifth floor end up getting finished?"

"For the most part, yes. There are a few finishing touches, but they're pretty much ready for people to move in."

I nod, following them both to the elevator while their sentries trail behind us. Ikelos still doesn't trust me, but Jackson came around pretty quickly, his excitement of another god living amongst them, pushing him to befriend me. I hope that in time, Ikelos won't be so guarded around me, but I can understand his hesitance. He knows my powers aren't just for making people fall in love, it works both ways. I can make people fall *out* of love as well, and I know he's fearful of my interference with his mate.

I have no desire to ruin what he has, and I only use the lead arrows against those who have wronged me, or who I feel is undeserving of such a visceral emotion such as love. Why would I ever want to ruin his happiness when he's known no such emotions for all his life?

I've always pitied him—his less-than-ideal upbringing—but I'm proud of what he's become and the life he was able to create for himself. He glares at me while Jackson smiles, the both of them pushing past me to stand with their respective woman. I chuckle, shaking my head and pushing the button to the club floor.

"Have you found yourself an assistant?" Mckenna asks the moment we step out onto the club floor.

"Not yet, but I have an interview set up with someone today. It's hard to find someone who is organized and can handle high-stress situations, *and* who doesn't bat an eye at what I'm trying to create with this club."

It took me quite some time, and having to cut through a lot of red tape to get a place like this properly set up to not draw unwanted attention. The main club is open to everyone, but the upper levels are members only, which I need someone who can vet thoroughly. The last thing I need is someone sneaking in and causing chaos or reporting my establishment.

We're legit, but I do plan to push the limits right to the edge of the grey zone. The menu rooms will be the most promising, allowing patrons to explore their desires and experiment themselves if they so wish it. The elevator has been modified to only allow access to specific floors with a keycard, and each keycard has its own level of clearance to members.

I figured a subscription system was the best option, having different levels of access and membership fees. The club itself is free, as well as the events I'll still be holding on the second floor, like the mix and mingles and speed dating that seems to be more popular than I expected.

The extra I added onto Mckenna's plate was to have rooms available for staff to move into if needed. My assistant—when I hire them—will have the only other apartment on my floor at the top. It's a little bit smaller than mine, but it still has everything they could ever need.

"This looks amazing, Mckenna," I say in awe as I take in the new club.

"Thank you. I took some of your initial ideas and modified them a bit to try and streamline the way patrons may move and mingle through them. I added in the private VIP rooms but still kept the private booths as well for those who don't want as much discretion.

I'm hoping with this setup, they'll aim to purchase the more secluded rooms, that way you don't run into people seeing things that they shouldn't."

"It's wonderful. I'm glad I went with your company for this because it's beyond anything I could have dreamed up myself."

"Good thing you had a dream lord on staff," Ikelos chuckles.

I smile at him, surprised to see him actually joking around with me since he still seems to hate me. "Yes, it's a very good thing. You're very good with your hands it seems, the construction is exquisite as well." I run my hands along one of the columns, admiring the intricate work he's put in.

"He's definitely good with his hands," Mckenna giggles, and I give her a sly grin while Ikelos looks horrified. She pinches him in the ass, causing him to grunt and lurch forward before whirling on her. "Aren't you?" She smirks, wiggling her eyebrows teasingly.

"Mckenna," he huffs.

"What? Are you embarrassed with me talking about our sex life?" She pouts, and Addison laughs at the disgruntled look creeping across Ikelos' face. Jackson is smiling as well, enjoying the interaction just as much as I am. "You're such a prude."

"Prude?" He scoffs. "I'll show you a prude." He lurches forward, tossing her onto his shoulder and smacking her ass while she squeals and giggles, wiggling in his grip as he carries her over to one of the VIP rooms.

"Looks like they're breaking the place in for you," Jackson laughs.

I laugh along with him, but a pang of jealousy hits me when his gaze softens as it falls on Addison. He kisses her, a small moan slipping from her lips. I swallow, turning away from them as the feeling of jealousy turns to sadness for myself.

I've never been in love. I've never had anyone truly love *me*. As much as it's been denied, I believe it's a curse thrust upon me. I've had to live my life, witness countless mortals and gods fall in love over and over again, but that emotion has never graced me. I've felt affection towards others, happiness spending time with mortals and gods, allowed myself to experience all the sensations that come with sexual desires and needs, but that's as far as it's gone.

No one ever stays or feels the pull towards me that tethers a soul to another. I've been close to falling for some over the ages, but nothing has ever felt like how it's described it should be. There has never been that spark or desperation to be *with* that person, or the feeling of panic when they're not near.

Ten minutes go by before Ikelos and Mckenna come back out, him with a smirk on his face while she frantically tries to smooth her hair back down. Her cheeks are flush, her lips swollen and red, but her eyes show how satisfied she is with his spontaneity.

"That was quick," Jackson snorts.

"I know how to work well under time constraints, don't you worry. I go for quality."

"What kind of quality could possibly come from ten minutes?"

He glances down at Mckenna, who is refusing to look anywhere but at the floor. "How many times?"

Her cheeks flush a deeper red and she clears her throat, peeking through her lashes at him. "Four," she squeaks out.

Ikelos grins, beaming with pride while we all laugh at Mckenna's expense. "Will you all attend my grand re-opening? My new sign will be here at the end of the week for the official rebranding."

"Are you changing the name of the club?" Addison asks.

"Yes. I felt it was time to fully commit to something a bit more...me. Amore will officially be known as Cupid's Hollow."

"Oh, I like that!" She says happily, clapping her hands while her mouth spreads into a huge grin. "When is the official opening?"

I grin. "Valentine's day." Moving towards the bar, I pour out five shots of whisky, motioning for them to join me. "Hopefully, I can get everything I need to set up before then."

"We'll help you with anything you need leading up to it," Jackson says, taking two of the glasses and handing one off to Addison.

Ikelos quirks a brow when I hold one out to him, and I sigh. "Are you ever going to stop hating me? What else do I need to do to prove to you that I mean no harm?"

He snags the glass and Mckenna pats him on the back as she grabs her own. "I don't hate you," he murmurs. "I didn't trust you—I still don't—but I don't hate you."

"I haven't had any real friends since coming here. I've been in the mortal world permanently for about ten years now, and in all that time, I've been alone in that sense. It's nice having you all here, where I can be myself and not worry about my true self being exposed."

"You think of us as friends?" He snorts, grunting in surprise when Jackson punches him in the arm.

"Don't be a dick," he snaps, glancing towards me. "I think of you as a friend, Eros, and I understand what you said completely. I felt the same way when we first started on this project. It's nice to have a group of friends that you can just be yourself with." He holds his glass up and smiles. "To friendships and new beginnings."

Mckenna and Addison clink their glasses, as do I, but Ikelos hesitates. "Nic?" Mckenna huffs.

"To friendships and new beginnings," he sighs, clinking his glass as well. He may seem like a hardened creature, but I catch the small smile on his lips when he brings the drink to his mouth.

CHAPTER THREE

EROS

My nerves are starting to get to me. I took Mckenna's advice in holding this interview in the new office on the main floor, instead of in my home. She said it would be a bit more professional for this setting and a bit less intimidating. I didn't think my home was intimidating, but I guess it's a bit ostentatious.

I've sent out notices to the rest of my staff to come in ahead of the grand opening to get a feel for the new place and to give those who no longer wish to work for me the opportunity to quit. I'll be offering most of them an apartment as an incentive because I do want to turn this business into something more than just a way to make money. I'm hoping to have a good group of staff that is as invested in this endeavour as much as I am, and I want us to be close-knit—like a family.

I've looked over the resume in front of me at least ten times, but I open the file and give it another look while I sip on some sparkling water. Venessa Daye, twenty-seven years old, previous experience in the hospitality industry as well as three years working as a personal assistant. I did check her references, all of which spoke highly of her and were disappointed to see her go. The strange part of it all is the fact her places of employment have been spread out across the country.

She doesn't seem to stay in the same place too long, the longest being about three years before she packs up and leaves town. Am I setting myself up for failure with this one? I want my assistant to be someone who is going to stick with me for quite a while. I don't want the same thing to happen like it did with Kevin, even if him leaving was my decision.

I smile as I think about him. I personally sent him an invitation for the re-opening, including a plus one for Luke. They've been going strong since that night, and Kevin finally told his parents. They were a bit hesitant at the idea of their son being into men, but they eventually fully accepted who Kevin really is. I'm proud of him, and I hope the both of them end up having a wonderful life full of the love they deserve.

I sigh, hating the way my thoughts spiral with the knowledge that others are able to find their true happiness. I'm happy for all of them, and I'm thrilled to help those who need that push forward into the unknown side of love, but I just can't shake the feeling of wanting and wishing for more.

The clicking of what sounds like heels greets my ears, and I straighten in my seat, holding my breath until the moment I hear the knock at the door. "Come in," I call out, cringing at how idiotic I just sounded.

"Hello, Mr. Knight. I'm sorry, I'm a little bit early."

I stare at the women slipping through the door. She's eclectically beautiful, an original sense of style and beauty I've actually never seen before. She's dressed in knee-high boots over pinstriped pants, and a gorgeous white blouse with frills of fabric down the front. Her frame is small yet curvy, and her height is definitely enhanced by the height of the shoes. Her dark hair is pulled up into a high ponytail that hangs down to mid-back, but that's not the most interesting part. Her fringe bangs and the strands framing her face are vampiric red, her blue eyes rimmed in dark coal liner that wings at the ends.

The look screams unique, and her presence is shy but confident in her appearance. "It's no problem at all, Miss. Daye," I smile, motioning to the seat across my desk. She gives me a small smile and nods her head, settling herself into the chair with a lethal grace about her.

Her scent wafts towards me and I can't help but inhale it, my lids fluttering at the smell of honeysuckle and something heady and thick like sandalwood. I open my eyes slowly, tilting my head as I glance over her again. She doesn't smell human, but the scent isn't potent enough to be other either. I can't place the scent clearly, but this girl isn't what she seems.

"Have you recently moved to the city?" I ask, glancing down at her resume like I'm actually studying it, even though I have it practically memorised at this point. I'll admit, I'm sort of avoiding real eye contact with her until I can fully process her smell. It settles completely in the room, leaching into every nook and cranny.

"I moved about a month ago."

"How do you like it?"

"It seems nice enough."

Have you worked in this type of establishment before?" I already know the answer to that, but I'm curious how she'll respond.

"What kind of establishment do you mean?" That gets my attention, and I glance up. She quirks a brow, a smirk tugging at her lips. "A club?" She muses.

My own smile pulls, and I settle back into my chair. "Among other things." If she wants to play the game, it would be rude not to participate.

She breaks first, shaking her head as she laughs, the sound twinkling like bells and settling into me in a way that sends heat rushing through my body. "No, I've never worked for a place like this before."

"Do you feel you would be comfortable in this environment and would be up to completing the tasks required."

"Do I get a list of said tasks, or at least a general idea? I'm basically your personal assistant, correct?"

"Yes. You'll be tasked with keeping track of the business itself. My other staff will answer to you when it comes to ordering things, and I require you to be my eyes and ears when I'm otherwise occupied."

"Do you participate in the events at your club?" I frown, leaning forward once more while she just stares at me. The question is forward and not typically something that gets asked on first meeting. "I mean—"

"I know what you mean, and the answer is no, not that it's actually any of your business if I do or don't. It's my club, and I'm pretty sure that allows me to do as I please within these walls."

"That was forward of me," she says quietly, shifting her eyes to stare at the table.

"Do you plan to participate? If we're going to dive into the personal side of things right off the bat, I think I deserve an answer from you as well."

"No," she says quickly, shaking her head. "I—you don't have to worry about that. I don't...I mean, I won't be participating in any of the events or visiting any of the rooms unless it's for business purposes to observe the members."

"Do you have an issue with sex, Miss. Daye? If you do, I need you to tell me now. I don't want things to get awkward for you and have to go through this process all over again a week into opening."

"Sex is fine," she mumbles. "I just won't participate."

"In general? Is there a reason?"

My mouth snaps closed at the vicious glare she tips my way, silencing me into an internal shock. "I don't think that's any of your business," she says carefully, using my own words against me.

She's defensive, and not in the same way I said the words. Does she not *like* sex? Is there some trauma behind her words that she doesn't wish to share? If that's the case, I might be pushing her too far with this line of questioning, but my curiosity is forcing me to file that away for a later conversation.

"You would be starting immediately. You will be paid weekly and have access to my business account to get anything that is needed for things to run smoothly. I'll have to be told beforehand of course, but I'm pretty lenient on spending costs when warranted. You'll have unlimited access to anything on the property, as well as one of the apartments on the top floor, my own is the only other one."

"Wait, you're providing accommodations with the position?"

"Yes, unless you have a home that you wish to stay in instead, but I'll be asking all my staff to move into the building if they so wish."

"I'm...staying in a hotel at the moment, so that would be amazing."

I smile, pulling a large envelope out of my desk. "You will receive a five thousand dollar signing bonus up front, bonuses quarterly, and you will be paid sixty an hour to start. This is your trial period, Miss. Daye." I slide the envelope across the desk to her, and she takes it hesitantly, opening it up. "That there is your upfront money, the key to your apartment, an access card to the building itself, and an access key to the elevator. That one there will allow you entry onto any of the floors."

"Thank you," she whispers, her eyes still fixed inside the envelope.

"Do you need assistance in moving your things?"

She shakes her head, tucking the envelope into her purse. "I don't have much with me. It makes it easier to travel when I have less to pack."

"Well, I hope you stick around and spread your roots a bit here. It would be a shame to lose you too soon."

"Thank you, Mr. Knight."

"You can call me Eros, and welcome to Cupid's Hollow, Miss. Daye."

CHAPTER FOUR

EROS

"I have the list of what we need for restock in the bar," Rex says, bringing over some drinks for myself and Venessa. She's been quietly working away on her laptop while I work on updating our social media. I didn't want to completely overwhelm her with tasks on her first day, but she's doing well to adapt to the quick pace I've set.

"I can take those," she says, holding out her hand to him as she rips her gaze from the screen. "Has the chef sent up his list?"

Rex quirks a brow, glancing at me quickly before turning his attention to her once more. "Not yet, no."

She sighs. "I'd like to get that order in before noon or they'll delay the shipment by a day, which is cutting it close to finalize opening night's menu."

I grin, impressed that she has enough mindset to see when it's best to put in orders. "I'll send him a message," I chuckle.

"I can do it. It's part of my job and you're already doing more than you should."

After yesterday's interaction I expected her to be less...docile. She's tamed her appearance as well, which is surprising, but maybe she was worried what the rest of the staff would think of her. She really didn't have much when she moved in this morning, two suitcases trailing behind her. I was coming out of my own apartment when she got off the elevator, and all she gave me was a nod as I told her to meet me on the club floor once she was ready.

"It may be a part of your job, but I hope you don't think my expectations are for you to take on so much at once. This is a lot to deal with on the first day, that's why I'm making it a point to be involved, Miss. Daye."

"Venessa." I frown, and she shakes her head. "You don't need to call me Miss. Daye...Eros."

I smile at that, giving her a small nod. "Very well." I push the drink closer to her. "I'll make the call."

She huffs but takes the drink, a smile playing at her lips as she takes a sip. The call is short, Kian not extremely thrilled about the time restraint, but I know he'll get it done none the less. I have a great team working for me, all of them working as a unit towards the success of this venture.

An hour later, Kian is strolling into the room with a cart topped with food and his list for the menu items needed. "I figured you would want some lunch, but I wouldn't mind you sampling some of the items I was hoping to make for the big night."

He hands Venessa the list and sets one of the plates in front of me. I stare at him, and he stares back, tipping his head in confusion when I don't move to try the food. I sigh. Grabbing the fork and spearing one of the raviolis.

"It's brazed duck, with a raspberry reduction inside and a blush cream sauce. I—"

He stops short when I hold the fork out to Venessa. She stares at it, her brows dipping. "If you may?" I say carefully. I expect her to take the fork from me, but she leans forward, slowly pulling it into her mouth. I gawk at her, not complaining in the slightest, but I didn't think she would do something that bold.

"Mmm," she hums. "That's really good. I think some lime zest in the raspberry reduction would elevate it further."

"I—" Kian chokes, shaking his head and clearing his throat when I glare at him. The last thing I need is him starting shit with her. I want her to feel comfortable in putting in her input on things like this, and I'm impressed with her palate as well.

I take a piece for myself, my thoughts on the fact this same fork was in her mouth moments ago. "She's right on both counts," I say, motioning to the next dish on the cart.

"Yes, Sir. I'll make the change and have you test it again," he mumbles, grabbing the next dish.

“Put it in front of her.”

He looks like I just slapped him, but he does what I ask, huffing when Venessa reaches over to take the fork I set back down. She glances up at Kian expectantly, and I swear the poor guy is going to blow a blood vessel.

“Uh, here we have a parsnip mash with honey glazed salmon and a lemon dill sauce.”

“The plating is beautiful,” she says, bringing a slight blush to Kian’s cheeks. Taking a bit of both, she pulls it into her mouth. I’m enamoured with her. The way she savours the bite, the way her eyes close as she processes the flavours melding against her tongue. The soft hums she lets slip have my body feeling strange. I wouldn’t call it lustful desires as I’ve felt with others, but it’s something similar.

“It’s delicious. I don’t think anything needs to be changed at all.” She scoops up another bite, surprising me when she holds the fork out to me.

I don’t want to push her by biting into it from her hand, so I settle for reaching for the fork with my hand instead. I almost drop it when she pulls her hand back quickly the second my fingers touch her skin, a look of panic flashing across her face.

“Apologies,” I murmur, frowning at her reaction. She shakes her head, plastering a smile on her face, but it’s fake and forced.

"It's fine," she says carefully, but I catch the slight tremor in her hand as she settles it onto her lap, hiding the evidence of how shaken up she truly is.

Seriously, what the fuck happened to this girl for her to react in that way? Does she not like touch? Is that why she took the food from me the way she did, so as to not touch my hand by accident? These small details slide into place within my mind, a puzzle that's still incomplete, but I'm desperate to succeed in finishing.

I don't focus on her reaction, pulling the food into my mouth, but no longer tasting it. I feel like I fucked up somehow, and I'm not sure how to fix it without making it uncomfortable. I can tell she's unsettled by whatever memory or sensation that was triggered from that small touch. It was barely anything, a simple brush of my fingers without intention, but she reacted like I just burned her.

"It's quite good," I say, not even registering any of the flavours at this point and only tasting the bitterness of doubt. "Thank you, Kian. We'll finish these up and I'll return the plates once we're finished."

One thing I pride myself on is respecting people's boundaries and not pushing them outside their comfort zone. It's something I need to be highly aware of in this line of work, not wanting to set myself or any of my staff up for a situation that may come back and bite us. I've had my fair share of hookups, and my staff isn't shy with allowing themselves the pleasures available to them within these walls. Some have found their forever lovers within this very foundation. Some have fallen into their relationships naturally, while others needed the push forward, just like Kevin.

At the end of the day, all that matters, is that people who visit my club or work here are happy. This is also a reason why we're thorough with our vetting, not wanting to bring in possible predators or people taking advantage of the desire to find a more meaningful connection.

"Is everything alright?"

My head snaps up at Venessa's question, her face shifting back to one of neutrality with a hint of concern. "Yes. Why wouldn't it be?" She gnaws on her lip; her hands still safely tucked away on her lap. I push my plate towards her as well, settling the fork along the side of the dish. "Eat," I murmur, opening my laptop once more.

"What about you?"

"I'm fine, I had a big breakfast," I lie, trying to focus on the screen in front of me, but it's impossible when I can feel her eyes burning into my face. Glancing up, I watch as her eyes shift from the plates now in front of her back to my face, the chewing on her lip persisting. "You can throw it out if you don't wish to eat it."

"That's wasting food," she murmurs.

"I rather waste the food than force you to eat."

There goes that fucking lip again, and the urge to reach forward and pull it from between her teeth gnaws in my chest. I curl my hands on either side of my computer to stop myself from doing that, but my mind wanders to what it would be like to bite it myself.

I shake my head, trying to dislodge these thoughts because I *can't* do that. Not only has she been clear that she's not even into sex, but she shies away from physical touch—and of course the fact she's my fucking personal assistant now. I can't even consider the option of taking advantage of my position because that is beyond wrong.

She's shown no interest in me, and I doubt she ever will. She's my employee and nothing more. I smile to myself when she grabs the fork and eats, each bite being savoured just like before. "So, I think that we should have some type of gift bags for the guests for opening day," I say, trying to shift the conversation to something safer.

"That's going to cost quite a bit if you're expecting a large amount of people. What if we do gift bags for either the first hundred people, or even people you already have on your list as members."

"Do you think we should do some type of welcome package for those that sign up?"

She nods, covering her mouth as she chews the last bit of food. "You could do a tier based goodie bag for sure."

Smiling, I type in the ideas into a separate document. "I have no idea what to even include," I admit. I have no experience in this side of things, having never actually done any type of grand opening or real promotion. It started off smaller and spread through word of mouth, but I want to build something that is open for people who might be too afraid to explore that side of themselves and offer them a safe environment to do so.

"Well, do you want the gifts to be sexual in nature?"

I clear my throat and glance back up at her. "Possibly?"

"I can head over to Eternally Yours and see what they may have there that would fit the theme then."

"Are you comfortable doing that?"

She frowns. "Why wouldn't I be?"

"Never mind."

She's so hard to read. I'm still trying to figure out where her limits and boundaries are in regard to sex and the club itself. She said she didn't have an issue with sex in general, and now she's willingly volunteered herself to go to one of the biggest sex shops in the city to pick out sexual favours to give our guests.

"Is there anything else you need from me at the moment? I'm going to put these orders through, and then I'd like to take a shower and get ready before heading out."

Get ready? She looks perfect as she is, even if she's dressed more subdued than she was yesterday. She can pull off any look without even trying, but who am I to decide what she should and shouldn't be wearing.

"Not at the moment. If I think of anything else, I'll either send you a message or email you."

"Okay." Carefully pushing the chair back, she lifts to her feet. "Thank you for lunch," she adds, tucking her computer into her bag.

"It's no problem at all." Even if I think the food she ate wasn't *nearly* enough to sustain her. Kian brought samples, not full meals, that's why I just forfeited eating anything other than the small tastes I allowed myself. It's not like I really need human sustenance, but I do enjoy the taste of food for the most part.

"Okay, well..." She fidgets slightly on the spot, hiking the strap on her bag a bit further on her shoulder. "I'll message you when I get back. I'll grab some samples of things, and we can go over what might be best to use."

"Don't forget to use the company card."

"I will, thank you."

I watch as she walks over to the elevator, her posture slightly stiff, stiffening further when she glances back at me as she pushes the button. I don't look away, not wanting her to think I'm embarrassed for watching her, but her own cheeks flush slightly before she turns to face the door again. She practically launches herself into the elevator, and I smirk as I see her jamming her finger over and over, trying to get the doors to close quicker.

She hasn't made any comments towards me acknowledging that I make her uncomfortable, but she's showing signs that prove she's slightly on edge around me. I don't know why though. *Am I intimidating?* I don't think I am, but I might not be the best judge of character of myself.

"Do you think I'm intimidating?" I ask Rex when he slides another drink onto the table for me.

"What? You mean, your looks?"

I shake my head. "All of me, not just my looks. Do I act or look like someone you should be wary of?"

"Um, no? I mean, you're pretty built so I can see it from that perspective, and maybe the slight broodiness of your face, oh and the tattoos, but other than that, you have a welcoming presence I guess, except when you're scowling like you want to murder someone. Yeah, like that!" He laughs, pointing to my face. He stops laughing immediately when his own words register. "Please don't kill me," he whispers.

"I'm not going to kill you," I grit out, irritated with his miniature rant. "Fucking hell, so I *am* intimidating."

"I think you would be more to guys than girls if it's any consolation. Girls dig that shit. You know, the mysterious, broody, I can fix him types."

I frown. "What the fuck are you on? Are you high?"

"Seriously? You scream I'm nice, but I have issues. You own a fucking sex club, Eros."

My teeth grind together, the urge burning in my chest to tell him, '*no, it's not just a sex club, it's a secret way of me using my powers to make people fall in love since they can't seem to figure their shit out on their own'*. Jesus fucking Christ, I *would* sound insane if I said that.

Nope, can't do it. I will not, and cannot, expose my true identity to fucking humans. He would have me committed if I started spewing nonsense like that, ending up in a place just as bad, if not worse, than the one Addison barely escaped.

"It's not *just* a sex club," I say, knowing full well how weak and pathetic that excuse is without context.

"Fine, call it your *oasis*, but a tomato is still a tomato no matter how you pronounce it."

CHAPTER FIVE

EROS

It's like we're in a staring contest. Neither of us moving, too afraid to be the first one to speak or shift. The elevator opened, and before I could take a step, Venessa's 'deer caught in the headlights look', made me pause.

"You're heading out?"

Fucking hell, you're so lame, Eros.

"Oh, uh, yeah."

She looks adorable in a really pretty white sundress, something I didn't expect her to wear since she seems to lean more towards the dark and gothic spectrum of attire, but it looks lovely on her. Her signature dark rimmed eyes shine brightly, like pools I want nothing more than to dive into. I shake my head, horrified where my thoughts are going.

Pull yourself together, man. What the fuck is wrong with you?

Clearing my throat, I shift closer to her, and she takes a step back before she realizes I'm trying to exit the elevator to give her space to get on. "Are you all done for the day?" She asks when I finally step off.

She turns to face me, stepping into the elevator and squeaking when the doors begin to close on her. I move on instinct, stepping forward and slamming my hand against the frame to stop it from crushing her. Fucking elevators are so temperamental. She's not *that* small, so it should have sensed her.

"Eros," she whispers, and I glance down, realizing too late the position I put myself in.

I've pinned her slightly against the frame as well, my body pressed to hers because she has no where to move. "Fuck, I'm sorry," I say quickly, shifting my hips back awkwardly to let her slip out into the cabin. "I didn't mean to invade your space, it's just the elevator sometimes decides crushing people is its job."

She laughs. She actually fucking laughs, and holy hell, the way it lights up her face is exquisite. She's stunning as it is but adding that to her arsenal is proving something to me. I'm in fucking trouble. That weird feeling I got when I first met her is manifesting again, pushing me to rub at my chest.

Her eyes follow my hand, and she swallows, stepping back further. "I'm sorry. I—I'm going to get a cab now, so I'll...message you when I get back."

I frown. "You don't have a car?" She shakes her head. "Do you drive?"

"I do, but the car I had broke down before I moved here, so I don't have one at the moment." I dig into my pocket and fish out my keys, tossing them towards her. She scrambles to catch them, nearly losing the purse slung over her shoulder. "What's this?"

"Take mine. I'm not planning to go anywhere today, so you're free to use it. There's a parking structure attached to the building that you can access with your main card and just swipe it on your way out."

"This is too much." I shake my head when she steps towards me, the keys dangling from her fingers as she reaches out to hand them back. "Eros, seriously, I'm fine with a cab."

"I'll see you when you get back. You can meet me in my apartment, if you'd like, I have a home office."

She hesitates to respond, making me wonder if I pushed it to far with that invitation. Mckenna made a remark after first meeting her, that Ikelos was pissed off that I set our meeting there and not in the club office, but at the time, I needed renovations done to my home as well. I guess I wouldn't think anything of it because it's not like I saw her or Addison in any form of sexual manner for them to feel threatened, plus the girls can hold their own against me.

The fact he thought so little of me was hurtful, not once having ever given him a reason to despise me other than just existing, but I can't blame him. I know how much both Ikelos and Jackson have gone through, but I just want their friendship, and that includes Mckenna and Addison as well.

I'd like to be friends with Venessa as well, but I have a feeling earning that from her is going to be more of a challenge than finally breaking through Ikelos' walls, and that's saying a lot.

"Yeah, that's fine," she says, pulling me from my thoughts.

"Really?" I ask, completely shocked after psyching myself out in thinking it was the wrong move.

Her perfectly arched brow goes up in question, and I hate thinking I just fucked it up by bringing it to her attention. "Did you expect me to say no?"

"Honestly, yes," I laugh, awkwardly. "Between the fact you seem uncomfortable around me, and the fact I just technically invited you into my home, I expected you to tell me to fuck off."

"I would never tell you to fuck off, Eros," she says quietly, her expression softening. "You've done nothing wrong, and I'm sorry if it seems like I've acted in a way for you to think that, but I promise it's nothing against you."

"Venessa, I hope you know that if there's anything I can do for you to feel comfortable in your new position here, all you need to do is ask it of me."

She gnaws on her lip, hooking the strap of her purse higher on her shoulder. I can't read her properly, and that irks me beyond belief. I pride myself on being able to see every part of someone—reading them being important to what I do—but with her...nothing.

“I’ll see you later,” she sighs, the tone dismissive enough that I back away to let the doors begin to close. I watch her, my eyes locked on hers until the metal clicks together, cutting her off from me.

CHAPTER SIX

VENESSA

What the fuck am I doing? My legs are trembling under me, enough that I need to brace myself against the elevator wall to stay standing. I've done well to keep my cool around Eros, but that interaction really tested my limits.

The natural attraction to him isn't surprising, not with the way he looks, but his personality seems genuine, too, and that makes it harder to keep my distance. Well, as much distance as this job will allow me, but it's hard to find jobs that keep you in isolation.

He's way too observant, noticing small things I do where no one else really catches them. I thought I was doing well to keep my aversion to touch under the radar, but he caught it almost instantly. My reaction around him may have been a bit more dramatic, but he's definitely not someone I can come in contact with since he's my boss. I don't want to hurt him.

Fuck, I don't want to hurt *anyone*, but least of all someone who has given me a chance at a phenomenal job with plenty of perks, and the fact he's a super sweet boss. I still can't believe he just handed me his car keys like it was the most normal and obvious thing to do.

Why is he so nice?

Taking on this job may end up being a mistake, but I really hope I can make it work. My past always seems to haunt me, and that haunting keeps following me to every town and every city I end up in. I wish this could be the end of me running away from my problems and mistakes, especially with how perfect this position with Eros is, but hope is a cruel thing.

Hope leaves room for lies and deceit, pain and suffering, as well as room for darkness to seep into the weakened parts of yourself. The worst is when that darkness takes root, clawing and scraping at every fiber of your being until you're struggling to keep yourself whole.

I think that if I remembered ever being loved, I wouldn't feel as though the world around me is out to get me, but I had no such luxury. Pulling in a rattling breath, I step out of the elevator, keeping my head down to not draw attention to myself. It's a habit I need to try and break out of, at least for a little while. I know I'm safe here—for now—and I need to allow myself to live, at least a little bit.

I still get random fragments of my mother, but half the time I wonder if it's actually a memory, or just a dream I've convinced myself is real. It's hard to know these days since it seems like my reality has been warped for the most part.

My foster parents weren't bad people, but they were quick to turn on me when things went south, and they sure as fuck went so far south it seemed like I would actually end up in the bowels of hell. At this point, I think I deserve to be there—the welcoming flames caressing my skin and burning away all the wrongs I've done.

I know I'm not a bad person, but my subconscious actions have made me do bad things. If I could go back and change things, I would. The desire to shift the path I'm currently on a constant nagging voice in my head. I wish I could be normal.

Why can't I just be fucking normal.

The lot is bigger than I expected it to be, with plenty of cars lined up in perfect lines. Grabbing the key fob, I hit the lock button, hearing the distinct beeping a short distance away. Hitting it again, I freeze when I see the car.

"Is he fucking insane?" I mumble, taking in the sleek black beast in front of me.

There's no way I can drive this thing. I'm going to end up scratching it and he'll fucking kill me. Why would he think giving me the keys to a fucking Ferrari is a good idea? Digging through my purse, I pull out my phone, finding his number saved in my favourites. He answers on the second ring, his huffing breaths giving me pause.

"Venessa? Is everything alright?" He pants, and fuck me, why does that sound so *hot*?

"Uh, sorry, did I interrupt you?"

"It's fine, I'm just working out. What's up?"

Of course he is. I have no doubt he works out plenty to keep up that insane physique. Not that I've seen anything more than his forearms, but the way his clothes strain against his body, leaves plenty to the imagination.

"I can't drive this," I say bluntly, my fingers carefully touching the shiny paint of the car in front of me.

"Oh, do you not know how to drive stick? I'm sorry, I didn't think of that."

"No, I do, I just...this car is too expensive to be letting *me* drive it."

"It's just a car, Venessa," he chuckles, and the sound radiates through my system in a way that sends tingles through my body.

"Just a car would be a Volvo or a Prius, this isn't just a car. I'll just call a cab."

"No." The finality in his tone has me swallowing hard. That is the voice of someone you don't mess with, the one word radiating like a command and not a request.

"Eros—"

"Listen to me very carefully, Miss. Daye. You would do well to do as I say. I give leniency in certain instances, but I'm growing tired of this game you seem to be playing. You are my employee, and you are to do as I ask because I don't feel as though I'm asking anything of you that is inappropriate or difficult to complete. Do you understand me?"

"Yes, Sir," I say quickly, not being able to refuse him even if I wanted to. Is this a kink? Am I *turned on* by this? Fuck, I'm in trouble.

"Good girl. Now...drive the fucking car."

He hangs up before I can say anything, but I couldn't speak if my life depended on it. My inside practically liquified at hearing him call me a good girl. I'm not in trouble—no, that's too simple—I'm already fucking dead, and maybe...he is, too.

CHAPTER SEVEN

EROS

Idiot.

I have no idea what I was thinking when I said that to her, but something about the way she acted made me want to demand things from her and no longer ask. Does she think I'm an idiot? I know full well what type of car I gave her the keys to, and it's not like I really care if she drives it. It's a car, and as much as I love that thing, it could be replaced if something happened to it.

It's easier to replace a vehicle than it is a person, and I don't want her going around in sketchy cabs if I can help it. She's new to the city, and I rather she feels safe in her environment.

Glancing at the clock, I grab myself a bottle of water and head back to my home gym. Normally, I don't answer phone calls at all when I'm in the middle of a workout, not wanting to ruin the flow I have going, but when I saw it was her calling me, I had to answer it. It's strange how easily she's changing my routine without even trying, but I was concerned that something had happened already.

I toss my phone on one of the benches and tap my stereo system to start playing again. The beat thrums through the room, vibrating through my body, and shoving me back into my usual mental headspace. I hum along to the sound of Bad Omens—a band I instantly resonated with since first hearing them—and get back to work on the bench press.

My old assistant hated that I would do this without having someone spotting me, but I found it pointless to try and explain to him that something like this wouldn't kill me if I fucked it up. He saw me press four-hundred pounds once, and sort of let it go after that.

Exercise has been my saving grace, an easy and quick way to expend excess energy and frustration. I could spend hours in here, and I have in the past, but since the other gods and their mates have come into my life, I haven't felt such a primal need to do so.

Today left me more frustrated than I expected it to, and I couldn't think of anything else to do other than this or drinking. This at least is the healthier outlet, but it doesn't mean I won't be drinking later.

Try as I might, I can't keep my thoughts focused on what I'm doing, but my body still goes through the motions while my mind wanders. Everything seems chaotic in my head, a jumbled mess that I'm struggling to put back in order so that I can control everything around me.

With everything going on with the club, I think I'm starting to feel the effects of being overwhelmed. A lot of it I had to take care of on my own since I haven't had an assistant in quite a few months, but Jackson has been a big help in stepping in when I needed him to.

They've all stepped up, even Ikelos when I've least expected it. I think they all started to notice my slowly deteriorating mindset, and took the time to bring me back to the present when there were signs I was beginning to slip. While the renovations were going on, I didn't have ease of access to use my powers, which after having used them consistently for so long, it slowly took a toll on me.

My ability works like adrenaline to my system, a form of endorphins that keep me stable for a while after use. With the club, it's turned into a sort of addiction, which I hate to admit, but it's the truth. In the long run, not using my powers over and over will help me restabilize, I just need to accept the fact that I can't keep going this way for long periods of time.

I'm still looking forward to using my powers during the opening, getting people together and falling in love with one another. Seeing that happen, fills me with joy, a small happiness for something I'll never get to experience myself.

I can give love, see love, and *feel* love, but I can never *be* loved. It's just not written in the stars for me, a curse I've grown to accept, but it still hurts to think about. I've been alone for a very long time, and the thought of spending the next millennia with no one by my side is daunting.

I know human touch very well, but what would it be like to say that touch is only mine, that the person by my side is mine and mine alone, to have someone that I can claim as my own, to love and worship a soul bound to me and no one else.

The need has grown into a desperation that gnaws and claws at my psyche, but I can't do anything about it. I control everything in my life and everything that happens around me to such a finite line that it borders on insanity, and I hate that there's one aspect of my life that I have no control over.

The task is the epitome of self-sacrifice. My own happiness forfeit for the happiness of others. All this time, I've accepted it—become one with the idea—but is there a limit to how much I can take? This feeling that I've had from first meeting Venessa is something I've never experienced before, the sensation foreign and new, and I don't know what to do with it.

The bar clinks and rattles against the stand as I drop it down, sweat clinging to my body and brow while my chest heaves. I pushed myself a little too hard it seems, my arms trembling as I sit myself up on the bench.

Maybe I can talk to the others and see if they've ever experienced what I've been feeling. It doesn't hurt to ask them, and I don't think they would be the type to judge me if it's something simple enough to understand. Maybe I'll call them tomorrow, give them an update on the opening, and just to check in with them.

For now, I need to get my head on straight and my flaring emotions under control before I end up scaring Venessa away with my odd behaviour. I need to keep this relationship as professional as possible, while still making her comfortable enough with me that she can feel safe in my presence.

My nose crinkles when the smell of my own sweat wafts around me, and I quickly get to my feet, having lost track of time. She didn't say how long she would be, but I need to make sure that I'm at least presentable before she shows up here.

CHAPTER EIGHT

VENESSA

I'll admit, driving his car was way too much fun. The looks I got once I got out of it in front of the store were pretty comical, but I think I played it cool enough to look like I owned it and didn't steal it from some rich hottie.

I can't keep the smile off my face as I ride the elevator back up to our floor, my hands cramping slightly from the number of bags I'm holding. I hope I didn't end up overdoing it, but I wanted to make sure I got enough options for Eros to pick through, especially if he plans to have different levels of gift bags for his guests.

I'm contemplating going to my apartment first and changing into something else, but the look on his face when he saw me wearing the dress is making me want to keep it on. I don't wear lighter colours often, but I love this dress enough that I had to get it, even though it only came in white.

My nerves are getting the better of me as I stand in front of his door, the sound of music playing, drifting through loud enough for me to recognize the band. I smile at the fact he seems to have the same taste in music that I do and awkwardly lift my hand up to knock. I wait a few minutes, but he doesn't answer, so shifting the bags into one hand, I knock again. Still nothing.

He said to meet in his home office, so I wonder if he wants me to just walk in. Does my key work on his room, too? Fuck it. I dig through my purse, pulling out the room key and try it, surprised it actually turns and unlocks.

"Huh, he's either really trusting or really stupid," I mumble, tucking the key away before pushing the door open and sneaking inside. "Eros?" I call out, realizing very quickly that this might be a bit weird.

It's weird, right?

I'm creeping around like a weirdo at this point, setting the bags down on his dining table before sneaking towards the music. I can't hear him, and I haven't seen any trace of him, but I don't exactly want to go checking out every room in search of him and end up walking in on him by accident. Most of the doors are closed in the apartment, so I can't slip into the office and wait if I don't take a peek.

Maybe the music is coming from his office and he's already waiting for me in there. Reaching for the handle, I startle when the door opens, revealing a very muscular, very fucking *naked* chest coming towards me. His eyes widen and he tries to stop, but his momentum has him crashing into me. I stumble back, tripping over my feet while he tries to steady me, our bodies tangling together awkwardly and toppling towards the ground.

Somehow, he twists mid air, grunting when his back hits the floor with me on top of him. How the fuck are his reflexes so fast? He should have crushed me under his weight with the way we collided, but he thought quickly enough to stop me from getting hurt.

I stare down at him, my hands braced against his chest while his hands slowly slide away from my rib cage. "Venessa—"

"I'm so sorry," I say quickly, panicking at the fact I'm a complete idiot.

Pushing myself up, my chest heaves at the fact I'm touching his skin directly. The hard muscle flexes under my palms, a thin sheen of sweat covering every inch of skin. The urge to run my fingers over the tattoos covering his body is overwhelming, and I struggle to pull my hands away from him. The motion forces me to settle my ass against his thighs, and I swallow, feeling the size and length of him in this compromising position.

"I'm sorry," I say again. "I knocked a few times, but you didn't answer. I heard the music so I thought maybe you were already in your office waiting, so I tried my key, and I was surprised that it worked, so I let myself in because I thought to myself *'if he gave you a key that opens his apartment, it should be fine to walk in'*. I know

now how stupid that was, and I didn't expect you to be half naked. I—"

He presses his fingers to my lips, sending a wave of heat through my body. "It's fine," he chuckles. "You don't need to panic."

He's touching me. He's fucking touching me, and he seems fine. More than fine actually, he looks completely normal. He slowly pulls his fingers away, letting his hand fall back to his side as he stares up at me. I can't really read his expression beyond the edge of amusement from my stupid rambling. I get like that sometimes, the word vomit taking hold and making me sound insane. I can't help it. It's a force of habit at this point to apologize and explain myself because of my desperate need to not upset the people around me.

It's hard to express my feelings when I can't reinforce my words with actions and small touches, so my voice is my only weapon in those moments. My eyes drift down to his throat, his Adam's apple bobbing in a way that feels sensual and slow. Fuck, I want to bite it and drag my tongue up the length of his throat to taste him. He licks his lips, the silence stretching on between us.

I shake my head and clear my throat, awkwardly lurching to my feet. "I'm sorry. I'll understand if you want to fire me for walking in like that," I murmur, wiping my hands down the skirt of my dress to straighten it back out.

He lifts up onto his elbows and quirks a brow. "Why would I fire you? You've done nothing wrong, Venessa. I gave you access to my apartment because it could and most likely will be needed in the future. I hired you on as my personal assistant, and for that, I need to trust you completely." He lifts to his feet, and I back up a few steps to give him space. "I didn't realize you would be back so quickly, or I would have been a bit more appropriately prepared."

"That's my fault, I should have messaged you that I was on my way back."

He smiles, the dimples in his cheeks popping adorably, and yup, I'm so fucked. He's way too perfect to be real, but he has to be real because he's right there, standing in his half-naked glory. His gym shorts hang low on his hips, showing off all the definition in his abs and the muscles dipping beneath. He's not like a typical gym bro either, with their pencil legs and upper body that barely moves.

He seems fully capable of moving flawlessly and with grace, and those thighs could crush a fucking watermelon. I know I'm gawking, but I can't seem to force myself to look away from him. We had physical contact for quite a while, but no matter how many times I look over his body, he's showing no signs.

I haven't touched anyone in a long time, so maybe whatever is wrong with me is no longer active. Or maybe the touch needs to be in a different setting. The last time it happened, I was about to have sex...

I slam my eyes closed, trying to push that memory from my head, but I can't forget his face, the way it was completely devoid of colour, his eyes staring blankly at the ceiling while his heart slowed until there was nothing.

"Venessa?" I startle when he steps towards me, his fingers brushing my elbow. I jerk back, his brows dipping further with concern. "Are you alright? You look pale."

"I'm fine," I squeak out, backing up again and turning away from him. "I'm going to go grab the stuff I bought."

"Alright. I'm going to take a quick shower, but you're free to make yourself at home. If you need some water, there are bottles in the fridge, and the office is off the living room with the glass doors."

The sound of his feet padding along the wood floor has me glancing back at him, my eyes taking in every inch of his back covered in intricate tattoos as though they tell a story. I wish I had just a few more seconds to stare at them and commit them to memory, but he slips into one of the rooms before I can.

CHAPTER NINE

EROS

I can't get the feel of her body pressed into mine out of my head. She seemed surprised that we were touching skin to skin, her reaction settling her right up against my cock. Fuck, the weight of her against me felt like bliss, her body perfectly moulding around my frame. It took everything in me to pull my hands away from her soft, supple body.

I need to get my head on straight before I end up doing something stupid and ruining the professional relationship I'm trying to build with her, but I can't shake the thought of what her lips would feel like against mine. The perfect cupid's bow pout, the delicate flesh like a pillow under my crushing mouth. Fuck, I want to feel that—taste that. Could I risk it? Just one taste, one brief moment of contact, just to ease this ache that's building inside of me, burning like a volcano ready to erupt.

A shuddering breath leaves my lungs as I lean against the tile wall and let the heat of the water pound into my back. My cock is solid between my legs, thickening painfully as my thoughts stay focused on her. I can't ruin this—I fucking *can't*. It took me months to find someone that could fit into this workplace and provide me with the assistance I needed to run a business like this. Addison offered to help if I was unable to find someone before opening night, but I don't think Jackson would have been too pleased with that.

That's another relationship I don't want to ruin, so I didn't want to risk taking her up on that offer and having them all despise me in the end. I palm my cock, shuddering at the heat building inside of me, and give it a firm stroke. Fuck, it feels good, my thoughts wandering to Venessa again, the way it would feel to have those perfect lips wrapped around me while those bright blue eyes stare up at me.

I can just imagine what it would feel like to be buried inside her pretty cunt, the heat of her pulsing around me, pushing me over the edge. My hand shifts quicker, my grip tightening on my shaft to the point it's bordering on painful bliss.

"Fuck," I groan, my hips bucking into my hand as thick ropes spurt against the wall, painting it in my fucked-up thoughts. I shouldn't be thinking of her—picturing her in this way—but I can't get her out of my head.

Is it because she doesn't fawn over me like all the other women I've come in contact with? Most have no issues expressing their desires and thoughts of me, few getting that level of attention, but I am a man with needs after all. I don't *do* relationships, but it's not because I don't want to, I just know it'll never work because my own emotions don't function in the same way mortals' do.

I don't feel nearly as satisfied with my actions as I should, the persistent tingling at the base of my spine starting to get irritating more than anything. Making quick work of drying myself off, I throw on some sweatpants and a t-shirt, not bothering to get dressed up for this meeting. Is there even a point? She's seen me half naked already, and I'm in my home. I should be allowed to be comfortable, and she needs to get used to the fact I won't always be dressed to impress.

I see her across the room when I head out into the hallway, her small frame dwarfed in the large-backed leather chair in my office. There's a shit ton of bags on the table, and she jumps in her seat when I step around her.

"Looks like you did well," I chuckle, peeking into one of the bags before glancing at her. An adorable blush creeps across her skin as she slides my keys towards me. "How was it?"

"The car was really cool. Thank you for trusting me with it."

"Of course," I smile, pulling out the chair next to her. "Alright, let's see what you got."

I start pulling items out of the bags, setting them all down on the table while I feel her watching me with that guarded gaze. I wish she would just relax around me since it's not like I've done anything to warrant her fearing me.

"Explain the idea here," I say, glancing through all the items now laid out in front of me.

"So, I have different things for different tiers as well as items specific to gender. Some things are unisex, so packing them into gift bags should be easy enough."

"What made you decide on some of these items?" I ask, grabbing a box with a very interesting looking vibrator in it.

"Oh, uh...I just...this is awkward," she laughs, leaning back and folding her hands on her lap.

"Personal experience?" I muse, giving her a wry grin.

She clears her throat, her face flushing an even deeper shade of red that stands out against her white dress. "Yes," she croaks. "I just figured knowing some of the products would be useful. Have I overstepped?"

"Not at all. I don't want to gift people with low quality items, so thank you for your input."

The thought of her using some of these toys and other various items makes my cock twitch, my mind wandering to what she would look like with something like this between her legs. As much as I would love to be the one positioned there, the chance to see her pleasuring herself is turning me on. Of course, I would never admit that—the thought alone too perverse to even think it. She's my employee, and I don't sleep with my employees.

"Excellent. Put it in motion."

"Which ones do you want?"

"All of it. I'm leaving it to you to place what you feel is appropriate within the assigned bags."

"Eros—"

"I trust you, Venessa. This is the point of having someone like you in this position." I lean towards her, inhaling her scent deep into my lungs. "Do you like the position I've put you in or not? Do you not enjoy the freedom I've given you? The luxury of doing what you wish, when you wish to do it? I think I'm being fair and lenient with this job as it is, so why wouldn't I trust you to make decisions?"

Her jaw is slack as she stares at me, her eyes darting to my lips when my tongue darts out to lick them. Does she secretly think of me the same way I think of her? Is this attraction being felt from both ends of this spectrum? A mortal and a god, her light to my darkness. I wish for nothing more than for this girl to find what she is looking for because from the moment I met her, I knew she was lost.

It almost feels like she's running from something, possibly a ghost from her past that needs to be removed for her to finally live and enjoy the precious life she's been given. I want her to thrive here, and I want her to spread her roots in the city. The thought of her running like she has in the past, creating a hollow hole in my chest.

"Are you like this with all your employees?" She asks, ripping me from my thoughts and forcing me to focus on her again.

"I trust them. Most have been with me from the beginning, but I needed to find a personal assistant."

"What happened to the last one, if you don't mind me asking?"

"He wasn't cut out for this. He had a hard time in the club setting, and he was battling with himself as well. He had been hiding the fact he was gay from everyone, including his family, but he's doing well now. He's happy, he's told all his loved ones, and he has a boyfriend that cares for him deeply. He's in a better place now, and I couldn't ask for anything more."

"You sound like you care for him," she whispers, her tone taking on a longing lilt.

"I do. I care for all my employees. I don't just want people working for me, I want this to be a family and safe haven for everyone under my roof. If there is something I can do to help or protect them, I won't hesitate to do so."

She blinks rapidly, turning her gaze away to stare at the wall. "Do you feel alright?" She asks.

"Why wouldn't I?"

"I just mean because of earlier. You went down pretty hard."

I laugh, leaning back again to give her some breathing room. "I feel fine. Nothing a massage can't fix."

"You don't feel sick or lightheaded?"

I frown at the question; not understand why she would think that. "I didn't hit my head, Venessa. I barely felt it when my back hit the floor."

"You swear you feel okay?"

"I feel exactly as I have all day." She lets out a heavy breath, her body slumping back into the chair in relief. I don't understand her concern for me, the way she's become insistent about my wellbeing. "Is there something else going on?"

"No, nothing," she says quickly, sitting back up in her chair to begin tucking the items back into their bags. "I'll get the list together for those that are returning as members, and I'm assuming just a general idea for numbers for possible future tiers will be enough?"

"Yes, that's fine."

"I'll let you get back to whatever you were doing."

"You don't have to leave yet. We can go over some of the other things I'm hoping to plan for the event. Please don't feel as though you're imposing because that's not the case at all."

"Are you sure?" She asks carefully, my internal self screaming at the hint of need in her voice.

"Yes, I'm sure. We can order something in and make an evening of it. Did you end up getting the orders out for the bar and the kitchen?"

"I did, yes. The bar order should be in by Tuesday, and the kitchen will be delivered Wednesday morning. Hopefully that still leaves enough time for Kian to come up with the rest of his menu."

"I'm sure he'll be fine. He does well under pressure, so I have faith that he'll be able to come up with something."

"He doesn't like me," she sighs. "I think I offended him when I put my insight into his one dish."

"A good chef can handle critique, and I rather the dishes be served to their full potential. I really want this night to go well, and I hope it'll be the beginning of something good for this city."

"What got you into this?"

I get up from the chair and head over to the small bar I have set up, pointing to one of the bottles of whisky while I glance back at her. She nods, and I pour out two healthy portions before walking back towards her, sliding the glass in front of her.

"It started off as a small diner, if you can imagine," I chuckle. "I held meet and greets and did speed dating with dinner. It did well, but I felt like it was lacking, so I strived for more. Eventually, we moved into this building, but with so much space, I had no idea where to start to create the vision I saw in my head. I had a decent set up with certain things on certain levels, but three months ago, some of the smaller incidents started getting more frequent."

"Incidents?"

"The night I relieved my assistant of his duties he came up to me to inform me that there was a couple fucking in the bathroom." She gasps, her hand flying to her mouth in shock. "It's not as uncommon as you might think," I laugh. "But the more I thought about it, the more I didn't want someone other than my own staff having to experience that if they weren't ready. I had an idea, and Rex helped me come up with a way to make that dream of mine a reality."

"That's when you hired that interior designer, right?" My brow slowly lifts in shock at her knowing that information. "Sorry, she's got a really good reputation, and she actually did a bit of renovations in the building I used to work in back in Cameron."

"Ah, I see. Yes, Mckenna is quite talented, so I'm glad I chose her to take on the task. We've become quite good friends, and it's convenient that I actually know both her husband and her brother-in-law."

"Seriously?" She laughs.

"It was an interesting turn of events. Jackson has been great, but—" I snap my mouth shut, almost slipping in calling him by his true name. "Nic has never been a fan of mine, so it's taken some time to win him over. He thought I was trying to move in on his girl, like that would ever be a possibility," I snort.

"Why is that? Is there something wrong with her?"

"No," I smile.

"Is there something wrong with you?"

My smile falters. "How about that food? What do you feel like eating?"

I know that changing the subject like that is rude, but I don't feel comfortable in trying to explain exactly what is wrong with me to a mortal girl that wouldn't understand. It's not like I can actually tell her the truth, and it'll end up making me sound like a pathetic fool who thinks he's both unwanted and undeserving of love.

Maybe someday, far into the future, there might be someone out there that will finally thaw my frozen heart. My love was never meant for me but for those around me, and feeling pity for myself, won't allow me to do my job correctly. Any moment wasted on selfish needs and desires might be a minute taken away from others who are meant to be.

"Is this a tough subject for you?" She asks, effectively steering the conversation back to the topic I've been trying, and clearly failing, to avoid.

"It's hard to talk about being with anyone when I know who and what I am. Someone like me doesn't deserve that type of love and devotion, and that's something I'll have to live with for the rest of my life. In the meantime, I try to live the only way I know how, and hope that others are able to find the people they're meant to be with. Seeing their happiness makes me happy, and that is enough."

CHAPTER TEN

VENESSA

His words send a wave of sadness through me. He says them and seems to wholeheartedly believe them, but I can see it on his face, he wishes for more. Has he had a rough life growing up? Is that why he feels as though he's undeserving of love? I don't think I've ever met anyone else with that mindset, my own reasoning being that anyone who tries to love me or touch me, ends up hurt or worse...dead.

My entire life is a curse, and I can't do anything but continue to run and run and run, but I'm getting so *tired* of it all. I wish for the same things that he hopes his patrons will find. He wants every single person who enters his building to find the one that's meant to be with them, and that they can find happiness for themselves.

He released his assistant for that very reason, knowing that he would never truly be happy if he were to stay tied to him and his place of business the way he was.

"Your former assistant...do you still talk to him often?"

"Often enough. I'm excited to see him at the opening, I haven't actually seen him in three months."

The longer we stay on this topic, the more I see his expression change, almost like a darkness is settling into him. His features continue to harden further and further, like a wall is slowly going up, brick by brick, right in front of me. The last thing I want to do is push him to the point that he ends up shutting down.

"I'd like pizza, if that's something you enjoy."

He blinks, the hardness in his eyes breaking a fraction as they focus in on me. "Sure, we can do that," he says, his shoulder slumping, and whether that's from disappointment or relief, I'm not sure. "Anything you don't like on it?"

"I'm not a fan of pineapple, but I'm pretty open to anything else."

He makes the call, my eyes widening as he continues to add more and more to the list of items. By the time he hangs up, my jaw is practically on the floor.

"What?" He asks, setting his phone facedown on the table.

"Are you having other people over?"

He tilts his head in the most adorable way, and I have to press my lips together to stop myself from laughing. How can someone who looks like he could bench-press me, look so cute when he does that? His blond hair drifts across his brows, partially covering his ethereal eyes. I've never seen eyes like his, a deep amber with flecks of gold that seem to burn with any fragment of light. He's breathtaking as it is, but those eyes...those eyes push his presence to a completely different level.

"No?" He says carefully.

"That's a lot of food." My control breaks and I smile, shaking my head. "I just mean, I don't think the two of us can eat all of that."

"I haven't eaten all day, and I feel as though you don't eat as much as you should either. Not to say you don't look good the way you do, but I want to make sure you're eating properly and taking care of yourself. I mean, it's really none of my business, but I do worry. Fuck," he grumbles dragging his hands down his face in frustration before shoving them up through his hair. The strands stick up awkwardly for a few seconds, his hair still damp from the shower he took, before falling over his eyes again.

"Are you alright?"

"I'm sorry, I'm rambling and sticking my nose in where it doesn't belong."

"It's fine, Eros, I don't mind. You're not being rude or anything, and it's nice that you worry, but you don't need to, I'm fine. I thought you said you had a big breakfast."

He blinks, his face going blank at my question. "I lied," he says carefully.

"Why would you lie about that?"

"I wanted you to eat the samples, and I didn't think you would if I hadn't said that."

Ducking my head to hide the smile trying to break across my lips, I lift the glass and take a tentative sip. "You didn't have to do that but thank you."

"Will you ever tell me more about yourself?" He says quietly.

"What is it you wish to know?"

"What are you running from?"

His words hit me like ice water against my skin. My back stiffens and my breathing shallows because this was *not* what I expected him to ask. Is it that obvious that I'm running from something? I thought I was doing well to act normal and not skittish or afraid of everything around me, but the fear seems to be deeply ingrained, right into the very marrow of my bones.

"Why do you assume I'm running?"

"Aren't you? You don't need to lie to me, but I don't want you to be uncomfortable if it's a subject that bothers you."

Can I tell him? Can I *trust* him? Bringing him into my mess *could* put him at risk, but I've been alone for so long and haven't had anyone to talk to about any of this. Can Eros be the person I can trust enough to even get a glimpse into my past?

"It's not a good story. I have a lot of trauma attached to my past, and I don't really want to burden you with any of it."

I can't stop my heart from pounding viciously against my chest from the way his eyes burn into me. They almost seem to glow in the dim light, flickering in a way that reminds me of a predator in the dark—watching and waiting for their prey to drop their guard. Even with that in mind, I don't feel danger around him, I feel...*safe*.

"Neither you nor your past would ever be a burden to me, Venessa."

The way he says my name sends a shiver rushing up my spine. The way he talks seems almost ancient at times, the words beyond just the thought of eloquence, but bordering on sophistication. It's as though he feels comfortable in that version of himself but has adapted to the world of today.

"How old are you?" I blurt out, cringing at the question.

A smile tugs at the corner of his lips. "How old do I look?" He muses.

"Oh, uh...you look to be about thirty at most."

"Then why did you ask?"

"The way you talk...you talk as though you're older, but your looks don't match the way you speak." He frowns, sitting back into his chair and putting distance between us again. It's strange how quickly my body reacts to the loss of heat from him. He wasn't close enough to notice that, but it's definitely noticeable now that he's shifted away. "I'm sorry, that was rude of me."

"Not at all. I take pride in the way I speak. It comes in handy when it comes to business ventures as words can make it seem as though you know what you're talking about, even when you're just blowing smoke up someone's ass." He laughs—that delicious laugh that vibrates through my entire body.

"I like the way you talk."

"Thank you," he smiles. "Anything else you might like?" He whispers, the tone teasing and playful.

"Your tattoos. I didn't expect you to have so many, but they're all beautiful, and seem to be really intricate in their designs."

"They are. Do you wish to see them again?"

"Yes," I say way too quickly. "I mean, no!" I try to correct, but now I just sound pathetic.

His grin widens. "Which is it, Miss. Daye? It's not a trick question...if you wish to see them..." His hands drift to the collar of his shirt, his fingers caressing and skimming against his own skin. I swallow, my eyes locked on those long digits like they're the most interesting thing in the world. "Just say it, Venessa. Tell me you want to see them again."

"I—" My throat is dry, and no matter how much I swallow over and over again, the lump in my throat is permanently wedged. "I want to see them," I manage to whisper, my breath hitching when he lifts to his feet and moves to stand in front of me.

"As you wish," he says, his voice lowering in a way that sends heat through my body and the need to squeeze my thighs together.

Slowly—so fucking slow—he grips the back of his shirt and tugs it up and off his body. How is it possible for someone to look even better the second time around? I just saw him, but it's like I'm seeing him for the first time again. I tuck my hands under my thighs, forcing myself not to reach out and tug him closer to me by his pants.

He must be a mind reader or senses my need because he steps closer to me, close enough I can feel his heat again and smell the clean scent of his soap wafting off his body. I can't stop the deep inhale I take, my lungs filling with every piece of him until they can't expand any further. My eyes flutter closed, a small sigh escaping me when I catch hints of the true smell of him underneath it all. The smell is dark, like smoked pine and myrrh, and it wraps around my body in a way that has me leaning towards him.

"Is this what you wanted?" He asks, that deeper tone vibrating through my bones.

I nod, staring at his stomach in front of me, my breath stopping when he carefully tucks his knuckles beneath my chin to tip my head up. He doesn't let them linger, knowing I don't like being touched—though, it's not that I don't *like* it, but that I shouldn't because of the consequences tied to those small touches.

But you touched him fully and he's fine.

"You can touch them if you wish. I won't touch you again," he whispers.

Can I risk it? A gentle touch should be fine, and I *really* want to touch him. I'll admit, I miss the feel of someone else's skin beneath my fingers, the contrast of softness and roughness, the heat and thrum of a pulse beneath the surface.

My hand trembles as I slowly lift it up to touch the arrows etched into his skin on each hip. He sucks in a sharp breath, his stomach dipping as I lightly graze the skin of his stomach up to his chest. His hands fist at his sides and his muscles tense, his body coiling in a way that seems painful by how still he's holding himself.

My eyes drift up to his face, his eyes closed while he quickly licks his bottom lip. I pause my fingers over a small scar under his left pec, the skin puckered and white in comparison to the rest of his tan skin. Slowly his eyes drift open, his chin dipping to look down at me.

"What happened?" I ask, rubbing at the area gently.

"I have a few wounds from the past, small blemishes that remind me that I may think I'm invincible, but this body is still fragile when faced with a greater threat."

"Someone hurt you?" He nods. "I'm sorry."

"Don't be. It was in the past, Venessa."

A heavy need to kiss the scar burns through my chest, my body aching with trying to restrain myself from doing just that. "Can I see the ones on your back?"

"Of course."

He turns and I suck in a sharp breath at the masterpiece in front of me. There are more scars, some which have been covered with ink, but seeing them this closely, I can tell they're there. The arrow theme continues on the back, the shaft of one going up his spine. The broadhead sits at the base of his skull while the fletch sits between the dimples on his lower back.

A collage of lilies and roses, stars and moons, snakes and skulls, completely cover his back, and even though the subject matter seems chaotic, it all blends beautifully. Finer detail links the designs together, the shading completing to look.

"They're so beautiful," I whisper, touching one of the hearts along his shoulder blade with a dagger pierced through it.

"Thank you," he says again, and slowly he turns back around to face me. His hands clench and unclench on his thighs, those eyes of his burning brighter than a few moments before. I hold my breath when one of those hands lifts to brush a strand of hair behind my ear, his fingers barely touching my skin. "Anything else?" He says, a slight growl clinging to the words.

"I—" I lick my lips, my eyes flicking to his as I crane my neck to see him towering over me. I'm in *so* much fucking trouble. I can't deny the attraction I have to this man. My rational brain is screaming at me to not get involved, to not risk hurting him, and to not fuck shit up with my fucking *boss*. A small voice in my head is screaming through the abyss of darkness, telling me to trust him, to touch him, to fucking *kiss* him.

The last time I kissed someone, I ended up on the run, but Eros seems different. Can he handle my level of fucked up? If anyone can, I would think it would be him, but I still don't know if I should risk it.

"I can't think of anything else at the moment," I whisper, feeling regret instantly when his face falls and the slowly crumbling wall visibly erects once more.

"I'm glad I was able to satisfy your curiosity then. Do you have any tattoos yourself?" He asks, stepping back to pull his shirt back on over his head.

I shake my head. "I've always wanted one, but I never got around to it. I can't—" I swallow, mentally working out the proper words to say without giving too much away. "As you know, I don't do well with touch," I say carefully. "The idea of having someone touching me for hours was a simple deterrent."

"So, you've had this aversion for a while?"

"A few years now, yes. I wasn't always like this."

"Did someone hurt you, Venessa? I have connections if that's the case."

I can't help but laugh at that. "Trust me, you don't want to get involved with that part of my past."

He sits back into his chair, shifting it close enough to me that his knees graze against my own. His eyes darken, and the next words out of his mouth are spoken like a threat all on their own.

"If someone hurt you, I will hurt *them*. This is not a question of whether or not I should get involved with your past, but I will not sit by and watch you live in fear."

"You don't even know me," I laugh awkwardly.

"That doesn't matter. I don't need to know you to know that you are a sweet, kind, and gentle soul. I doubt you've done anything in your life that would warrant someone hurting you in turn."

"You don't know me," I grit out, my emotions bubbling up inside of me. They're thrashing against my control, pushing and prodding against the wall I've put up. "I am *not* a good person."

"I'll be the judge of that," he snarls.

"You wouldn't even entertain me if you knew what I've done!" I snap, hating how easily he's able to shatter the fragile dam. "You would fucking run from me if you knew anything about me!" Tears are streaming down my cheeks now, the first sign of weakness—the first sign that I'm officially losing my battle.

"Do you think so little of me that you think I would judge you based on your past? I'm not innocent either, Venessa. I have no right to judge the supposed wrongs you've done."

Just tell him, you fucking coward!

"I—"

A knock at the door has Eros' head snapping to the side, a growl ripping from his throat as he lurches to his feet. "The food must be here," he mumbles. "Come on, let's go eat."

CHAPTER ELEVEN

EROS

I let my anger get the better of me, but this girl is starting to piss me off. Clearly, she has trauma, but why can't she just give me *something*. I don't need her entire story, but she needs to talk about some of it before it completely consumes her. I recognize the darkness inside of her very well, something has buried deep inside of her, and if she doesn't confront her past, she'll never have a chance at having a future.

Being that close to her and feeling her hands explore every visible inch of me was something I never thought I would experience. Her scent slamming into me, that familiar knowledge that she is not fully human, hitting me like a truck. I can't place what she is, but she doesn't show any outward signs of being supernatural. She's not a god, and she doesn't show any familiarity when around me. If she were one of us, I would know it, like a warning bell that someone of our own blood is near.

"Logan," I murmur, opening the door to let one of the kitchen staff into the room.

He glances into the dining room, noticing Venessa making her way to the table with her head down. Her body trembles slightly as she settles into the chair, her hands coming up to rest clasped on the dark wood surface. "Just the two of you?" He asks, glancing back at me over his shoulder as he wheels the cart into the room.

"Yes. Neither of us have eaten much today, so I figured why not splurge."

"Well, hopefully, we've made it to your liking. Did you need plates and utensils?"

"Of course not," I scoff, following him in. "I have everything I need here, and I would have cooked, but we're currently working on the plans for the opening."

He starts to set everything down on the table and accidentally brushes up against Venessa. She jerks back and Logan sways, almost dropping the bowl of salad.

"Logan?" I say quickly, lurching forward to steady him. His face is pale, his eyes blinking slowly as he tries to focus on me. "Are you alright?"

"I—" He shakes his head, blinking a bit quicker now. "I just got a bit lightheaded. I think I need to eat something."

"Leave the rest and go take care of yourself. Don't worry about the cart for now, I'll take it back down later." He nods and I slowly release him, watching him stumble slightly as he heads for the door. Venessa is deathly pale as well, her eyes wide while her bottom jaw trembles. “Venessa?” I whisper, carefully touching her shoulder.

“No!” She screeches, pulling away before I can make proper contact. “Please don’t touch me,” she chokes out, her hand flying up to cover her mouth on a sob. “I—I need the bathroom.”

“Second door on the left,” I say, pointing down the hall.

She scrambles out of her seat, her feet slapping against the floor as she breaks into a run towards the bathroom. She looked ill, almost as pale as Logan, but I feel it was for a different reason. Once again, she snapped at the idea of me touching her, and now my thoughts are whirring, trying to figure out what the fuck is going on.

I don’t understand what happened. One minute he was fine, but the second he moved closer to her, he looked about ready to pass out. Did he actually touch her? There are only a few creatures that affect humans with physical contact, none of which match her scent. It’s been a while since I’ve come into contact with any of them, but I would think I would be able to pick them out.

The minutes tick by and she’s still not out, the food slowly growing cold on the table. I sigh, lifting to my feet and heading towards the bathroom, pausing when I hear the quiet sobs coming from inside.

“Venessa?” I call out, giving the door a light rap with my knuckles. “Are you okay?”

"I'll be fine!" She calls back, the sound of the toilet flushing barely covering the sounds of her sobs and quiet sniffling. The door opens suddenly, Venessa stumbling back when she notices me hovering. "Eros—"

"Tell me what the fuck is going on with you," I grit out, trying my best to keep my growing anger at bay.

"I can't," she whispers. "This was a mistake—this *job* was a mistake."

"Don't say that. I picked you because I felt you were perfect for the position. Are you trying to tell me that my opinion is incorrect?"

"In this situation, yes. You would be better off without me, and I can't risk letting that happen again."

"Letting *what* happen? I still don't know what the fuck is going on."

"I'm fucked up," she chokes out, the words breaking as she says them. "I'm the most fucked up person you'll ever meet," she laughs, the sound holding no humour.

"I doubt that. You're special, Venessa, and there's nothing wrong with being special."

She shakes her head, her breath shaking on an inhale. "I'm not." I step into her, wrapping my arms around her. Her body stiffens—frozen in my arms for a moment—before she snaps. She screams, thrashing in my grip. "Let go! You're going to get hurt! Let me go!" She wails, wriggling in my hold.

What?

She's worried about *me* getting hurt? The touch doesn't seem to have anything to do with her, and everything to do with the people that she touches or who touches *her*. "You won't," I snap, tightening my grip enough that she can no longer squirm. "I'm right here, Venessa, and I promise you, I'm fine."

I feel fine for the most part, other than a strange tingling sensation rippling across my skin the longer I'm in contact with her. I feel no pain, and the feeling isn't uncomfortable exactly, but this just proves there's something going on with her.

She sniffles when I pull back, dropping down to look at her face as she wipes at her eyes. "See? I'm fine. I'm still standing and there's nothing wrong with you."

"But Logan—"

"Logan must have already been feeling under the weather. You're worrying yourself for nothing."

"You don't understand," she mumbles, sniffling again. "Fuck, I didn't want you seeing me like this." She wipes at her eyes, trying to clear the streaks from her eyeliner and mascara.

"I see nothing wrong. You're beautiful," I whisper, brushing my thumb against her cheek to clear away some of the tears. She stares at me with wide eyes, her lips parted. "Apologies."

She shakes her head. "You're really sweet. I know I look like a racoon," she laughs, fanning herself with her hands. "Sorry for breaking down like that."

"Come on. Let's eat and get some more work done," I say, settling my hand lightly against the small of her back to lead her back into the dining room. I smile to myself at the fact she's not moving away from that touch, a small accomplishment that I'll take as a huge win with this girl.

CHAPTER TWELVE

EROS

"Hey, Eros!" I glance up from my computer to see Mckenna standing in the doorway, a huge smile on her face. Ikelos strolls in behind her, his brow lifting when he gets a good look at me.

"What the fuck happened to you?" He laughs. Mckenna punches him in the gut hard enough to grunt and curl over from the blow.

"Don't be a dick," she snaps, turning back to look at me. She walks towards the desk, hovering next to me a moment before bending down with her own frown. "He's right though, you look rough. Is everything okay?"

"Just peachy," I sigh, motioning for her to have a seat across from me. Ikelos flops down in the chair next to her, and I glare at him when he clunks one booted foot on top of my desk and then the other. "You're seriously a neanderthal, you know that?"

"Hmm, I think you're too prim and proper. You need to loosen up a bit, live a little. When was the last time you got laid?"

"Coming from the former virgin god?" I taunt, regretting it instantly when his smirk falters. "Sorry. I'm a bit on edge at the moment. Between some personal issues and trying to get everything ready for the opening, I'm a bit stressed. I didn't mean that, Nic."

He waves me off, turning his head to stare at the wall. "It's fine."

"What's going on? I thought you hired a personal assistant to help you with everything, did that not work out?"

"It worked out fine, but I told her to take the day off. She didn't have a very good day yesterday, so I thought it best to let her rest."

"Didn't she *just* start?" Ikelos asks.

"Yes, but there's something not quite right with her. She won't tell me much about her life before moving here, but I can tell whatever it is, is taking a toll on her."

"Why do you look so...dishevelled? I don't think I've ever seen you in such casual clothes," Mckenna points out.

"I slept longer than I normally would and felt exhausted when I was finally able to drag myself out of bed. I doubt I'm coming down with something, but who knows."

"Gods don't get sick like that, Eros," Ikelos states, turning his head to look at me. He drops his feet, leaning in closer to me over the desk. "If you're feeling off, that's more than likely a power issue. Have you been overusing?"

I shake my head. "I've barely used it since closing down for renovations."

"Have you come in contact with anyone supernatural?" When I don't respond right away, his brow goes up. "Explain."

I sigh, settling back into my chair and tipping my head back to stare at the ceiling. My mind feels a bit cloudy this morning, but there really shouldn't be any reason for that. "Venessa isn't human, at least not completely. I can't figure out what she is, but there's something off about her. I can't figure out the scent on her."

"Your new assistant? You hired someone without doing a background check?" He asks, but the words have a bite to them.

"I *did* a background check and she's clean, at least on the surface. I didn't think I would have to deep dive someone for this position. She's hiding something, I just need to figure out what it is."

"Eros, if she poses a danger to you—"

"No," I snap, glancing at Mckenna, who closes her mouth and turns to look at Ikelos. "I have it under control. She's not dangerous, she's just scared, and I think a little confused. I don't actually believe she even *knows* that she's supernatural."

"I think you need to do a bit of research. It's not to say you need to fire her just yet, but if she's refusing to disclose information that could be important, you need to find out what you can."

"Fine, I'll do it."

"You're going to do it yourself?"

I glare at him. "Who else am I going to ask to do it? I can't exactly trust my very *human* staff to look into her, just to find out that she is in fact supernatural."

Ikelos sighs, tucking his hands behind his head. "Fine. Jackson and I will help you. He's pretty handy with a computer, and I've gotten better over the years. The both of us can also phase through planes if we need to actually physically go anywhere in order to dig deeper."

I stare at him in shock. Ikelos, the god of fucking nightmares, the same god that wanted to murder me for even *looking* at his mate in a way he didn't approve of, is offering to help *me*. Am I dreaming? Has Morpheus slipped into this realm as well and decided to completely fuck with me because there's no way this is actually happening.

"Eros?" I blink, focusing in on Ikelos frowning at me. "You good?"

"You're serious? You're actually offering to help me? I thought you fucking hated me."

Mckenna smirks when Ikelos rolls his eyes. "I don't *hate* you—hate is a strong word. I just didn't trust you...in the beginning. You've grown on me, and I sort of feel bad for you. I couldn't imagine continuing the life I was living before and not having someone to share the best moments with."

Those words hit me hard, slamming into my chest and stealing the air from my lungs. I know he didn't say them to hurt me, but it doesn't stop them from cutting deeply.

"I appreciate you, Ikelos. I hope you know that."

“What are friends for?” He grins, and those words settle into me, easing the burn from his previous comment. He’s my friend. The fact he’s actually acknowledging it, out loud and in front of his mate as a witness, means more to me than I think he even realizes.

“Friend,” I smile, reaching across the table to hold my hand out to him. He stares at it for longer than I had hoped, but ends up taking it, giving it a firm shake. “Now,” I smile, leaning back into my chair. “Will you be confirming your attendance to the opening?”

“We wouldn’t miss it, Eros,” Mckenna smiles. “Assuming it’s formal attire?”

“You can wear whatever you wish, Mckenna. I know you’ll look lovely either way.”

“Watch it,” Ikelos growls.

“Oh, stop it. You can’t get mad at me for acknowledging the fact your mate is gorgeous no matter what she wears. I just want her to come and enjoy herself, wearing whatever she’s comfortable in.”

His face softens at that. “I agree, she should wear what she wants.”

I feel as though this is a topic that has been covered in the past, and the way she looks at him—with nothing but love and adoration in her eyes—proves that they are the perfect match for each other.

“As for you,” I say, pointing towards him. “You need to dress up. None of this, ripped jeans and t-shirt look, at my party.”

“Seriously? I look sexy as fuck in this shit, what do you mean?”

That makes both Mckenna and I laugh, though I can't deny it, he *does* pull off the look quite well. We're all silenced when a knock comes from the open doorway, shock rippling through me when Venessa peeks inside with a shy smile on her face.

"Sorry to interrupt your meeting," she says, taking a cautious step inside.

"I gave you today off. What are you doing here?"

"I have too much to do, Eros. I have plenty of time to take a day off when the opening has already happened."

I groan internally at the attitude on this girl. Sure, it's admirable, but it's also irritating as shit when she doesn't fucking *listen*. "What do you need?" She steps further into the room, glancing down at Mckenna, who is looking up at her with curiosity written all over her face. "Oh, yes. This is—"

"Mckenna Black," Venessa smiles. "It's a pleasure to meet you. I've seen your work, and can I just say, you're extremely talented. Your ideas and vision for spaces are like nothing I've ever seen before."

Mckenna holds out her hand to her, and Venessa's smile fades, her eyes darting towards me. "Venessa, that's Mckenna's husband and partner in crime, Nic."

She nods and smiles, turning her attention back to me and leaving Mckenna to close her fingers around air before dropping her hand back to her lap. "Two choices came in for the curtains. Did you want to go with the red or the black for opening?"

"I'll leave it to you, Venessa. This is what I pay you to do. You make decisions in my stead without having to check in with me every step of the way."

"But—"

"No buts. I trust you to do this job, that's why I hired you."

"Very well," she mumbles, turning towards the door. She bows towards Ikelos and Mckenna, a tight-lipped smile pulling at her lips. "It was nice to meet you," she says, leaving the room without another word.

"So, that's her?" Mckenna asks.

"Yes, that's her."

"I see what you mean, she's not fully human."

"You smelled it, too?" Nic nods. "I don't know what to do."

"We start by trying to find out who she was in the past."

CHAPTER THIRTEEN

EROS

At least I feel better by the time I finish my makeshift meeting with Mckenna and Ikelos. Hopefully, in a few days, he'll have at least some information on Venessa, but I don't know if I really want to know until after the club opening. The last thing I need is to be stressing myself out over knowing something about her that she doesn't want me to know. It's already going to be a violation of privacy, I just hope that when she finds out what I've done, she can forgive me.

I'm doing this to help her and break down the walls she's put up around herself. Every day seems to be a struggle, for her more than me, but I understand very well what she's going through. We both have a secret we wish to keep hidden, but the difference is, I have people I can talk to. Venessa has no one to turn to and no one to trust, and I hope that with time, I might become that person for her.

The moment we shared in my office still replays in my mind, and I don't feel as though I'm imagining the tension that was building between us. I know I should go check on her because of the way she left my office. She seemed upset with the dismissal, but that wasn't my intention at all. I want her to take time for herself, and yet, she keeps pushing herself harder and harder. The way she's bending is eventually going to lead to the moment that her branch can no longer hold under the pressure and she breaks.

It doesn't take a genius to notice how close she is to that moment, and I vow to not be the catalyst to her undoing. Everything seems to be running smoothly, all the orders are put in, and Mckenna is helping with the final touches on the decorations and layout for the opening. I honestly have no idea where I would be or what I would have done if I hadn't have met her.

It's only been three months, but it feels like I've known her and her sister for much longer than that. The two gods are also on that list for the simple fact I know them, but I don't *know* them. I love that I've gotten the chance to become friends with them, and I wouldn't change our chance encounter for the world.

The elevator pings on the top floor, the sound blaring in my eardrums more viciously than usual. I stop at Venessa's door, leaning my ear against it when I catch the faint sound of music drifting through. I smile, laughing to myself at the fact she likes Bad Omens like I do.

I knock, knocking again a few minutes later. It's quite possible she's sleeping, but the volume of the music is making me think she's up. I knock one more time before deciding to walk into her home. Normally, I wouldn't do this, but with the way we left things, it wouldn't sit right with me, and I know I won't be able to rest until I clear the air between us.

I stop short, my hand frozen on the handle as I take in the sight in front of me. I swallow hard, willing my body to move, but it's rooted to the spot, my eyes locked on her. Fuck, she's bendy. I don't think I've ever seen anyone doing yoga with this type of music playing in the background.

I can't take my eyes off of her, the way her body flows from one position to the next, the way her body bends and moves like liquid beauty, the way her skin glistens in the dimmed lights of the room. She's absolutely breathtaking, and my own body moves on its own, like a string is controlling it and drawing it in to its true center.

I'm behind her before I realize it, my memory glazing with confusion on how I got here. It's like my body was on autopilot, driven by the sudden desire to be near her. "Venessa," I breathe, grunting in surprise when I'm suddenly being flipped through the air until my back hits the ground. My breath wheezes out of me when her hand makes contact with my jugular, robbing my lungs of air.

"Fuck, Eros! What were you thinking?!" She squeaks, lurching to her feet while she stares down at me in shock.

"I clearly wasn't," I wheeze, rolling onto my side while coughs rock my body. Fuck, she's vicious.

"You can't sneak up on me like that."

Bracing myself on all fours, I glance up at her. "Were you anticipating someone else?" I laugh, stopping almost immediately when the action burns my throat.

"No, but I also wasn't expecting *you*. I didn't know you had access to my apartment."

"Of course I do." I slowly drag myself up to my feet and step back from her. She frowns but says nothing, tipping her defiant gaze up to me. "I'm sorry."

"Why are you here?"

"I came to check on you. I didn't like the way we left things, and I hope the conversation didn't come off in a way that seemed as though I was demanding things of you."

"Really? I had the feeling you preferred when people submitted to your will."

"Depends on the setting," I say a little too quickly. Fuck, I didn't mean to let that small kink slip through, but it isn't like she doesn't already know that part of me. I've already flexed my dominant side, but it was never my intention to use that on her. She really has a habit of bringing out the darker side of me.

Her brow quirks at that, a smile pulling at her lips. "I'm fine, Eros. I didn't mean to take you down like that."

"Hmm, I don't mind. It was interesting to be put in a position of submission." That statement is definitely true, and the fact she was able to subdue me so quickly and easily says a lot about her. She must be thoroughly trained in some form of mixed martial arts because I didn't see any of that coming, and it takes quite a bit to take a god by surprise.

"I don't take you as the submissive type," she giggles, a wide grin spreading across her face.

"Again, it depends on the situation." Her eyes dart to my lips, her chest heaving quicker than it was moments ago. "You're definitely an exception," I add, watching as her breathing changes again, the pulse in her neck fluttering as her heartrate increases.

I'm not just imagining things between us at this point, but it seems we're both too stubborn and idiotic to make the first move to see if there's something more than just an initial attraction. I can't deny the fact I'm attracted to her, more so than any other woman I've come in contact with, and that list is *not* short.

"Well, as you can see, I'm fine."

"What colour did you choose?"

"What?"

"For the curtains."

"Oh, I went with black for the semi-private rooms and red for the divisions in the upstairs level. I have the decorator coming tomorrow to put in all the final touches, so the rooms and levels themselves will be ready well ahead of schedule, but at least that's one less thing we need to worry about."

"Excellent. Have you started on the gift bags yet?"

"I was going to do that tonight."

"While you relax?" My brow lifts in question.

"It's not hard to shove things into a bag while I watch TV. I already have everything separated into tiers, so it's just tossing them in."

"Would you like some help?"

"It's not your job, Eros. This is why you hired me."

"I see. I just figured you may want some company, but if that's not the case, I'll leave you to it. Sorry to have bothered you."

I turn away from her and head for the door, hating the fact I let myself say those things to her. I don't want her to feel guilt or pity, but I honestly would have loved to just hang out with her. I don't do that often and never did before Ikelos and Jackson came into my life. I don't exactly have friends in this world since apparently, I'm intimidating.

"Eros, wait." I pause at the door, not wanting to turn to her and let her see the way my emotions are slowly slipping through to the surface. "If you want to hang out for a bit, I'll make some popcorn, and we can put on a movie to watch while we pack bags."

I turn my head enough to glance at her from the corner of my eye. She's no longer looking at me, her eyes locked on the floor in front of her while she fidgets with her shirt and gnaws on her lip. "I don't want to make you uncomfortable."

She glances up at that, her eyes locking onto mine. "You don't. You're honestly one of the first people in a really long time that I've actually felt comfortable around. So please...please stay."

A hum vibrates in my throat at the sound of her begging, my mind wandering to other begging words I wish to hear from that pretty mouth of hers. At this point, it's only a fantasy, the reality being that it'll never happen. A man can dream though. That's one thing that can never be taken from us, and as long as we can dream, we can have hope.

CHAPTER FOURTEEN

VENESSA

Why am I panicking so badly? I'm running around like an idiot, cleaning up what I can of the mess I've made in such a short amount of time. I change into comfortable clothes, settling for some baggy sweats and a tank top that might be a little snug, but who cares?

He went to his own apartment to change into something more comfortable as well, though he was dressed pretty casual today in comparison to his typical attire. I *do* like him in the sweats though, the look making him seem more human and more attainable. I shake my head at the thought.

Get your shit together, Venessa.

I can't think like that because he's *not* attainable. I can tell he's interested in me, and I can't help the small moments of flirting I shot back towards him, but I know that it won't go any further than that…it can't—but I *really* want it to.

I'm fidgeting awkwardly on the floor in front of the couch, two large bowls of popcorn sitting on the table, the delicious smell wafting through the room. I keep shifting the items back and forth, trying to find the best place for them to make this work with two people. I don't want to risk touching him at any point if I don't have to, that being one of the reasons I made two separate bowls of popcorn for us to munch on.

"Oh, fuck. I need drinks."

I bounce back to my feet, darting into the kitchen to dig through the fridge. I was beyond thankful that he had the place stocked for me before I moved in, the basic necessities and things that wouldn't go bad for quite a while. I still need to go to the store to get myself fresher ingredients to cook, but it's not really at the top of my list of things to do.

A knock comes and I call out. "Come in!" Quickly grabbing a couple of beers, I head back towards the lounge area as Eros walks in.

Fuck me, he looks good. He's dressed like the other night, his hair tousled over his brows in a way that makes him look younger and more innocent than what he clearly is. I know a man like that has plenty of experience, where I have the bare minimum. It's not my fault, but there's also nothing I can really do about it until I can figure out a way to get control over myself—If that's even possible.

"The popcorn smells amazing," he says, giving me a huge smile as he heads into the living room. "I haven't had any in a while, so this will be a nice treat."

"Really? Popcorn is so easy to make though."

"It is, but normally I'm either too busy or too tired to actually sit down and enjoy time sitting and watching TV. Thank you for allowing me to hang out with you, even if we'll still be working."

Why is he so adorable? I watch as he grabs one of the pillows, drops it to the floor, and flops down on top of it. He smiles as he inhales the smell of popcorn again, grabbing a couple of kernels to toss into his mouth. The small moan he lets out resonates deep in my gut, the sound drawing me closer to him. I set one of the bottles on the table, popping the top on the other one, and handing it to him. He stares at it for a moment, carefully lifting his hand to grip it, being mindful to not touch my hand in the process.

Even though I *do* appreciate the effort not to touch me, it also makes me a bit sad that he's given up so easily. He's the first person who's touched me in a long time and has walked away completely unscathed. Look at Logan, he barely touched me, and he almost passed out just from that small contact.

Eros has held me fully, his arms completely embracing me in a crushing hug that felt like he was trying to hold my broken pieces together, and yet, he stepped away unharmed. How is it possible? Are there certain situations that trigger whatever it is inside of me? What the fuck am I?

"Venessa?" His voice draws me back to the present and I blink, glancing down at him. "Where did you go?"

"What do you mean?"

"It looked like you got lost in your head there for a second. Do you want to talk about it?"

I smile, settling myself into my own cushion and grabbing the other bottle of beer. "The last thing I want to do is go back into my head," I say quietly, pointing towards some of the bags. "Those there will go into the black and blue bags while those go into the red and black. I got bags to match the theme but used red and blue for genders."

"That's clever. I knew you would be the perfect choice for this job."

"You don't need to keep buttering me up, Eros."

"That's not my intention. I'm being honest, and I want you to know how much I appreciate your hard work."

"I think anyone would be lucky to have you as a boss. You've been beyond good to me, and you've already had to deal with so much because of me, and it's only been like two days."

"The first of many I'm sure," he laughs. "I can't complain, I enjoy a bit of entertainment in my life. The last few years especially have been lacking a bit, but I think it comes with the territory. Even though this club is fun and exciting, it starts to get monotonous over time."

I can't help but watch him. He's speaking, but his hands are busy completing the task set in front of him, his hand occasionally dipping into the bowl of popcorn, happiness etched into his features. I don't know a lot about Eros, but from the small bits of interactions I've had with him, this is my favourite side of him. I know he can seem intimidating and broody, but he's so fucking sweet and caring. I know if I asked anything of him, he would drop everything to do it. If that's not commitment, I don't know what is, and it's crazy to think I've become deserving of such loyalty from someone that doesn't want anything from me but to complete the jobs he gives me.

Honestly, if he asked me to drop to my knees and suck his cock, I would probably do it, especially if the act didn't end up killing him in the process. I already know he's packing from that small feel I got from him, and he wasn't even hard. I think a man like this would end up destroying me, but at this point, I would welcome the pain. I would take it and ask for more because I know I deserve it for everything I've done.

I've only had sex once, and let's just say it didn't end well. Hell, my first kiss didn't end well either, that kid having ended up in a coma. I still remember his face as he stared at me with wide eyes, his face going deathly pale until he collapsed on the bed. That was the day my foster family practically disowned me, but they didn't want to officially get rid of me since those monthly cheques came in handy.

I never saw a dime from those cheques, the money going towards their own luxuries while I struggled to scrape together enough cash to keep myself fed through school. The official end to my relationship with them was my first real boyfriend. Whatever I am, woke up fully that day, and I couldn't do anything but run. I ran and kept running for years until I finally ended up here.

I've never killed a person before in my life, but I vowed that his life would be the last to fall by my hands. The only thing that tied the two together was the fact we were intimate, but I won't risk even a touch now. The darkness inside of me has grown to the point that even a small brush from my fingers can drain a person to the point of falling into a coma.

"You're being really quiet," he says, once again snapping me out of my thoughts. At least these ones weren't just depressing, though the fact I'm fantasizing about sucking my boss's cock, *might* be a little bit inappropriate.

"Sorry, I tend to get lost in my own head when I'm doing things like this. I'll admit, I'm used to doing things on my own, so I stay quiet most of the time. Plus, I don't really know what to talk about with you."

He grabs his beer, taking a long swig of it. I love watching the way his throat bobs, the corded muscles in his neck flexing with the motion. "We can talk about anything you want to talk about. I would love to know more about you, but I also know you don't like sharing."

"It's not that I don't like sharing, I just don't feel comfortable sharing my past. It's nothing against you, I don't think I would even tell my family."

"So, you still have family?"

I shake my head. "I don't know who my birth parents are. I was in the foster system from a young age, but that family was awful. I ran away when I was seventeen."

"Because of them?"

"Partially. I had a boyfriend at the time, and something happened that sort of forced my hand."

"You were just a child. No one should be on their own at that age, Venessa. How were you able to survive?"

I shrug, turning myself to lean my back into the base of the couch. I grab the remote to turn on the TV, picking a random movie for background noise at this point. "I spent some time in group homes and women's shelters, but I spent most of my time on the streets while I worked. I did end up going to school when I turned eighteen thanks to a few scholarships and bursaries. I wouldn't be where I am today if I didn't stick to it and end up going to school, but I don't regret doing it the way I did. If I would have stayed, my life would have been hell, and quite possibly my life would have ended."

"You're very brave," he says quietly.

"Brave or very stupid," I snort.

"This...boyfriend...is he the reason you are the way you are?"

He's too clever. I knew this subject was bordering on dangerous territory, but I thought I could avoid the direct subject a little better. "If I say yes, will you drop the subject, or will you continue to pry?"

"I just want to know who you are."

I tip my head towards him, but his eyes are fixed on the TV screen. His jaw ticks, his hand clenching around the bottle of beer. "Yes, it was because of him, but what happened then…I can't let it define who I am. Who you see here is the real me, Eros. I'm not faking it or pretending to be someone I'm not."

"Fair enough."

Surprisingly, he lets the subject go, going back to his work in silence while I continue to steal glances at him and allow myself to fantasize about the what ifs.

CHAPTER FIFTEEN

EROS

It doesn't take us long to finish packing all the gift bags, and I'm thankful she didn't kick me out the moment they *were* completed. She actually asked me to stay and have another beer with her once we shifted ourselves onto the couch. I polished off my bowl of popcorn and eyed hers enough that she finally laughed and handed it over for me to finish.

I've done well to avoid touching her, but the temptation remains there, nagging beneath the surface with every opportunity she gives me. I swear I catch her expression change to one of disappointment every time I do it, proving that this girl is an enigma I can't even begin to understand.

Does she want me to touch her or doesn't she? Do I risk it anyways and brace myself for the backlash that comes from it? I *really* want the information on the prick that ended up hurting her all those years ago, but even from her story with the lackluster details, I could tell she was still hiding something from me.

My body freezes when she goes freakishly quiet as her head rolls towards me. A cute little hum escapes her, followed by her lips smacking together in the most adorable way. Her head hits my shoulder, and I don't dare to move, my breath pausing in my lungs. I just about die inside when she curls herself closer to me, her head dropping to my chest while her hand moves across my stomach. She hums again, and my body aches from how hard I'm clenching every muscle, stopping myself from moving even an inch.

"Venessa," I whisper, not wanting to startle her, but I'm concerned that she'll wake up and lash out when she realizes what she's done. I could stay like this for the rest of the night if it meant being able to have her near.

I just about melt when her body slumps further, her head drifting down to settle on my lap. This is definitely a dream, a warp of reality that will crack and crumble the second I decide to move, but I want to *touch* her.

Slowly—ever so slowly—I lift my hand and settle it against her head. She sighs at the contact, nuzzling further onto my thighs. Her hair is soft, the fringe of her bangs falling across her closed lids. I carefully tug the hair tie, releasing her dark locks to run my fingers through the strands.

I've never had moments like this with anyone, all my encounters being purely physical. With her, I want more, even these small moments that seem insignificant but settle into me with a weight that feels important to me. The fact she feels comfortable enough around me to let down her guard and fall asleep means more to me than she could ever know. This is something I can hang onto and cherish, a new memory that I can lock away and look back on when I need to feel wanted.

I let my fingers trail across her cheek with the lightest touch I can muster, feeling a slight tingle against my skin. Whatever she is, it's seeping out, even in her unconscious state, but I still don't think she realizes it. Maybe she does, but it's a lack of control because she may not know what she is. Is that a conversation that I can safely bring up? I have no idea if she knows anything about the supernatural world, but if she knows nothing of her birth parents, it's a very real possibility that she was thrown into this world unprepared.

Her fingers curl into my thigh, bunching the material of my pants as she lets out another sigh. "Eros," she whispers, my name on her lips pausing my gentle strokes. The hum that vibrates in her throat sends a shiver up my spine and heat flooding my body.

I shouldn't have such primal reactions to simple sounds like that, but with her, I lose all sense of reason and control over my body. She stays asleep, and the thought of her dreaming about me has my mind wandering to what type of dream she's experiencing. Am I a villain in her dreams, or does she see me as someone she can trust and care for?

I don't want to move and risk waking her, so I settle myself back into the couch, tugging the blanket off the back of it to cover her body. I try to focus on the movie still playing in front of me, but my thoughts keep drifting to her, especially with the feel of her silky strands slipping through my fingers.

I can feel my own lids growing heavy, my body sinking further into the couch. This might not be the best place for her to fall asleep and there's no way my legs are a comfortable pillow for her.

"Venessa," I whisper, dragging my fingers down her cheek. "You should go to bed."

She groans, shifting a bit closer to me. "No," she whines. "Stay."

My chest tightens at the small, exhausted plea, and I don't have the heart to deny her because I would love nothing more than to stay a bit longer. "Promise you won't be upset in the morning if I do."

She smacks her lips together and hums out a breath, curling further under the blanket. "I...promise," she says sleepily. And that's all I need to hear. I shift myself further down, getting comfortable myself, and let my own exhaustion take over me.

CHAPTER SIXTEEN

VENESSA

The blaring of an alarm jolts me awake, my eyes struggling to focus on where the fuck I am. A groan behind me has my body stiffening, and I blink, realizing it isn't a pillow under me. Slowly I sit up, my eyes going wide when I see Eros sleeping with his neck bent at an awkward angle on the back of the couch. His brows bunch together and he shifts a bit, pushing his hips up into my hand, which is still sitting on his thigh.

"Five more minutes," he grumbles. Fuck, we fell asleep. I fucking fell asleep *on* him, curled up into him like a fucking cat. I try to shift away to grab my phone and stop the incessant noise, but his hand comes up and grip my hair, yanking me back down. "What is that *noise*?" He growls, his voice thick with sleep.

"My alarm," I whisper shakily, my eyes fluttering closed when his fingers drag through my hair in gentle strokes. "It's just going to keep screaming until I turn it off."

He sighs, sliding his hand away from me. "Fine."

I take the moment of freedom and lurch off the couch, my knees slamming into the ground as I scramble to grab my phone off the table. "Piece of shit," I grumble, tapping the screen but failing to turn it off. I sigh in relief when it finally stops, the silence stretching through the room.

The squeak of leather has me glancing back to see Eros sitting up, his hand pushing through his hair to reveal his hooded eyes staring down at me. I swallow thickly, my heart pounding heavily against my ribcage when I realize I'm kneeling in front of him. My eyes drift down for a second, taking in the not-so-subtle bulge between his legs.

"I'm sorry I stayed the night," he says carefully, taking my silence as something I don't mean him to.

"I'm sorry I fell asleep on you," I snort, frowning when his eyes drift closed again. "Do you feel okay?"

His eyes snap back open, and I swear I see them glow for the briefest of seconds before settling back into their normal, but beautiful, amber hue. "Other that being rudely awakened by that blasphemous sound burning into my ear drums, I'm fine," he chuckles. "I don't normally set alarms, so that was a bit jarring."

"How do you wake up on time?" I shift myself a bit more, settling my knees onto the pillow still on the floor. He watches my movements carefully, his tongue darting out to lick his lips in a way that send heat flooding through my body.

"What is considered on time? I work for myself, Venessa, and so any schedule is based on my time, no one else's."

"Must be nice."

"It is, and your schedule can be planned the same way as well. You don't *need* to get up at the ass crack of dawn."

I glance at my phone before tossing it back onto the table. "It's not *that* early." He turns to look out the giant window in my apartment, the curtains still drawn back to show the city skyline below. The sun is barely peeking over the buildings, so my argument is totally a lie.

"I would assume it's pretty early since we're up before the sun," he laughs.

"Yeah, it's a force of habit. I usually work out in the morning and then sit and enjoy a cup of coffee while I watch the world around me wake up." I smile to myself, dropping my eyes to my lap. "I always imagine having a home with a cute wrap-around porch, where I could sit and watch the sun come up and the sun go down, where I could curl up and experience a storm rolling in through an open field." I close my eyes, picturing the scene in my head. "I can just imagine the smell of that storm breaking in the distance, the sound of thunder clapping overhead."

"It sounds lovely," he whispers.

Slowly opening my eyes, I tip my head up to meet his gaze again. I half expected his expression to hold some taunt or doubt, but it only shows interest and curiosity. "Sorry, that was stupid of me to say," I laugh awkwardly, a choked gasp stopping the sound when his long fingers grip my jaw.

"Nothing you wish for or dream of is stupid," he says, his voice dropping in a way that has my insides screaming. He sounds dangerous and dominating, and I can't do anything but stare up at him with wide eyes. He's touching me, the feel of his warm skin against mine so foreign, but so welcoming. I want to melt into that touch, and no matter how hard I search his face, I see no signs of drain or pain. "You will not speak ill of what you want and who you are, do you understand me?"

When I don't answer, his grip slides down until his fingers are wrapped around my throat. I swallow, his hold on me pressing tight enough that I feel it push against his hand on the motion. His grip is tight, but it doesn't stop me from breathing. Why am I turned on? Heat builds between my legs, my thighs squeezing together at the wetness building inside my panties. His nostrils flair and he leans in closer to me, his pupils dilating right in front of me.

"Answer me," he growls, and fuck me, I'm officially a puddle.

"I—I understand."

My breaths are panting now with every second that ticks by. My lips part when his hand shifts again, his thumb lightly grazing against my bottom lip, tugging it down slightly. This is wrong on so many levels, but I can't deny the attraction I feel towards this man. I've warned him away on multiple occasions, but he takes those warning as a challenge, pushing my boundaries and doing the one thing that I've been afraid of for the last ten years.

I don't want to allow myself to dream and hope that Eros is someone that can tame the monster that's living inside of me, but he's making it difficult with each passing day. I crave his touch, the warmth of him, the strength of his mind and body wrapping around me in a protective cocoon from the outside world.

A small whimper slips from my lips when he pulls away, my body swaying towards him, following the contact that it's desperately trying to cling to. I've never craved physical contact as much as I do in this moment, but the nagging voice in the back of my mind continues to beat at the wall, reminding me that I could very well kill him.

That thought cracks through my mind like a whip, the sensation physically jerking my body back to put some much needed distance between us. I clear my throat and pull myself to my feet, turning towards the kitchen.

"Do you want some coffee?" I ask, glancing at him as I grab the kettle to fill with water.

"No." The word is blunt, almost angry, and I watch as he lifts to his feet and heads towards the door. "I'll talk to you later. I have some things to take care of."

I can't do anything but gawk at him as he walks out of my apartment without a second glance back at me, the sound of the door sliding shut, resonating through the room. I'm left speechless, wondering if I ended up saying or doing something wrong to make him react so coldly all of a sudden. I can't get a proper read on him, but I know that my mixed words and actions are leaving him confused. I'm not helping the situation any, but I'm doing what I do best, I'm fucking everything up.

CHAPTER SEVENTEEN

EROS

I fucking slipped again. I keep doing that, letting my urges take over my body when I *know* I need to keep control over myself. I glance down at my fingers, rubbing the pads of them against my thumb. They're still tingling even though it's been minutes since I touched her. The feel of her neck gripped in my hand sent a pulse of desire though me.

My cock twitched, desperate to sink into her, to see how she would feel tightly wrapped around my length. The way her lip pouted out on that gasp was just begging to be touched, my thoughts pushing me to claim her with my own mouth, but I settled with just touching her with my thumb.

Her whimpering breath when I pulled away just about sent me over the edge, the sound needy and desperate as well. She didn't shy away from me until I had pulled back, her own mind clearly warring with itself on what it wants, versus the need to protect her.

I need to put some distance between us. I need to stay away from her until I can get control over myself again, but her being my personal assistant is going to make that nearly impossible. I need to get away, get the fuck out of here until opening night. It's not like I'm actually needed here, that was the whole point in hiring Venessa to begin with.

The moment I get to my apartment, I head for my phone, having left it behind last night so I wouldn't be interrupted. I'm surprised to see four missed calls from Ikelos, and quickly dial him, since he didn't even bother leaving a voicemail.

"What the fuck, do you not keep your phone on you?" He says, answering on the second ring.

"I was busy with the party favours for opening night, and I left my phone in my apartment."

The silence for a few beats gives me time to realize that I just fucked up. "You were out all night?"

"Was there something you needed, Ikelos?"

"Jackson found something that we think you should take a look at. We can head over in the next hour if you're available."

"I'll come to you if that's alright?"

"Really?"

"Yeah, I need to get out of here for a little bit...clear my head."

"Did something happen?"

"I'll see you in an hour, Nic."

I hang up on the sound of him pushing the subject, but I mentally can't deal with it right now. I know he'll continue to pry the moment he sees me, but at least this gives me time to get my thoughts in order and control over my emotions.

I startle when my phone rings in my hand, my heart thumping loudly at the name across the screen. If I ignore it, it'll end up being worse in the end. "Yes," I sigh, pinching the bridge of my nose.

"Did I do something to upset you?"

Her voice is timid, breaking slightly on the words. "You've done nothing," I murmur, and it's true. I already knew going into it how she would react in certain situations, and yet, I kept pushing her boundaries until I chipped at the walls erected around her.

"Okay. It's just...the way you left—"

"I told you, I have things to do today. I'll be out of town, possibly for a few days. You'll be able to manage everything leading up to the opening, correct?"

"You're leaving?" The disappointment laced in her voice has my heart beating faster. I don't want to leave, but I know I need to if I have any chance in getting a handle on myself.

"Yes. I'll have my phone and computer with me if there's anything that absolutely needs my attention, but I trust you'll be able to oversee everything. I'll remind the staff that you are in charge in my absence."

"Okay," she whispers, and the sniffle she tries to hide rings through my ear, piercing through me.

I've upset her with my actions, but at the same time, she's left me no choice. She's been adamant on her rule of no contact, even *if* we can't seem to stay away from each other. I know it, deep down in my soul, that we're both drawn to each other, but I can't figure out for what purpose. Why would I be drawn to someone who can't be physical, when I myself am a physical being.

Is that what this is? Are we opposites drawn together? Where she holds emotions that I don't understand, I hold the physical side of things which she hasn't been able to explore. I need to find out what happened to her for this creature in my presence to be the way she is. I swear if someone hurt her, I will hunt them down and show them the meaning of pain.

"Enjoy your day, Venessa, and make sure not to overwork yourself."

"Bye, Eros."

"Goodbye, Venessa."

A strange sensation ripples through my body when I end the call, the act feeling too final and almost cruel. I rub at my chest, setting the phone down on the counter before heading to the bathroom to take a shower. I still feel some edges of exhaustion through my mind and body, but as the hot water pelts against my back, my thoughts are on her.

I can't get her out of my mind no matter how much I claw and scrape at the thoughts. In such a short amount of time, she's been able to leach into me, turning me into this obsessive being that I don't even recognize.

CHAPTER EIGHTEEN

EROS

"How is it possible for you to look even more like shit?"

I glare at Ikelos as he steps back to let me into his home. "Nice to see you, too," I grumble.

"Seriously, what's wrong with you?"

"I'm stressed out, and not in the usual way. This feels heavier than the stress I feel in running a business or everyday situations."

"Where were you last night?" He asks, walking past me to lead me further into his home.

Jackson is sitting on the couch with his laptop open, tilting his head up and giving me a smile when he hears us come in. "I was with Venessa."

Jackson's eyes widen, his gaze darting to Ikelos. I can hear the girls laughing in the distance, the sound sending a pang of jealousy through me. "Have a seat, Eros," Jackson says, patting the cushion next to him.

My anxiety spikes at his tone, but I do as he asks, settling into the seat at the same time Ikelos flops into the single chair next to Jackson. "You found something?"

"I think so. I put her photo into the system and ran her name through the foster system. There was only one Venessa with that spelling, but she's changed her last name legally once she turned eighteen. Venessa Tulpa was her name before. Her foster parents are Julia and Derek Tulpa, one other foster sibling, her name is Candace."

"A name change isn't all that surprising, she mentioned she ran away when she was younger."

"It's the reason *why* she ran. There's an article stating her as a person of interest for a suspicious death. The guy who died was the son of a pretty brutal organization, though that's more known in the dark web. He's a lawyer on paper, but the family has mafia ties. Anyways, the son was found dead in his room, and it was deemed a heart attack."

"Okay? What's this have to do with Venessa?"

"The kid was eighteen. How many eighteen-year-olds do you know that suddenly die of a heart attack? He was healthy from the medical records I was able to get my hands on."

"Was he, her boyfriend?"

Jackson nods. "They had been dating for about six months before he was found dead. The news report states that she was over that day, but when his brother went in to talk to him, she was gone, and he was dead on the bed...naked."

"Are you trying to say the kid died while they were having sex or something?" I laugh. "That sounds like the kind of shit that would happen to a seventy-year-old."

He nods. "So, you understand why this is weird, right? I got some photos from the coroner files, and the kid didn't look right. Only a few hours later, he seemed like he had been dead for a few days. The weirdest part, his eyes were white, the iris completely devoid of colour, like it had been sucked out."

He shifts the computer to show me the screen, the images horrifying. I can't imagine the trauma this must have caused Venessa if she witnessed this, but I still can't figure out why they would think she would have anything to do with this.

"I dug further and there was an incident a year prior, but the kid didn't die...at least not right away. He fell into a coma, face drained of colour, and the reports say that his eyes changed, too. He had brown eyes, but after he fell into a coma, they were blue."

"What's the connection?"

"The kid was Venessa's boyfriend, too. Whatever she is..."

"She's the one causing this. She's afraid of touch...I wonder if she's afraid of this happening again."

"This doesn't make sense," Ikelos murmurs, resting his elbows on his thighs as he leans towards us. "For one, a supernatural being should have control over their powers at her age. Clearly, she was able to touch people prior and in between the time of one boyfriend to the other. The only thing I can think of is..." He sucks in a deep breath, his eyes landing on me. "Sexual arousal being the trigger of the ability."

"If that were the case, why is she leaching her power now?" I ask, and he frowns. "We've...touched."

"And you've felt it?"

"I don't feel drained exactly, but I feel a tingling over my skin from where we've made contact."

"If she doesn't know what she is, she probably doesn't realize she needs to feed. If she's been starving that side of herself, it would make sense that her supernatural blood would be trying to pull on life energy any way it can."

"She has no control. If she did, she wouldn't have killed her boyfriend."

"She's adopted. Without guidance from her birth parents, she would have been thrown into this life blind."

"Do you know why I wouldn't be affected by her the way she's been draining others? I'm pretty sure she accidentally siphoned from one of my staff when he brushed against her, and she went into full blown panic-mode."

Jackson sighs and flops back on the couch, stretching his arms above his head. "I don't think she'll affect other supernatural beings the same way she would a human. If she's as starved as I think she is, she could still end up draining a lot of your essence." Glancing towards Ikelos, he quirks a brow. "Have you ever had a run in with one of them?"

Ikelos shakes his head. "It's not like I have much experience in the human world, but within our realm, I've never seen one. I think they've slowly gone extinct, so I'm curious what her parentage actually is."

"I haven't seen one either," Jackson murmurs, glancing at me.

"I've had a run in with one about two hundred years ago, but nothing since. I don't even know what I can do to help her at this point without information to give her to guide her control."

"Fucking her might help," Jackson laughs, and I roll my eyes. "Seriously though, she needs to balance herself out and she can't do that with a human at this point. The best way for her to learn control is by practicing, and she can't do that if she keeps avoiding contact. Normally, they feed through a kiss, but she's evolved enough to not need that intimate touch out of desperation."

"The fact the best way to help her is by sleeping with her is pretty fucked up. She'll never go for that, and she'll think I'm just trying to get in her pants."

"Aren't you?" Ikelos teases.

"No. She's different. I...*feel* different around her, and I can't explain it."

"Hmm," Jackson hums. "Do you feel all tingly around her, and like, it's hard when you're not around her?"

"Maybe?"

"You like her, man."

"I've known her for two days."

"So? Sometimes it's not up to you. Sometimes it's your soul that tells you how to feel."

"You don't understand," I grumble.

"What is there to understand? You like her, and from what Nic said, she seems to like you, too, so what's the problem?"

I never wanted to have this conversation because I didn't want to actually admit to *anyone* the internal struggle I've experienced my entire life. It's not the fact I don't trust them, but acknowledging my issues makes them real and not just something I feel. Both Ikelos and Jackson stare at me, waiting for a response, but neither of them show signs of judgement on their faces.

"I can't...fall in love, and no one can love me," I say quietly, the words feeling like acid on my tongue.

"Why do you think that? I didn't think anyone could love me either, but Mckenna proved me wrong."

"Same for me. I didn't have anyone until Addison came along, and without her, I would still be an unseen god in this world."

"It's my curse. In all my years, I've never been granted that feeling within myself. I don't think I even know *how* to love."

"Everything happens for a reason, and maybe Venessa is your path to understand that which has been out of reach for you for so long." I stare at Ikelos, my jaw popping open on its own for the sheer fact he sounds *smart*. "What?" He snorts. "Don't look at me like that. I understand this more than you think, Eros. I didn't think I would ever be capable of loving anyone, especially when I didn't even know how to love myself. Mckenna showed me that I was worth something and being important…being the center of someone's universe, changed me for the better."

"I don't know how to even act around her. I keep fucking everything up, and her aversion is subconsciously a challenge for me. It's like, the more she doesn't want me to touch her, the more I need to. It makes me feel like a pervert." I admit.

He smiles and settles back into his chair while Jackson laughs. Both their heads tip towards the entrance to the living room, and seconds later, Mckenna and Addison walk in. They both smile when they see me, and my heart thumps at seeing true happiness on their faces at my presence.

"Hey, Eros! We made some breakfast, if you guys want to come into the dining room."

I swallow thickly, trying to tamper down my emotions at how welcoming they are. It's a strange feeling—having friends—though I feel they're more like my family at this point than my own. They've accepted me into their group, even if I had to work a bit harder with

Ikelos to prove myself and to show him I mean them no harm. I don't know what I would do if I didn't have them to talk to about any of this, and I will fight to keep them in my life.

CHAPTER NINETEEN

EROS

"Do you think I can stay with you guys for a few days? Just until opening night?"

Ikelos glances at me while his dogs run off to chase one of the squirrels in the park across from his home. He shoves his hands in his pockets, tipping his head back against the sun beating down on us. It warms the chilly day in a comforting embrace, making the wintery temperatures more tolerable. I think either Jackson or Addison have been manipulating it a bit since I've shown up here, since it seems it's gotten a few degrees warmer from when I arrived.

"You know you can't run away from this," he sighs.

"I know. I just—I just need some time to think. I'm acting more impulsively around her than I normally would, and I'm just worried I'm going to end up saying or doing something I shouldn't. I don't want her to run again, least of all because of me."

He stays quiet for a while, making his way towards one of the benches at the edge of the park. He sits, but I stay standing, feeling as though I've pushed my luck with him. I don't want to fuck up my relationship with any of them, and now I'm starting to regret asking the question.

"Sorry, that was too forward of me. I'll just grab a hotel somewhere and take the time on my own to think."

He leans back into the bench, his legs falling open slightly as he pats the seat beside him. I take it hesitantly, too nervous to glance at him when he continues to stay silent. I know how fearsome the god of nightmares can be, that thought permanently etched into the back of my mind. I can feel the edge of power within him, but he does well to keep it contained.

"You're really struggling with this, aren't you?" I nod, lacing my fingers together to stop my hands from shaking, but it's useless. I feel nervous around him, not wanting him to judge me for my poor decisions and actions. "You can stay, but you have to promise me that you'll deal with these feelings once you get back. You can't just hide from her, and you hired her, Eros, you're sort of stuck with her unless you fire her. Is that what you want?"

"No, I can't. It's not even the fact I don't have the heart to do that, especially now, knowing what I know. I don't think I could handle not seeing her anymore if I end up letting her go."

"Alright. We'll help you if you need it, but you would do well to try and handle this yourself in regard to her. More than likely, she doesn't know what she is, and so she can't control her powers. You need to talk to her, Eros."

"I will when the opening is over. I don't want to stress her or have her freaking out before that. She's already got enough on her plate, especially with me just leaving the way I did."

"Has she contacted you?"

I shake my head. "She called me after the way I left this morning, and I just told her I would be gone for a few days, and to handle everything as best she could. She knows she can call me if she runs into any real problems, but at this point, I don't know if she would reach out to me."

"She's probably really confused."

"As am I. The moments we've had, I can tell she craves the contact I've given her, but then it's like something snaps her back in her mind and she recoils. I can see the fear in her eyes, clouding over the want and desire." I sigh, leaning back into the bench as well. "She's so beautiful, and really sweet, and I hate that she's had to live this way with no knowledge of who she is."

"Hmm," he hums, ripping his gaze from his hounds to look at me. "You seem smitten."

"I am. I don't know what I'm doing though. I've never had any form of relationship in my life, and I'm scared I'm going to end up fucking it up."

"You're both in the same boat though. Neither of you really have any experience with that."

"I'm more experienced than she is. It's not even the fact I'm so much older than she is, and it scares me a little bit. I don't want to frighten her if I end up being too intense for her. I've had a few moments where I think I've pushed it to far, but she hasn't acknowledged she's uncomfortable."

"You mean your dominating personality?" He snorts, and I roll my eyes. "She might even welcome that version of you. She's had to have control over herself and her life for so long, so the idea of letting go *might* scare her, but be a path to freedom at the same time."

"Maybe you're right."

"That happens sometimes," he chuckles. "I know I've been hard on you, but I think this is a good thing, Eros." He glances up at the sky, a smile tugging at his lips. "This life—the one I have with Mckenna—I hope you can find the same peace and comfort that I've found. I don't know where I would be if I didn't go against the life thrust upon me, but I think it would have remained dark, slowly chipping away at my sanity."

"That is very kind of you, Ikelos."

He huffs, tipping his head towards me once again. "The fact you still call me that is a bit irritating."

"I introduce you as Nic for the sake of the life you've created, but the name was given to you by your mate, and I don't feel I deserve to call you that quite yet."

His eyes widen, my words stunning him into a brief silence. I've never admitted that to him, but it's the truth. He worked to have the name, just as I have to work to be truly accepted into his life. I'm getting there, little by little, but even if he's come around, I know I'm not at a level where he fully trusts me yet.

"Eros, I—"

I shake my head. "It's the truth. I'm grateful to you and your family for being in my life, but I won't claim to be a part of it. I have a lot of respect for you and what you've done with yourself. You're stronger now, and that is something to strive for."

"I'm stronger *because* of Mckenna. If it weren't for her, I wouldn't be here in this form. I would still be a lost god, trying to find my place in this world. Love is a very powerful emotion, Eros, and it took me too long to realize that. You wield that emotion as your power, and with that, you may be the strongest of us."

"I may wield it, but I don't seem to understand it as well as I thought I did. Having access to that, but not being able to *feel* it for myself, it's a bit discouraging."

"You will in time. I have faith in you, and I can see how much you want this. You're opening up without even realizing it and allowing yourself to actually care for this human."

"Human," I scoff. "I don't know whether to say I'm happy or sad at the fact she's not fully human."

"It could be a blessing. I couldn't imagine life without Mckenna, and if I hadn't turned her, I would have lost her in time. I'm sure Jackson feels the same way. We both lost our human mates but gained someone who can stay with us for eternity."

"How did they handle becoming supernatural beings?"

Ikelos smiles, looking out towards the boys and blinking quickly. "Hey! Leave the squirrel alone!" He yells, and I laugh at the sigh of exasperation that slips from his lips. "Mckenna adjusted well for the most part. She didn't come into her powers as quickly as Addison, and she did have some moments where her emotions came to the surface in full force, but once she settled, she seemed content. She's happy, and I plan to keep her that way for the rest of my life."

"I'm envious of you both. They fact you fought for what you wanted and came out of it happier than ever."

"We both suffered plenty in the process. Seeing Mckenna dying in front of me, feeling her life slipping, her tears as she fought to cling to life while blood pooled from her body, it fucks with you. It's an image I'll never be able to purge from my memories, and they still haunt me to this day. There are moments I wake up with the scene playing behind my lids, and I scramble to grip into her, to make sure she's with me, and the life we have now is real."

"Do you plan to have children?"

"Eventually. Neither of us are in a hurry for that, but we have talked about it. I think she would make a wonderful mother, but I'm worried about being a father. I don't know what I'm doing and I'm trying to learn as I go. I also don't want to lose Mckenna's favour quite yet, which I know would happen once a little one is born. She's everything to me, and it worries me that I'll become second to her. Is that selfish of me?"

It *is* a little bit selfish, but I can't blame him for fearing that and feeling the way he does. He's had nothing and no one that has cared for him the way Mckenna unconditionally loves him. The fear of losing even a fraction of that love would scare me as well.

"No, I understand your mentality completely. Take all the time you need until you feel confident in yourself. Mckenna would never love you any less, if anything, I think she would love you more because not only are you her mate and husband, but you would be the father of her children, a child that is a piece of both of you combined."

"I'm scared," he admits quietly. "I think Mckenna will want children eventually, but aside from all my other fears, I'm honestly afraid if I'll be a good father. I don't want to disappoint them or make them feel less than, the way I felt growing up."

"Have you talked to your family?"

"No," he grumbles. "After they crashed my wedding, they tried coming around a few times, but I refused to entertain them. The last time they tried to contact me was about six months ago."

"What are they trying to accomplish?"

"They want to know how I did it. The fact I'm powerful enough now to hold a human form in this world seems to fascinate them, and they're trying to find a way to recreate that power surge. They don't understand that it's not something that can be willed or forced. They'll never gain this level of power because they'll never accept that it was because of Mckenna and the fact she fell in love with a monster like me."

"You're not a monster," I whisper. "You have to know that you aren't the way you are because you chose to be this way."

"They *made* me this way. I *do* understand, but it doesn't chase away the darkness that has clung to me for eons. I know in my heart that I can be good, and I will be whatever Mckenna needs me to be for all of eternity."

He lifts to his feet and whistles for the dogs, turning to look at me once more. I hate seeing the edge of sadness in his features, but I hate it more knowing that my questions and the line of conversation that I've pushed has been the cause of his mood shift.

"Let's go home and grab some lunch. I'll get you set up in the guest room for now, too. It's not much, but it should be what you need for now."

"Thank you," I sigh, lifting to my feet as well and smiling when the dog he calls Dom slams into the back of his knees, almost taking him to the ground.

"For fuck's sake," he grumbles as they run off, barking and whining as they go. "Don't thank me yet, the hounds can get pretty annoying, so I'll apologize now."

CHAPTER TWENTY

VENESSA

"Okay, the D.J. is booked, the chef has the meal planned out, the bar is fully stocked, decorations are up, party favours are ready to be distributed, I've set up the system for new members to sign up for verification, and the cake has been ordered for midnight."

I sigh, grabbing my glass of whisky from the bar top and shooting it back in one go. The burn of it down my throat is welcoming, but lackluster. I've been frequenting the bar over the last few days, hating the feeling of being alone in my apartment more and more with each passing second. Every time I'm in there, I think of Eros and the last time I saw him. The feelings swirling inside of me are mixed, the memories of lust and happiness, tainted by the sudden change in him and how quickly he shut down when I rejected him once again.

"I think I have everything covered," I murmur as Rex fills my glass again.

"Did you get yourself something special to wear?" He asks, setting the bottle down and leaning his forearms on the counter to look at me fully.

"I'll just pick through the clothes I have."

He rolls his eyes. "I don't think Eros will be too pleased if you do that."

"I don't want to waste money on a dress or anything for one night."

"You don't have to. You have Eros' card, don't you?"

I frown. "I would never do that."

"Why not? If he were here, he would tell you to do it. It's technically a business expense since it's for an event for the club, and you're going to be the face people see right away. You may not want to admit it, but you're Eros' right hand now, and you're more likely to get attention than he is."

I chug back the glass again, and he quirks a brow, shifting to grab the bottle to top me up again. "Doubtful," I murmur. "Have you *seen* him? He's admittedly gorgeous, so I'll be in the background the whole time."

"Have you seen *you*? You're beautiful, Venessa. Not my type, but still beautiful."

I smile at him, a giggle slipping through when he gives me an exaggerated wink. I've really grown to like Rex over the last few days, and he's been a big help. Not only has he been someone I can bounce ideas off of, but he's also helped me feel confident in my job. I was surprised to find out he's gay, but the man is stunning and a beautiful person inside and out.

I haven't had the nerve to call or message Eros at all, even though he told me I could, but he hasn't contacted me either. In the back of my mind, I keep thinking he left because of me, and not for the reason he gave me originally. With the opening so close, I wouldn't have expected him to just take off like that, but he did. I felt so lost that day, keeping to myself and burying all my time and energy into planning this night and making it perfect for him.

Opening night is only a few hours away, and I can't get control over my clashing emotions. The excitement for it is warring with my nerves, the anxiety that I'll end up fucking this up somehow.

He's still not back yet, and with each passing hour, I wonder if he'll even end up showing up for his own event. He has to, right? He invited Mckenna and her team, so he can't exactly blow it off for the sake of being mad at me.

Is he mad at me?

Fuck. I can't get out of my own head, and the longer I sit here trying to figure out what else I need to do, the more my thoughts hyperfocus on me being the reason he's basically abandoned ship.

"Venessa?" I blink, realizing Rex is snapping his fingers in front of my face with a look of concern on his own. "Are you okay?"

I sigh, sliding my tablet into its case and stacking my files on top of it. "No, but it is what it is. I think I messed up with Eros, and I'm worried he's not coming back for tonight."

"Don't stress over it, he does this sometimes."

"Has he…ever had a relationship? I assume he hooks up with people, seeing as how he owns a place like this."

"Why? Are you interested in him?" He laughs, and when I don't answer, he sighs and grabs my empty glass. "He's never been in a relationship. I honestly don't think he knows how to be in one, but I haven't seen anyone show interest in him outside of hooking up. It's weird since he seems like a genuinely good person. He cares about us as people and treats us like family, not staff. It's a little sad, if I'm being honest."

"I don't understand why. He seems perfect in so many ways, so how hasn't he been tied down yet?"

Rex shrugs, wiping a towel across the counter. "I'm not sure. Plenty of people end up finding love because of the events he holds here, but he doesn't seem to have the same luck. He's not really affectionate with any of them, and it's not to say he doesn't give a shit exactly, but there's no care, if that makes sense? The hookups he's had never stay the night either. I don't think he's ever actually *slept* with anyone."

That surprises me enough to almost drop my tablet. He's never actually spent the night with anyone, yet he stayed with me. I mean, we sort of fell asleep, but he didn't want to get up in the morning, like he *wanted* to stay with me longer. Would he react differently if we had been intimate? I'd like to believe he wouldn't just bone and dash, but I don't know a lot about his personal life.

I wish I could talk to Rex in more detail, but I know that would end up being an invasion of privacy when it comes to Eros. I wish I had *anyone* to talk to, but I can't let myself get too close without risking them being put in danger as well.

"I'll see you in a few hours," I say to Rex, sliding off the stool.

"Are you going to buy something?" I nod. "Good girl," he laughs, giving me a nod as I walk over towards the elevator.

"Miss. Deye!" The receptionist in the lobby calls out to me the moment I step out. "A package came for you."

She slides a black box with a glistening gold ribbon wrapped around it towards me, and a small black envelope. "Who is it from?"

She shrugs. "A courier came and was adamant it got to you, but we were put under strict orders from Mr. Knight to not let any outside guests into the building before we're officially open."

"Thank you, Hannah."

She smiles as I turn to walk towards the door. I really want to open it right now, especially since I don't want to be carrying a box with me while I go shopping. I quickly move towards the lobby and take a seat, resolving myself to open the package before messaging for an uber to come pick me up. The store I want to go to isn't exactly far, but the weather is pretty chilly today, and I don't want to risk getting caught in a snowstorm if it decides to change on me.

I carefully tug at the ribbon and slowly open the box. I blink, confusion washing over me at seeing two more boxes inside. I open the smaller one first and stare at the random car key inside.

"What the fuck?" I mumble to myself, setting it back in the box to open the next one.

A small gasp slips through my lips, my hand trembling as I run my fingers over the gorgeously delicate necklace inside. The thin chain is white gold, gleaming in the overhead lights of the lobby. The pendant is stunning, a white gold arrow with the heart-shaped tip covered in tiny diamonds. The chain is long enough that if I were to wear it, the arrow would settle just above my cleavage.

Glancing around, I catch Hannah watching me, but she quickly turns away when she notices me looking towards her. I set the box down on the seat next to me and open the envelope, my emotions getting the better of me as I read it over and over again.

Venessa,

I'm sorry I left you to deal with everything in my absence. I've gifted you something I know will be essential for you to complete your job, as well as a small token from me. I hope it isn't too forward, but someone as kind as you, deserves something to make your internal light shine brighter in the darkness that seems to cloud you.

I know you, and I know you'll think it's all too much, but it's not. Don't ask questions, and please...wear the necklace. The key is to a car already parked in the lot, and it is for you to own. Think of it as your bonus for having to put up with me and my difficult personality.

Be the person I know you are without worrying about what happened in your past. We'll talk soon, but for now, just know that I am not letting you go, so don't run from me.

I will see you tonight. Save a dance for me.

Eros Knight

I can't stop the tears from streaking down my cheeks as I read the letter one more time. How am I supposed to feel about any of this? This seems well beyond the actions of someone who is supposed to be my boss, and I know I should keep that boundary erected, but he's blasting away at it brick by brick, and at this point, I don't want to stop him.

Grabbing the box, I make my way towards the parking lot, tapping the button a few times until I hear the beep of the car. "Seriously?" I huff, a laugh slipping through as well. "Why am I not surprised?"

A black Porche sits in the spot next to the one Eros' Ferrari was parked in last time, the leather seats a deep red. It's a beautiful car and definitely way too extravagant of a gift. This is worth at least ten years of bonuses and he just handed me the keys like it was the most normal thing on the planet. I feel guilty now at the thought I was going to take Rex up on his suggestion to buy something pretty with Eros' card. He's coming tonight, so I know I need to be dressed to impress, but will he be upset with me?

I settle into the driver's seat, setting everything in my hands on the passenger side before pulling out my phone. I haven't talked to him in days, and my hands tremble when I pull up his contact. I can't call him. I can't guarantee I won't get emotional at hearing his voice while my own breaks on my words.

Me: ***Sorry to bother you, but I just wanted to confirm the dress code for tonight.***

Gnawing on my lip, my leg jiggles as I type out another message.

Me: ***If I should be wearing a dress, I need to go out and buy one.***

The dots pop up, bouncing for a few seconds before disappearing. It feels like forever before I see them again, and a few seconds later, a message comes through.

Eros: ***You can wear whatever you wish, but I would love to see you in a dress. Charge it to the company card.***

I sigh in relief, knowing that Rex was right about doing just that. The ache in my chest hits me suddenly. I miss him. I barely know Eros, but being away from him this long makes me realize how far he's buried himself under my skin. I want to hear his voice again, the soft whispers, the laugh, the sensual words dripping with hidden desire.

I contemplate saying thank you to him for the gifts, but it seems so stupid to be doing it over text. I rather thank him in person so I can see his face and the emotions swirling in the depths of his hypnotic eyes. I just need to wait a few more hours, and I hate how that still feels too long.

Me: ***Thank you, Eros. See you soon.***

CHAPTER TWENTY-ONE

EROS

My hand tightens around my phone as I read her message again. I wonder if she got the gift I sent her. She would have said something if she did, right? Fuck, what if she got it and she hates it? Fuck me, is the car too much? She probably thinks I'm some pretentious asshole that loves to throw around money just for the sake of it. God fucking damn it, I'm going to punch myself if I ended up fucking this up further because of my impulsive decision.

I nearly jump out of my skin when a hand settles on my shoulder. "Fuck, are you good?"

A nervous laugh escapes me at the look of concern on Jackson's face as he quickly pulls his hand away. "Yeah, sorry. I was lost in thought and didn't hear you coming."

"Are you okay? Are you ready to see her again?"

"No, but I can't keep hiding out here either. I know I need to go back, not just because of the club opening, but because I owe it to her to not be a coward when it comes to this."

"Are you afraid?"

I frown. "Of what?"

"Of her. Are you scared about what will happen once you talk to her?"

"She might run. It's not a fear exactly, more like a worry. I don't want her to run from this. I want her to be comfortable enough to confide in me and trust me. I know that's asking a lot since we don't know each other very well, but I feel like I know her better than I should in such a short amount of time. I think...this obsession might be a bit unhealthy."

Jackson shrugs and flops down on the couch next to me, bumping into my shoulder. "Preaching to the choir," he chuckles. "I know my obsession with Addison wasn't normal either, but I couldn't imagine not feeling the way I did towards her. I didn't want to leave her for even a second, and when I did, it felt like I was losing a piece of myself."

"She texted me."

"Oh? What did she say?"

"She wanted to confirm the dress code for tonight."

"Ah. That's the first communication you've had since you left, right?" I nod. "You haven't reached out to her at all?" I shake my head, and he sighs. "You're not going to be able to avoid her when you get to the club."

"The club is pretty big," I mumble, but hating the thought of not seeing her tonight.

I don't *want* to keep avoiding her, and I don't want to deal with the conversation that we're inevitably going to have to have. It's going to blindside her completely and she may freak out enough that she ends up running anyways. If that happens, I need to prepare myself for what I'll do. Will I let her go? Or will I chase her down and drag her back, even if it's kicking and screaming?

"That's not the point, Eros. You *can't* avoid her. If your goal is to try and help her, you need to see her, and you need to make her feel like she can trust you."

"She *can*."

He sighs, tipping his head back on the cushion. "I know she can, but you need to convince *her*. I'm not going to sugar coat it, Eros, this isn't going to be easy for her to just accept. It sucks that she didn't grow up in the world she was born into, and I can't imagine the struggle she's going through to try and feel normal, when deep down, she knows she isn't."

"I think I'm going to head out," I mumble, lifting to my feet and shoving my phone in my pocket before turning to look at him.

"Do you plan to see her before the party?"

I shake my head. "It'll take me a bit to get back to the city, and I still need to pick up my suit from the tailor. I didn't want to task her with doing something so mundane, and I'm sort of glad now. I'll see you guys later. Can you let Ikelos know that I've left?"

"Of course."

Nodding my head, I make my way to the door, grabbing the bag of clothes and essentials I bought while staying here. They were beyond welcoming to me, Mckenna showing true happiness with my visit. Jackson and Addison came over every day, the guys keeping me company while the girls worked on another project they've been commissioned for. Ikelos was kind enough to show me around his town, the area peaceful and quite beautiful in the winter months. I can only imagine how nice some of the parks and landscapes are during the spring and summer, but I didn't have the heart to ask him if I could visit again.

As welcoming as they were, I don't want to impose on them in the future or push my luck on their hospitality. A thick frost coats my car, a stupid move on my part to bring it here when I should have just driven my truck. Venessa's scent still lingers faintly in the cab of it, and that's the only reason that pushed me to drive the thing. It's a fucking death trap in the winter, but Jackson was kind enough to ease up on the snow to make it safer for me to drive home.

Cranking the heat in my car, I let it warm up enough to thaw out the intricate designs of the frost, watching it slowly melt away into nothing. I quite enjoy winter, the snowfall and crystalline beauty that clings to nature. It's peaceful and ethereal, a welcoming escape from my ever-present chaotic thoughts.

The traffic to the city is thankfully scarce, my timing pushing me before rush hour. I drive by the club, wondering if Venessa is in there and what she might be doing. The entrance is set with the grand re-opening sign, and I catch sight of Toby setting the heating towers out for the anticipated line. I have about two hours before the doors officially open for the night, giving patrons ample time to hit up the restaurant beforehand.

Pulling up to the tailor twenty minutes later, I stare up at the sign out front, the words *Take a Knee* gleaming with frost along its metal edges. Maybe someday I'll do just that, a thought that has crossed my mind more times than I'd like to admit, but never having anyone attached to the other side of that image. Now? Fragments of blue eyes and dark hair shimmer in my mind, my chest tightening at the teasing thought.

My body is trembling as I step out of the car, carefully making my way up to the double doors. "Mr. Knight," Devon says happily when he sees me. For being an older gentleman, he's still attractive, his greying hair slicked back away from his face. His own trousers are perfectly tailored, which is to be expected, and the dark green dress shirt is a perfect match to his olive complexion. His smile reaches right up to his dark brown eyes, the edge of crow's feet peeking through.

"Hello, Devon. Do you have my suit ready?"

"Of course. Your event is tonight, correct?"

I nod. "In a few hours, yes."

"Let's get to it then. I want to make sure I did everything correctly, so if you don't mind trying everything on one last time?" He points towards the dressing area, where my suit is already hanging. "I went with a deep red for the dress shirt, but if you prefer a different colour—"

"The red is perfect." It really is. The colour is almost a perfect match to the red in Venessa's hair, and it fits well with the theme I have throughout the club for tonight. Red and black, two colours of sex and sin, love and lust, passion and obsession. The colours are a mirror of myself in so many ways, leading the humans towards the path they can't seem to find for themselves.

I can feel Devon watching me as I snag the hangers and slip into one of the spacious rooms to change. The material of the suit is butter soft, the shirt like silk slipping through my fingers. It feels good against my body, the suit moulding to my form in a flexible embrace. I can't help but stare at myself in the mirror, no longer recognizing the person staring back at me.

I don't exactly know what I expect to see, but the dishevelled man with overgrown scruff and darkened eyes, wasn't it. The thought of having to confront Venessa is taking a bigger toll on me than I thought it would, the secret I'm now holding, slowly eating away at my insides.

I thought taking the time to think about it and come up with a plan would help, but the time away from her, knowing how confused she must be, tore at me the entire time I was with Ikelos and the others.

"Is everything alright, Sir?" Devon calls out through the closed door. A heavy breath rattles my lungs before I open the door and step out to greet him. The smile spreading across his face shows clear admiration for his handiwork, and he motions me up onto the platform at the center of the blinding lights. "I think the fit looks amazing, but how do you feel in it?"

"It feels good," I murmur, moving my arms and squatting down a bit to test the seam reinforcements. "I think I need a tie though. Maybe a thinner one in black."

"Of course," he says, moving to one of the tables to pick through the selection there and bringing one over in a satin material. I make quick work of tying it around my neck, smoothing it down over my stomach before doing up one of the buttons on the jacket. "Very sharp, Sir," he says with a smile in his voice.

"I'm always impressed with your work, Devon," I murmur, catching his eyes in the mirror.

"That's very kind of you."

"It's the truth. This might be the nicest suit you've made for me."

"Well, I hope others appreciate how you look in it as well," he chuckles.

I stare at myself, picturing Venessa on my arm. "I hope so, too."

CHAPTER TWENTY-TWO

VENESSA

My nerves are getting the better of me. The opening has been in full swing for an hour now, a lot of the patrons heading to the restaurant for dinner, while some went straight to the club. I'm hovering like a fucking mother hen, waiting for something to go wrong, but the staff has done well to manage everything flawlessly.

I.D. is being checked as it should, members are being handed their new access cards as well as their welcome gifts, while others handle the new members and the background checks needed for elite entry. My eyes keep drifting to the doors as soon as someone walks in, and each time, disappointment settles into my chest.

"I'm heading to the club," I say to Holden, glancing over the counter he has to keep track of every soul that gains entry. "Will you be okay?"

"We got this," he says with a smile, making a shooing motion to me. "Go. We'll be fine, and if we need you..." He taps the earpiece. "I know how to reach you," he murmurs, his voice radiating into my eardrum.

Smiling at him, I head towards the elevator, glancing back to the entrance as I wait for the doors to open. The club is doing well, the lineup wrapping around the building with eager patrons dying to get a look inside at the new place.

"How are the memberships looking?" I ask, tapping the earpiece and walking into the elevator.

The crackle resonating back causes me to wince, but I should have know better than to ask when I climbed into the metal box. "It's looking good. We have a few returning members that have upgraded to the private floors already, and a slew of others wanting to join. We're still running background checks on a lot of them, but we told them we would be in contact, and to head into the club in the meantime."

"Thank you, Cole. I'm headed to the club level now."

"How's it looking out there?"

"The line is a bit ridiculous," I chuckle.

"Have you seen Eros yet?"

My chest tightens at the question, more so because I can hear the hesitation in the question. Most of the staff were surprised that Eros left the way he did, but mainly because of the fact it was so close to the big day. That knowledge had guilt ripping through me, further proof that I was the cause of his sudden departure.

"No," I say quietly, fighting back the burn of tears threatening to break through.

"I'm sure he's on his way."

"Yeah, you're probably right. He must be caught up in whatever business he had to deal with."

The words taste bitter in my mouth, my voice cracking on the lie I'm trying to tell myself as well as everyone else who has asked me if he's been in contact. I know that it's my job to take care of things when he's not around, but the pressure of it all is starting to get to me. I hate how much faith he put in me to have this event run smoothly without his hands directly in it. I hate it even more because my stupid ass is trying so hard to impress him and not just as my boss.

Is it wrong of me to try and do my best because I want to hear the praise fall from his lips? Is my need to feel appreciated and needed something I shouldn't desire? I don't even recognize myself because of my mindset. I haven't felt this desperation to be acknowledged in a long time, not since I gave up any hope of that when my family practically disowned me. If they could see me now, I know that they would feel nothing but hatred and disappointment towards me.

Fuck them. I shouldn't care what they think of me, and I'll do everything I can to stay off their radar. They're the least of my concerns at this point, the bigger threat being the Volkov family. At the time, I didn't think anything of it, feeling the thrill of danger in knowing I was involved with someone that had such powerful ties.

Why would I feel any fear around them when I was no one—nothing but a notch on the youngest son's belt.

Little did they know that the meek mouse was the true danger, the one to bring down a mafia son without even trying. I never wanted him dead, my emotions for him bordering on love, even if he didn't feel that way towards me. No. I know he cared for me, memories of the way he would talk about our future, the promise of me becoming his princess in the dark life his family set before him.

His death brought on the death of my own life, the unraveling of everything I ever knew, and the destruction of any chance at creating a future for myself. I can't stop the tremor from ripping through my body at knowing they're still out there, hunting me down.

The elevator pings and I pull in a deep, rattling breath before the doors open. The music in the room thrums through my body, the lights flashing in a heady glow. A twinge of pride settles into me at how good the club looks and how packed it is. Bodies move and bounce on the dance floor, the VIP rooms filling and curtains closing, the promise of sin radiating through the space.

"Venessa!" I startle at the sound of my name, turning to see Mckenna walking towards me with a huge smile on her face. Her hand is gripped tightly around Nic's, whose eyes dart around as though anticipating something happening. "You look gorgeous!" She squeals, pulling away from him to run up to me, taking my hands instead.

"You look gorgeous, too," I smile, slipping out of her grip as panic settles into me. She *does* look gorgeous. The silver dress clings to her body, hugging her every curve.

She motions towards another couple walking up to stand next to Nic, thankfully ignoring the way I pulled away from her. She shows no sign of being affected by my touch, and I let out a small breath of relief. "That's my sister, Addison, and her husband, Jackson."

"It's a pleasure to meet you," I say, giving them the warmest smile I can muster.

Mckenna's eyes travel around the club, a frown line forming between her brows. "I haven't seen Eros yet. Do you know where he is?"

Another crack through my armour at her words and my smile falters. "He's not here."

Her frown deepens, her eyes darting to Nic and the others before quickly turning to me once more. "What do you mean? He should be here by now."

I shrug. "I'm not sure."

"Have you spoken to him?" Nic asks, stepping closer to Mckenna to slide his hand across her lower back.

"A few hours ago, when I messaged to confirm the dress code for myself." I catch Jackson's eyes widening as he looks towards Nic at my comment. "What's wrong?"

That snaps his attention back to me, and he quickly shakes his head. “No—nothing! He invited us, so we assumed he would be here for the opening.”

“You and me both,” I mumble before I can stop myself.

CHAPTER TWENTY-THREE

EROS

I'm a fucking coward. The fact I've been sitting in my car for the last hour just proves how much of a fucking piece of shit I am. My nerves got the better of me when I drove by the club again and saw the massive line already forming and wrapping around the building. I didn't see her near the entrance, but I could *feel* her.

My phone vibrates on the seat, my heart thumping viciously when I see Ikelos' name come up on the screen. My hand trembles as I grab it, sliding my thumb against the glass to answer the call.

"Where the fuck are you?" He snarls, the bumping bass of the music vibrating through the speaker.

"I don't know if I can do this." My voice shakes on the words, and I pinch the bridge of my nose, closing my eyes when he sighs.

"Stop it. There's zero reason for you to be acting this way. This is your night, *your* fucking event, and you're not even here. I thought the whole point of you leaving early was for you to get here on time and fucking deal with this."

"You're right," I mumble. I know he's right, and I know I'm acting like a child, but my body struggles to move with the fear that tonight won't go as I had hoped. I don't give a shit about the club opening at this point, I worry about *her*.

At this point, she is more than likely assuming that the reason I left was because of her and for no other reason. I can only imagine the guilt she must feel in thinking that, the anger that must be coursing through her at knowing I basically abandoned her. She's going to hate me at the end of this and probably leave my ass behind. I did it to myself—there is no one else to blame but *me*.

"Are you in the building?" Ikelos' voice pulls me back to the conversation, and I shake my head, trying to dislodge the thoughts trying to burn themselves into me.

"I'm in the parking structure."

"How long have you been there, Eros?"

"I—since before the opening."

"Fucking hell," he groans. "Seriously, get your ass in here. We already ran into Venessa, and she seemed pretty upset at the fact you're not here."

That perks me up a bit. Does that make me an asshole? It must, since finding joy in the fact someone is upset with my absence, is something that shouldn't make me happy. "Really?"

“Come and see for yourself,” he grumbles, ending the call before I can respond.

“Fucker.”

I hate the fact he’s right in all of this. He has less experience with human interactions and socialization, yet he’s able to read the atmosphere and emotions better than I can. It shouldn’t surprise me as much as it does, seeing as how his power is fully based on emotion as well. Fear can be extremely potent in scent compared to love and lust. Wait. Has he sensed fear in Venessa?

That thought is the catalyst, pushing my body to move. I’m practically running towards the elevator that leads to the bridge attached to the main building. My body is shaking as I make my way towards the member elevator, where I tap my card and watch as the numbers tick by, leading me to *her*.

The doors open and I blink, coming face to face with Ikelos and Jackson. They’re both scowling, arms crossed across their chests. “About fucking time,” Jackson says, lurching forward to grab me, dragging me out of the elevator before I can second guess my decision and get the fuck out of here.

Their behaviour draws a bit of attention from some of the patrons. Some smile, some widen their eyes in seeing me, while others blink and grin in a seductive way. So much for sneaking in here to slink in the shadows until I’m ready to confront my problems.

I stumble, tripping over my own feet while Jackson hauls me towards the bar, where Mckenna and Addison sit with drinks in hand. "Jackson," Addison grumbles, smacking his hand away from me and releasing me from his grip. "Are you okay? You look a bit pale," she says, touching my cheek with more care than I deserve.

"I just need a few minutes."

"You've had over an hour," Ikelos grumbles. "Rex! Can you get your boss a double?"

Glancing up, I catch Rex watching me with wide eyes. He quickly grabs a bottle, pouring out a not-so-healthy helping of the amber liquid I practically live off of. Instead of sliding it across the bar top like he normally does, he walks it right over to me, setting it down in front of me as he leans in towards my ear.

"Are you okay?" He whispers, his breath tickling my heated skin.

"I'll be fine. Where's Venessa?" I ask, grabbing the glass and chugging back the contents in one go. The liquid burns like molten lava down my chest, settling into my stomach like a lead weight.

"She's in the club. I haven't seen her since she came up, but she's doing well to interact with the guests."

"Did she do okay while I was gone?"

He pulls back and frowns. "You left her to deal with everything on her own as someone who just got hired, Eros. You know that was a shitty fucking move, even for you."

"I know," I sigh. "I feel like shit for doing that to her, but I needed to get out of here for a while. I—I know I shouldn't have done that."

"Why the fuck did you leave? Venessa was sure you did that because of her, but I told her you do weird shit like that from time to time. Please tell me she wasn't right in her assumption." I can't look at him, a new burn ripping through my chest, but this isn't from the alcohol, this is guilt. "Eros," He groans. "What the fuck happened for you to react like that? Did she do something?"

"No. She's done nothing nor said anything for me to react the way I did, but I just needed some time to get my thoughts together, and I couldn't do that if I was still in the building."

"You like her," he says, his voice getting lost in the sound of the music radiating around us. His eyes widen and he leans in closer to me once more. "Eros, I don't think I've ever seen you *like* anyone, and I've known you for quite a while. Does she like you back?"

I shrug. "I'm not sure, but I know that starting a relationship with her is inappropriate. She's my employee, Rex, I can't put her in that position, and I refuse to fire her."

I can feel the others watching my interaction with Rex, listening in with their supernatural hearing, and giving me no reprieve from the thoughts that have haunted me for the last few days. Thoughts of her have consumed every aspect of my mind, burying beneath every layer and seeping into every crevice until I can only see and think of her at every turn. Her existence has turned into a parasite within my being, overtaking every cell in my body until there is no me without her.

“Well, you don’t have many options here. You can’t keep avoiding her when she fucking works for you as your personal assistant, Eros.”

Heat creeps up my spine causing my body to shudder. My back stiffens at the feeling of being watched, and I catch Rex shift his gaze past me, his eyes widening slightly. He doesn’t need to tell me who it is because I *know*.

Slowly, I turn my head, my eyes searching through the flashing lights in the dimly lit room. My breath hitches when my gaze meets hers. Fuck, she’s beautiful. I swallow the lump forming in my throat, my breath catching in my chest as my lungs tighten at the sight of her.

The dress is absolutely gorgeous on her frame, the black satin clinging to her curves in a sensual invitation. The thin straps leave her shoulders bare, the neckline dipping to tease the delicious expanse of her sternum. The glint of diamonds between her breasts has my heart thumping faster. She’s wearing the necklace I bought her, the delicate chain catching in the strobing lights.

My eyes drift back to her face, to her hardened eyes rimmed in dark coal liner. The firm set of her plush lips has my heart stuttering and guilt ripping through me once more. There is no light in her eyes, no hint of a smile on those perfect lips, and the sudden stiffness of her shoulders causes me to stutter to a stop.

I didn't even realize I was moving until her look of anger and disappointment rooted me to the spot. I startle at the sudden smack of a hand against my back, my eyes reluctantly ripping away from her to see Ikelos standing next to me with a worried expression on his face.

"She looks more pissed than she did earlier," he says. His gaze shifts towards Venessa, his brows lifting in surprise. "Fuck, she's running."

"What?" I whip my head back to look at her, only catching her hair flipping across her shoulders when she turns quickly, giving me a view of her bare back, the dress plunging low and to the edge of her ass. "Fuck."

I take off, ignoring the soft laugh from Ikelos behind me as I weave my way through the crowd while panic settles into me.

Please don't run.

I will the thought towards her, wishing that I hadn't waited as long as I did to come in here. My actions have been nothing but a series of mistakes, layer upon layer of errors I can no longer take back.

"Eros!" A hand grips at my arm, and I glance down to see one of the regulars—Fiona, if I'm not mistaken—smiling up at me. "Dance with me!"

"Don't touch me," I snarl, ripping my arm away from her. Her eyes widen, but I don't even feel an inkling of remorse at my reaction. It's always been like this, but her touch no longer brings me any calm, it brings disgust and pity to the surface. I don't want her—I don't want *any* of them—I only want *her.*

I feel violated from her touch, like I've done something wrong in allowing my guard to be down enough to not see her advance towards me. My eyes scan the floor once more, panic settling into me again when I no longer see her, but I head in the direction she was headed, popping out at the sideline that leads to the bathrooms.

"Venessa!" I call out in desperation, my chest heaving with each breath. I notice a few girls stumble out of the bathroom, their faces pale and eyes slightly glazed over. "Fuck," I grit out, pushing through the line towards them.

The closer I get, the more I realize they're not drunk. No, they have the same look on their faces that Logan did. I shove my way through the door, ignoring the protest from the girls trying to get in.

"Go to the other one!" I snap, throwing my hand up to point to the bathrooms on the other side of the room. They don't hesitate to run away, shocked by my anger and behaviour. There are a few still lingering in the bathroom itself, some glancing towards the stalls with wary looks while others sit in the lounge area. "Get out," I say through gritted teeth.

"Oh, fuck, Eros," one of them squeaks. "Wh—why do you look so angry?"

"I said get the fuck out, Melody. I won't ask again. All of you, get the fuck out of this bathroom before I throw you out."

They all scramble to do as I command, panic written all over their faces. When the last one slips out, I flip the lock, officially cutting off Venessa's escape. I know she's in here, I can feel her presence like an electric current running through my system. She's leached her powers without meaning to, and I know her—I know that slip in judgment will push her to spiral.

One by one, I push the stall doors open, each one empty. A sniffle pulls my attention to the last one in the line, my strides eating up the distance until I'm in front of it. I try to push it open, but it's locked, my teeth gritting together in agitation. I knock my knuckles against the metal, her quick gasp of breath cutting through the silence.

"Go away," she hisses.

"I can't do that," I snap back.

"Leave me alone, Eros!"

"I can't do that either." She makes no move to open the door, forcing me to pull in a long breath to try and calm myself. "Open the door, Venessa," I sigh, resting my forehead against the cool metal while I brace my hands on either side of the frame.

"No. I don't want to talk to you. I don't want to fucking see you!"

That comment hurts, slicing through my chest like a serrated blade. "You're upset with me."

"You left me," she sniffles.

"You did your job perfectly without me. The place looks beautiful and it's running smoothly. I knew you could handle it on your own."

"You said you would be here for the opening. You lied."

"I know. I'm sorry."

I stumble back when the door rips open, her furious, but broken gaze, locked onto mine. "If you were sorry, you would have been here." She tries to squeeze past me, but I grip into her elbow to stop her. "Don't fucking touch me!" She screams, whirling hard enough to rip from my grip at the same time her other hand comes up, slapping me across the face.

I'm stunned, blinking from the shock of her attack. Slowly, I turn to look at her again, her chest heaving on broken inhales. Her makeup is beginning to run slightly, dark streaks marring her cheeks while her face contorts from fury to pain. Her eyes bow, a flicker of regret slipping onto her expression.

"You look beautiful," I whisper, pointing to the necklace around her neck. "I'm glad you're wearing it."

"Fuck you," she chokes out, her hand coming up to grip the pendant. My heart pounds viciously in my chest, the fear she'll rip it off her slim neck rattling around inside of me. "This was a mistake. All of this was a fucking mistake, and I shouldn't be here." Her hands tremble as she lifts them to the back of her neck, carefully undoing the necklace. She stares at it in her palm for a few long seconds before holding it out to me. "Take it back."

"No."

"Take it back, Eros."

"I refuse," I grit out, my throat burning from holding back my emotions.

"Fine." She opens her palm, the necklace slipping through her fingers and falling to the floor in a soft clink, but the sound echoes through my head like the thrum of a gong. "I quit," she whispers. "I'll be gone by the morning."

My body is frozen as I stare at her. How did this happen? How did I end up fucking this up so royally? "Venessa—" I manage to stumble a step forward but stop when she takes two steps back with her hands up to halt me.

"Don't. Don't come near me."

"What can I do to get you to stay? I don't want you to go, Venessa."

"You'll find another assistant and forget all about me, Eros. This is for the best. I'm sorry I wasted your time." She drops her head, her fingers running gently over the dress. "I'll return the dress and send you the money for it, and I'll return the car as well."

"No." She glances up, tears still streaking down her cheeks. "You can't."

"I have to," she whispers. "I'm a stranger—a fucking nobody to you."

"You're not."

CHAPTER TWENTY-FOUR

VENESSA

I step back in shock when he sways on the spot and drops to his knees in front of me. His hands settle into his lap, open in submission as his head bows in defeat. I stare at him, horrified at the fact I've broken him to this level. I'm nothing to him, an employee that he showed a bit of interest in, but he's reacting harder than I expected him to.

I can't give him anything. I can't provide him with comfort or calm in his life, only pain and misery, and more than likely, death. I hate myself for entertaining the idea that we could be something more, something that could grow and evolve.

When I saw him walk off the elevator, my heart skipped a few beats, but my steps paused on my way to him because his attention was never on me. He didn't even try to look for me, being dragged off by Nic and Jackson to start drinking while I worked my ass off to pull off this event.

The longer I stared at him, the angrier I got, and the harder my resolve became. I'm not good for him, and being in an environment like this one, will end up with someone getting hurt. Those few girls that I pushed past felt the poison within me, stumbling away while I tried to run and hide from him.

He looked panicked when I took off, leaving everyone behind to seek me out, but it was too late. My mind was made up, and I knew if I waited for his explanation, I wouldn't have the will to fully pull away from him.

Seeing him now, on his knees in front of me, practically begging me to stay, I need to know. "Why didn't you come find me right away?" I ask, my voice trembling as quiet tears continue to fall down my cheeks.

His shoulders slump forward, and his head dips deeper. "I was pulled away the moment I stepped off the elevator. I had every intention of trying to find you. I looked the best I could while Jackson dragged me off, but I couldn't exactly slip away easily. I never meant to hurt you, Venessa. I know I shouldn't have left the way I did."

"Why did you? Why would you just leave like that, Eros? I know you lied when you said you were leaving to deal with things. You left because of me, didn't you?"

His hands curl into fist on his thighs, his head tipping up enough for those amber eyes to gleam at me through the fringe of his blond hair. His eyes are glassy, his emotions burning through, right into my soul. "Yes," he sighs. "I left because of you."

I knew. Deep down, I knew it was because of me, and I thought I was prepared to hear it confirmed by him, but the words hurt deeper than I thought they would.

"Then I guess you just made this decision easier for me. I won't be a bother to you any longer."

"You were never a bother, Venessa. Please just listen. At least give me the chance to explain myself."

"It won't change anything."

"It may not, but I need you to know."

"Fine."

He grabs the necklace and slowly gets to his feet, hesitating his steps when I move away from him again. He sighs, running his fingers through his hair in frustration. He looks rough, the scruff on his face longer than it was days ago.

"I left to put distance between us. I—I was having indecent thoughts about you. I know you don't feel anything towards me, and I didn't want to make you uncomfortable if I slipped again and made an inappropriate comment that would end up causing you to leave. I thought if I stepped away from the situation for a little while, I would be able to gain control over my emotions."

"And did it work?"

He shakes his head. "No. Every second I was away from you, only had me thinking about you more. I know how fucked up that is—how fucked up *I* am for thinking that way—but I tried, Venessa." He drops his eyes to the ground, taking a step back from me while his hands fist at his thighs. "I looked into your past," he says quietly.

It feels like I just got doused in ice water, my body swaying as his words settle into me. "How...?" I croak out. None of it makes sense. I've been careful to hide every single part of my past, and it's not like I gave him enough information for him to piece any of it together.

"Jackson is good with computers. Venessa, you need to know that what happened in the past wasn't your fault. You didn't kill him on purpose."

My knees buckle and I stumble back, bracing myself against the wall while my lungs stop working. He dug deep. If he knows that, he must know *everything*. He steps towards me again and I throw up my hand, my breath wheezing through my lungs. "Don't come any closer."

"It wasn't your fault."

"It was. *I'm* the one who killed him."

"Do you know *how*?" I stare at him a moment, his gaze kind and unwavering. I shake my head. "I think you need to sit down. There's a lot I need to tell you, Venessa. I had hoped to do this tomorrow instead of during the event, but I can't let you walk away from this—from *me*."

CHAPTER TWENTY-FIVE

EROS

In my desperate attempt to keep her, I'm about to ruin everything she's known about herself. I hope she doesn't freak out, but explaining to her that she's a supernatural being, won't sit well with her. None of this is her fault, that wasn't a lie. She was thrown into this world, forced to live a human life with no knowledge of what she is. If she were any other being, she may have been able to survive without knowing, but her chemical makeup requires her to feed, and she's slowly starving herself. If she doesn't get a hold of this side of herself, she may implode, pulling in everyone around her without meaning to.

She settles into one of the couches in the darker corner of the bathroom, her hands trembling as she folds them on her lap. I stay standing for now, not wanting to encroach on her personal space when she very clearly wants me to stay away from her.

"Do you know anything about your birth parents?" I ask, trying to keep my voice calm and low.

She shakes her head. "They died when I was a kid. I don't even remember what they looked like."

"So, you have no memories from before...from when you were a child?"

"Sometimes I get bits and pieces, small fragments where I wonder if it was just a dream or an actual memory."

I file that comment away, wondering if Ikelos might be able to tap into her subconscious mind when she's ready in order to uncover some further truths. "Venessa, you're not human. Not fully at least."

Her face pales and her jaw drops open. "What?" She laughs awkwardly. "What do you mean? I'm not human? What else would I be?"

"Your scent has supernatural hints to it."

"Supernatural...like vampires and werewolves?" She scoffs. "Those things don't exist, Eros."

"They do. There's a world that exists, hidden in the shadows, one most humans don't know about. There are a few that actually sell themselves to vampires in order to gain the high from their venom, and the hope to be turned, but that's not the point. You're not like them, you're something different."

"Stop fucking around, Eros. This isn't funny."

"I'm not trying to be funny."

"If that society is so secret, how do *you* know about it?"

"Because I'm not human either." She shakes her head and tries to lurch to her feet, but I shove her back down, crowding into her space to hover above her. "Listen to me. Look at me and tell me I'm lying."

Her eyes burn into mine, searching for the lie that doesn't exist. I let a small portion of power bleed through, and her eyes widen. "Who...*are* you?" She whispers, her hand slowly coming up towards my face. She catches herself before she makes contact, quickly tucking her hand back into her lap.

"I'm Eros."

"I don't mean your name," she murmurs, rolling her eyes.

I have to admit, she's taking this better than I expected her to, but I don't think she actually believes what I'm saying, even with the small bit of proof I've given her. I don't have extravagant powers like Ikelos or Jackson, my abilities bordering closer to stealth and subtlety.

"I'm known by many names, Venessa. Eros is the one I prefer. Do you know what Eros means?" She shakes her head. "Love."

"Wait...are you trying to tell me you're Eros, as in, the *god* of love? Like fucking Cupid?"

"Yes," I chuckle. "Like fucking Cupid."

"So, this club—"

"It's a ruse. A place I can use my abilities freely and without repercussion or worry."

"Prove it."

"How do you wish for me to do that? My powers aren't exactly extraordinary in any way."

"Your eyes were glowing...that wasn't a trick of the light?"

"No, that was me flexing my powers."

"You're insane," she laughs, dropping her gaze to her lap.

"That might be true, but not in this situation."

"Say I believe you...say I buy into the fact that the supernatural world exists..." She glances up at me through her tear-soaked lashes, but the tears have finally dried up on her cheeks. "What am I?"

"You're a succubus—at least half."

"A succubus. Isn't that a sex demon? They're dream demons, are they not?"

"You're only part, so your human half is more than likely allowing you to feed and exist in the waking world." I'm surprised she knows that much about the creatures. They're portrayed in films in different ways, so her knowing anything close to the truth is quite impressive.

"So, I'm a freak of nature," she murmurs, her voice cracking on the word freak.

I drop to my knees in front of her, pushing the boundary, and getting as close as I can to her without touching her. "You're not a freak, Venessa. You're special, and you've lived a hard life because you didn't know who and what you are. There's nothing wrong with you, and you're not a bad person."

"I kill people that touch me, Eros," she whispers. "I'm evil. What I can do is evil, and how am I supposed to go on living, knowing that I've killed someone just because they cared about me and wanted to be with me?" She wipes at her eyes but doesn't look at me. "I can't risk you getting hurt, too."

"I'm an immortal, Venessa. That's the reason why your touch doesn't affect me the same way it does others. The reason it's happening so aggressively is because you haven't allowed that side of yourself to thrive. You're starving for energy, and it's your body's way of trying to get what it needs. It's not your fault because you didn't know this is who you are, but I'll be here to help you...if you'll let me."

"I don't know what to do," she sniffles.

"Let me help you." Slowly, I lift my hand up to cup her cheek, hoping she doesn't pull away from me. My heart thumps loudly in my ears when she leans into the touch, a soft whimper slipping through her lips.

She finally looks at me, her eyes swimming with emotion and glistening like pools of turbulent water. "I'm scared," she sobs. "I'm so fucking scared, Eros. I haven't talked to anyone about this. I ran and pushed everyone I knew away."

"No more tears," I say, gently swiping the new tears away from her cheeks and the muddled streaks of her makeup. "We'll figure this out." I grip her hand, turning it palm side up and settling the necklace into it. "Please, put it back on."

She nods and clasps it back around her neck with trembling fingers before dragging those fingers down the pendant. "It's really beautiful."

"It's nothing compared to you." I lift to my feet and hold out my hand to her, smiling down at her when she glances up with wide eyes. "There's one more thing I hope to get from you."

She settles her hand into mine, letting me pull her up to her feet. "What's that?"

"A dance." I can feel the tingle of her power against my skin, but tonight isn't the night to test her power. I don't want to overwhelm her further than I already have, and when the reality of what it means hits her, she might end up hating me or fearing me in the end.

"I'd like that," she whispers, giving my hand a small squeeze.

It'll take some time, but I hope that she'll allow me to help her. Even if she's not comfortable with the true intentions of a succubus—that she won't choose *me*—I want her to be confident in her own skin and capable of living a long and normal life.

CHAPTER TWENTY-SIX

VENESSA

I can't stop the nerves from battering around in my system as Eros leads me out of the bathroom. We get some strange looks from the girls impatiently waiting outside the door, but no one dares to question him or his intentions.

What *are* his intentions?

I can't even begin to wrap my head around the information he's dumped on me, but I can't deny the fact it makes sense since nothing else has. I'd be lying if I said I hadn't looked into supernatural reasons for what I've been able to do, but my search always came up empty. I didn't have enough details to fully form any proper theories, so the fact that Eros knew exactly what I was just from my history, says a lot.

Wait. Does Jackson know what I am, too?

"Eros?" My voice is quiet, drowned out by the music, but he still turns his head back to look at me. "What's Jackson's last name?"

His brow quirks up at that, a smirk playing on his lips as he leads me towards the DJ booth. "Eros!" Ethan smiles, tugging his headphone a bit further off his ear. "What can I do for you?"

He leans in closer to him, his voice low enough that I can't catch what he says to him. Just when I decide to ask him again, he tugs me onto the dance floor, a gasp slipping through my lips when my body collides with his. His warm hand grips mine, while his other hand slides across the small of my back in a strong embrace. I glance up at him, tipping my head when I catch the music changing.

"Bad Omens!" I laugh, my heart kicking up at notch at the smile he gives me.

"We seem to have the same tastes, so I figured we could make this our song."

I stare at his chest, trying to hide my own smile at the fact he's picked out a song for us. I'm not complaining, Specter is amazing, and I wouldn't reject the idea, even if someone paid me.

"Frost," he says, his warm breath creeping across my cheek as he leans down towards my ear.

"What?"

"Jackson's last name. It's Frost."

"You're joking." He shakes his head, the smile still playing across his lips. His eyes hold a hint of mischief in their depths, and I know he's being serious. "Jack Frost." He nods. "*The* Jack Frost?" He nods again. "Fuck."

"Don't tell him I told you. I'm sure he'll mention it eventually, especially now that you're technically one of us."

"One of us..."

"There are plenty of supernatural beings living among us, Venessa. It's not just me or Jackson." His jaw ticks as he straightens back up, glancing around. "Nic, Mckenna, and Addison, are also *other*. There are a few shifters here as well, and I'm pretty sure I scented a witch or two."

"Wait, roll back. Nic, Mckenna, and Addison, too?" He nods. "How did I not see that."

"In time, you'll come to understand the subtle tells that give away someone who is supernatural. Their scent is the most obvious one, but it could be something as simple as their looks and presence."

"I should have known you were a god," I mumble.

Slipping his hand from mine, he tucks his fingers under my chin, tipping my head up to look at him. I don't think I'll ever get used to feeling his skin against mine, the warmth of his touch, the gentleness he grants me as he stares down at me.

"Why do you say that?" He asks, his head tipping in curiosity.

"Look at you. You're practically carved from stone, and your eyes...I've never seen eyes like that my entire life."

He leans down towards me, my breath hitching at how close his lips are to mine. The desire to lift onto my toes and close the distance between us is overwhelming, and my body trembles at the strain to stop myself from doing just that. "You like my eyes?" He muses.

I swallow thickly, licking my lips as my eyes drift from his mouth to his eyes, and back again. He's close—too close—and it's taking everything in me to not kiss him. He's my boss, and as much as I hope his words were true and that he likes me more than an employee, I still don't have the confidence to risk losing him. It's hard enough to manage the fact he's touching me so freely, when every instinct inside of me is screaming at me to pull away and put distance between us.

"Yes," I whisper, a whimper slipping through my lips when he shifts a fraction closer. I can feel his warm breath fanning against my already heated skin, the smell of mint tempting me to taste him.

"Is there anything else you like?" He asks, the grip on my chin shifting down to gently circle my throat.

My heart pounds harder and more frantic, my breaths coming in sharp pants as heat floods through my body. I stare at his eyes, the glow from before more subtle than it was earlier. He's showing no signs of weakness or drain, yet he's been touching me this entire time. Is he someone that I can actually be with without risking killing him? That thought gives me a small fraction of confidence as I shift my hands across his hips, up his stomach, and settling them against his chest. His body stiffens, like he's anticipating me pushing him away.

"Everything," I say, giving him a small smile. "I like everything, Eros."

"What do you want, Venessa?" His fingers curl into my lower back, gently tugging me closer to his body. My heartrate quickens at the feel of his cock pressed against my stomach, slowly hardening with each passing second.

"I—I don't know. I can't get out of my head," I admit.

His eyes drift to my lips, his Adam's apple bobbing in a way that makes me want to run my tongue against it and nip at the skin. "Say the words," He growls, his fingers tightening around my throat.

I need to know. I *need* to know that this could work between us. He's willing to test the theory and put himself at risk. I know he's strong—more resilient than the humans I've come in contact with all this time.

"Kiss me," I whisper, the words so low that I wonder if I actually spoke them out loud.

CHAPTER TWENTY-SEVEN

EROS

The words are barely through her lips before I grip her neck and pull her into me, crashing my lips against hers. She moans into my mouth, her body melting into mine as I pry her lips apart with my tongue. Heat burns through me, her fingers gripping into my jacket before she slides her hands up to grip into the back of my neck.

Releasing her throat, I slide my other hand down her body, digging my fingers into her hips and rolling them into me as I press myself against her body. The kiss is feral and primal, her desperation bleeding through with every nip and suck, gasp and moan, but I devour every single sound and taste of her.

My lips tingle from her touch, my heart pounding frantically in my chest with each passing second. I can feel the energy being pulled from me into her, but her kiss is an addiction I have no desire to quit.

Her body trembles within my hold, another gasp slipping through before she tries to break the kiss. "Eros," she says shakily.

"A little more," I moan, nipping and sucking on her bottom lip before plunging my tongue deep into her mouth.

Seconds later, she pulls back again, but she doesn't try to completely remove herself from my hold like I expected her to. She drags her hands back down my chest, brushing her fingers over my pecs as she looks up at me with wide eyes.

Those pools of blue are glowing softly, my own energy revitalizing the beast within her. I can see the hunger within those depths, the desperation for more, to taste again, to feed until it's satiated. It'll take some time to balance the need within her, but little by little, I will feed that side of her until she regains control.

My skin prickles, the hair on the back of my neck creeping up. Glancing over, I startle at the sight of Ikelos and Mckenna staring at me with smirks on their faces, while Jackson and Addison stare with wide eyes.

"What?" I grumble, pulling Venessa against my hip and turning to face them.

"Let's go grab drinks," Ikelos says, jerking his chin towards one of the VIP rooms before gripping Mckenna's hand and pulling her along.

I wait for Jackson to follow, but he lifts a brow, motioning with his hand for us to go first. It's a weird sensation, being sandwiched by two gods, but I do as I'm told and follow Ikelos to the room.

"Get in," he says. I sigh, pulling Venessa with me, deep into the circular booth at the back of the room. Ikelos slides in next to me while Mckenna gets in on Venessa's side, Addison sliding in next to her.

"I'm going to grab us a bottle and some glasses," Jackson says, closing the curtains on us.

"So," Ikelos starts, leaning back into the bench with his arms draped across the back of it.

"So," I repeat, feeling suddenly nervous by his attention.

"Did you work your shit out?"

"I told her everything," I admit, squeezing Venessa's hand when she tries to pull away.

"You were making out pretty hard and for a little while. How do you feel?"

"I feel fine. My adrenaline is a little spiked, but nothing I can't handle."

His eyes drift to her and my spine tingles with apprehension. "You haven't run away, so I can only assume you've come to terms with what you are."

"I don't think I would be able to run away, even if I wanted to. I think Eros would hunt me down and drag me back," she snorts.

I bring our joined hands up to my lips and kiss her knuckles. "And then I would tie you up so you couldn't escape me again," I whisper. She shivers at the words, a light blush creeping up her neck and cheeks.

Ikelos turns his head towards the curtains, where seconds later, Jackson walks through with a bottle in one hand and a tray with glasses in the other. He sets everything down on the table in front of us, pouring out large portions for each of us and flopping down on the bench next to Addison. He drapes his arm across her shoulder and leans into her, placing a small kiss on her cheek.

"How much did Eros tell you about what you are?" Jackson asks.

"I mean, I know a bit about it because of myths and legends, but he explained that my composition seems to be a bit different because I'm part human."

Jackson nods and takes a drink, setting the glass back down on the table. "We won't know until later on if you'll age like a human or a succubus either. It's hard to know what characteristics take hold when crossing is involved. Knowing that, you still need to be careful to not put yourself in dangerous situations that may risk your life."

"I've been living as a human my entire life, so I doubt I'll be able to break the habit ingrained into me. Self-preservation is at the top of my list, that's why I've been running for as long as I have. I've avoided contact with everyone because I didn't want to risk hurting or killing someone again without meaning to, and then getting caught and thrown away or worse, killed."

"Do you understand what needs to happen for you to gain control over these powers?" Ikelos asks, leaning towards Venessa across the table. She frowns, glancing at me for a second, like I hold all the answers. "Eros," Ikelos sighs.

"I didn't want to overwhelm her. Be thankful she's no longer shying away from physical contact, Ikelos. I wasn't going to throw everything at her at once."

"Ikelos?" Venessa murmurs, her frown deepening.

Fuck, I slipped up and called him by his true name instead of the one he's adopted in this world. "I meant Nic," I say quickly.

"But you *said* Ikelos." She turns to him again, cocking her head. "Who are you?"

"How much has Eros told you?"

She nods towards Jackson. "He told me you were all considered *other*. He didn't go into detail on who you were though."

I sigh in relief that she didn't throw me under the bus for already exposing Jackson. My anxiety spikes with the fear that all this information will be too much for her. It's one thing for her to deal with one god, but three? Technically four, since Addison has the same abilities as Jackson now, making her a lesser god as well.

"I'm Jack Frost," Jackson says, giving her a crooked grin before planting another kiss on Addison's cheek. "Addison is like me, adopting the same abilities that I have, but she started off as human."

"Wait, what?" Venessa gasps, shifting her gaze to Addison.

"Jackson was made as well, just a long time ago. It's this whole self-sacrifice thing with this stupid bird," she says, waving her hand dismissively and rolling her eyes.

"He's definitely a stupid bird, but he's still the god of winter," Jackson chuckles.

"Since Eros already exposed my true name, I may as well go next," Ikelos grumbles. "I'm the god of nightmares, and Morpheus is my brother. Mckenna here, was also human, but in order to save her life, I had to turn her into one of my nightmares and tether her soul."

I glance down at Venessa from the corner of my eye, watching as her eyes go wide, jaw slackening, and her face paling another shade. "What the fuck," she whispers. "That...all of that sounds insane!" Her eyes dart from Mckenna to Addison. "You guys died?" They both nod. "Do you guys have powers?"

Addison grins, shuffling in her seat and clearing her throat as she settles her palms flat on the table. A thin sheet of ice spreads from her fingertips towards her glass, creeping up the sides of it to frost it completely.

Venessa leans towards it, her eyes going wider than I thought humanly possible. "That's so cool," she whispers, reaching her hand towards the glass.

I snatch it away, glaring at her when she turns her head quickly to look at me. "I wouldn't touch that. It may look pretty and seem harmless, but that could physically harm you if you touched it at the source."

"He's right. Jackson had to tell me off when I tried to touch his show of power, too."

"What about you?" She asks, shifting her attention to Mckenna.

"My powers are based off of Nic's," she says, lifting her hand up, where shadowy smoke tendrils caress her fingers, slowly dissolving the skin into a dark vapour.

I haven't seen her powers in action, but it's definitely like the hounds he keeps in his company. I got to see them phase through the doors on multiple occasions as they tried to get away, which was both horrifying and entertaining when Ikelos tried to run after them. Mckenna is very different from the hounds in looks alone, the eerie red gleam of their eyes not gracing her features. From what Ikelos said, Mckenna's eye colour did in fact change, taking on a lighter hue from her original tone.

Her hair changed as well, having been a darker blonde than Addison's current locks. Addison shifted in appearance as well, not only her eyes and hair colour, taking on lighter tones, but her skin as well. The skin tone was a surprise, since Jackson has a rich, dark hue to his own flesh, which makes his white hair and stormy grey eyes stand out in a way that draws attention. Having been hidden from the world for so long, I don't know how he manages with the influx of attention because of his appearance. I've witnessed Addison on multiple occasions, threatening to end lives when girls look at him a little bit too long with seductive eyes.

"Wow, I wish I had cool powers like that," Venessa murmurs, her shoulders slumping as she stares at the table in front of her.

"As do I, but just because our abilities can't be witnessed and put on display, doesn't mean they're not vital to our purpose."

"I don't feel like what I can do really *has* a purpose. It's not used for good in any way, and it's not exactly something I can claim to be used as a defense."

"That's where you're wrong. Your powers could save your life if the situation presented itself. The fact you can drain someone's life force if you so choose to do so is an impressive weapon. All you need is one small touch, Venessa."

She glances up at me, her eyes darkened by the weight behind my words. "A defense shouldn't jump right to murder."

"Those results are only happening at the moment because you've strayed away from what you are. Once you get control over that part of you, you'll have the choice on whether or not to feed. You're only doing that right now because you've starved yourself since coming into your powers."

"If I'm starved, how long will it take me to be satisfied?"

"It'll take time," I say quietly, rubbing my hand across her shoulder blades and loving the way her eyes flutter as she leans into the touch.

"It would be quicker if you just fucked," Ikelos murmurs. "Ow! What the fuck?" He grumbles, glaring across the table at Mckenna.

She's glaring back while he leans down, rubbing at his leg under the table. "You're such an asshole, you know that?" She growls.

"How am I an asshole for simply telling the truth? It's not my fault he's only giving her half the information."

"It's not really your place to be throwing that information at her in that way," Jackson interjects.

"Well, a succubus *is* a sex demon, so I sort of figured that was the whole point of it," Venessa says quietly.

I lean down towards her ear, smirking when her body shivers against the feel of my breath against her skin. "You don't *have* to do that. We can stabilize you with touch alone, it'll just take a bit longer, that's all. No one is forcing you into anything."

"You don't want to have sex with me?" She asks, tilting her head enough to glance at me from the corner of her eye, her brows dipping in a way that has a slight panic creeping inside of me.

"I didn't say that," I say quickly, cringing when she smirks. My own words settle into me, and the others snort out laughter at how easily I caved into acknowledging my desires. "I just mean, I don't expect that of you."

"No?" She muses.

"Your company is enough, Venessa. The fact you've allowed me to touch you so freely tonight, makes me unbelievably happy. So no, I don't expect anything else from you." I frown when her brows dip again, her expression seeming almost...disappointed. "Do you...want to?" I ask hesitantly, not wanting to get my hopes up at the idea of actually getting a chance to be with her in that way.

The kiss was amazing. My body burning from the inside out in a way I've never experienced before. It was like I could feel everything. Every touch, every cell in my body lighting up, and every small fraction of her body shifting against mine. It was like that kiss merged us—fused our souls a little closer together, but not quite completely tethered. I know that this possible relationship is still quite precarious, but I don't want to do something that may end up ruining my chances with her.

Pressuring her into something like that—a truly intimate encounter—would most definitely ruin things if she's not on the same wavelength as I am. I want her to make this decision for herself and not let herself feel pressured into it. I don't want her to use me either, but I would let her if that was all she wanted in order to help herself and the situation that she's currently in.

With her condition, I know that I'm the logical choice for her *to* be intimate with someone. There's no way she can risk being with a human, when past interactions have resulted in such severe reactions. A gentle graze from her alone was enough to almost make Logan pass out where he stood. She would most definitely kill someone if she tried to kiss or have sex with them in her current state.

“Maybe,” she says, her voice trembling on the word.

CHAPTER TWENTY-EIGHT

VENESSA

I can't believe I just admitted that to him. No, not just him. With the way all their eyes widen, I know that my voice wasn't low enough for these supernatural beings. I still can't believe half the shit they've been saying, but the proof was right there—right in front of my eyes. Unless I've gone completely insane, I can't deny the power that was flexed in front of me tonight, and deep down in my heart, I *want* it all to be true.

Acknowledging the fact that the supernatural world exists would make everything that's happened in my life make so much more sense. It would make things easier for me, knowing that I can trust this man and his group of friends to help me in a way my family never could. If my parents wouldn't have died, would I have ended up in the situation that I was in? I doubt it.

"Hmm," Eros hums, a shiver raking up my spine when he drags his nose gently up the length of my neck. His soft inhale causes my body to shudder and subconsciously lean closer to him.

I missed this. The touches, the warmth, the care he flexes towards me with each gentle caress of his fingers. The way those strong hands curl into my side, urging me to move closer to him. Everything about him has my body aching and begging for more, but I can't voice those desires to him. Even with knowing everything, I can't get out of my own head, and I can't let go of the fear that has weaved and wrapped its way around my entire being, stitching itself into my very soul to prevent me from ever giving anyone a chance.

"Maybe is better than no," he whispers. "But I won't force you into anything. You have all the control here, Venessa."

"What if..." I hesitate in my words, my body trembling and my cheeks heating with embarrassment. "What if I don't *want* control?"

He pulls back enough to look down at me, and instantly I regret the words. I'm being too forward and too presumptuous in my admittance of wanting him to take the reins on this. It's bad enough I've admitted to wanting him, but to basically say I'll throw my will away so that he can do what he wants...

His eyes begin to glow, the amber burning like an ignited coal. They sear right into me, freezing me to the spot and making it so I can't look away from him, even if I wanted to. The low growl that rumbles in his chest has my body shivering, but not in fear, in delicious anticipation. The sound is primal and filled with desire, and maybe I'm not regretting my words as much as I was moments ago.

He cups my cheek, his hand burning against my skin, and locking my gaze on his. "Is that what you want?" He asks, his brows dipping as his eyes search mine for the hesitation that was there a few seconds ago. I swallow, giving my head the barest of nods, and gasp when his eyes flare to life and widen.

He crashes his mouth against mine, prying my lips apart with his tongue to delve into my mouth and taste everything I have to offer him. I whimper and moan, leaning into him and parting my mouth further to clash my tongue against his. An internal fire erupts inside of me, and my body shifts towards him as my hands snake up his neck to tangle into his hair. I tug and pull him closer, locking him against me. My chest tightens and my body heats further as I gasp into his mouth, feeling an electric current snap between us.

He pulls away too soon, the both of us breathing heavily as he rests his forehead against mine. His hand is trembling as he brushes it through my hair, his breath puffing out in a long, slow burst. "I'll give you what you want...soon," he whispers. "I don't want you to rush into this and regret your decision to be with me." I try to shake my head and argue that I won't regret it, but he buries his hand into my hair at the nape of my neck and presses his lips to my forehead. "Please," he murmurs, kissing me again.

I don't know if he's doing this because he's actually afraid I'll regret it and is giving me the time to change my mind, or if he's actually afraid of what I'm capable of. The way his body trembles slightly, shows that the kiss we just shared affected him in a way that may have been a drain on his power. He's still standing, and he still looks fully here, but with the way I am, I could still very well be risking hurting him.

I don't want to hurt him, and I'm fighting against that fear to try and listen to him and allow myself to experience things I've only dreamed of. This god is giving me the chance at living a normal life, and I'll take it as slow as he needs me to.

"You two are going to have your work cut out for you. This isn't going to be easy to start, but over time, you should be able to live normally, Venessa."

I turn to look at Nic, a pitying smile on his face that makes my heart clench in my chest. I know he's right, but I hate that they know so much about me and the things I need to do to get my life back. I don't think they're against my relationship with Eros, if anything, they seem to be encouraging it, and I'm not sure why. I have nothing to offer him except the possibility of his demise.

His life would be so much simpler if he were with someone else—someone that could be with him and care for him in the way he deserves without risking his wellbeing. For some reason, still unknown to me, he wants to be with me. I'm nothing—no one—but what am I to him in his eyes? What does he see in me that has forced this strange pull between us?

"We'll figure it out as we go, but I'm willing to try as long as Venessa is," Eros says, his grip on my hip tightening possessively. I glance up at him, shocked at the way he's staring down at me with those ethereal eyes glowing softly. "Are you willing to try?" He whispers.

I swallow; the lump lodged in my throat growing thicker the longer he stares. *Am* I willing to try? I want to. I want to give him the chance he seems desperate to have, but that nagging voice in my head is pounding away, telling me this is stupid, that this is wrong, and that I'll end up destroying him. His brows crease at my hesitation and his nostrils flair as he leans down towards my ear.

"Answer me," he whispers, his breath sending a shudder through my entire body. The tone of his words isn't harsh, but the edge of darkness within them still makes my chest tighten and my lungs struggle to pull in a proper breath. I practically stop breathing when he drags his nose up the length of my neck, inhaling deeply once he reaches my hair. "Tell me you want this," he purrs, his lips brushing delicately against my skin.

My body heats, a flush spreading across my skin in a way that makes me want to tear off my clothes to relieve the fire building inside of me. It's been so long since I've been touched in any way, and the sudden attention has my body craving each caress he offers me. I want to melt into him and let him do what he wants. I want him to taste and touch every inch of me, to kiss every starved section of flesh.

The thought of having sex with him has anxiety building inside of me. It's been so long—too long. I haven't seen him fully, but I've gotten glimpses of what is hidden beneath his clothes. He'll break me. He'll tear me apart from the inside out, and my depravity is craving that thought. There will be pain mixed with that pleasure, and every cell in my body is desperate to experience that amidst the fear of hurting him.

Fuck it.

"I—I want this," I murmur, my voice trembling on the words. I turn my head, sucking in a sharp breath at how close his lips are to mine. "I want *you*."

"Fuck, Venessa," he growls, cupping my jaw as he presses his lips to mine. The kiss is gentle, nothing like the one we had moments ago, but something inside of me slides into place, like a puzzle piece that was waiting to slide home.

"Let's go enjoy the rest of the night," Nic says, drawing our attention back to him. "You haven't really socialized with your patrons, and I'm pretty sure you scared the shit out of a few of them when you were hunting Venessa down."

"I saw you snap at that one girl," Mckenna points out.

"She fucking touched me," Eros snaps. "She tried to stop me, and I don't appreciate being stopped when my efforts are set on one goal."

"Hmm, you know you can't act that way, especially in this type of setting," Jackson snorts.

"It's my club, and therefore, I follow my own rules. There is only one person that I will allow to touch me from this point on, and it doesn't include any of the desperate twats in this building. They only want one thing from me, not seeing me for anything but a conquest in their own game."

His words send a thrill of joy through me. He doesn't *want* anyone else but me. He could have any of the women in this building, plenty of which are better looking than me, but he's proving once again that he wants *me*.

"So, only I can touch you?" I ask, knowing the answer, but still needing the reassurance for my fragile ego.

"No one but you. Until you decide I am no longer worthy of your time, and even then..."

That's beyond anything I would have expected from him since I would have been perfectly happy with a simple yes. The fact he's implying he won't allow anyone to touch him even if I decide I no longer wish to be with him has my heart beating a little faster. Once again, I have no idea *why* he's so focused on me, and what about me has gotten under his skin enough to pursue me, even when I was adamant on never being with anyone for the rest of my life.

“Please don’t say things like that,” I murmur, hating the feeling of guilt settling into me at the thought of him being alone if I’m no longer with him.

He frowns, tucking a stray strand of hair behind my ear. “What do you mean?”

“If we’re no longer together, I don’t want you to not try to find someone else to be with. We barely know each other, Eros, so there’s no reason for you to express that level of devotion.”

“There is no one else,” he says again, his tone harsh and filled with promise. “I’ve never been in a true relationship, and I’ve had no desire to even pursue that with anyone until I met you. My born curse hasn’t allowed me to even try any form of relations, but not once have I had the desire to do so. You’re the first person I’ve *wanted* to try for more. There’s something about you that draws me in, and the thought of not seeing you or being around you makes me extremely uncomfortable. I know we don’t know each other, but I hope in time, we have the chance to get to know one another.”

“You’re serious? Eros, you’re not cursed. What could you possibly mean by that?”

The question is enough for a shield to go down over his features. His face hardens, and his jaw ticks with barely restrained agitation or anger. Which, I’m not sure. “I can’t love, and in turn, can’t *be* loved,” he says bluntly.

His eyes shutter closed, and I glance around at the others, but none of them meet my gaze. They all have pitying looks on their faces though, so I know this is a subject he's talked about before. I don't understand how he could possibly believe that.

"That can't be true," I saw quietly, my throat drying up when he finally looks at me again. He looks so lost and so broken, the weight of his admission settling into him heavily. If it's true, what future could we truly have?

CHAPTER TWENTY-NINE

EROS

The last thing I wanted to do tonight was admit to her my darkest secret. She deserves to know the truth though, and letting her go into this blindly, would only end up hurting her in the end. I brace myself for the rejection, the words that will crush me the moment they come out of her mouth. The smartest thing for her to do would be for her to walk away from me and end this before it truly begins.

I know my limitations and I'm still willing and eager to give this a try, but she needs to know that true emotion from me will be the farthest from my mind. It's not on purpose of course, I *want* to care for her, and I do in my own way, but the thought of loving her feels like a whisp of smoke that I could never grasp onto.

"You're wrong." I blink, watching her as her lips press into a hard line, and that chin of hers tipping up in defiance.

"Excuse me?"

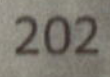

"I'm going to prove to you and to everyone else that you're capable of the emotions you think are out of reach. I don't know who made you believe this, but from the small interactions I've had with you, I can see for myself that it's a lie. If you didn't care, you wouldn't have gone to the lengths you have to keep me in your presence."

"You assume that it's not just some act," I retort, earning a vicious glare and an epic eye roll from her.

"Is it?" She snaps back.

I contemplate the answer, digging through my own thoughts to try and draw the truth from within myself. It must be a ruse, right? No, it can't be. I would never chase anyone else, even if the ones playing hard to get with me have been few and far between. I've never put this much effort into convincing someone I'm a good person in the hopes that they'll like me and trust me. I let her drive my fucking car for fuck's sake, and no one drives my car. I chased her through a room of people, pushing past women begging for even a second of my attention and ignoring them just to get to *her*.

"No," I admit before I can think better of it. My chest tightens at the look of triumph on her face. She's tearing at my walls without me even realizing the damage she's done with each blow against the foundation. If she keeps it up, there will be nothing left but my bared soul for her to see in all it's darkened glory.

"Good. If you want this, I want you to let yourself feel everything you wish to feel, without allowing yourself to be caged by your self-imposed curse. There is no proof of that, Eros, you just haven't found someone to bring that side of yourself out."

I fight back a grin. "And you think that *you're* that person?" I muse.

"Aren't I?"

She very well could be, but I don't want to get ahead of myself and end up disappointed if it doesn't end up working out. She's right though, I can't put limitations on myself if I have any hope of this working between us. Ikelos is right, we have our work cut out for us. She may very well end up killing me, but at least then the torment of my existence will no longer haunt me.

"We'll give you two a minute," Ikelos says, motioning for the others to slide out of the booth. He gives me a nod once he reaches the curtains and I have no idea why I'm suddenly so nervous being alone with Venessa. It's not the first time, and it certainly won't be the last.

"We should head out there and make sure everything is still running smoothly," I say quickly, trying miserably to end this awkward feeling building inside of me.

"Okay," she whispers, and my breath puffs out of me in relief. Sliding myself out of the booth first, I hold out my hand to her, hating the way she still hesitates to take it. "Thank you." Her hand trembles in my grip as I help her to her feet.

"After you," I say, motioning for her to move ahead of me, and I don't miss the small frown that forms between her brows and the slight shake of her head, like she's trying to dislodge whatever thought just invaded her mind. I shamelessly take in her form, loving the way the dress hugs her sensual curves, and the way her hips sway with every step she takes. The material leaves plenty to the imagination as it clings to her perfect ass, the swoop of the dress stopping just shy of revealing that part of her.

Fuck me, she's beautiful. She has her moments of unconventional beauty, but only a blind man would miss the glaring features that scream perfection incarnate. My heart thumps a little harder, beating a little faster, just in her presence alone. The thought of being with her in an intimate setting has heat flooding through every cell in my body. I don't know what will happen when that moment comes, but I'm sure it'll bring pleasure laced with unavoidable pain.

Kissing her felt like kissing a live wire, the touch electric and volatile, but addictive enough that it took everything in me to pull away. The music blaring from the speakers can't hide the hitching breath she takes the moment she opens the curtains. Her steps stall when she notices Mckenna and Addison standing guard. I notice the guys over by the bar, Jackson's eyes drifting towards us the moment we step out of the booth. Another nod of acknowledgement, and having both their support, sends a wave of relief through me.

I don't know what I would do without them. It's been nice, having people to talk to who understand me better than I understand myself. They've witnessed my control cracking, and the flurry of emotions I've been battling with firsthand.

"Here," Ikelos says, handing a drink off to me while he juggles two others. Jackson does the same thing for Venessa, a blush scattering across her cheeks as she carefully takes it from him.

You don't have to worry about touching me, Venessa. We're all supernatural, so a random touch won't affect us like a mortal. Once you get a handle on your power, you'll be able to touch them as well, but just know that you're safe with us."

I don't miss the faint gleam in her eyes as she fights back the emotions at his words. "Thank you, Jackson," she says quietly. "I–I appreciate all of you being so kind to me, even knowing what I've done."

"It was out of your control," Mckenna mumbles. "Don't blame yourself for something you had no say in. If you were brought up how you should have been, none of that would have happened."

"Eros?" My head whips over to the sensual voice next to me, disgust rolling through me when fingers drag down my arm. I'm really starting to hate this. I fucking hate the fact these women think they have a right to my body, to touch me in this way, at expecting me to bend to their will.

"Do not touch me," I snap, jerking away.

"But the last time I saw you—"

"Maxine," I snarl. "I've never given you permission to touch me at your leisure."

"But—"

"He said no!" Venessa hisses, sliding herself between us to glare at her. Her back is flush against my body, and Maxine's eyes drift from me to her, narrowing with irritation.

"Who the fuck do you think you are?" She huffs.

"His fucking assistant. Now, if you don't want to be escorted out of here, I suggest you leave him the fuck alone. I won't say it again."

"Just because you're his assistant, doesn't give you the right to interrupt us. We were talking, and quite frankly, someone like you should still know your place. Eros and I have history, and you would be smart to step away before things get ugly."

"Excuse me?" Venessa says coldly, her body swaying forward with the sudden urge to step into Maxine's space. I slide my hand across her stomach, pinning her to my chest to stop her from doing something she shouldn't.

Maxine's eyes drift from my hand around Venessa, up to my face. Her jaw twitches and her lip curls into a sneer. "You need to keep your bitch on a better leash, Eros. She should know who I am."

I blink, my fingers curling around air when Venessa suddenly lurches away from me to grip Maxine's jaw in her hand. "Venessa!" Ikelos roars, and it takes me a second to realize the reason for his reaction. A thin whisp of iridescent smoke trails from Maxine's parted lips towards Venessa. While one's eyes slowly dull and turn vacant, the other's gleam like a predator, ready to devour.

CHAPTER THIRTY

VENESSA

It's like the world around me fades into nothing. The sound of the thrumming music dulling until all I hear is the vicious pounding of my own heartbeat in my ears. My vision fragments, my breathing growing heavier with each passing second while the girl in front of me blurs and then sharpens into focus, only to blur once more.

I swear I hear my name being called out, but it's like I'm hearing the voice while I'm being forced under water. The vibrations of the club continue to strum through my body, but it's like I'm no longer here. I'm locked in some unknown place that I have no idea how I fell into, and I'm struggling to claw my way out of the encroaching darkness bleeding into every vein and blood vessel inside my body.

A shimmer of light flickers in front of me, and a roaring begins deep within my mind.

Take it. It's right there, begging to be consumed.

Is that me? Is that the sound of my own voice speaking to me within the hazy blackness encroaching on my mind? My hand is shaking and cramping around something hard and barely yielding, but I don't let go—I *can't.* My body is working on its own, my mind glazing over with a desperate need to consume. To destroy. To fucking *devour.*

Something grips my jaw painfully, wrenching my neck to the side before heat and warmth crash against my lips. A shudder rips through my body as a cool wave washes down my throat, satiating the raging hunger attempting to consume me, mind, body, and soul. A whimper has me blinking, the club coming into blinding focus before the source of the heat and cooling breath fragments into my vision.

Eros?

His eyes are screwed shut, his hand trembling as it begins to lose its grip on my face while Nic and Jackson try to wrench him back from me. I'm left gasping when he's pried away, my body swaying at the loss of contact from him. I watch in horror as the scene unfolds in front of me. Eros staggers, his knees buckling out from under him. He would crumple to the ground if it weren't for the hold Nic and Jackson have on him, their faces straining at the sudden drop from his weight. Addison is gripping the girl from earlier—I think her name is Maxine—while Mckenna smacks at her face to bring colour back into her cheeks.

A few of the patrons notice the commotion, their eyes widening as they take in their surroundings, and they slowly back away to give us all room. My own body is shaking, both from panic, and from a sudden jolt of energy coursing through my veins. My breaths are heavy, panting through my parted lips as the scene finally settles into my brain.

I did this.

"Eros," I croak out, my body wanting to move towards him to check on and make sure he's okay, but the moment Nic snaps his head up to look at me, I'm frozen in place. My mind is screaming at me to run—to rid them of the monster standing before them. It's me. *I'm* the monster, and no matter what Eros says, there's nothing he can do for me.

I had no control over my actions, the memory of the rage I felt when Maxine wouldn't back down and had the audacity to put a claim on him, like he *belonged* to her. He's mine.

I shake my head. No, he's not mine. He's never been mine and he never will be, not after what I've just done. I hurt him. The one thing I was afraid would happen, actually happened, and the guilt and pain at knowing I possibly ended another life and almost destroyed the one man who has shown me kindness, even knowing what I am, was almost torn from this world.

"I'm sorry," I sob, backing away just as Eros' face tips up to look at me. His eyes widen, like he knows, deep down, what I'm planning to do. "I'm so fucking sorry."

I bolt, turning away from him and hearing him grunting and swearing at Nic and Jackson to let him go. I hope they don't. I hope they cling to him and give me time to run from him and from this city. This was a mistake. I let my walls collapse because Eros was great at beating into them until they gave way. I let myself believe and have hope that I could finally have a life. One that's somewhat normal, where I could finally have control over this *thing* inside of me, but that was all a dream that was easily destroyed, floating away like whisps of smoke that are impossible to hang onto.

Everything I own is in the apartment upstairs, but I can't go there. If I go up there, he'll find me, and I can't face him after what I just did to him. I pound into the button on the elevator, begging and screaming in my mind for it to come to the floor faster. I wish this place had stairs, I would tear down them until my lungs burn and my legs scream in agony.

"Venessa!" My back stiffens at Eros screaming out my name.

"Come on," I whine, squeezing through the door the second it opens and pressing the button over and over for them to close again. I glance up just as they start to close, my heart breaking at the look of pain on his face as he runs towards the doors. I flinch, closing my eyes when his body slams into the now closed doors, a sob slipping through my lips when the elevator begins its descent down to the lobby.

My legs shake under me, and it's taking everything in me not to drop down to the cool tile floors and sob, but I need to get out of here, I need to keep myself standing and not let the need to break take hold of my quickly weakening mind and body.

I choke out another breath when the doors open, pushing past the guests waiting on the main floor, waiting to get on. The bouncers call out my name when I rip past them, concern lacing through their words, but I keep going, keep running until I'm out in the street, dragging down the crisp night air of winter. My skin feels like it's on fire, and soft snowfall scatters around me, burning away the second it touches my heated flesh.

I can't breathe, no matter how hard I force my lungs to expand and drag in air. My desperate attempts to calm myself feel completely useless, my body swaying as I tip my head back, closing my eyes to the darkened sky above me and wishing for this to all just be over.

Tears streak down my cheeks, and I pull in a shuddering breath when my resolve finally settles into me. Slowly, I open my eyes, glancing back at the club and the few people watching me with wary looks and concern on some of their faces. My feet move forward, my heels slipping on the quickly freezing ground beneath.

Stepping off the curb, my feet drag until I'm standing in the middle of the road, and the bright lights of the vehicle burn into my retinas for a moment before I close my eyes again.

It's finally over. I should have done this years ago. I should have rid the world of my existence so no one else could get hurt from just knowing me. At least I can die knowing someone cared for me, even if it was only for a short while. Knowing death is coming has a wave of relief settling into my bones. Heat floods through me, burning away the chill I felt moments ago as the snow fell around me. I can almost feel those final lingering touches from Eros. Those moments of peace and safety he granted me, and I'll take those memories with me, clinging to them like the precious gems that they are.

CHAPTER THIRTY-ONE

EROS

"Fucking elevator!" I scream, prying the door open the second it hits the floor again. "Move!" The patrons inside scramble out of the box, fear scattering across their features the second they see me. A hand stops the doors from closing, and I glance up to see Ikelos holding it open. "Step away before I break your arm," I snarl.

He sighs, stepping into the box with me and casually pushing the button for the doors to close again. I glance at the glowing button, frowning when I see it set for the lobby. I step forward to push the button to the apartments, but he slaps my hand away and turns around to face me. "She's running," he says bluntly.

"Right, so why are you getting in my way?"

"I'm not. She's running, Eros. She's not going to risk going to her apartment, knowing you're going to follow her. If I were her, I would make a break for it and escape this place completely."

"All her shit is still upstairs."

He lifts a brow. "Do you really think mundane things will matter to her when she's in this state? She knows she hurt you, and she probably assumes she killed the girl. She's going to feel guilt and pain and probably regret for ever coming here. She thought she had a chance of making it through this, but in the blink of an eye, everything was ripped from her."

"She didn't know," I say quietly.

"I know that and so do you, but she doesn't. Clearly, her succubus side took hold and was triggered by that twat trying to lay claim to you." He turns back around, giving me his back. "I probably would have done the same thing in her shoes, but I would have been fully aware of my actions. I don't appreciate people talking to me in the way that bitch talked to her, and I sure as fuck don't share what belongs to me. You claimed her, and then some random hoe decided to encroach on what she deemed was her territory. Basic instinct kicked in and now she's paying for that side of herself coming into the light uninhibited."

"Since when do you talk so much?" I murmur.

"When I have something important to say, I tend to ramble."

"Why are you here?"

He glances at me over his shoulder seconds before the doors begin to open. "Do you honestly think you can track her on your own? I'm here to help you, even *if* I think she's beyond dangerous with the amount of power slipping out of her without her knowing." He steps through the door, and I quickly step out to follow him. "She could have killed you."

"But she didn't. She stopped, and that's all I need to know that she's still herself." Screams at the entrance draw my attention, and my feet are pounding against the lobby floor on impulse alone. The moment I step through the doors with Ikelos on my heels, I see her. "No," I choke out.

"Fuck," Ikelos swears. Shadows pulse out of him, but they struggle to break through the encroaching light, headed towards Venessa. He won't make it in time. I might not make it either, but I need to try. "Eros!" He screams, but I can't hesitate in my actions, or this will be the end for her.

My heart clenches painfully in my chest at seeing the broken girl in front of me. Her body relaxes and her head tips back, her eyes closing as a serene look settles over her face. She welcomes death. Her actions today and the ever-present looming darkness that has tainted her heart and soul have pushed her to this moment.

I don't think, I run towards her, grab her body, and fling her towards Ikelos while my own body careens in the other direction. Her eyes open and widen when they lock on mine, Ikelos' arms cradling her while the screaming sound of a horn blares through my head. Blinding light floods through my vision, blurring Venessa from my sight before searing pain rips through my body.

The car collides into me, the screeching of the brakes ringing through my ears painfully while I get launched forward. It takes a little bit before my body stops tumbling and rolling over the cold, rough asphalt, but the moment it does, pain rips through every muscle and bone. The screams ringing out around me get drowned out by the sound of my own heart beating in my ears, and the rushing of blood to my brain.

I struggle to lift my head, blinking through the thick, wet heat, dripping into my eyes as I try to focus in on Venessa and Ikelos. She's screaming and sobbing, clawing against him, but his grip is like a vice, holding her tightly against his chest while her mouth moves. What is she saying? Is she calling out to me?

"Eros?" I blink, my head falling back against the ground. "Eros!" I blink again, Jackson and Addison coming into my line of vision before darkness washes over me.

CHAPTER THIRTY-TWO

VENESSA

Guilt. Pain. Regret. Disappointment. All the dark emotions in existence run through my mind and body while I sit in the waiting room with the others. Nic has appointed himself as my guard dog, not trusting me to not run off again and make matters worse. The only thing worse than this would be Eros actually dying, which once again, would be my fault. Why couldn't they just let me die. They would have been free of me and been able to live their lives as they were before I came into their lives.

"He won't die," Nic says, as though reading my thoughts. He settles back into the shitty plastic chair next to me and relaxes his legs wide as he crosses his arms across his chest. "He's a god, he can't die from something as mundanely stupid as a car hitting him."

"But there was so much blood," I whisper, pinning my hands between my thighs to try and quell the tremor still running through them.

"Hmm, yes, there was."

"I thought gods didn't bleed by normal means."

"They don't," he says bluntly, and I glance over at him. He shrugs his shoulders, shifting himself again to lean his forearms against his thighs. "I guess I should say, they don't normally. I never used to bleed either and neither did Jackson, but yet, we both do now. Do you know why?" I shake my head. "We have someone to fight for—someone we hold dear and would sacrifice everyone and everything for."

My eyes widen. "He—he doesn't even know me."

"Maybe not in body, but in soul. He clearly has a pull to you, even if he can't quite understand the feelings and intentions behind that sensation. He didn't even hesitate tonight, Venessa. I would have done the same thing if it were Mckenna in your position."

"I never wanted this," I admit, my skin itching with the need to run still burning through my entire body.

"But you need it. Do you honestly think you can survive without leveling yourself out? You lost control of yourself tonight, allowing your internal creature to take over your body and run rampant in our world. We told you you've been starving that part of yourself, and that was completely apparent tonight."

"I—I don't know what happened."

"Let us help you. Let *him* help you. I know what you were doing tonight, Venessa, and death is a coward's way out of it."

I flinch at his words, hating that he's right. Allowing myself to die is the easy way out, instead of dealing with the problem that is my supernatural heritage. I don't know how to respond to him because anything I say at this point will just seem so stupid and insignificant. His head pops up, his back stiffening when Jackson lurches to his feet. A code gets called out and a slew of nurses go running down the hall.

"Fuck," Jackson laughs awkwardly, taking off down the hall to follow them.

"What's happening?" I ask when Nic gets up to follow Jackson and the girls as well.

"He's awake," he sighs, shoving his hands into his pockets. He watches me as I slowly lift to my feet, my legs trembling under me. I startle when he settles his hand against my lower back, guiding me and keeping me stable. "Come on," he murmurs, his touch gentle, but still hesitant.

"Get this shit off me! I'm fine!" My steps stall at the anger in Eros' voice streaming from one of the rooms.

"Calm down, man. You're freaking out for nothing," Jackson says just as we reach the door frame.

Eros is trying to rip out his I.V.s, getting shoved back by Jackson when the nurses attempting to settle him back down, fail. "Get off me!" Eros snaps. "Venessa. Where's Venessa? Is she okay?"

My chest tightens at the concern in his voice, and the panic on his face before his eyes finally find me. His eyes widen and his body stills. Jackson glances back towards me, slowly stepping away from Eros with a small bow of his head. "Hi," I say quietly when all other words fail me. It's pathetic, I know, but what can I say to him right now, surrounded by prying eyes and strangers.

"Venessa," he whispers, his throat bobbing on a heavy swallow. His face is clear of cuts and bruises, his supernatural healing having kicked in, and making the nurses and doctors question everything if their whispered voices are any indication.

I glance at Nic when he gently guides me forward, and my steps stutter a bit when fear tightens my muscles. I know he's angry, and I don't know if I can handle him yelling at me. "Let's give them a bit of privacy," he murmurs, glaring at the nurses when they try to argue. "He's not going anywhere as long as she's here," he snaps, shifting out of the doorway and motioning for them to quicken their steps.

The moment the last one trails through, along with Jack, Mckenna, and Addison, he turns to me and gives me a small nod. He slips through himself, closing the door behind him and leaving me with *him*.

The room is eerily silent except for the steady beeping of the machine hooked up to monitor his heartrate. I pull in a deep breath and lift my gaze to him again, taking a hesitant step towards him.

"I'm sorry," I whisper.

"For what exactly? For running? For trying to kill yourself? For feeling that my life would be better without you in it? Tell me which part you're sorry for, Venessa, because there are plenty of reasons."

"All of it, but I'm the sorriest for hurting you. I—I almost killed you...why would you risk yourself to save someone who almost killed you?" He continues to rip out his IVs, wincing when the needle snags and causes blood to well in the puncture. "You shouldn't do that," I say quickly, stepping closer to him.

"I hate needles," he grumbles, tossing the offending things to the ground before tipping his gaze to me again. "You were about to feed off Maxine tonight. I had no choice but to step in because I knew I could handle it. You did nothing wrong, Venessa. You didn't attack me; it was my decision."

Is that what happened? I don't have any memory between the moment Maxine started bad-mouthing me and Eros being ripped away from me. I take another hesitant step towards him, wringing my hands against my stomach. He shifts the covers off his body and slides his legs over the side of the bed, pulling in a deep, steadying breath.

"You—you shouldn't be moving, Eros."

"I'm fine," he grumbles, but his arms shake as he closes his eyes.

"Why didn't you just let me die?" I finally ask, needing to know if what Nic said could be true.

He lifts his head to look at me, settling back onto his hands while his expression darkens. "Because I care about you. Losing you would be a devastation to this world, Venessa, not just to me. You have a bright future ahead of you. You're full of light and life and love, even if you don't care to admit it. You can only keep those emotions and feelings locked down for so long, but they're there, and they *will* burn through the walls you've put up around yourself. I wish you could see for yourself what I see in you," he says, his voice dropping to a quieter tone.

"I have no one. I have *nothing*."

His eyes lock on mine, filled with care and longing that turns the air in my lungs into flames. "You have me."

CHAPTER THIRTY-THREE

EROS

She's such an idiot, I swear. How has she been conditioned into this broken creature in front of me that doesn't see the value of her own life? She's had a tough upbringing and never had anyone who cared for her the way she deserves to be cared for. She's a kind soul, and I just wish she would be able to see that for herself. She's done nothing wrong. She may have killed someone and had a hand in hurting countless others, but she had no control over her actions because she didn't know who or what she was.

She needs guidance and a helping hand, and I've willingly offered myself up to her. If she doesn't want to take the arrangement further than stolen touches and chaste kisses, then I won't push for more.

She looks surprised at my words, her mouth parting in shock and her body going deathly still. Are my words that hard to believe to be true?

"Are you okay?" I sigh, needing to know she wasn't hurt during that entire ordeal.

"I—I'm fine," she squeaks out, clearing her throat and taking another tentative step towards me. I don't even think she's doing it on purpose, her body being pulled towards me subconsciously because deep down, she knows she needs me.

When she's close enough to me, I reach out and grip her tightly clenched hands and pull her towards me, settling her body between my thighs. She blinks, realizing too late where she ended up, and her body stiffens once more. She tries to pull out of my grip, but the motion is half-hearted and weak, and I easily pin her between my legs.

Her eyes widen and her body trembles when I reach up and slowly place my hand against her cheek, willing her to accept my version of affection. I may not be able to love, but I want to give her every piece of myself to make up for that lack of emotion.

"Don't" she whimpers. I slide my hand down to cup her jaw, her body trembling harder. "Please," she chokes out, fighting back a sob as she slams her eyes shut. I can see the internal battle going on within her mind. The need to pull away from me, but the desperation to feel *something*.

"Please what?" I whisper.

"I—I can't handle you touching me."

"Why?" I curl my fingers into her nape, and she shudders.

"I don't deserve it." Her voice is but a breath in the stillness of the room, barely audible over the incessant beeping from the machines behind me.

"You deserve it all. You've gone your entire life without knowing a gentle touch or kind words, and you deserve far more than what I can offer you, but this is me, Venessa. This is all I am and all I'll ever be, and I willingly give it to you. I don't want you running, and I don't want you shying away. I want you to want this and to take what you deserve and desire. You may think your soul is tainted and black, but it shines bright like a white light, fighting off the corruption that is desperately clinging to you."

I want to devour that corruption to allow her light to shine brightly as it deserves to be. The cacophony of emotions rumbling through my body only seem to be tampered down in her presence, through the briefest of touches and stolen glances. I need her more than she even realizes. All my life I've shuffled along, doing the job thrust upon me while the world around me muted and faded in life and in colour. With her, I see the purity and the beauty of the world around me, her vibrant soul shining and flushing the dim world, bathing it in a sea of colour and beauty.

"Why you felt that your life wasn't worth fighting for and you were willing to throw it away...I just don't understand. Why, Venessa? Why would you try to kill yourself? I saw you. I saw the resolve and peace on your face as death neared you. We know nothing of your composition, and therefore, we're unaware of the state of your immortality. You went out there, wanting to die. *Why*?"

My grip on her tightens, her breath puffing and turning sharper with each passing second. She sways in front of me, her face paling the longer she stands, staring at me.

"*Why!?*" I snarl, pulling her head down, mere inches from my own. Her eyes turn glassy, the welling of tears pooling on her lashes. "Tell. Me. *Why*."

We gave her hope for a future, and the moment something went wrong, she gave up. She was willing to throw it all away—willing to throw *me* away.

"I didn't want you to get hurt because of me. I should have never applied for the job, and I should have never gotten involved with you. You would be safer not knowing me. This world would be safer without me in it."

"You regret...meeting me."

Her eyes bow, her tears finally breaking through the dam to cascade down her cheeks in steady streams as she sobs and hiccups in front of me. "I don't regret meeting you," she sniffles. "I regret the darkness I've brought to your doorstep."

"The darkness was already here, love. You can rest now. You no longer need to migrate in search of somewhere safe and warm to live out your life. Let this city be your home. Let *me* be your home."

Surprise radiates through me when she lurches forward and wraps her arms around me, her face buried into the crook of my neck. A tingling current skates across my skin at the full contact but I don't even care. I wrap my arms around her, hauling her up onto my lap, and running my hands up the bare skin of her back. She pulls in a shuddering breath, and I shiver at the feel of her lips pressing against my skin.

She shifts her hips against me, and the thin material of the gown is doing me no favours in hiding what the feel of her is doing to me. She leans back, looping her hands behind my neck to look at me fully. I want to smooth the small frown line forming between her brows, but I can't take my eyes off hers as they stare at me like she's trying to pry open my soul. Her fingers gently trail up and down the nape of my neck, scraping through the strands of hair in a way that has my skin pebbling and my heart beating faster.

I need her to realize that the world doesn't tell us who we are. That people around us can't decide our fates and the paths set before us. We're the ones to choose our path and make the decision to do better and be better, and to accept our identity and the help that's being freely given when it's needed. She needs to learn to feel for the intention of those around her and accept the care and emotion surrounding her when those few people that want her to thrive offer it to her.

I blink, my eyes closing on the groan ripping through my throat as her lips press against mine. She's kissing me. She made the first move and showed me what she wants. My fingers dig into her back, pulling her closer to me when she slides her tongue against my lips, a silent plea to let her in. I do. I open my mouth to her in invitation and melt into her when she takes it and plunges into my mouth, pushing her tongue against mine.

She whimpers against my lips, her fingers curling into my strands and tugging against them. The sensation ripples through me, and I gasp out a breath when I feel the pull on my life energy. She breaks the kiss, panting an inch from my mouth. "Sorry," she whispers.

I curl my hand around the back of her neck and pull her towards me again, letting myself fall into the feel of her against me and the vicious tug against my power. Her hands shift to my chest, her weak attempt at pushing me away, but this is my decision. I feel good, her powers muted in comparison to earlier where she was unaware of the actions of her internal creature. This feels normal and stable, a slow, subtle trickle being siphoned into her.

"Take it," I breathe against her lips, nipping at the bottom one playfully.

She whimpers, her panting breaths puffing against my skin in a hot wave. Her eyes glow with an internal light that has my own breath hitching in my throat. I groan when she pushes through her hesitation and presses her lips back to mine.

"Looks like you two made up."

CHAPTER THIRTY-FOUR

VENESSA

I jerk away from Eros at the sound of Nic's voice behind us, losing my balance enough to surprise him. He scrambles to grab me, but ends up getting a fistful of my dress, which can't handle being man-handled apparently because the sound of tearing rips through the room.

I let out the most non-sexy sound as my now half-naked ass hits the floor with a thump. A low growl rumbles from above me, and my eyes widen when Eros' begin to glow. He has scraps of my dress gripped within his fist, the knuckles turning whiter and whiter with each passing second.

"Whoops. You alright there?" Nic says, drawing my attention back to him. I quickly cover up my chest, startling when the material of my dress flutters over my body.

"Don't you knock?" Eros snarls, lifting to his feet and stepping around me in an attempt to cover me from view. My eyes widen at his bare back and ass, clearly visible with the gown open at the back.

"I did," he says, a hint of a smirk in his voice. "You must have been too busy sucking face to have heard me."

"You made me rip her fucking dress, Ikelos."

"I did no such thing. *I'm* not the one who gripped into it and tore it from her body like a barbarian."

"You little—" He stops when I reach out and touch the back of his calf. "Venessa."

"It's fine, Eros," I sigh.

"But the dress, and the fact you're naked in a hospital with no access to your clothes."

I glance over when I see Nic move further into the room, making his way towards one of the cabinets set off in the corner. "They usually keep spares around the entire hospital, just in case," he says, pulling out a set of scrubs that seem *way* too big for my frame.

I can't exactly complain since it's better than what I have access to currently, which is barely a scrap of cloth. Eros rips the clothes away from Nic when he holds them out to him, Nic's feet making their way towards the door again.

"We were able to convince the doctor to let you go and calmed down the nurses you terrified with your actions."

"I don't like needles," he grumbles, pulling a laugh from Nic and forcing me to press my own lips together to stop myself from laughing. He huffs out a breath and shifts to crouch down next to me, turning his head to glare at Nic one last time. "You can go now."

"Your clothes, or what's salvageable, are in the bag on the table at the end of the bed."

"Fine."

"So snippy," Nic snorts, the door clicking shut behind him.

"I'll head into the bathroom to get change. Let you have some privacy. I'm sorry about the dress, Venessa. It was beautiful and looked lovely on you."

He helps me to my feet while I hold the material tightly against my chest. He averts his gaze, holding the scrubs out to me. He's being really sweet, even with the situation we've both fallen into. I take the clothes, my fingers brushing lightly against his. He moves to pull away, but I reach out quickly and grip his hand.

"You don't have to go," I whisper, dropping my eyes to the ground the moment I catch him turning to look at me.

He uses the grip on my hand to pull me towards him, a gasp slipping out when my chest collides with his. "You want me to stay?" I nod my head, peeking up at him through my lashes. "Do you...want me to *see* you?" I nod again, and his sharp intake of breath has me looking up at him fully.

"I'm sorry your opening night was ruined," I say. I can't stop myself from apologizing over and over again, and I don't think I'll stop anytime soon.

He brushes my hair back before sliding his hand back along my jaw, his fingers curling into the nape of my neck. I don't know what it is about that move, but it sends a flush of heat coursing through my body and a ripple of energy across my skin, causing the hair on my arms to raise.

"That night wouldn't have succeeded as well as it did it if weren't for you. I left you to do all the work, too afraid to confront you and the feelings I held towards you."

"I'm not sure how well we did since we had a few incidents. I know they were all my fault, but I hope I can do some crowd control in the morning and that you don't lose any of the subscribers to your venue because of it."

"Fuck it. I don't care if I lose every single one of them, Venessa. The club could shut down completely, and I wouldn't bat an eye because the one thing I wanted out of tonight is within reach now." I tilt my head in confusion, my brows furrowing as I try to figure out what he could mean. He smiles, shaking his head through a soft chuckle. "You. The only thing I cared about tonight, was you."

After everything I've been through, all the rejection and hate, how did I get lucky enough to find someone like him. Someone who sees me for me and not the monster inside of me. It feels unreal—a fever dream. I'm scared. I'm scared of waking up and realizing that none of this is real and that my mind has finally broken enough to show me something I've always wanted, only to be ripped away in the waking world.

I let the scrap of the dress fall between us, catching the sharp intake of breath from Eros as his eyes drift down to look at me. His Irises rim with light, his lips parting in awe. No one has ever looked at me the way he looks at me. A look filled more than just lust and longing. A look void of resentment and hatred. I've gotten so used to that look that I forgot what it was like to have someone show even an inkling of affection.

"You're serious," I whisper, tipping my head further back to look at him fully.

"More serious than I've been with anything else in my entire life. I've lived for a very long time, Venessa, but nothing has compared to this or elicited these emotions that I know nothing about from me. I'll admit, I was wary of these feelings, not knowing or understanding the true nature of their intent, but now that I know what they are...I can't handle not having you in my life."

He leans down and presses his forehead against mine, a heavy breath rattling out from his lungs. The feel of his skin against mine is something I feel like I'll never get used to, having been deprived of human contact for so long. It's nice. The warmth from him, the softness of his skin against mine, the feel of his rough thumb brushing gently against my jaw, all of it turning into something I welcome and desperately need.

"I—I don't think I can do this without you," I admit quietly, and it's the truth. I was willing to end my own life because of everything that's happened and the darkness that has been following me around for years. If I don't have him, I don't think I'll survive. I'm so tired. Tired of running, tired of hiding, and tired of constantly fearing myself.

"That's the thing though, isn't it? You don't have to. You don't have to do anything alone anymore as long as you allow me into your life, Venessa. Let me into your heart, I promise you I'll protect you. I'll help you, care for you the best way I can, and I promise to be there for you."

"But you'll never be able to love me." The words choke out of me, something I didn't want to say, but his words have been picking and clawing at my mind since he spoke them.

"I..." He pauses, pulling back enough to watch my expression fall, my own emotions bubbling up as the weight of my own question settles heavily between us. "I don't think I can in the way you want me to. I told you before, that emotion doesn't exist within my heart. Love is for everyone else in this world. I give and take and give again, but I can never hold onto that feeling for myself. I've never loved anyone in my entire existence, and I can't promise you that it'll be different with you."

Sadness wells inside me at his words. I never thought I would ever have anyone love me so I shouldn't feel as broken about this, but I can't help it. Is his version of love enough for me? I don't think anyone else in this world would ever look at me the way he does, but I don't want to use him for my own selfish reasons either. I *do* care about him, and I want to see where this may lead, but I don't want to hurt him in the process.

"Please don't pull away," he says quickly, and I didn't realize I had actually tried to step back from him. "I—I know you deserve so much more, but please give me the chance to make you happy."

My heart breaks at the plea in his voice. He wants this—wants *me*. Do I even have a right to deny him the chance at this point? He's done so much for me in such a short amount of time that I feel indebted to him in some way.

"Don't speak so little of yourself, Eros. I don't even think I deserve you or the kindness you've shown, knowing what I've done. If anything, *you* deserve better."

He chuckles and grips my hips, tugging me back towards him. "Doesn't that make us perfect for each other? If we both have the same mentality, then maybe we're meant to be with each other."

I wrap my arms around him, settling my cheek against his chest and smiling to myself. "Maybe you're right."

CHAPTER THIRTY-FIVE

EROS

I can't keep the grin off my face as I step out of the room with Venessa's hand gripped in mine. Everyone is waiting for us, their expressions ranging from amusement to hesitance. The girls seem more wary than the guys, but I can't blame them. They're the ones that had to deal with Maxine, making sure she was taken care of. Thankfully, the brief contact she had with Venessa didn't kill her instantly.

"How's Maxine?" I ask once I stop in front of them.

Venessa tucks herself slightly behind me when Mckenna's gaze shifts to her. "She's stable. I think she'll be fine, just needs some rest and fluids."

I squeeze Venessa's hand, trying to reassure her, and tug her to my side. Mckenna's eyes stay locked on her, and I glance down to see

Venessa staring at the ground, avoiding the piercing gaze pointed her way.

"Thank you for your help today, Mckenna. We both appreciate it."

"Are you feeling okay? You looked pretty beaten up when they brought you in."

"I'm fine. Nothing my healing couldn't handle."

"That's what Nic used to say," she grumbles, ripping her eyes away from Venessa to glare at Ikelos when he laughs. "It's not funny."

"You worry too much. I told you immortals can't die by normal means."

"It's still not a fun feeling. Seeing you bleeding out, especially when I was the cause of it."

The edge of sadness gripping at her features has me gripping into Venessa tighter, knowing that she felt the same way when she saw me getting hurt in that way because of her. I'll never blame her. I mean, how could I? It was my decision to push her out of the way, even if that meant me taking the brunt of the hit myself. I would do it again in a heartbeat. I don't think there would be anything I *wouldn't* do for this girl if presented with situations like that.

She's fought most of her life to survive. It's time someone else gives her a hand to ease the strain on her mental wellbeing. "Let's head back. I'm assuming you're all staying at the club tonight?"

Ikelos pushes away from the wall and walks over to Mckenna, slinging his arm across her shoulders. "That would be great, thank you."

"We drove here behind the ambulances that brought you and Maxine here, but there aren't enough seats for all of us," Jackson says, gripping into Addison's hand and tugging her to his side.

"We'll cab back. Just wait for us in the lobby and I'll set you guys up with some rooms." They nod their heads and head out while I pull Venessa along towards the counter to put through my discharge papers. I fucking hate that I ended up in this ridiculous building, something I never expected to happen in all my life.

"Do you have insurance to cover the costs of your stay?" The nurse asks.

"No."

Venessa gasps next to me, her hand trembling in mine. "Alright, we'll send you the bill then to the address we now have on file."

"That's fine." She slides over some paperwork for me to fill out, and I make quick work of it, giving her a curt nod before heading towards the exit.

"You don't have insurance?" Venessa asks the moment we step into the lobby just outside the doors.

"Why would I need it? It's not like I can get sick or gravely injured where I would need mortal intervention. I provide the means for my employees to have such things, but there's no point in me spending money on something I won't use."

"But you needed it now," she grumbles.

"It's fine, Venessa. I can pay for it on my own. I don't expect to be having a repeat of today, but if I do, I'll pay for it again." I dig for my phone in my pocket, making the call for the cab while Venessa stares off through the glass doors, her eyes focused on the snow falling in fluttering sheets to the ground.

I sigh, leaning myself back against the far wall as the exhaustion of today finally catches up with me. I want to reach out to her and pull her into me. I want to grip her hips and plant her between my legs so that I can feel the heat of her body leaching into my own, but I don't. I stand here, watching her as she gets lost in her own thoughts, unsure how to break the sudden silence between us.

I would love nothing more than for her to want those things for herself, and for her to make the first move as she did earlier. It was a pleasant surprise when she kissed me of her own volition, but I feel that may have been a heat of the moment thing, and possibly something she now regrets.

She's hesitant in her movements, even though she exudes confidence when she needs to in order to portray herself as someone strong and unyielding to the world around her. Inside—deep down—she's broken and fragile, struggling to keep up this mask that she's tried to glue to her face.

I can see all those cracks and the damage that's been done to her overtime, but I don't see something that can't be fixed in front of me. I see a girl trying desperately to survive and silently pleading for someone out there to help her mend the broken pieces that are slowly chipping away from her. I want her armour to crack, but I want the being protected within to stay whole.

I open my mouth to speak, stopping short when she turns her head to look at me. We stare at each other for what feels like an eternity, the world around us fading away as though time is deciding to slow to give us this moment to ourselves. She's so fucking beautiful; a unique creature that has stolen my heart and all rational sense within my mind. I can't think straight when I look at her, thoughts and words getting jumbled into a tangled mess of incoherent fodder.

My breath hitches, freezing in my lungs when she turns to me and slowly starts making her way towards me. The scrubs hang loosely on her petite frame, drowning her sensual curves. She looks tired and drained, no doubt feeling the same heavy weight of exhaustion after the events of tonight.

I regret leaving her the way I did, and I wish I would have had the courage to just talk to her. She deserved the truth from me, even if I didn't want to admit it to myself.

She stands in front of me, my hands clenching at my sides with an incessant itch crawling across my palms with the desire to reach out to her and do the one thing I've wanted to do from the beginning. I know this relationship will be difficult, but I'm willing to try as long as she is as well.

She's like a feral animal that has shown up at my doorstep, surprised by my care and attention and desire to care for her. Her guard has been up right from the beginning. The distrust ingrained into her very being because all her life she's had nothing but hatred and pity thrown towards her.

I don't understand how her foster parents didn't care for her the way they were tasked to do. Is that not the point of taking on children? Is it not for the need to take care of children and make their lives better after they've had everything they've ever known ripped away from them? She lost her birth parents, and then she was thrown into a world with new ones that didn't *care*. They never cared. If they had, they wouldn't have let her run. They wouldn't have ostracized her for what happened in the past, and they wouldn't have made her feel as though she were a burden—a stain on this god-forsaken planet that humans are hellbent on destroying.

"Eros," she whispers, tipping her head up to look at me. Her fingers curl into the edge of the scrub shirt, her teeth digging into her bottom lip.

"Yes?"

Those eyes. Those cool blue eyes burn into me for a moment longer before being shutter by her dark lashes. She shakes her head, stepping back from me once more. She turns her head to the glass doors. "The cab is here."

And just like that, the pull between us snaps, jarring me back to reality. I know she wanted to say something to me, but whether through fear or regret, she refused to speak the words.

She shudders the moment we step into the cold night air, and the need to pull her into my body to warm her burns through my chest. She's quick though, darting across the nearly frozen ground towards the cab while I lag behind, trying to get my thoughts back in order.

She slides into the back, scooting over to give me room to get in as well. "Can you take us to Cupid's Hollow, please?" I say to the driver, closing the door just as frigid air whips through the backseat.

The drive is quiet except for the soft music playing through the speakers. Venessa has her body practically pressed into the opposite door, giving me ample room for my wider frame, but I don't take advantage of the space. She seems nervous, but I thought we were past that point and had moved on from the awkwardness into finally accepting what is going on between us.

The drive ends quickly enough, and I pay the driver before sliding out of the car, holding my hand out to Venessa to help her out. She hesitates, and that small motion makes it feel like the crack between us is slowly widening into a chasm. She's quick to release my hand once she's out of the vehicle, heading to the double doors in front of me at a hastened pace. The club itself is officially closed for the night, the night staff to the hotel portion now working their shift.

"Eros!" Hannah calls out from behind the desk. "I didn't expect you to be up and around after that."

"It looked worse than it was," I reassure her, her eyes trailing after Venessa as she heads for the elevator. "How did the rest of the night go?"

"It was good. We got a bunch of new member applications, and I'm pretty sure those have been sent to you for review in the morning if you're up for it."

I nod. "Very well." I motion towards Ikelos and Jackson, who are also watching Venessa basically run away from me. "Can you set them up with rooms please?"

"Oh, sure," she says quickly.

I give them a nod, barely glancing at Hannah as I jog after Venessa. "Have a good night, Hannah." The elevator pings open and I quickly head towards it, my heart plummeting at the memory of Venessa running from me earlier and using the doors as a barrier between us. She slides her hand against the frame, holding it open for me to get on. "Thank you," I say quietly, a rattling breath slipping through my lips.

"Of course," she replies, no doubt sensing my unease.

The silence between us is really starting to get to me. I hate it. I hate that she isn't speaking or asking questions or telling me *anything* that is going through her mind. My own thoughts are chaotic, and I need to know if she's feeling the same things I am. I don't push her though, keeping the deafening silence between us until the moment the elevator pings to our floor.

I head out first, leaving her to trail behind me. I'm just passing the door to her apartment when I feel her trembling fingers grip into my forearm. Stopping, I turn to look at her, but her eyes are downcast, avoiding my own gaze.

"Did—do you want to come over?"

"You should rest," I say quickly, wanting nothing more than to go into her home, but knowing better.

She looks up, her exhausted eyes dark and troubled. "Stay with me." It's no longer a question but a plea.

"You want me to stay with you?" She nods. "I'm going to take a shower and change out of these clothes, but I'll be over shortly. Is that alright?" She nods again, dropping her hand away from me. I watch as she opens her door and slips inside, my own mind running a mile a minute, trying to figure out what is going on inside her head.

One minute she's desperate for my touch, the next she's shut off and quiet, only to turn around again and ask for my company. Her personality swings are starting to give me a bit of whiplash, but I feel as though *she* doesn't even know what's going on in her own head. She seems confused by her words and actions, and I know for a fact she doesn't have experience with any of this.

I mean, how could she? She's never even been in a proper relationship. I don't know how long she dated the boy before they attempted to have sex, or how deep her feelings ran for him. Did she love him? Did she see herself spending the rest of her life with him? Is she *still* heartbroken over what happened and fearful of those emotions being the root of the evil she feels residing inside of her?

I don't know what's going to happen tonight, but I hope that she can find it within herself to finally open up to me and show me the person she really is inside. I don't want her to run or hide or be fearful of what I may think of her, and I just want her to be comfortable within her own skin. I want to see that badass girl I first met during the interview, not this shell of a person that has been completely gutted and strung up with her secrets bare for everyone to see.

CHAPTER THIRTY-SIX

VENESSA

What was I thinking? I can't believe I asked him to come over and stay the night. I mean, I expected this weird relationship to progress to that point eventually, but I didn't think I would have the balls to have that happen now. I don't know what he's expecting from me tonight, and the more I think about it, the more my own panic settles into me.

I bolt for the bathroom the second I'm through the door, ripping off the scratchy scrubs and turning on the shower. I would love to take a bath to soak away all the aches and pains and exhaustion I'm feeling, but I doubt I have that much time.

The water burns the instant I step under the stream cascading from the too large shower head, but I welcome it, hoping the sting of it will burn away the hatred I feel towards myself for letting tonight go the way it did. I scrub every inch of skin, hating myself more and more to the point tears begin to streak down my cheeks. I can't seem to get a handle on my emotions, and I've cried far more than I have in a long time.

I scrub at my face, trying to clear my cheeks of the black marks I'm sure are etching their way into my skin from the makeup no longer holding against the constant flow of water it's had to endure. I grab my razor like an idiot, thinking I need to shave every inch of myself, even though I already did this routine earlier. Settling myself on the ground, I quickly swipe the blade against my legs over and over, trying to smooth out the already clean skin.

"Fuck," I hiss out when the blade snags against my knee, cutting my skin. Blood wells instantly in the wound, the burning water stinging against the fresh cut. I watch in horror as the skin begins to stitch itself back together right in front of my eyes until there's nothing left. Nothing. Not a scratch or scar, only the pink tinged water still around it being the only sign that something just happened.

Panic ripples through me. This has never happened before. I've gotten cut and injured in the past and not once have I ever seen my skin heal the way it just did. What is happening to me? Is it because of what I did to Eros? Is what I took from him changing my own body, turning it more into the monster it's so desperately trying to become.

I don't know if I should tell him what just happened; the fear of him freaking out over it settling into my mind. I'm a freak; a fucking abomination to this world, but he keeps fighting for me. He must be pretty fucked up himself for wanting anything to do with me, knowing I could kill him at the drop of a hat.

I haven't had a blackout moment like I did tonight in a long time, but in the past, I don't remember doing anything that hurt anyone either. *Did* I actually hurt someone, and I just don't remember it? Could I have killed countless others and have no fucking clue just how dark I am and how covered in blood my hands really are?

"Venessa?"

I startle out of my dark thoughts, scrambling to my feet and slipping on the wet floor. "I'll be out in a minute!" I call out, my arms shaking as I brace against the glass door.

"Are you okay?"

"Fine!" My voice squeaks out awkwardly, and I cringe on how panicked I sound. What the fuck do I do? I'm still trying to wrap my head around the fact that I can fucking heal now, and he's already here. I can't tell him, not yet. I think it'll just end up ruining the night further than it already has.

I make quick work off shutting of the shower and drying myself off, wrapping the towel tightly around my body before stepping out the door. Eros is standing by the large windows, staring out at the dark city below, the glittering lights flickering as the snow falls in front of the gleaming glow from the buildings.

He's gorgeous. His hands are clasped behind him, the sweatpants hanging low on his hips and the t-shirt stretching across his broad chest, showing every ripple of muscle hidden beneath. He could literally have anyone in the world, and yet, he's chosen me. He's set his sights on me and wants to give me his full attention. He showed disgust when that woman touched him tonight, as though her attention tainted him.

I don't say a word, but he senses my presence, tipping his head towards me. A genuine smile spreads across his face, his damp hair falling across his eyes in the sexiest way imaginable. Fuck, I love his eyes. They're beyond beautiful, glistening in the dim light of my apartment. There's no glow at the moment, his emotions more under control than they have been tonight.

What does he see in me? What does he actually see when he looks at me with those ethereal eyes?

"I'm sorry, I came as soon as I was done. I thought you would have been decent."

"It's fine. It's not like you haven't seen me already." It's the truth. I did end up changing in front of him at the hospital, and I did get a decent look at his ass since he, one, had a gown on, and two, changed in front of me as well. I can't let myself be shy around him if I have any hope in getting myself out of this aversion to being exposed to others.

"Hmm, yes. I did see quite a bit of you, but not nearly enough to satisfy me." I blink as his words settle into me, my body freezing to the spot when he closes the distance between us in a few long strides. He leans down towards my neck, his nose skimming across the skin on a deep inhale. "Yes, not even close to being enough."

"Eros," I stutter, my body swaying towards him when he pulls back to look down at me.

"Am I being too forward?"

"I just—I don't know what you're expecting."

He frowns, his eyes drifting down to my lips. "I don't expect anything from you, but I'll take whatever it is you wish to offer me."

I settle my hand on his chest, the heat of his body seeping into my palm. A low hum vibrates in my throat, thick heat spreading through my body and settling into my core. "I'm going to get changed and then go to bed," I say quietly. His face falls slightly and he steps back, my hand sliding away from his chest. Taking a deep breath, I walk past him, pausing at the edge of the hallway that leads towards the bedroom. "Are you coming?" I ask, turning to look at him over my shoulder.

His eyes widen and I fight back a grin. Did he think I would invite him over here just to kick him out? I asked him to stay with me, which I thought was an obvious intention at the fact I wanted him to *stay* with me.

He practically jogs to catch up to me, a laugh bubbling up my throat. I can see the need in him to touch me as he walks with me, but he's doing well to hold himself back.

"You can hop in bed," I say, pointing to the lavish set up with the large mattress set in the middle of the room, the ornate headboard lending a decadent view of wealth and the promise of sin.

He heads towards it, tugging back the covers to climb in. I spare him another glance, watching him prop himself up against the headboard as he gets comfortable. I drop the towel, glancing back again at the sharp intake of breath.

"What?"

He shakes his head. "Nothing at all. It's still surprising to me how much you're willing to show me."

I smile, turning back to the dresser and opening the drawer to the small amount of clothes nestled inside. I don't have much to my name, only the essentials to get me by, but with that man sitting in my bed, I wish I had so much more.

I don't bother with underwear at this point, pulling out a soft set of boy shorts and a thin camisole. I don't need to turn around to know he's watching me, the feel of his eyes burning into me a clear sensation across my skin. I don't think I'll ever get used to that feeling. The feeling of a predator watching me, waiting to devour me whole.

CHAPTER THIRTY-SEVEN

EROS

I can't take my eyes off of her. The fear that if I do, she'll disappear from my reality. I never expected to be here, in her room, with her willingly changing in front of me. If she only knew the perversive thoughts that were running rampant through my head as my gaze drifts across her exposed body, the swell of her ass, the way the material she's covering herself with clings to her like it's meant to be against her flesh.

I would prefer it if she stayed naked, but I will admit, I do enjoy unwrapping a package like her. I want to touch her. I want to trail my tongue against every inch of skin, and it still wouldn't be enough. I shift uncomfortably, hating the way my body is betraying me as I watch her. I know she's not expecting anything to happen between us tonight, but I don't know how to act in this situation. I don't sleep with anyone; not in the sense of actually sleeping. This will be twice now that I spend the night with this girl with nothing happening between us.

She quietly makes her way over to the bed, pulling back the covers and hopping in before turning off the bedside lamp and plunging the room into complete darkness. My eyesight quickly adjusts, focusing in on her form as she tucks herself under the covers, snuggling herself against the pillow, facing me. I smile at the fact she did that instead of completely shutting me out and turning her back to me.

I shift myself lower in bed, getting as close as I can to her without touching her. She surprises me when she reaches out, her fingers brushing gently against my cheek.

"Is this okay?" She asks.

"Why wouldn't it be?" I feel nothing coming from her. No power flare, not even an inkling of a tingle from her gentle touch. She shrugs, and I shift myself a bit closer, testing the waters a bit more. I'm close enough now that I can feel her breath cradling against my skin and the heat of her body seeping into my own.

"I want this," she says.

"What exactly?" She leans in closer, closing the distance between us to press her lips against mine. "Mmm, I can get behind this." I smile against her mouth, fighting back a laugh at the disgruntled breath she lets out.

"Can't you just let me enjoy this?" She huffs.

"This is what you want?" I ask, pressing my lips to hers again. She nods. "How about this?" I tentatively slide my hand down her ribcage to settle against her hip.

"Yeah," she says breathlessly, shimmying her body closer.

My own heart is pounding viciously against my chest as I let my hand slide further down, trailing along her outer thigh. My heart skips when my skin meets hers, the edge of her shorts teasing the delicate flesh that I want to ravage.

"And now?"

"It—it feels nice," she says, her breaths panting and mingling with my own ragged breathing. I shift my hips into her, hiking her leg up against my thigh until I'm flush against her. She gasps, her body trembling in my grip. "Eros—"

"Tell me to stop," I say quickly. I don't want her to tell me to stop, but if she doesn't, I don't know if I can control myself any longer. "Tell me to stop and I will, Venessa, but if you don't..." I let the words hang between us, giving her the room to choose.

Her hand slides down my chest, squeezing between our bodies until it settles against my cock. My eyes slam shut, a feral groan ripping through my lungs at the feel of her hand pressing against me.

"Don't stop."

CHAPTER THIRTY-EIGHT

VENESSA

This is happening. Fucking hell, do I want this? Fuck, his hand feels amazing and hot against my skin, and the way he trails his mouth up my throat sends a flutter of butterflies soaring through my stomach. I don't think I could tell him to stop even if I wanted to, my body reacting to him in a way that seems completely out of my control.

I rub him through his pants, feeling the thick length running down his thigh. Fuck, he's huge, and the thought of it inside of me sends a wave of panic through me.

"Fuck, Venessa," he groans, his voice dropping to an unbelievably sexy baritone. "That feels good." His fingers dig in harder at my thigh while he shifts his hips into my hand, putting a harder pressure along his cock. "Can I touch you?" he whispers.

"Yes," I whimper, fighting back my own groan when his fingers dip under the edge of my shorts to grip into my ass. He rolls into me, pushing me onto my back, and braces his weight against his forearm to hover over me. Shifting his other hand across my stomach, he teases his fingers at the edge of my shorts, looking down at me with those amber eyes.

"Can I keep going?" I nod, my breath stuttering in my lungs when his hand plunges down, his fingers gliding down between my legs.

"Fuck," I squeak out, my body bowing into his at the sudden flood of sensation ripping through my body.

"Fuck, you're so wet for me."

I can't catch my breath. With every strum of his fingers against my clit my body jolts like a live wire is running through me. I moan when he slides one of his thick digits into me, thrusting it slow and deep, sensual strokes that pull a whimpering breath from my lips.

"Mmm, I love the sounds you make, Venessa. They're better than I could have ever imagined." I cry out when he slips out of me, shifting back on the bed to settle on his heels. The covers pool around him, the motion tugging them away from me and exposing my body to him. "I want to taste you," he says, but he makes no move to touch me again.

I give him a nod, hoping he can see the subtle motion in the dark. Who am I kidding, of *course* he can, and I can see the feral grin spreading across his face, his teeth gleaming in the darkness and his irises rimming with light. He grips my shorts, ripping them down my legs, and the soft thump of them hitting the floor radiates through the room like a gong in my mind.

I can't stop my body from shaking as his hands trail up my legs and press my thighs apart while he slowly lowers himself down between them. He inhales sharply, his nose trailing up my inner thigh. I want to squeeze my legs together at the sudden embarrassment I feel, but his grip leaves me no room or give to do that. His lips leave hot trails along my skin, his tongue stroking the sensitive flesh leading right to my core.

"Oh, god," I whimper, my head tipping back against the pillow the second his hot tongue swirls against my clit. He moans against me, the vibration radiating through my entire body. Heat builds in my chest, my breaths turning more ragged when he dips his finger into me again.

"You taste so fucking good, Venessa. Fuck." He licks and swirls, his finger thrusting deeper and curling into me before he presses another one against me. My back arches off the bed, a cry slipping through my lips. " Hmm, I need to get you good and ready so you can take my cock. You're so fucking tight."

He's going to tear me apart. I've only had sex once. Well, if toys count, then it's been more than that, but I don't think I've put anything inside of me as big as he is. Nothing has felt as good as his mouth on me either, a wave of heat flushing through me, building in my spine and stomach in a way that has me squirming against his hold.

My fingers curl into the sheets in a death grip, my heart bounding against my chest painfully as all the air rips from my lungs on a scream. Oh god, it feels so good, but I feel like I can't come down from the high he's pushing through my body. He's ripped an orgasm from me; completely blindsiding me and overloading my senses until there is nothing but him and the feel of him.

He pulls away from me, his eyes burning brighter than I've ever seen before. The rustle of clothes hits my ears, and I catch his movement as he rips his shirt from his body before shifting over me to slowly lift my own shirt over my chest. I pull it off the rest of the way, my arms shaking as I slowly lower myself back down to the bed.

My eyes dart down when he hooks his fingers into the waistband of his pants, pushing them down for his cock to spring free. My eyes bulge at the sheer size of it, my mouth going suddenly dry when he palms it, giving it a firm stroke.

He stops, my eyes drifting to his face to see a frown forming. "Fuck," he grumbles, the word sounding pained. "I don't have condoms on me."

I swallow the lump lodged in my throat. This would be the perfect excuse to step away from this situation, but of course my mouth is moving faster than my brain. "I'm on the pill."

His eyebrows go up and a wicked grin spreads across his face as he slowly crawls towards me. His body is hot against mine, the feel of his bare skin both intoxicating and addictive. The heat rolling off of him is comforting, and I welcome every inch of him. He hasn't made any comment about my powers, no sign that I've drained him or even dared to touch his energy.

His lips press against mine, sensual and soft, but desperate and claiming all at the same time. It's impossible to not get lost in the feel of him. He doesn't even need to pry his way in, my mouth willingly parts for him, begging him for more, and fuck me, he gives me more.

"I love kissing you," he murmurs, his mouth trailing hot kisses along my jaw and down the front of my throat. He nips at the sensitive flesh, pulling a small whimper from my lips. "You're so perfect. So fucking beautiful. You're doing so well, Venessa." He drags the underside of his cock against my clit, the pressure sending a jolt of pleasure through my body. Why does this feel so fucking good? My insides tighten and clench around the thought of him seated deep inside me.

He presses the head of his cock against me, pausing when my entire body tenses. He inches his way in slowly, shallow thrusts that have him groaning against the crook of my neck. My fingers drag against his sides, trailing up to his shoulders, where his muscles ripple and tense with how hard he's trying to hold himself back.

He's being gentle with me, trying not to hurt me, and taking it slow so he doesn't scare me away. My heart swells in my chest, tears burning in my eyes at the lengths this man is going through in order to make me comfortable with him, and with myself.

CHAPTER THIRTY-NINE

EROS

Fuck, she's so fucking tight. It's taking everything in me not to slam into her and just get it over with, but I don't want to hurt her, and I don't want to scare her with my aggression. I nip at her shoulder, thrusting in a bit deeper. Her fingers dig into my shoulders, gently clawing at the skin while her heart pounds against my own chest. He breathing is ragged, small whimpers slipping through.

She's soaking wet, but this is still difficult for her. I know she hasn't been with a human for a long while, but she made it pretty clear that she wasn't shy to sex, having her own vast opinions on the toys she bought as party favours. Fuck those toys. I never want her to rely on something like that ever again. I want to be the one she turns to when she seeks pleasure. I want to be the only one who makes her come. I don't want anyone else to fucking touch her ever again, and I swear to the fucking gods, I'll tear anyone who tries limb from limb until they're a screaming lump of meat on the floor in front of me.

"Eros!" She gasps, her knees curling around my hips, opening herself up further to me. I groan, sinking myself completely into her, and taking a moment to just enjoy the feel of her pussy fluttering around me as it tries to adjust.

Fuck, I can't believe I'm inside her. I never thought this moment would come. Not with the way she was deathly afraid of me touching her and shying away from the simplest of touches. In anyone else's mind, this would be a conquest, but I don't and won't think of her in that way. If she would have told me to leave her alone, I would have tried my best to respect her wishes, but I knew, even then, that it wasn't what she truly wanted.

I could see it in her eyes, the desire within her was apparent, even if she couldn't admit it to herself. She can't be with anyone else anyways, her succubus composition making it nearly impossible for her to be intimate with any mortal. Maybe in the future, once she has full control of her powers, but at that point, I won't allow it. She's mine, and I refuse to let her go.

"Fuck, you're so tight," I grunt, slowly dragging my cock out and slamming it back into her. She whimpers again, clawing at my back with her nails and sending stinging pain across my skin. "Are you okay?" I should have asked this right from the start, but I got lost in the feel of her and the sheer shock at the fact that this is actually happening.

"I—" She chokes out a breath, and I pull back enough to get a look at her, my entire body freezing. She's crying. Tears are streaming down her cheeks, settling into her hairline.

"Did—did I hurt you?" I'm stumbling over my words, full-blown panic settling into me. I try to pull away, but she shakes her head, digging her fingers into my arms to stop me. "Venessa—"

"It's not you. I just—" she sobs, screwing her eyes tightly shut and pushing more tears through her lashes. "I didn't realize what I was missing out on. I mean, I did, but I didn't know it would hit me this hard. The feel of your body against mine, how good you make me feel, even through the small pain I felt...it's a lot to take in, Eros."

"You still felt pain?" I cringe at the knowledge. I knew it would be a possibility, but I thought I held myself back enough to give her time to adjust. Her small frame can't handle me, but she's trying her best to see this through.

Her hand comes up towards my face, her fingers pressing between my brows. "I'm okay," she whispers. "You didn't *hurt* me, Eros. I promise."

"I can't fuck you while you're crying?"

She frowns, her lip pouting out in the most adorable way. "Why not?"

"I don't have a pain kink, and pain kink usually involves tears."

"Well, what do you want me to do? I can't exactly command my tears to stop," she huffs.

I shake my head, letting out a small chuckle for the sheer ridiculousness of this girl. "I don't have a good answer to that," I smirk, leaning back down and darting my tongue out against her cheek to clear away the tears. She sucks in a sharp breath, her body trembling under me. "What do you want me to do?"

"Keep going," she says breathlessly. Slowly, I drag out of her, nestling the tip of my cock just inside before slamming back into her. "Oh, god," she cries, her hands sliding up my arms, up the back of my neck until her fingers are buried aggressively into my hair. She tugs at the strands, pulling a low growl from deep within my chest.

I've slept with many women in my life, but nothing has compared to her. The feel of her, the building of pressure in my chest as I watch her face morph with pleasure. The innocence and desperation within her to feel something other than the self-hatred she's felt for the last few years. Everything about her presence sings and draws me in, like a true devil laying a trap, but she doesn't even know that she's set the trap.

Succubi, in general, naturally draw people into them to make it easier to feed, but with her, she's pushed everyone away for most of her life. I grunt in surprise when she pulls me down towards her, her lips crashing against mine. We both moan at the visceral pleasure of our mouths parting, tongues clashing, and teeth nipping.

A shudder rips through me and thick heat spreads through my body when I begin to feel the pull on my life energy. It's definitely tamed in comparison to earlier, but it's still aggressive enough for my body to tremble in the wake of it's hooks digging deep into me. I thrust into her again, the hooks sinking deeper and deeper until my body is moving on its own, throttling into her until she's a mewling mess beneath me.

"Take what you need," I groan, dipping my tongue into her mouth again and relishing in the cold pull of her power against my own.

"Are you okay?" She pants, moaning with each press of my lips against hers.

"Yeah," I huff. "I can handle it." I don't think I could stop or pull away from her, even if I wanted to. She's a magnet—a fucking siren that could destroy me if she wished it. Her allure is difficult enough to deal with when she's in a protective state, and I'm quickly beginning to realize she'd be impossible to resist once her powers are in full swing and completely under her control.

The thought of her turning her power on any other man to draw them to her has me ramming into her harder, willing her body to only accept me and be mine. She can't leave me, and that thought has me claiming her mouth once again.

Her muffled scream vibrates through me, her pussy tightening around me hard enough that my hips stutter and my cum explodes into her like a burning wave. We're merged together so thoroughly that I don't think either of us can move. It's taking everything in me not to collapse against her, but she wraps her arms around me and pulls me down, pressing my chest flush against hers to crush her with my body.

The pounding of her heart thumps through my own chest, the feel of it mingling with my own until I swear our heartbeats merge into one rhythmic beat.

That went better than I expected. There's a bit of drain on my power, my body feeling the effects and straddling me with a sudden wash of exhaustion. My eyes feel heavy, and the gentle brush of her fingers through my hair and down across my shoulders has me sinking deeper into her. I know I should move and give her a reprieve from my weight, but it feels nice being close to her like this, the warmth of her cunt still wrapped around my softening cock.

"Eros?" She whispers.

"Hmm?" It's all I can muster, the mere thought of speaking at the moment feeling like a distant memory. My tongue feels thick and heavy in my mouth, my eyes drifting closed.

"Thank you."

I huff out a sigh, pulling enough energy into my body to turn my head and kiss her on the neck before nuzzling my face further into it. I love her smell, the scent seeping into every cell in my body and lulling me into a comfortable haze.

CHAPTER FORTY

VENESSA

I smile when I feel his body completely relax against mine. It's strange, I don't feel panic in the fact he's touching me completely, skin to skin. The beast inside of me is quiet, my thoughts muted and satisfied with tonight. I felt the link between us, the feel of his energy streaming into me like water from a tap. I swear, feeding on him heightened my senses further, the orgasm he tore from my body, completely consuming me.

He fucked every fear out of me, showing me just how completely he planned to claim me, and claim me he did. The thought of losing him rattles around in my head, the thought of that moment happening sending a sharp pain through my chest.

I don't know where I would be without him. If I hadn't stumbled upon this job, and in turn Eros, would I have ceased to exist? They all told me that I was starving myself, slowly killing my supernatural origin without even realizing it. Without knowing about this world, I would have continued to avoid everyone, fearful of any human contact, forever empty and destined to be alone.

With him, I no longer need to fear that future. With him, I *have* a future. The fear of my past catching up to me still hangs over my head like a dark cloud, but I'm trying to convince myself to at least let myself enjoy these few stolen moments in the peaceful, safe cocoon we've created.

Tomorrow is another day with another set of challenges and tasks, but tonight...tonight I'll hold him, cradled against my chest. My eyes flutter shut, even though I'm fighting the pull of sleep because I don't want to sleep yet. I don't want this moment to end only to wake up to the idea that all of it was a dream. It feels too good to be true, and I don't want to lose this. I want to fight for him and this life, even if he can't love me the way I had hoped he would.

That emotion seems far out of reach, and we're too early into this relationship to even entertain the idea of love, but he thoroughly believes he can never feel that way towards me. Can I handle his version of love? I doubt it'll be some watered-down version, but a mimicry feels like a lie.

This must be what sociopaths feel though. The information given to them on what an emotion is *supposed* to feel like, and how it should be expressed, but feeling it for themselves is never something they can experience because their brain doesn't know how to process such a thing.

Eros isn't crazy, but there's definitely something broken inside of him. Who would have thought that the god of love, can't love.

CHAPTER FORTY-ONE

VENESSA

Groaning, I roll over in bed, my hand pausing on the sheets when I feel nothing next to me, or should I say, no one. I bolt upright, instantly regretting it when pain radiates through my entire body. Eros is gone. Did he get up in the middle of the night? He fucking left me, and now I'm alone, naked and feeling suddenly used.

I tug the covers up over my body, trying to fight back the tears burning at the back of my throat. The bedroom door swings open, and my head snaps up, my jaw dropping in shock at the sight of Eros in just his sweatpants, and his arms loaded down with a tray of food.

"You're up!" He says cheerfully. "How'd you sleep?" I watch as he sets the tray down on the dresser, coming over to me with a steaming mug of coffee. "What's wrong?"

"You...made breakfast?"

"Of course I did. I had to run to my apartment since you don't have anything useful in your fridge. You really need to go shopping for supplies today so you're not living off canned soups and noodles." He holds out the mug to me, waiting patiently until I take it before leaning down to press his lips to my forehead. "I hope you're hungry."

What the fuck is happening right now? This is the last thing I expected from him, especially after he bitched before about how early I typically get up in the morning. He was up before me and fully functional, not a single trace of hesitation in his steps or look of exhaustion on his face.

"Do you feel okay?" I ask, shifting back slightly when he slides the tray of food onto my lap.

"Surprisingly, yes. I thought I might be a bit tired this morning, but I feel pretty good. Now, I might nap later, but that'll depend on what we do today," he chuckles, grabbing his own tray and sliding back into bed with me.

Wait.

"What do you mean, what *we* do today?"

He shoves a whole piece of bacon into his mouth and quirks a brow in question. "We need to go over the subscription list and get that in order for tonight in case they come back again and want access. Of course, if you have anything else you wish to do..." He wiggles his brows, pulling a laugh from me. "I wouldn't be opposed to you doing me," he grins.

"You're ridiculous," I snort.

"Hardly. You're a succubus, Venessa. You're naturally going to have a high sex drive. I have no idea how you've managed for so long."

"That's what the toys were for," I mumble, biting into my own piece of bacon and letting out a soft moan at the greasy goodness.

"Are you…do you plan to keep using them?" He asks, his voice timid enough that it pulls my attention back to him.

"Do you not want me to?" He shrugs, dropping his eyes to his plate. "Does it bother you that I use toys?" Another shrug, and now I'm getting irritated. *He's* the one that brought it up, but he won't give me a straight fucking answer. "Eros," I sigh. "Just tell me what you want from me."

"I don't want to seem controlling," he says quietly.

I'll take that answer as a no, but I still can't figure out why it bothers him so much. "I want an answer though. If you don't tell me the reason, then it feels like you're hiding things from me."

"I want to be the one to give you pleasure. Not your toys, and definitely not another man."

"Would you be opposed to using the toys on me yourself? I'm not saying you're incapable, but they can be fun." I really don't want to give up my toys. Those things have gotten me through some fucked up times, and he's right, I have a major sex drive. Obviously, I didn't know the reason why. I just chalked it up to the fact I must be a bit weird since it's not like I've had real sex that I can brag about. My boyfriend literally died before we even got fully into it, and that's a trauma I didn't think I would get over.

He perks up at that, glancing over at me through his long lashes. "You would allow me to do that?"

I fight back a grin. "Why wouldn't I? It would still count towards your demands since it'll be you controlling them. I even have one that's controlled with an app, not that I ever gave anyone the code," I say quickly, not wanting him to think I've gone that route of giving some random stranger access to my fucking sex toy like a sociopath.

"Wait...they make those?" I nod. "Do people seriously just...give out the code like that?"

"Yeah. I think it's just some kink that people get off on in general, but I never went that route."

"Why would you buy one that has that function if you never planned to use it?"

"I mean, it's cool to have something like that in case I *do* want to use that feature. I swear I haven't." His frown makes me tack on that comment again because I feel like this is turning into dangerous territory with him.

He doesn't respond, instead, he continues to eat his food quietly. I sigh, turning my attention to my own food and eating it in awkward silence. I don't want this to be something that ends up coming between us, but I don't know if I can just give up my toys completely like that.

He finishes his food before me, chugging back the rest of his coffee before getting up and setting his tray down on the dresser. Just when I think he's going to leave the room, he shifts to the drawers, opening each one like a fucking weirdo. "What are you doing?" He opens another drawer, rummaging through my underwear now. I shift the tray from my lap onto the bed. "Eros, what the fuck are you doing?" Another drawer gets drawn open and his body stills, the same as mine. He shifts the thin blanket I have set on top and carefully pulls out one of my toys, rolling it around in his hand.

He sets it down and moves to another, his brows drawing together as though in concentration. "How could this possibly satisfy you?" He says, bringing the small vibrator up to his face. He clicks the button, and the deep hum sounds so fucking loud in the silent room. "Hmm." He shuts it off and moves onto another, pulling out one of my favourite dildos and turning to me with a quirked brow. "This is...small."

"Compared to you, maybe," I scoff, feeling my cheeks heating with embarrassment. I don't know what to do in this situation. If I freak out and go to him to get him to stop rummaging through my unmentionables, he'll more than likely get defensive, but sitting here has my anxiety spiking to an uncomfortable level.

"And this has satisfied you?"

"It's not one of my favourites, but it does the job."

"Better than me?"

"We've only had sex once." His face falls and he turns back to the drawer, setting the toy back into it. "I didn't mean it like that. The sex was good, Eros. Better than good, but...fuck, this is getting awkward."

"You're basically saying the toys are better than I am at satisfying you, so the truth is awkward to you?"

"That's not what I said!"

"Your words imply it," he snaps.

I can't handle the fact he's upset over this. Getting up from the bed, I pad over towards him, hating that I'm still naked, but knowing that if I were to grab clothes he would more than likely take offense to it. I slip in behind him, wrapping my arms around him and pressing my cheek into his strong back. The muscles tense under me, his walls going up brick by brick, but I know I need to tear them down before he shuts me out.

"I'll get rid of them," I say quietly.

"You don't have to do that."

"Yes, I do. I don't want this to be the thing that comes between us, Eros. I can see how much this upsets you, and I don't want you to be upset." I let my fingers trail across his stomach, feeling every stitch of muscle rippling under my touch. "You're enough."

His chest expands on a heavy breath, and then his fingers come up to gently touch my forearms. I love his warmth. I love the feel of his perfect skin against my body, so much so that it brings me to the brink of tears. I could have had this right from the beginning if I just knew what I was from the start. If I had control over these powers, I wouldn't have been alone my entire life, but if things hadn't happened the way they did, I would have never met him.

Fate has a strange way of working, and I don't know if I'm grateful for the fucked-up way of doing things or not. My life hasn't been easy, but I don't regret the things I've learned in the process. I've hardened myself to the outside world, but this man might be the key to finally letting my walls crumble.

He turns around in my grip, my hands sliding away from him as I stare up at his troubled face. I hate seeing him upset, and I just want to smooth the frown line forming between his brows.

"I'm enough?" He whispers. I nod, tipping my head up to him. He cups my cheek and brings his lips down to meet mine. The kiss is gentle, nothing like the ones we shared last night, but it still sends a flutter of excitement through me.

I loop my arms around his neck, locking him to me as I deepen the kiss, prying through his lips with my tongue. He growls against my mouth, his hands shifting down over my hips to grip into my ass. I gasp when he lifts me onto his hips, turning us both and walking towards the bed. He lays me down, crawling up over my body to stare down at me with those unwavering eyes of amber.

"You know I will never put a limit on when we have sex, correct?" I quirk a brow in question, and he smiles. "No matter when or where, when you feel the need to be ravaged, I'll happily oblige."

I smirk, brushing my thumb against his jaw and the stubble that has grown in over the last few days. "Oh really?" I muse. He nods. "So, if we're in the middle of a meeting and I feel a sudden...*need*, you'll take care of me?" He nods again. Fuck me, this could be fun and it's oh so tempting. A bit scandalous but still tempting. "You realize people will side-eye us if we do that, right?" I giggle.

"Do you honestly think I give a fuck what people think? I'd take you right in front of them if you weren't a shy little thing."

That gets my attention, and my heart thumps a bit quicker in my chest. "You mean, like in the rooms at the club?"

"I mean anywhere. On my desk." He kisses my stomach, trailing his tongue up to my breast and pulling a nipple into his mouth. "On the floor," he groans, shifting to the other one. "On the bar in the club," he sighs, nipping the skin on my collarbone. "In the fucking elevator." He hovers an inch from my face, a wide grin pulling at his lips. "I'd fuck you in front of the club where the entire city could see you, just so everyone knows that you're mine."

"Pretty bold," I whisper, my body trembling under him.

"I've never been shy, but I've also never had a desire to flaunt what belongs to me. You are perfection, and I want to keep you."

I tip my head to the side, avoiding his gaze as embarrassment washes through me. It's useless though. He grips my jaw, turning my head back towards him, a frown forming on his face. "Don't say shit like that," I sigh. "I can't handle you throwing around words like that."

"Like what?" He seems genuinely confused, his head tipping in the most adorable way.

"Calling me perfect when I'm far from it. Even when you call me beautiful, it gets to me a bit."

"You don't like me calling you beautiful?"

"I'm not."

"You are though. I don't understand why you would think otherwise, but if I think you're beautiful, my opinion should matter. It's not just your looks, Venessa, it's all of you. You're sweet and kind, determined and strong in your own way, you don't shy away from a challenge, and you stand your ground when it matters. Everything about you makes you beautiful and perfect, even if you don't think those things qualify in your own mind."

He grunts when I buck my hips into him, rolling him off of me to fall on his back against the bed. His eyes widen when I shift over and straddle his knees, slowly lowering his pants down. I lick my lips when his cock slips out, the monstrosity looking even larger in the daylight.

This thing was inside me. He's right, my toys are way smaller than him, but I wouldn't dream of buying something as big as he is because in my mind, this thing should have torn me apart.

"What are you doing?"

I palm his cock, running my fingers over the length of it, enamoured by the feel of the soft skin stretched over his member. Thick veins run along the underside, and I watch in awe as it hardens in my hand. He lets out a slow breath, and I glance up, watching him tip his head back against the pillow. His throat bobs on a thick swallow, and I can't help staring at the way the muscles in his neck tense and shift with the motion. I want to bite the skin there and feel that motion under my tongue, but right now, I want to give him what he's given me.

I lick my lips again, bringing my mouth down towards his quickly hardening cock, and dart my tongue out to taste him. Precum beads at the tip, the taste subtle and salty and not as bad as I thought it would be.

"You don't have to do this," he whispers, and I glance up at that.

"I want to," I smile, dragging my tongue up the length of him and swirling it around the head. I don't have a ton of experience in this department either, but I hope I can make him feel good.

"Fuck, Venessa," he groans, his hips shifting into me when I take him into my mouth. Every muscle in his body tenses and his chest heaves when I take him further. "Fuck."

My jaw screams from the sheer size of him and I try my best to relax my mouth, inching him in bit by bit. My eyes water when he hits the back of my throat and I fight not to gag around him but fail miserably. The tightening of my throat has his hand lurching out, his fingers tangling into my hair.

I glance up at him, moving up and down his length while his hand rests on my head, each bob pushing his fingers to tighten against my strands. His eyes are glowing, getting brighter with each passing second, and fuck me, I'll never get used to that. It's something that should scare me but seeing it up close and knowing that I'm the one causing his emotions to break through his hold, sends a thrill through my body.

I love seeing him like this, the subtle tell that he's far more than a mere human. He's a god in every sense of the word, even if he doesn't think his abilities are enough to call him anything more than a lesser-known god. Cupid was nothing more than a myth and legend, a little cherub that went around in a diaper with tiny wings and a chubby face. I am so fucking glad that was all false claims and manipulated knowledge.

Eros is fearsome and gorgeous and everything anyone could hope for in a man, and this man wants to be with me. *Me*. I want every inch of him, and after last night and the way he made me finally feel whole, I don't think I could let him go, even if I wanted to.

I moan around his cock when his breaths turn heavy, his body tensing further under me as I lick and swirl my tongue. Fuck, this is turning me on, and I clench my thighs together to try and seek some friction without making it blindingly obvious what this is doing to me.

I didn't think I would like sucking dick, but the sounds he's making and the way his body is reacting to me has me feverishly lapping at him until he's a moaning mess beneath me.

"Fuck, Venessa. Fuck, I'm going to come." He tries to rip me back by my hair when I refuse to back away, and I dig my nails into his thighs, anchoring myself to his body. "Fuck" he grunts, his body curling forward and his fight to pull me away weakening as he completely unloads into my mouth. The taste of him exploding against my tongue has me moaning around him and my tongue lapping up every drop.

He's breathing harshly, his chest heaving as I pull away and swipe my thumb across my lips. I take the lingering bits of him and dip my thumb into my mouth while my eyes stay locked on his. He swallows hard, his tongue darting out to lick his lips as his eyes follow the motion.

Everything about him is sensual. The angle of his jaw and cheekbones, the slope of his nose and the deep set to his eyes that hold a promise of sin and seduction. The way his lips curve and pout out, perfectly plump and pink. They're beyond kissable, and the memory of them on my body has me shivering at the thought.

"Are you okay?" He asks, snapping me out of my mental daydreaming.

"Yeah. Why wouldn't I be?"

"Do you feel okay? You haven't fed this morning, so I'm just making sure you feel alright."

"I think I took plenty from you last night. I'm actually surprised you're functional with everything that happened."

"I mean, I felt the pull from you when we were intimate, but it felt different from the times before. It didn't feel as volatile."

"I don't think I did anything different."

"I believe you were more aware and subconsciously had the intention to feed. The fact you know that it's safe to do so with me could very well be all you needed to gain control over yourself."

"Maybe," I say quietly, but I'm having a hard time believing that to be true. Could that really be all it took to gain control over myself? With him being a supernatural being, it would take a lot for me to drain him completely in comparison to a human, but he felt the heavy effects of my power when I blacked out for those precious moments in the club.

CHAPTER FORTY-TWO

VENESSA

I thought I had been out of control before, but that was something I never want to experience ever again. I never want to be completely out of it like that again, completely void of any rational thought or reasoning. The being I became in that moment scares the shit out of me, and I never want it to see the light of day again.

I'm pathetic. I hate how weak I seem to everyone around me, even though I've tried my best to make myself seem strong and put together. I'm far from the person I pretend to be, the mask slipping off my face too many times to count.

Eros has been the worst for that, shattering any line of defense I've put up like it's a wall made of fucking Legos. The brute basically kicked it down and laughed at the destruction he created.

I still feel fear in being here for too long, not wanting to draw attention to myself, or bring chaos to Eros' doorstep. Leon Volkov will stop at nothing to find me. I know he wants revenge for what I did to his brother, even if I never meant to hurt him. His father passed away a few years ago, something that ended up in the news due to his title as a business mogul. If they only knew the true business that family was in. I know a lot of people *do* know, but there's an ingrained fear to never speak of their dark workings and ties to the underground.

Leon, being the next in line to rise to the Volkov throne, will let his anger and obsessive nature take hold. It's only a matter of time before him and his men find me, and I don't want Eros or the others to get caught in the crossfire of my imminent demise.

I need to allow myself to enjoy these small moments, even *if* they're fleeting. I know I could tell Eros about my concerns, but I don't want him getting directly involved in this. I know he can be hurt now, and that's also because of me. I won't be the reason that he ends up killed because he's suddenly become vulnerable.

I can feel my mind slowly caving in on itself, all the thoughts scrambling and destroying the small joys I've allowed myself to experience. Quickly glancing at him, I shift myself back off the bed and head over to the closet to pull out some clothes.

"What's wrong?" He asks, and my spine stiffens when I hear the bed creak and the soft pad of his feet as he walks towards me.

"Nothing. It's getting late in the morning so we should get going."

His fingers brush against my elbow, but I quickly shift away, moving past him to set my clothes down on the bed. I glance at him again, hating how dejected he looks, but I push myself forward and head to the bathroom to clean myself up and get presentable for the day. My heart is processing some mixed emotions as I put on my makeup and brush my hair. Part of me wants him to just escape, leaving me here to wallow in my self-hatred. The other part of me hopes that he sticks around and fights to break through the mental ward I'm slowly putting up.

My lungs ache as I pull in a deep breath and head back into the bedroom. My heart drops when I see it empty. He left. He cleaned up and took the plates of food out of here, but he left without saying anything. The slight hope that he's just in the kitchen is quickly destroyed when silence greets me throughout the rest of the apartment.

I'm pretty sure I just fucked this up before it even truly began. I know I should fix this, but it might be for the best. He said he wanted to be with me, but he left without saying anything, so maybe he just said those things to make me feel better about myself. I'll admit, it worked. I felt special in his eyes, even if it was only for a short while.

I gasp, stumbling back when I open the door to see Eros standing there, fully dressed now, and waiting for me. He quirks a brow, his eyes roaming over every inch of my body before settling on my face again.

"Why do you look so frazzled?" He asks, shifting out of the way to let me by.

"I didn't expect you to be standing there."

"Where did you expect me to be?"

"Not here," I huff, walking past him and hiking my laptop bag up on my shoulder before pushing the button to the elevator. I don't need to turn around to know he's come up behind me, his steps quiet, but his presence looming and hot. His aura literally presses into mine, sending a bone-chilling shiver up my spine.

His warm breath caresses my ear, and I'm begging for the fucking elevator to come faster. "Did you think I left you?" He whispers.

"No." My voice squeaks out awkwardly, and I cringe internally at how pathetic I sound.

"You're lying," he says, a hint of amusement in his tone. It takes everything in me not to jerk away from him when his tongue slips out to touch my earlobe. He gently sucks it, his hands moving down my sides to rest on my hips. His touch burns through the thin material of my skirt, my body reacting instantly to his touch and leaning back into him.

"Fine, I thought you left."

"Hmm, why would you think that?" The elevator opens and I quickly shift into the box before he completely melts my brain of any rational thought. I turn, my eyes widening when he steps in as well and the door closes behind him. Why the *fuck* did I think an elevator would be a better option than the hallway? "No more running," he growls, his eyes flaring with light.

"I—I'm not," I stutter, backing up another step.

"You are, but you have no where to run and no where to hide. You're trapped, butterfly, and I'm about to pin you to the wall."

My eyes widen when he reaches back and presses the giant red button on the panel. The elevator sways and jerks, coming to an abrupt halt. Fuck, I fucked up. He takes a step towards me, and I take another step back, squeaking out when my back hits the wall. I'm trapped; left with no where to run, just like he said.

CHAPTER FORTY-THREE

EROS

She looks terrified, as she should be. I don't understand what her fucking problem is all of a sudden. We seemed fine, but then a wall erected between us and she's turned distant. Her body still reacts to me, and I'm planning to take advantage of that fact right now.

If I can't break through to her consistently with my words, I'm going to mould her with my body. She won't deny me, not when she's desperate and starving for attention and affection. Every touch I grant her has her leaning into me, where before, she was shying away and fearful. She knows I won't hurt her, and it'll take a lot for her to drop me down in power. She could very well kill me if she wished to do so, and with the chain she's shackled me with, tying me to her, I don't know if I would have the will to fight her.

I crowd into her, fighting back a smirk at the awkward sound that slips through her parted lips. She grips into the strap of her bag, but I pry it from her tiny fingers, ripping it from her body, but gently setting it down.

I grip into her hips, pressing my body against hers. “Eros, no,” she says, but her voice is quiet and weak, like *she* doesn’t even believe the words spoken.

“You’re going to tell me no?” I whisper, dropping my head down towards her ear. I tuck my nose in against her neck, inhaling her sweet scent. Gods, I could get lost in her smell. Drown myself in the intoxicating aroma until there’s nothing left of my own essence and all that surrounds me is her.

Her throat bobs against my lips on a swallow, her breathing growing heavier. I nip at the skin, the sexiest whimper from her sending a shot of adrenaline coursing through my veins.

“Eros,” she says again, weaker than before. “I—we can’t.”

“Why not?”

“We need to be professional right now.”

“Says who? Pretty sure I’m the boss, and whatever I say, goes.”

“People are going to wonder what’s wrong with the elevator.”

“I don’t care.” Another lick and nip, and another whimpering breath from her greets my ears.

“They’re going to wonder where we are,” she says shakily.

“I. Don’t. Care.” Each word is emphasized with a kiss to her skin, and each touch has her leaning closer to me, seeking out the contact without her realizing it. "They could all fuck off for the day, and I would be ecstatic."

I growl at the feel of her plump ass gripped in my hands and hoist her up onto my hips. Her arms loop around my neck instinctively and her legs curl around my waist. The heat between us builds and I grind my hardening cock against her core. She whimpers, rocking back into me. The skirt is a fucking tease, something she doesn't typically wear, but something she must know I adore. It brings her femininity to the surface even though she still shows her defiant nature with the rest of her appearance and gothic flare.

"Tell me, Venessa. Tell me you don't want this."

I think I've become as insatiable as she is, her presence alone completely shattering all my control. I'm not normally forward when it comes to sexual needs, not needing to seek out partners or practically beg them to give me their time. Women throw themselves at me, which has become monotonous and boring and only serves to scratch the itch of physical contact and gratification.

With her it's different. With her, I *want* more. I want everything from her, not just her body and submission. I want her mind and emotions, her very being and soul. I want every inch of her, both visible and that which is hidden beneath her layers of defense and fear. She doesn't need to fear me, and I truly believe she's learning to trust me more and more.

Someday, she'll completely open up to me, telling me about her past and her childhood. Things that aren't surface level and that give me a true glimpse into the person she was before she became hardened to the outside world.

My fingers grip into her loose strands, tugging her head to the side and exposing the expanse of her delicate neck. Trailing my tongue against the soft flesh is pure bliss, a feeling I could easily get lost in for hours. Every inch of skin is begging to be devoured, by my mouth and touch and eyes. Drinking in her form and beauty has become an addiction I do not wish to break, a deadly surrender of my sanity.

She's wanted to me to run and hide and be afraid of the monster that's inside, but I welcome her self-created insanity and the darkness within her. I may seem innocent myself, but I'm far from it. Gods are never innocent, even the ones that seem quiet and unassuming. I was a warrior once, and I've broken enough hearts in my lifetime to know all too well what it's like to kill a person.

Heartbreak can be devastating, enough so that the physical vessel ceases to exist. The term *'dying of a broken heart'* isn't a myth or an endearing phrase to show the connection of souls. It's truly something that happens when someone's reason for living is taken from them. Souls exist and they're built to take a tremendous amount of pain, but when it merges with its other half, the damage is nearly irreparable.

Soulmates exist, though it's rare for the pairing to find each other. When they do, the world fades around them and everything just *makes sense*. Life becomes easier and harder at the same time. It's difficult for them to be apart, and the thought alone of losing them tears at the mind, completely destroying the mental walls they thought they had in place.

This is why souls are precious and so valuable, the fuel used in the divide. Kept safe or tormented by the reapers who collect them. Those lucky enough to earn a new life are granted that and lifted from the divide to live a new life. Their other half may be in that world at the same time as them, and there will always be a pull to find them.

My mouth pauses on her throat, the feel of her panting breaths against my own chest sending raging heat careening through my body. I've had a natural pull to this girl form the moment I laid eyes on her, with no rhyme or reason to the workings of such a visceral sensation. Is she truly mine? Could Venessa be the elusive soulmate that has failed to come forth in all the centuries of my existence? Could she be the one to break this curse?

She may truly be the death of me in the end. She'll either kill me with her power, or I'll finally know how to love and have my heart torn from my body when she leaves me. I know I wouldn't survive it, the thought pounding within my mind like an incessant drum.

CHAPTER FORTY-FOUR

EROS

The feel of her fingers digging into my hair snaps me out of my thoughts, throwing me back into my body. Fuck, I keep getting distracted, too focused on the fucking what ifs and where this relationship could end.

She's desperately trying to pull me closer to her, the heat of her body moulding me against her. She rubs against me, her legs tightening around my hips to draw me in. Her succubus origin is both a curse and a godsend when it comes to sex. She'll always want touch, the natural instinct pulling her to give into her needs and desires. I just need to give her a little nudge, urging her to let go completely by manipulating her body the way it needs to be.

"Eros," she pants, her hips grinding harder against me and drawing my cock to its full attention. It throbs in my trousers, not-so-silently begging to be released. She grips my jaw with her hands, yanking me down to crash her mouth against mine. "Fuck me," she growls, pulling my bottom lip between her teeth and nipping it hard enough that I fear she'll draw blood.

"Hmm, I thought you wanted to get to work," I tease, loving the disgruntled breath she lets out at my sass.

"The quicker you get inside me, the quicker we get downstairs."

"Now, why would I ever want to make this quick? I should torture you for hours. Draw out your pleasure until you're whimpering and mewling, begging me to let you come."

She's shaking now, the threat of extending her pleasure both horrifying and enticing. I won't do that to her just yet because she's right, we *should* get some work done. The sooner we get done what we need to, the sooner we can play again.

I press my body into hers, pinning her to the wall while I fumble with my belt and the zipper on my pants. She tugs up the edges of her skirt, exposing her soaked panties to me. Fuck me, she's so wet and I'm practically salivating at the thought of putting my mouth on that wet cunt and licking up every drop of her arousal.

She tugs her underwear to the side, clearing the path for my cock. I nestle the tip against her and we both groan when I sink into her. Her pussy flutters and tightens around me, sucking me in deeper and further all on its own. Her head thumps against the wall, her hands trembling as she grips into my shoulders.

I grip her hips, shifting her to tilt her pelvis so I can slam into her fully, dragging out slowly just to slam into her again. She cries out, clawing and scraping at every inch of skin within her reach. My fingers dig in harshly, puckering the flesh of her ass while I rail into her harder and deeper, a chaotic rhythm that pushes the both of us quickly to the edge.

"Eros. Oh, fuck! FUCK!" She screams, and I'm so fucking thankful I didn't let the elevator move even a fraction towards the lower floors. I don't want anyone else to hear her screams of pleasure. I'd kill anyone who did. Her sounds and moans are mine, no one else's.

Fuck, when did I get this psychotic about a fucking girl? I've never had the desire to kill anyone, let alone over a woman. She clenches so fucking hard around my length my hips stutter. I grunt, my own body shaking as I try to keep going, wanting to push her even further and completely unravel her from the seams.

She breaks, crying out, screaming, writhing, and gripping into my arms hard enough to cause pain. "Fuck," I roar, slamming into again and unloading into her.

We're both panting, shaking, chests heaving. Curling my arms around her, I draw her up, pulling her flush against my body while we both try to steady our breaths and trembling limbs. My knees shake under me, forcing me to lean into her and the wall to stop myself from dropping to the ground.

Fuck, that was one of the most intense orgasms I've ever felt in my life. I felt the pull of her power, but it was subtle enough to mingle in with the building pressure that ripped up my spine. Her head is tucked in against my shoulder, my fingers stroking and brushing through her locks that are now slightly clammy from the heat of her body.

We're still joined together, and I have no desire to pull apart from her. I want to stay buried for as long as possible, the flutter of her inner walls against my cock feeling so fucking good. Fuck, I just want to take her back to bed, cocoon her in the blankets and hold her hostage until I've had my fill, which won't be for a very long time.

Her fingers claw at my back gently, her lips pressing against my neck. "That was…" She sighs, her body slumping further into me to the point I don't even know where my body ends and hers begins. "So fucking good."

"Is everything alright?" My back stiffens at the sound of the speaker in the elevator crackling and what sounds suspiciously like Ikelos' voice.

"Fuck." Turning my head, I glance back, seeing the blinking light in the corner of the camera I completely forgot was in here. The fucker can't hear me, but I glare at the camera with as much venom as I can.

"Oh my god," Venessa groans, burying her face deeper into my chest.

"That mother fucker. I'm going to fucking beat him if he saw us fucking." Sure, he may not have been able to see her, but having a full view of my epic ass is still enough to piss me off.

"There's a camera?"

"Unfortunately. An error on my part, but I wanted to make sure every part of this building was under surveillance, and since this elevator works as a universal access point, I didn't want to risk leaving it unsupervised."

"Fuck. This was a bad idea." She tries to push me away, but I grip into her, tipping my head back enough to look at her. Her cheeks are flushed, her hair completely disheveled.

"I told you before, I have no issues fucking you anywhere at anytime, including in front of others." I say that but I'm pretty pissed off at the fact Ikelos saw us, and probably the security crew as well. Why the fuck was he in that room to begin with? Was he going in there to spy on us and see if we were up already? I think I'm more upset about it because I didn't *know* anyone was watching.

I don't want something like this to happen again since Venessa seems uncomfortable by this turn of events. She's still trying to push me away, her small hands gripping into my chest with a deep force.

"Put me down."

"Venessa—"

"Put me down, Eros."

CHAPTER FORTY-FIVE

VENESSA

My stomach drops at the dejected look that crosses his features. I wince when he finally pulls out of me, the sensation of emptiness feeling like a void suddenly swallowing me up. My body is getting way too comfortable with the feel of him inside of me, and each time I feel like I'm merging with him further.

I feel hopped up, the pull on his power still coursing through me like an electric current lighting up my veins with ever pulse of my beating heart. The act of feeding is coming naturally, and each time it feels easier and gentler. The monster residing within me feels almost satiated with the consistent meals it's getting. Eros is doing everything he's promised me so far, and I feel bad for treating him in this way.

I can't help the embarrassment coursing through me at the fact we were watched. How much did Nic see? Who else fucking saw Eros fucking me against the wall? My cheeks heat as I remember the sounds I made when I lost control of myself. I screamed so loud that if we were on any other floor, they would have all heard me. Thank fuck the elevator has a push button for communication to the security detail or I would be darting out of this building as quickly as possible.

No. I can't ever do that to him again because I know he would follow, and after the last time, I can't handle him getting hurt again. I can feel his cum seep out of me, pooling along my panties and slightly dripping down my inner thighs. I can't help watching him as he tucks away his dick, his body completely covering me from view to the camera.

My body relaxes a bit at that, my heart clenching in my chest at how protective and sweet he is, even after I just pushed him off me. I catch the small tremor though his body, his hand trembling as her lifts it up to brush through his hair. His eyes are still glowing but dimming with each passing second. That's where my attention stays, those gorgeous eyes like pools of gold.

"I'm sorry if that made you uncomfortable but I don't regret it and I hope you don't either."

Do I regret it?

I shake my head, smoothing my skirt over my legs as I step towards him, closing the distance between us. He seems surprised when I reach up and cup his cheek in my hand. The way his eyes flutter closed, his thick lashes fanning out against his tanned cheeks, makes my heart tighten in my chest. How easily he gives into my touch, seeking it out like it's the best thing in the world. He's so sweet, nothing I would have expected of a man like him. Someone that is notorious, good looking, successful, and can have any woman he could ever dream of, but he chose me.

"I don't regret it," I whisper. His eyes open slowly, hooded and darkened to their natural amber tone. They focus in on me, burning into me until everything around us melts away and blurs. "I don't think I could ever truly regret any moment I spend with you. I have plenty of regrets in my life, but you, Eros, you've granted me something I never thought I would ever experience."

"What's that?"

"Affection, respect, the chance at actually living a life where I don't need to be afraid."

I say that, but I *am* afraid. I'm afraid of losing him and the life he's shown me is possible. The fear of being hunted down and found by Leon isn't something I can just let go of. I don't know what to do. I've always ran; kept myself on the move so that he couldn't pin down my location. I don't know if I've been able to shake him or not, but with his connections, I know it's only a matter of time.

"Those are all things you deserve, but you deserve so much more, Venessa. You've been trapped by your past. A prisoner of your own mind for far too long. You need to spread your wings and allow yourself to thrive and be free. Unshackle yourself and allow yourself to *live*. You truly are a butterfly. A transformative being that learns to change and adapt to its surroundings in order to live a full life."

"I'm trying." My voice shakes, my fingers tracing the stubble along his jaw.

He grips my wrist lightly, shifting my hand to his mouth and placing the gentlest of kisses on my palm. That small kiss just does something to me; another crack on the dam holding back my emotions.

"I know you are, and I'm so proud of you for how far you've come in such a short amount of time."

My lip trembles, my throat tightening while tears burn at the back of my eyes as I fight back the tsunami of emotions flooding over. Proud. He's *proud* of me. No one has ever said they were proud of me for *anything*. Not once while I was a child, and even while I put myself through school. I never did anything spectacular to warrant anyone acknowledging me in that way, but Eros is. He's seen my struggle and my fight to come out of this on the other side. I'm not succeeding unscathed, but I *am* trying, and he *sees* that.

He cups my cheeks, and I can't stop the sob that bubbles up my throat. I want to hide from him, but he keeps me pinned, forcing my gaze to stay locked on his while tears begin to stream down my cheeks. His eyes bow, an edge of pity marring his features, and I just fucking can't. I break. I sob harder. Bone rattling sobs that feel uncontrolled and vicious, but he holds me still.

He presses his lips to mine softly, resting his forehead against my own while his arms curl around me. There's so much warmth and comfort in his embrace, his grip tightening like he's trying to hold the shattering pieces of myself together.

"Please don't cry. I hate seeing you upset."

"I can't help it," I sniffle. "You keep breaking through every barrier I try to put up around myself like it's made of glass."

"Your walls *are* made of glass. We both know that deep down you don't want to be shut off from the world. What kind of life is it to never experience the joys and normalcy of life? I'm giving you the chance to have that, Venessa...even if at the end of it all you no longer choose me."

My heart throbs painfully at the thought of no longer having him in my life. I haven't known him for long but trying to picture that day where I never see him again is painful. I don't want his smile to fade from my memories or the feel of his strong hands cradling me. I can't let go of the warmth and comfort he provides me or the sense of calm. He makes me feel wanted, which is something I've never experienced, and I don't want to let it go.

I don't think I could ever find anyone like him anywhere else. I might get lucky and find another supernatural being that can handle me, but it wouldn't be him. They wouldn't have those ethereal eyes that can literally see right down into my soul.

What does it look like to him? Is it as black and bottomless as it feels? He's good and light and everything I'm not, and once again the fear rages forth. I may very well break him and taint him. Darkening the light that burns inside of him until there's nothing left but the blackness seeping out of me like dark sludge, ready to devour and extinguish everything in its path.

"I'll always choose you." I say it so quietly that I wonder if he heard me, but seconds later, his body tighten around me, and his arms pull me in closer to his chest. "It'll always be you."

CHAPTER FORTY-SIX

EROS

I was a fool for not realizing how deep her emotions went. Her past is clinging to her like tar, and I know it'll take quite some time to clear her soul of the darkness lingering in every crevice and every hallway of her mind.

My grip on Venessa's hand tightens when the elevator opens, revealing a smirking Ikelos and Jackson. The girls aren't with them, but that doesn't mean they aren't lurking in the shadows, ready to pounce at the information I'm sure Ikelos divulged to them.

"You're lucky I like you or you would be dead right now," I growl, pushing past him and tugging Venessa along behind me.

Ikelos laughs, jogging with Jackson to catch up to us as I lead the way towards my office. "Are you mad that I saw your ass? It's decent, I'll give you that. Nice and perky, and admittedly biteable."

Venessa snorts next to me, but Jackson is less subtle, cackling like a hyena at the comment. "I don't want you biting my ass, Ikelos."

"Just a little nibble?" He teases. I take a swing at him, missing by a mile due to his quick reflexes. His genuine laugh pulls a smile to my lips. He's lowered his walls around me over this last week, and I think it has something to do with Venessa. He's always been cautious of me, no doubt experiencing an internal fear that I may try to take his mate away from him.

"Fine, you can have a nibble."

"Fucking hell," Jackson snorts.

"Were you on the other end of that camera?" I ask, turning my attention to him and trying my best not to let my anger get the better of me.

His eyes widen and he shakes his head vehemently, his white locks whipping across his face. "Nope. I knew better than to do that shit. To be fair, Nic was a bit worried about you two, so he thought it was a good idea to check the hallway cam to watch if you guys would come out of your rooms." A grin spread across his face. "Then he saw you coming out of hers towards yours."

"So, you watched us the entire time. There was no reason to be watching us in the elevator if you knew we were coming down."

"Well, with the way you both looked a bit pissed off, I wanted to make sure neither of you did something stupid, like beat the shit out of each other."

He's got a point. We both got on that elevator in a shitty mood, and I had every intention of preventing it from reaching its destination before I said what I needed to say. I didn't mean for us to have sex, but something about her just makes me fucking feral for her.

"We weren't going to kill each other," I grumble. "We just had...a moment of disagreement."

"That ended with you nine inches deep?" He chirps.

"Eleven," I grin. Venessa smacks my chest, and I tip my head down to look at her. "What?"

"Stop talking about your dick size."

"Why? You should be proud of yourself for handling me."

"That's not the point!"

All of us laugh at that, bustling into my office with grins on our face. Mckenna and Addison are sitting off at the side table, their brows quirked at our shenanigans.

"What are you guys laughing about?" Mckenna muses.

"Eros' dick size," Jackson giggles, flopping down on the leather couch with his arms draped across the back.

Mckenna grimaces, her gaze shifting to me. "I'm sorry. Is it small?"

I blink, coming to an abrupt halt at the comment. "No."

"Then why would they be laughing?" A wry grin spreads across her lips and Addison blushes, darting her eyes to Jackson when he laughs again.

"Apparently he's got eleven inches that he loves bragging about."

"I did no such thing," I huff, guiding Venessa over to the seat across from my desk. She's quiet through the interaction, but I don't miss red tinge on her skin creeping up her neck. Her lips twitch like she's fighting back a smile, and that's all I need to know that she's okay with this conversation. "I'm sorry you weren't privileged enough to see that, so you'll have to settle for my biteable ass."

"Biteable?" Mckenna asks, her brows dipping in confusion.

"Yes. Your husband wants to bite my ass. He loved the view I gave him while he was being a Peeping Tom."

Her head whips towards Ikelos as he drops on the couch next to Jackson, looking every bit the dark god that he is in his dark jeans and black henley. "*That's* what you were doing? What the fuck, Nic! That's an invasion of privacy."

"I wanted to make sure they were okay."

"Did you *stop* watching when you realized what was happening?" He tips his head back, staring at the ceiling and officially avoiding Mckenna's horrified face. "Nico!" She snarls. "What the fuck!?"

"I didn't see *her*."

"Not the point."

"It *is* the point. Eros hasn't tried to kill me, so that has to count for something."

I roll my eyes and take a seat at my desk, watching Venessa setting up her laptop with reddened cheeks and her eyes down. "Anyways, what are you all still doing here? I figured you would have headed home by now."

Mckenna huffs, ripping her gaze away from Ikelos. "We figured we would help you guys out for a bit today in case you still weren't feeling the best after yesterday."

"I feel fine, and as far as I know, so does Venessa." She glances up at that, her coal rimmed eyes burning into me.

"I feel fine," she says quietly.

"I'm sure you do after the elevator," Ikelos snickers.

"Enough." He snaps his mouth closed and glares at me. "Let's move on, please," I add, not wanting him to storm out of here if he thinks I'm pissed off. I can tell this continued conversation is starting to get to Venessa and I don't want her uncomfortable for the rest of the day. Plus, if they keep picking on her for what happened she's more likely to not allow me to do something so bold again.

His eyes drift to the back of her head and his gaze softens on a sigh. "Fair enough."

Mckenna comes over with a tablet and a stack of papers, setting it down on the edge of my desk. "These were dropped off this morning. I went through a few of them, just a quick glance. Do you want us to help with the background checks?"

"You don't have to do that. I think Venessa and I can handle it on our own."

"Are you sure? There are quite a few submissions here, and with all the background checks, that'll take you most of the day on your own."

"I have no where else to be." I glance back down to Venessa. "Unless *you* do."

She clears her throat, pulling one of the files towards her and grabbing the tablet to boot it up. "You said I needed to go grocery shopping, so I plan to do that today at some point."

"I'll go with you." Her head snaps up at that. "What?"

"I—I can handle shopping on my own."

"Do you not *want* me to go?"

She gnaws on her lip, her eyes drifting to Mckenna still standing at the edge of my desk. "I'm sure you have better things to do."

"I don't."

"Eros."

"Venessa." She sighs and rolls her eyes. "If you tell me you don't want me to, then I won't, but you have to say it. Out loud."

"I—" Her fingers curl into fists on the desk, her agitation and hesitance apparent to everyone in the room. "I want you to go," she whispers, her shoulders slumping.

I grin. I can't fucking help it at this point since I thought for sure she was going to fight me on it with a bit more conviction. "It's a date."

CHAPTER FORTY-SEVEN

VENESSA

The fucker shouldn't have such a nice smile. It's not fair. With those blasphemous dimples and perfectly white teeth that could blind me with the right lighting. He's way too happy about this whole grocery shopping thing, but I can't help my own small smile at the fact he called it a date.

Is it a date? *Are* we dating? I don't even know how to label what's going on between us. We haven't made it official, but we've been intimate more than once now. It's not just hooking up, that's blatantly obvious, but is there a term for what we are? I want to ask him, but I don't want to have this conversation in front of the others.

I'm embarrassed enough with what happened this morning already, and the comments from Nic just sent my anxiety skyrocketing. I know he means well and he's just beating the piss out of Eros, but I'm not used to that type of banter.

I've never had anyone to share their type of relationship with. The easy-going nature, the banter, the subtle jabs without ill intentions. I want that, and I can't help but hope that I may get that type of relationship with Mckenna and Addison.

Addi is quieter than Mckenna for the most part, but I think she's still holding back a bit on her personality. They're sisters and similar in so many ways, so I doubt they're actually much different when it comes to being vocal about things.

I can't get a full read on Nic or Jack either. Nic is the god of nightmares, but he seems tamer than Jack in a lot of ways. There's something about the winter god; something that lurks beneath the surface. I think he would have no issue or hesitation in taking someone out, especially if they threatened Addison. Who am I kidding, Nic is no different in that sense, and I'm starting to realize that Eros is the same as them.

"Alright, we'll head back home for now but keep us posted if anything comes up or if you need anything." Mckenna squeezes my shoulder, giving me a warm smile.

I blink, realizing too late what just happened. I didn't flinch away. They've all broken through my walls, slowly mending my fears and trauma with the lack of hesitation in their movements. They've never been truly fearful of me, understanding my life and powers better than I ever could.

"Thank you!" I call out to them, turning enough in my chair to see them all glance back at me as they head towards the door.

"They like you."

"More like tolerate. I know they weren't happy after what happened to you," I say, turning back to face him but quickly focusing my attention on my laptop and the file in front of me.

"They know it wasn't your fault, Venessa. Anyone with the trauma you've experienced would shy away and question the motives of those around them."

I don't respond, mainly because I don't know what to say anymore. I feel like I've turned into an idiot around him, losing track of myself and my own strategic plays. He doesn't push it once I inadvertently end the conversation, but he does let out a sigh. The sound of our combined typing is the only sound within the room, and I'll admit, it's sort of getting to me.

I have a hard time with complete silence and the need to turn on one of my playlists is gnawing at me. My leg bounces while I research profile after profile, trying to find anything that may flag the applicants from participating in the exclusive club settings.

My fingers pause on the keys when music begins to quietly play through speakers in the room, the sound of Bad Omens filtering through. I stare at him, my jaw slack.

"What?" He says without glancing up at me.

"You like Bad Omens that much?"

"They're one of my favourite bands."

"They're one of my favourites, too."

"Have you ever been to one of their shows?" He asks, finally look up past his computer. I shake my head. "They're playing in Chicago in a few months. Would you want to go with me? I can get tickets."

My heart thumps hard against my chest. He's thinking about the future. A future that includes me. The fact he's easily thinking about it and making plans that involve me has tears burning at the back of my throat.

He takes my silence as rejection, his face falling slightly and his eyes shifting down to look at his keyboard again. "If you don't want to that's fine, Venessa. I just figured I'd offer."

I want to go so badly but my dark thoughts are nagging at me, telling me not to commit to anything because we probably won't be here in a few months. I don't want to run anymore. I want to stay here, with him.

"I'd really like that."

His eyes widen as he looks up again. "Really?" I nod, and the smile spreading across his face eases some of the panic building in my chest. "Okay," he laughs. "I'll buy the tickets right now."

He's so happy. I love seeing him this way; normal and fun and carefree. Witnessing his true self and the care he's capable of showing others is something I wish to burn into my memory. He keeps that giddy grin of his plastered on his face as he stares at his computer, probably buying the tickets as we speak.

The clients I'm running through vary from run of the mill to people with records, my piles quickly evening out. "It's crazy that some of these people even applied. You would think they knew we would run background checks on all of them for safety purposes."

"You would think," he sighs. "You'd be horrified by some of the people who try to get in. We don't restrict the club as heavily as we do the private sectors, but those that we deem really bad don't gain entry into the building. We have a list that gets cross-referenced when they hand over their I.D. at the entrance, and we've had a few that have tried to come back. Now, those that are questionable but haven't submitted an application still get through the door since we can't exactly run scans on everyone who just shows up."

"Your setup is still really good. It's impossible to keep all the bad ones out, but you're doing a great job in limiting access to those who would be vulnerable to those types of people."

"We try our best. I want this place to be a sort of sanctuary for people, where they won't be judged or ridiculed for what they like and enjoy. It's my home. A place that I cherish and hold dear. I don't know what I would do if I no longer had it in my life."

"What did you do before you owned the club?"

"I dabbled a bit into business, doing my cupid duties on the side. I knew that if I wanted to live in the mortal world full time, I needed to establish myself as someone of normal standing. It was difficult at first—adjusting to the mundane way of living. I don't think I would change how I did things because that path led me to meet some amazing people and to create longer friendships. It was humbling to start from the bottom, but not being of this world didn't really leave me any other option. I had to start from scratch, but I think I did well for myself."

"I would say so," I laugh. "You're pretty well known through the city, and you've done well for yourself. It's sort of inspiring, knowing your background and that you had to start from the beginning. It makes you a bit more attainable—a bit more human."

"I'm closer to human in comparison to some other gods for power level alone. I don't hold animosity for that though. I know my limitations, and the fact I have the body of an immortal is still far more beneficial than being mortal myself."

"I wouldn't complain about your body either," I mumble, heat creeping into my cheeks when he lets out a hearty laugh.

"Why, Miss. Deye, are you hitting on me?"

Rolling my eyes I pin him with a half-hearted glare. "Don't let it go to your head." My amusement must be clear on my face because he laughs again. Damn this man and the way he makes my heart thump faster just by being in his presence. My hand pauses on the next file, my eyes focusing in on the name.

No. There's no way.

"What's wrong?" My hand trembles as I bring it closer to me and open the file, the polaroid paperclipped to the inside making my blood run cold. "Venessa."

"This—This guy was here last night?" I ask, my fingers hovering just over the picture.

"Everyone in these files were here last night in some capacity. What's wrong?"

This can't be happening. My worst fear is here, and my past has finally caught up to me. The name and photo practically burn a hole into my retinas. I haven't seen him in years, but I know it's him. He looks so much like Alexi, right down to the mole on his jaw. The difference is in the eyes. Where Alexi got his mother's hazel eyes, Leon got his father's brown—though darker and even more sinister. Those voids stare at me now, the promise of pain written in the hard planes of his face.

I startle when Eros is suddenly beside me, his hand settling gently on my shoulder as he leans down to look at the photo. "Do you know him?"

"He's—" I swallow around the lump threatening to choke me, robbing me of precious air. "He's the brother...of the guy I killed. My—my boyfriend's brother."

CHAPTER FORTY-EIGHT

EROS

She's shaking. Her chest heaves harder with each passing second as her eyes stay focused on the photo of the man in front of her. How the fuck did they find her? I should have had Jackson look further into the Volkov family to see what the dynamics were in their organization, but this could be trouble. No. It *is* trouble.

I had hoped that they would just leave her alone after all these years, but they clearly feel she's responsible for the brother's death. They're not wrong, but it wasn't her fault. The fact they've been following her and hunted her down has fury rolling through me. Is this why she's been running all this time? Because of *him*?

"Venessa—"

"I need to go. I need to get out of here before he comes back."

"Venessa, you are *not* running. Now that we know what he looks like, he won't be allowed back into the building. This is the safest place for you." A sob rips from her lungs, and she buries her face in her hands, trying to block out the fact she's breaking right in front of me. "Hey," I whisper, crouching down next to her and shifting her chair to face me. I settle onto my knees and scoot in closer to her, placing my body between her parted thighs. "Look at me."

"I can't. I'm so sorry, Eros. I'm so fucking sorry."

"For what?"

"I didn't mean for this to happen. I thought I had more time. I usually get a few months before I feel like I need to move on. I'm sorry that I brought my past right to your doorstep." She peeks up at me through tear-soaked lashes, a look of anguish ripping across her face. "I've put your home in danger," she says through a broken sob.

My hand palms her jaw, my thumb brushing away the steady stream of tears cascading down her cheek. The touch doesn't seem to comfort her, bringing heavier sobs to the surface. She's shattering in front of me, all the pieces falling to the ground at our feet with barely any hope of being pieced back together.

"You're safe here."

"I can't," she hiccups. "I can't just stay here, locked up in your ivory tower. That isn't a life."

"Neither is running. I won't let anything happen to you, okay?" She nods her head, but I don't think she believes me. The fear she has of the Volkov family is too ingrained into her, and every instinct inside her is telling her to run away like a frightened rabbit. "I'm going to make you some tea to help calm you down. Just stay here, okay?" She tries to turn away but I grip her chin, forcing her to look at me. "Please. Promise me you won't take off. We'll figure this out, Venessa. Tell me you understand."

"I—I understand."

I press my lips to her forehead, my eyes closing in anguish at the broken sob that chokes out of her. "Good girl," I whisper, ripping myself away from her when everything inside of me is pushing me to stay with her and comfort her.

Snagging my phone, I quickly make my way out of the room and down the hall to the staff breakroom, punching out a call to the only person I know that can help me.

"Didn't expect—"

"Nic." Silence greets my ears, the pounding of my own blood the only sound.

"What's wrong?" His voice holds no amusement, my own tone and the use of his mortal name pushing him to realize something is amiss.

"They found her. The Volkov family is here, and they were in my club last night."

"How do you know?"

"Leon Volkov submitted an application to the private sector. I don't know if he's just trying to fuck with her or if he knows he'll have further access to her if he were to get in."

"Why not just let him in? It would be easier to keep an eye on him and monitor his movements."

My hand is practically crushing the kettle at his words, and it's taking everything in me not to whip it against the wall and shatter it into pieces. "I'm not doing that to her. You didn't see her, Nic. You didn't see what she became when she saw his photo. She's terrified."

"He won't touch her."

"I'm not letting him anywhere near this property. This is supposed to be a safe place for her."

" You can't just keep her locked up, Eros. If you treat it like a prison, she's going to resent you in the end. He's in the city so how do you expect her to live her life if she's not allowed to go out and do things she enjoys?"

I know he's right, but I don't know how else to deal with this. "I'll hire guards for when I can't be with her. I won't let her be unprotected at any point."

"She'll still hate you for that. She's not going to want to be under watchful eyes while she's going about her day."

"Then what do you suggest because I can't think of any other way to do this. I need to fucking deal with this prick before he ends up hurting her. He's clearly a vindictive prick if he's been following her this whole time."

"Do you really think he would hurt her?"

"He's fucking mafia. He wouldn't be going through all this trouble for shits and giggles."

"Fine. We're turning around and coming back to you."

I pause dipping the tea bag. "What?"

"We'll handle it."

"I don't want you getting involved."

"Why?"

"It's not your fight. You all have lives, and you've all been through enough. I don't want any of you getting hurt because of this. It's Venessa's problem and therefore mine, so I'll deal with it myself. I'm sorry I called you."

"Why did you?"

"I—" Why *did* I call him? I shake my head at the fact the first thing I thought of doing after finding out this information was to call Ikelos of all people. "I think of you as family, even if you don't feel the same way. I didn't know who else I could call or trust with something of this magnitude. I'm sorry."

"We'll be there in twenty minutes." He hangs up before I can argue further, and I don't know whether to be happy or upset with the fact he didn't listen to me.

"Fuck." I should have just kept my mouth shut and dealt with this myself. The last thing I want is something happening to them. I couldn't live with myself.

I'm careful with the steaming cup of tea as I walk back to my office, my thoughts running a mile a minute as I try to come up with the best solution to all of this. Ikelos is right, I can't just lock her up in here like a prison, and having guards won't give her a sense of freedom either.

My hand tightens on the doorknob, my body frozen in place while my eyes widen and dart around frantically.

"Venessa?" I call out, rushing into the room and setting the mug down on the desk. She fucking promised but she left me. No. Not again. I can't do this again. My heart breaks at the fact she didn't trust me or believe in me and decided to run when I trusted her. The sound of water running and a door opening has me turning suddenly, Venessa's small frame standing in the doorway to the bathroom. Air wooshes out of my lungs, my body sagging in relief at seeing her.

"Is everything okay?" She asks, walking carefully towards me while my body shakes and sways. "What's wrong? Did something else happen?"

"I—" My voice cracks, my emotions bubbling to the surface, and in this moment, I know. I'm fucked without this girl. Just the thought of her not being here is crushing my soul and the relief in knowing she stayed lifts that devastating weight off my shoulders. "I thought you left."

Her eyes widen and she quickly rushes towards me, gripping into my hands. "I said I wouldn't."

"I know, I just—I thought you were gone."

She cups my cheek, giving me a weak smile. Her eyes are rimmed in red, puffiness settling into the underside of them from her crying. "I won't do that to you again," she says quietly. My breath rattles out of me when she squeezes my hands reassuringly. "Thank you for the tea."

She settles back into her chair, and I snag the file on Leon, feeling her eyes on me as I round the desk and take up my own seat. I want to do my own research on him, but I know that Jackson will be able to get more info once he gets here with the others. Do I tell her they're coming back? She may think that she's become an imposition if I do that, thinking that she's a burden to us while we change our lives to accommodate what's currently going on in her own life.

I keep stealing glances at her, watching her taking small sips of her tea. Her eyes close on a soft hum every time, and that small gesture fills me with joy. Something so simple makes her happy. An act of kindness with no motives other than to make her feel seen and cared for.

Her body jerks in surprise when a knock comes from the door. "Come in," I call out, tipping my head in question when Ikelos walks in with Jackson. "I'm surprised you knocked," I muse.

"Hmm, I didn't want to accidentally walk in on you guys again."

"We're not fucking all the time." He quirks a brow. "You just have impeccable timing apparently. Where are the girls?"

Venessa turns around to stare at them. "I thought you left to go home."

Ikelos glances towards me and I quickly shake my head, hoping he understands. "We went for breakfast and decided we wanted to stick around for a bit longer." I sigh in relief, but he gives me a look that basically says, *'you owe me one'*. "The girls are in the lobby. They're planning to go to lunch if you want to join them."

Venessa turns back to look at me, panic written all over her face. "Go. You'll be fine with them."

"But—"

"Trust me. Trust *them*." She nods her head and stands up from the chair. Closing her laptop and setting it on the small pile of files. "Come here." She startles, gnawing on her lip as she rounds the edge of the table to stand next to me. I stand, cupping her jaw and leaning down towards her ear. "They'll protect you," I whisper, pulling back to look down at her. She nods again, her throat bobbing on a heavy swallow.

"I trust you," she says shakily, propping up on her tiptoes to place a gentle kiss on my lips. I groan, gripping the back of her neck when she moves to pull away, and slam my lips against hers. The small whimper she lets out has heat building inside of me, and when she plunges her tongue into my mouth, I just about come in my pants.

This girl is ruining me. Turning me into a barely contained teenager with her body and sexual need. The way her powers touch and tug at my life energy makes me want to give her everything. It makes me want to satisfy her in *every* way possible.

She breaks the kiss too soon, granting me a beautiful blush across her cheeks as she turns around and walks past the guys with her head down. Ikelos follows her exit with his eyes, not speaking a word until the door closes behind her.

"Let's see the file," he says, motioning to Jackson to step forward, his own laptop in hand. Ikelos flops down on the couch while Jackson slides into the seat Venessa was in before.

I push the file towards him and he opens it, frowning when he sees the picture. "I saw him in the club last night."

"You did?"

He nods. "He was with four other guys. I thought it was a bit weird that they weren't really being social. They stayed off to the side and only had one drink the whole time I was watching them. All they did was watch the people in the club."

"Did you notice any of them watching Venessa?"

"I mean, yeah. A lot of people were watching her last night. Not only for the fact she's your assistant and was at the entrance for a lot of the night, but also because of both incidents last night. She wasn't quiet about shoving her way through the crowd, Eros. That shit draws attention."

"Fuck."

How the fuck did I miss all that? My attention was so focused on her that my surroundings were a complete blur. I didn't care about anyone else or how they perceived my reaction to everything; all I cared about was getting to her any way that I could. The fucking snake snuck into my home and has now threatened what is mine.

"I'm going to kill him," I whisper harshly.

Ikelos sits up on the couch, his brows drawn together. "Gods can't kill humans, Eros. He hasn't done anything yet, so you can't even justify it that he's done her harm. We were able to come out of our punishments unscathed, but there's nothing to say that they will show you mercy for something like that. You're not violent by nature."

"Because I choose not to be," I snarl. "I don't give a fuck about the consequences. I will not allow this insect to threaten Venessa, even if it means I get put away in order to protect her and allow her to have a full, normal life."

"She wouldn't want this, man. She'll be pissed if you sacrifice yourself for her," Jackson murmurs, typing away on his computer and not looking up at me for even a second. He's too focused on whatever he's doing to help Venessa in his own way.

Ikelos sighs and flops back into the couch, tipping his head up to stare at the ceiling. "We'll find him and keep an eye on him. In the meantime, the girls can keep Venessa company when she needs to go out. It won't be as suspicious if they use it as an excuse to get to know her. She doesn't need to know they're here to watch over her. They're both pretty powerful and have abilities beyond what you can do for her."

I wince at that. He's right. I'm fucking useless in comparison to them, but Leon is mortal. It shouldn't be difficult to take him out and protect Venessa from him and his minions. I just can't let them get close to her since as far as I know, she's basically human as well. I know nothing about her body composition and whether she can be hurt or not, but that's something I'm not willing to risk finding out. I would never hurt her on purpose just to find out if she's invulnerable or has healing. The fear that I could damage her permanently is something that doesn't sit well with me.

"You didn't have to help me—us. Not to this extent. I didn't want to drag you into this, I just—I wanted someone to talk to."

"You're family, and family needs to stick together."

Fuck, he's going to make me cry. This fucker went from hating me to fucking calling me family. What am I supposed to do with that?

He tips his head towards me when I don't say anything, a grin spreading across his face. "You didn't expect me to say that did you?" He laughs. "Yes, Eros, I'm admitting to the fact that I think of you as family. All the gods are connected in some way, and I rather choose my family. I hate my real family. They're a bunch of assholes who never cared how I felt or what I wanted for myself. They always dictated what I should and could do, and they hated that I rebelled against the path set before me and paved my own way. I don't regret it, but I do regret the pain Mckenna had to go through because of me."

"What does loving someone feel like?" I hate how quiet my voice just got asking the question, and I hate the pitying looks both Jackson and Ikelos give me.

Jackson is the first to answer, closing his laptop and giving me his full attention. “Do you honestly believe you can’t feel that emotion?”

“I know it. I can’t love because my powers won’t allow it. The emotion is housed within me, locked behind a glass wall and only available to those who are worthy of it. I grant them that feeling so they can live happy lives with the people they’re meant to be with. If I were to ever love someone, that love would no longer be available for others.”

“Why do you think that? Love is a vast emotion. It’s unconditional and capable of being given to multiple people, even if the intention behind it is different. There are many forms of love. Those between siblings and parents, as well as those reserved for friendships and lovers. To say you can’t feel the emotion doesn’t make sense because that emotion isn’t limited, Eros. I think that you can and will love and it’ll be reserved for someone who truly deserves it from the god of love himself.”

“Don’t do that.” He tips his head in question. “Don’t give me hope,” I sigh.

“Why not? Hope is the one thing we can cling to and believe in. Hope is there to show us that life can be better if we believe in it and want it for ourselves. I love Addison. I knew I was falling for her from the moment I saw her. I felt it deep in my chest, like a chain weaving its way around the both of us, tying us together. I would do anything for her, including killing and dying for her.”

"I agree with Jack. I think you've been conditioned into believing this about yourself, that you can no longer see the light at the end of your dark tunnel. Mckenna loved me and cared for me before she knew who and what I was. I came into this world weakened. A mere fraction of my power only allowing me to hang onto an animal form. I didn't care. I still cared for her and would have done anything to keep her safe. My love for her granted me access to more of my power, which was locked within the dream world, just out of reach. There's something special about feeling that, knowing that someone else can make you stronger. We were taught that those emotions were a weakness and we could only be all powerful when we're fueled by anger and rage. They lied to us, Eros, and for that reason they will always remain stagnant within their power."

"I never want to go back to a world where I don't have Addison in it. It's like Nic said, we're stronger now. For years I couldn't be seen, and now I'm seen by everyone. That's because of Addison and her sacrifice for me. Her love for me and my love for her has fundamentally changed me, too."

"That doesn't really tell me anything," I grumble.

Jackson laughs, opening the laptop again. "Well, love feels different to everyone. For me, I can't imagine being away from Addi. It hurts my heart to not be with her, to see her upset, to see her cry. Everything inside of me *wants* to make her happy and I would do anything for her. My love for her puts her above my own life and needs."

"I would have to agree with Jack," Ikelos adds. "Before Mckenna got her job as a designer, I was anxious when she would go to work. I know that the events of her past had a hand in those feelings, and knowing my family was watching us had me on edge."

Half of the things they're naming off I already feel myself. I thought there would be more to love, some universal signal that the emotion was present. I can't fathom love being so simple. If it were, why am I even necessary to this world? There must be some other reason why so many mortal have been hesitant and reluctant to fall for those they're meant to be with.

"Do you experience any of those feelings when it comes to Venessa?" Jack asks.

"I feel protective of her," I say carefully, not wanting to delve into everything else cycling through my mind because I don't understand it quite yet.

"That's a start."

CHAPTER FORTY-NINE

VENESSA

This is fucking awkward. Mckenna and Addison flank me as we walk down the street towards Carson's Eatery. They insisted we go for lunch, acting strangely friendly with me. I don't know them, and their behaviour is sending warning bells through my head.

"How are you liking the city?"

I snap out of my thoughts, glancing at Mckenna with wide eyes. "What?"

She smiles, her eyes drifting to Addison next to me. "The city. How do you like it?"

"It's fine."

"You and Eros seem to be doing better."

"We're fine." I cringe at how short I'm being with her, but I can't shake this feeling, like she's trying to pull for information.

She sighs, no longer pulling for conversation and walking quietly next to me. Fuck, I just made this even more awkward. Like, how is that fucking possible. I suck at social interactions, never holding friendships while I was younger right up into my adult life. I suck at being friendly. I wouldn't even know where to begin with becoming a good one.

"I'm sorry," I whisper just as she reaches for the door.

She pauses, glancing back at me. "For what?"

I wring my hands, hating how nervous I feel around them. "I'm not...good with people."

"You don't have to be so guarded around us. We're not going to hurt you."

"I have trust issues."

"Clearly," Addison snorts.

"I don't know what to do or what to say. I never allowed myself to get close to anyone, for obvious reasons."

Mckenna motions for me to walk in ahead of them, the warmth of the restaurant a welcoming sensation against my chilled legs. I wouldn't have worn a skirt if I knew I was going outside right from Eros' office, but here we are. At least the place wasn't too far of a walk.

The hostess blinks when she breezes past her, ignoring her weak protests and leading us to one of the booths at the back. The poor girl runs after us, huffing out a breath and dropping the menus on the table for us. She opens her mouth to say something to Mckenna, but she pins her with a glare, her eyes flashing a brighter blue. The girl actually yelps, tripping over herself, trying to get away.

"Mckenna," Addison chastises.

"What? I don't need someone telling me where to sit when the place is barely full."

"When did you get so vicious?" She snorts.

"The day I died," she snaps back, rolling her eyes. She grabs one of the menus just as the waitress comes over to us. "A pitcher of margaritas and three glasses," she says without glancing up at her. The waitress snaps her mouth shut, her eyes drifting to me and Addison. "Oh, and we'll have the spinach dip to start."

I give the girl an apologetic smile before she turns away. "You're acting like a bitch," Addison grumbles.

"I'm hungry."

"You ate like an hour ago."

"My metabolism is fucked. I need to eat every hour or I get grumpy. Nic has to always keep snacks on him to keep me satisfied."

"What are you, a dog?"

"Woof."

I can't help it, I laugh, a snort slipping out when Mckenna quirks a brow. "I'm sorry," I giggle.

Her face softens, a small smile tugging at her lips. "There you are." Heat creeps into my cheeks and I just can't meet her eyes. It's like she's trying to see into me, blowing past the walls I try to keep up. "Venessa, just be yourself."

"I don't know who I am, okay? I don't have friends. I don't have people to talk to and I sure as fuck never talk about myself to anyone. I mean, why would I? You know about my past, and that's traumatizing as it is. I can't handle being judged for my actions and people knowing I'm not a good person."

"But you *are* a good person. Your past doesn't define you and it wasn't your fault. If you had control over your power, I know you would have never hurt that boy."

"But I did hurt him and now—" I cut myself off before I tell them what's going on. I don't want to drag them further into my drama. They're being nice to me, and if this could turn into a true friendship, I don't want to ruin it.

"And now?"

I shake my head. "It's nothing. Just my thoughts getting jumbled in my head."

I'm a terrible liar. She narrows her eyes, seeing right through my bullshit, but she doesn't push it, instead, turning her attention back to the menu. The waitress drops off the pitcher and appetizer, taking our orders before running off again. I can't rip my eyes away from Mckenna and her small frame, taking in every detail after she ordered an asinine amount of food.

"Seriously. Are you pregnant?" Addison asks.

Mckenna settles her elbow on the table, propping her chin on her hand. "Do I *look* pregnant to you."

"Girl, I have a high metabolism, too, but I'm not eating anywhere near as much as you."

"We're different. You were reborn, but I was recreated. I think it's because I'm using power to pull on Nic's abilities, so it uses a lot more energy. He eats a ton of food, too, and it's so he can keep a stable connection to his nightmares. If he's weakened, they're weakened…same as me."

I'm fascinated by their conversation. I only heard the basic story of what happened to the both of them, but knowing a bit more of the details has me staring in shock. I don't know how they're so *normal* when they've both died and come back.

"Fine, but if you're pregnant, I'm going to lose my shit."

"What? Why?"

"Because! I thought I would have kids first!"

Mckenna's eyes widen. "Wait. Are you two *trying*?" Addison blushes, snapping her mouth shut quickly and turning her head away. "Addison!" Mckenna squeals. "Oh my god!"

"Shut up," Addison grits out. "It hasn't happened yet, and I don't know when it'll happen, but we both want kids."

Their excitement and focus on the conversation send a pang of jealousy through me. I never pictured myself being a mother—the fear of not being able to touch my own child because I would kill it is a horrifying thought. It could happen now if I can get full control of this volatile power. Eros would be such a good dad.

Wait.

Why would I think that? That type of conversation is so far in the future that I can't even fathom speaking to him about something like that. We haven't even gone on a date yet, even though we've already fucked and he's very clearly obsessed with me. I'm obsessed with him, too. Irrevocably.

CHAPTER FIFTY

EROS

I'm exhausted. Mentally, I'm at the point where I feel like I can't handle this day anymore. Physically, my body is aching with the need to have Venessa cradled within my arms. My distance limit has been shrinking the more time I spend with her. It was awful being away from her as long as I was, but now, it's fucking torture. I keep glancing at my watch, my eyes darting to the door every time I think I hear the sound of heels on the tiles outside.

"Will you relax?" Jackson sighs, glancing up from his laptop with a frown on his face. "She's fine. She's with the girls and nothing is going to happen to her. She'll be back soon."

"My skin feels itchy," I grumble, gripping into the collar of my shirt and tugging it away from my neck. My throat feels constricted, each breath more laboured than the last.

"If you need to take a break you can. We're not going anywhere."

"Yeah. Maybe I'll go grab some air."

I can feel their eyes on me as I get up from my chair and make my way to the door. The room felt suffocating the longer I sat there waiting for Jackson to find anything useful on Leon. I don't pay any mind to the staff, barely waving at them when I walk by them and make my way towards the lobby entrance. The day seems nice enough, the sun deceiving to how cold it is when I step out the door.

The frigid air is welcome against my clammy skin, easing some of the unease I was beginning to feel. They've been gone for a few hours now, and the temptation to call Venessa has been nagging at me for the last hour. I know they're right and that she's safe with the girls, but with knowing that fucking psycho is watching her, I can't help but be on edge.

Twinkling laughter draws my attention down the street and my heart clenches in my chest at the sight of her. She's smiling cheerfully, talking and laughing with Mckenna and Addison as they walk back towards my building. She seems happy and carefree, and a pang of jealousy hits me at the fact *they* were able to bring this side of her out.

She's still been guarded around me and hesitant to fully open herself up to me, but I know that I can't rush it. She's told me enough about her past to at least ease some of the burden that has been weighing down on her, but how much more trauma is she holding onto?

Her eyes meet mine, widening when she realizes it's me, and a blush of pink creeps across her cheeks. She ducks her head and stares at the ground when she stops in front of me, the girls giving me small nods of their heads, leaving her behind.

"Did you have fun?"

"I did," she says quietly. Her body trembles in front of me, her arms wrapping around herself. I quickly pull her into me, engulfing her small frame within my arms. She sighs, leaning her cheek against my chest. "Thank you."

"You're not dressed well for this weather. Especially if you're walking around."

"I didn't want to bother them by going up to the apartment to grab a jacket."

"They would have waited, Venessa. You need to realize that you're not a burden to anyone."

She tips her head back, gracing me with her beautiful eyes that glitter in the sunlight like an endless pool. "Not even to you?"

"Especially not to me." Planting a kiss on her forehead I squeeze her tighter, loving the way she melts into my hold. I hate that she still thinks so little of herself. Have I not done enough for her to realize she's important in this world? That she's important to *me*? A prickling sensation creeps up the back of my neck, but when I glance back over my shoulder, nothing is there. "Let's get you inside and warmed up. I'll make you another tea."

"Did you eat lunch?"

"Not yet, but I'm not very hungry."

"Hmm. I don't like that you're skipping meals."

"I don't need mundane food to survive, Venessa. I do it mainly because I enjoy the act and the taste of food." I tuck her in against my side and lead her through the doors into the warmth of the lobby. She shudders, curling further into me.

"You're really warm," she sighs, settling her hand against my stomach. It still surprises me how naturally she's falling into expressing herself and her needs with touch after being deprived of contact for so long. I *like* how affectionate she is, and I'll take every gentle touch and desperate need.

The temptation to bind her to me is strong. Rope might chafe though, but I could invest in some padded cuffs. At least then she wouldn't have the option to run away from me like she has in the past. Hmm, maybe a collar would look better on her. Something elegant but still an obvious claim that she's mine.

The moment I open the door to my office, everyone goes quiet. Mckenna is sitting with Ikelos while Addison hovers over Jackson's shoulder. "Have a seat and I'll grab you a tea," I say, motioning for her to head into the room. Ikelos tilts his head in confusion, but I just shake my head and head back out of the room.

I'm taking care of this girl better than I take care of myself, but I don't mind in the slightest. I happily make her a tea, heading into one of the lounge areas to grab her a blanket as well. By the time I walk back into the room, Venessa is sitting on the couch with Mckenna now, while Ikelos lounges in my chair like he fucking owns the place. I glare at him, my eyes drifting to his booted feet propped up on the desk.

"What?" He murmurs.

"What the fuck are you doing?"

He shrugs. "I figured the couch would be more comfortable for your girl, so I took the chair."

"And the feet?"

He lounges back further in the chair, giving me a wry grin. "It's still a comfy chair," he chuckles. "I can see why you like it so much. Very kingly."

I roll my eyes and head over to Venessa. The smile she gives me when I hand her the tea completely drains the irritation towards Ikelos out of me. "Thank you," she says happily, blowing against the rim to cool down the steaming mug.

I settle the blanket around her legs, tucking the edges under her and giving her a quick kiss on the lips. "Hopefully that warms you up." She hums out a cute breath, leaning towards me when I move to pull away and plants another kiss on my lips.

"You're adorable," Ikelos snorts. Sighing, I pull away from Venessa to sit next to Jackson in the other chair. "Does that make you uncomfortable?" Ikelos laughs.

"It's common courtesy."

"Hmm, I think the tea would have been enough if it wasn't something more." He leans towards me, lowering his voice enough that only me and Jackson can hear him. "I would consider that a sign that you do in fact love her." I stiffen at that, hoping Venessa didn't hear him. He shrugs, settling back into the chair with a neutral expression on his face. "You can fight and argue all you want, but from what I've witness, I believe you don't give yourself enough credit."

"It's common courtesy," I say again, and I can't help biting it out through gritted teeth. I don't like how he's pushing this. The way his words settle into me and give me a false sense of hope. Because of him, I can't help but hope. Hope for a real life and a real future. One that revolves around the girl that has somehow stolen my heart.

"Alright, I hacked the CCTV system, and I'm running my program for facial recognition to try and pin him down. It should give us some warning if he tries to come within fifty feet of the building. I was able to pull your security footage as well and spot him quickly enough. He's right here," Jackson says, pointing to the screen.

I'm glad I invested in higher technology for the cameras, the image clear enough to see all his features, including his goons. The image of him on the camera shows his soulless eyes and hardened features as his gaze follows Venessa through the club.

"What are you doing?"

My back stiffens at the sound of Venessa's voice ripping me from my thoughts. "Fuck," Jackson murmurs, turning the screen back towards him. "Sorry, man."

I can't blame him. He was focused on the task in front of him and didn't register the fact that Venessa was back in the room. It's not like we could avoid it forever. She would have realized soon enough *why* the four of them were here.

"You brought them in? So, the girls taking me out was just a distraction so you three could go behind my back and try to deal with my problems without me?"

"Venessa—"

"You tricked me!" Venessa snaps, shutting Mckenna up with a click of her teeth. "You didn't want to hang out with me. You were forced to do it."

"We weren't forced to do anything," Addison says, trying to tamper down Venessa's quickly growing agitation.

"How am I supposed to trust any of you when you can't be honest with me?" I'm on my feet the moment she lurches up, the blanket sliding to the floor and pooling at her feet. "Don't," she snaps, her eyes fixed on me.

"Venessa—" I step towards her.

"No. Don't fucking come near me right now."

Her teeth are gritted together, her hands clenching at her sides hard enough to turn her knuckles white. I can feel the buzz of power flickering under her skin from her. Her agitation shifting her power into an unstable state.

"I'm trying to protect you," I whisper.

"By hiding things from me? By *lying* to me? This isn't protecting me, Eros. This is pushing me away because you're doing things behind my back. This is my life and *my* problem to deal with. It was one thing having you know about Leon, but you went and brought *them* in?"

"They care about you as well."

"No."

"They're family."

"They're *your* family, not mine. I'm nothing to them. The only reason they're here is because of you."

"Venessa, if you would have called us yourself, we would have come for you. Why can't you see that we're in this together?" Mckenna tries to placate, shifting herself off the couch as well.

She looks like a trapped animal trying to escape predators ready to devour her. Her eyes are wide, her chest heaving harshly while her body trembles. The mug of tea in her hands sloshes with the tremors wracking her body, but she doesn't react to the burning liquid. The skin reddens instantly, and she catches my line of sight, quickly dropping the mug to shatter on the tile floor.

The sound is like a starting bell, pushing her into motion. She's fucking quick, darting through the door fast enough that I'm scrambling after her. I can't fathom the thoughts running through her head, not when her first reaction is always to run. The little rabbit has been conditioned into this, running being the only way to outrun the wolf that's been hunting her down.

Mckenna tries to cut me off, and I snarl at her, her eyes widening in shock at the glare I throw her way. "Eros—"

"You've done enough," I snap.

"Eros," Ikelos warns.

"No. I asked for your help, and you've gone and made it worse because you couldn't keep your mouths shut. Any progress I've made with her has just been completely destroyed because she believes we're all fucking manipulating her. Can't you see how fucking broken she is?"

"She just needs time," Addison adds.

"What she needs is *me*."

I swear, I need to put a god damn tracking device on the girl with how much of a flight risk she is. She's upset, and I doubt she would go to the apartment when she's in this mindset. Memories of the night before flash through my mind, and I take off, heading towards the main level and the lobby.

I sigh in relief when I catch sight of her pushing through the glass doors, bolting after her as quickly as I can. My fingers graze against her arm, her reaction time quicker than I anticipate. My head snaps to the side, my cheek stinging from the full hit she just knocked me with.

"Fuck off!" She screams, taking off down the street.

"Damn it," I grumble, rubbing at my cheek while anger and frustration bubble up inside of me. "Venessa!"

"Leave me alone, Eros!"

"You shouldn't be out in the open!" I yell, jogging to catch up to her.

She whirls around, stopping me in my tracks. "What are you going to do, huh? You going to throw me in a cage and keep me locked up in your little ivory tower for the rest of my life?"

"We'll find him and deal with this, but in the meantime, you're safer inside. I don't want you wandering around alone."

"I've handled myself this long. I don't need you and your fucking *family* butting into this. It was a mistake to even tell you about Leon."

"I'm sorry. You weren't supposed to find out like that."

"Or at all. Isn't that right? You took what I told you in confidence and fucking ran to them the first chance you got. How can I trust you if you keep talking about me behind my back?"

I don't know what to say to her because she's right. I didn't know how to handle the information on my own. The situation completely different from the shit I usually deal with. I knew I needed help trying to deal with this, and I thought reaching out to Ikelos was the best option. I didn't think that Venessa would react this badly, but she already has severe trust issues due to her upbringing and the events of her past.

"Venessa, I care about you, and I want to help you any way that I can. I'm sorry if my actions feel like a betrayal, but that wasn't my intention."

"Care about me," she scoffs. "You're just like everyone else who has claimed to *care about me*. They all wanted to control me and make me feel weak." My eyes widen, my feet moving on their own towards her. How did this happen? "I won't let you break me," she sobs.

"I'm not trying to break you; I'm trying to help you!" She shakes her head, tears flying off her cheeks while her hair whips in the cold wind around us. "Please."

She turns, sobbing as she takes off again. Fuck this shit. What do I do? How do I make her *see*? A growl rips up my throat, and I run after her, following her into the alley next to the building. She screams when I grip into her arm and turn her, slamming her back against the brick wall. She tries to hit me again, but I grab her wrist before she can make contact and lift both her arms above her head, stretching her body out completely.

We're pressed close enough to each other that each of her breaths heaves her chest against mine. She wriggles in my grip, trying to rip her hands out of my hold, but I press them harder into the wall above her.

"Let me go!"

"No."

"Let me fucking go, Eros!"

"No," I snarl, shoving my leg between her thighs and completely pinning her to the wall. "I will not let you run from me again. You are *mine*, Venessa. Fucking mine. I vowed to protect you, yet you take every chance you can to push me away and put distance between us. Get it through your thick skull, I'm not going anywhere. You can yell at me, hit me, fucking hate me, but I will protect you no matter what. You are not alone, and you never will be because I am here for you until the bitter end."

Her eyes glisten with tears, her body stiff and unyielding. She shakes her head, crying out in frustration. "Let me go!" She screams. "Help! Someone he—"

I slam my lips against hers, silencing her desperate attempts to draw attention to us. Her fear and desperation pushed her to seek the help of others to get away from me. *Me*. Like *I'm* the one doing her harm. Her lips stay pressed together, fighting my attempt to delve into her mouth. I growl low in my throat, sinking my teeth into her bottom lip until she gasps. I take her moment of surprise and plunge my tongue into her mouth, forcing it against her own.

Her fight weakens, her body slowly slumping against mine. She no longer struggles to free her hands, her body bowing into mine as she clashes her tongue against mine. Her whimpers and needy nips and sucks of my tongue and lips have me pressing into her further, completely restricting her between my body and the unforgiving wall behind her.

"Stop fighting me," I murmur, nipping at her lip again. "Stop trying to make excuses in your head to give you an out." I kiss her again. "There is no out, and there's no escaping me." She moans into my mouth and fights against my hold on her. I let her go, groaning when her arms curl around my neck, her fingers digging through my hair with sharp tugs. "Tell me you still want me, Venessa," I whisper.

"I want you."

"Good." I pull away and she squeals out in surprise when I lift her up and toss her over my shoulder. "Let's get you back inside."

"Put me down!" She screams, smacking my back over and over weakly. "Eros, I can walk!"

"Hmm, I don't trust your little escape legs at the moment," I chuckle. She smacks my ass. "Careful. I quite enjoy rough play, if you haven't noticed already. Smack me again and you'll have a permanent mark on your own pretty ass when I'm done with you."

That shuts her up and stills her body. She huffs, letting herself dangle down my back like a little ragdoll that I want nothing more than to play with. Fuck, I'm fucked up. What is it about this girl that keeps me chasing her? Seriously, I've never had to put this much effort into keeping a woman. I'm usually the one being chased. I'm the one that women flock to, as is only natural due to who I am.

They don't realize the reason for the pull they have towards me, but Venessa was the opposite. She did everything she could to stay away from me, never giving into the temptation that is weaved through them because of my power. Maybe that's *why* I like her. The reactions from her are genuine and not a manipulation from my presence.

Addison and Mckenna are waiting in the lobby when we get back, their eyes widening at the now limp Venessa on my shoulder. "Is she okay?" Addison asks. I feel her push against my back, propping herself up against it to look at Addison. "Uh..."

"She's fine. I'm going to take her home and I'll meet you all in the office once I'm done with her."

"Done with her?" Mckenna says carefully.

"Hmm. I think Venessa needs some rest, so I'll be sure to put her to sleep." I grin at the look of surprise on her face, her eyes drifting to her sister. "She'll be fine."

Venessa lets out little huffs the entire ride up in the elevator, quietly grumbling under her breath. She's not fighting me at least, and in my books, that's progress. The fact she allowed me to carry her this whole way says a lot about her. She doesn't *want* to run, but she keeps letting her doubts cloud her mind, taking over all reasoning and making her reactive instead of rational.

She squirms in my grip as soon as I'm in front of her door, and the little shit smacks my ass again when I don't release her. My fingers dig into her thighs, my own hand coming down hard enough to make her scream in surprise.

"You spanked me!" She cries out.

"I fucking warned you, but you didn't listen."

"So, you fucking spank me?!"

"That's the least of your concerns." I breeze through the door and head right for her bedroom, her squirming stopping when she realizes the predicament she's in. She squeals when I toss her, her back hitting the mattress and her body bouncing up from the force of it.

"Eros, what the fuck?" She scrambles back, eyes wide when I step towards the bed. Her gaze darts around frantically, but there's no running, not here. "What—what are you going to do?"

I tilt my head, a grin spreading across my lips. "Whatever I want. You've run from me again, hit me again, and denied me once again. What do you *think* I should do?"

She gnaws on her lip, her eyes drifting down to my hands when I slowly pop the first button on my shirt. Her thick swallow is audible, her gorgeous neck bobbing sensually. "I—I don't know," she whispers.

"Think, Venessa. What do you think you deserve for your actions?"

Her body trembles as I step closer still, stopping just at the edge of the bed and popping another button. She stays quiet, giving me ample time to completely expose my chest to her. I tug my shirt out from the waistband of my slacks, letting it slide off my shoulders to fall to the floor.

"P—punish me?" She chokes out.

"Hmm, yes. I think you deserve to be punished. Do you know how I'm going to punish you?" She shakes her head. "I'm going to make you cry and scream until you beg me to let you come." Her eyes widen at that, her mouth popping open in shock. I slide the belt from my waist snapping the leather between my hands. "Hold out your hands." She shakes her head, her chest heaving harshly now. "Show me that you trust me and hold out your hands, Venessa." She gulps, shifting herself closer to me.

Setting the belt down on the edge of the bed, she watches me carefully as I grip the edge of her shirt, pausing to look at her. She gives me a small nod, and her willingness brings a smile to my face. Slowly I pull it off over her head, exposing half of her body to me. Reaching behind her to undo the clasp on her bra, it pools against her chest, allowing her gorgeous tits to settle into their perfect, natural position.

Fuck, she's breathtaking. Every time I get to look at her, I feel like I'm a starved man with food being dangled in front of him. My mouth waters at the thought of tasting her again. Of being *inside* her again. My fingers tremble, touching every inch of skin visible to me.

"Gods, you're so beautiful."

CHAPTER FIFTY-ONE

VENESSA

There must be something seriously wrong with me. Sure, I feel fear at the thought that he's going to punish me, torturing the pleasure from my body, but why do I feel an edge of excitement at the thought? I'm fucked up, right? No one in their right mind would willingly submit to something like that.

That's what I want to do. I want to submit to him. I want to let him do what he wants with me and relinquish all my control. The belt is making me a bit *more* nervous though, the idea of being tied up and not having the option to use my hands freely. Deep down, I know he won't take it too far. If I ask him to stop, he will...right?

"Eros, I'm not sure about this," I say quietly, hating how weak my voice sounds. His eyes bore into me, taking in every detail in front of him. He keeps telling me how beautiful I am, over and over again, and each time I feel my walls crumbling further.

"About what exactly?"

I roll my eyes and point to the belt. "I don't know if I can handle being restrained."

He said that if I trust him, I'll do as I'm told, but there's still that nagging voice in the back of my mind that is screaming at me to not trust *anyone*. Eros has proved himself time and time again, but yet, I ran from him once more. I keep doing that. I keep fucking running like my legs have a mind of their own. My brain isn't communicating with my heart the way it should, taking over like a defence mechanism.

"Do you think I'll hurt you?"

Do I? Physically, I don't think he would—not on purpose anyways. Mentally, I think I'm hurting myself more than he's hurting me. He's done everything he can to level me out, both in emotional aspects and the fact he's vowed to help me with my succubus heritage. I wish I knew my parents. I wish they would have never died. Things would be so different if they were still here, helping me and guiding me through this fucked up life.

"Honestly? I don't know, Eros."

His features soften, his hand coming up to cup my cheek in a gentler touch than I feel I deserve after everything. "I'll never hurt you," he whispers, and fuck me, I believe him. His thumb brushes against the sensitive skin under my eye, a frown forming on his face. I blink rapidly, trying to quell the tears bubbling along my lashes, but it's no use, I can't stop them. "Please don't cry."

"I trust you." The weight of fear slowly eases at admitting that, but I know in my heart that it's true. I'm an asshole for losing my shit earlier on him and the others. I felt panicked and trapped, like they were manipulating me and working behind my back. My reactive nature wouldn't allow my brain to think about the situation. Now? With the way he looks at me, even after I yelled at him and hit him, I know he's not in this for selfish reasons.

"Give me your hands." I do, holding them out in front of me and swallowing hard when the leather bites in against my skin. It's slightly uncomfortable, but I don't feel pain from it. I can't help the spike in my heartrate when he gently pushes me back to lie down on the bed. His fingers skim across my stomach, down over the material of my skirt before gripping into the band.

My breath hitches as he slowly draws the material off of me, the soft fabric tickling my skin and the warmth of his fingers causing goosebumps to erupt in their wake. All that's left between us is the soft cotton underwear that's still soaked through from this morning.

"Mmm, I love that you're still covered in my scent," he sighs, running his fingers against the wet material. "How did it feel walking and sitting so casually with my cum dripping out of you?" His eyes drift up to meet mine; the amber hue darkened with desire. "Hmm?" He brushes his thumb against my clit, pulling a whimper from my lips. "Tell me, Venessa. I want to hear you say you liked it. Tell me how good it felt knowing I was inside of you all day."

Fuck, he's got a dirty mouth. Why are his words alone turning me on further? Seriously I am *fucked up*. I figured I would like sex if I ever got to experience it again, but I didn't expect it to be like this. The dirty talk just does something to me, sending me right to the edge. I want to take control. I want to push him down, straddle those thick thighs of his and ride that monstrous cock until he breaks me in two. Fuck.

Get your shit together, Venessa.

His thumb pauses its torturous circling. "Say it," he growls.

My body aches for more, my hips shifting into his hand to try and gain that blissful friction he was giving me, but he snaps his other had out and pins me down, forcing my body to still. "I...I like it. It feels good to have you inside of me."

"Fuck," he groans. "Do you want my cock buried into you?" I nod. "Use your words."

"Yes." Fuck, yes. "I want you to fuck me."

He grins, his tongue darting out to lick his luscious lips in a sensual stroke that make my own lips part in anticipation. "That's a good girl. I'm going to fuck you...but not yet. I told you you're going to be punished for what you've done. Do you understand me?" I nod again, hating it more and more that I allowed my emotions to betray me. He would be fucking me already if I didn't act out the way I did.

My breath stutters out of me when he finally pulls my underwear down off my legs, exposing my sensitive flesh to the air and his burning gaze. He hums low in his throat, the sound sending a wave of heat coursing through me.

"I'm about to show you how much better I am in comparison to your toys."

His lips and tongue trail up my inner thigh like molten lava. My body trembles, every fiber of my being wanting to grip into him, but I hold back, allowing him to do what he wants to me. I know I deserve his punishment, but this is one punishment that I feel will be something I'll be begging for again and again. The leather of the belt bites against my skin when that wicked tongue flicks out against my clit and my body bows.

He moans, the vibration radiating through my hips and right into my soul. "Oh god," I whimper.

"That's right, love. I *am* your god."

He licks and sucks and nips, delving his tongue right into me and making me jolt at the sensation of its invasion. Fuck, it feels so good. The way he pushes into me, licking at my walls only to drag it back out to press against my clit. I'm so fucking close, my back bowing off the bed while I squirm against the restriction of the belt on my wrists. My fingers flex, hands shooting out to grip into his hair as the orgasm builds and builds and—

"No!" I cry out, panting as I stare up at Eros, his lips glistening with my arousal.

He smirks, licking his lips. “Yes,” he chuckles. “This is your punishment, Venessa. I’m going to wind you up tight enough you’ll beg me to break you.”

CHAPTER FIFTY-TWO

EROS

She's going to be so easy to break, I can already see it. The way her chest heaves with each breath has my cock throbbing in my pants. I'm glad I kept the barrier between us, the desire to sink into her building with each passing second.

The taste of her on my tongue makes me feral. I need more, and I think that at this point, I may struggle as much as she does. This punishment may end up affecting the both of us, which was not something I anticipated. Oh well. I *could* switch it up a bit in a way that benefits the both of us, but I still want to play with her a bit longer.

Her eyes follow me as I shift myself off the bed, biting back a groan when I finally allow my cock free, my pants sliding down my legs to settle against the floor. She visibly swallows, her chest heaving again when I move over her, pressing my body against hers before claiming her mouth.

I love kissing her—love the sounds she makes and the way her body reacts to every nip and suck. Her tongue clashes against mine, needy and begging for more. I give her more, slanting my head to deepen it and pulling a low moan from deep within her throat. My own moan filters into her mouth when I drag the underside of my cock against her wet cunt, putting pressure on her clit.

"You're making this very difficult," I admit against her lips. "You're so fucking wet for me, Venessa."

"Please," she pants. My fingers skate down her side, the soft touch making her shudder under me. She trembles harder as I slide back up her inner thigh, brushing my knuckles against her wet heat. I keep a slow steady rhythm, driving my hips into her in blissful friction as I slide one finger into her. "Oh fuck," she whimpers, widening her legs to me in an attempt to have me push deeper.

The fact she feels this good without me even fucking her is a bit of a mindfuck. I've never done anything like this, my previous ventures being simple and straightforward in the intention. With her, I don't want to just fuck her, I want to consume every inch of her.

Her breaths turn harsh when I slide a second finger into her, my own mouth devouring her moans. I can feel her walls tightening and clenching around me, and it takes everything in me to stop.

"Fuck!" She cries, trying to shift her hips into my hand. She's desperate for a release, doing everything she can to pull that last bit of friction that will push her over the edge.

I bury my face into her neck, kissing and sucking on the skin while my own chest heaves. My cock throbs, desperate to be seating inside her warmth, but I keep my body still, allowing her to ebb from that peak of orgasm.

"Eros, please! Please!" She whines, her voice breaking desperately.

"Not yet." My voice sounds strained, my own desperation bleeding into my words. I want to give her what she wants, but I need to prove a point. She's mine and always will be. This isn't just a punishment but an official claim.

Her bound hands between us press against my chest, her trembling fingers tracing against my skin delicately. "I don't think I can handle this."

"You're doing so well," I reassure her, kissing her jaw before pulling back enough to look at her face. I pump my hips slowly, watching her eyes slam shut, head tipping back as she pulls her bottom lip between her teeth. "Do you want me to fuck you?"

"Yes," she rattles out.

"Beg for it. I want to hear you beg me to fuck you, Venessa. Tell me you're sorry. Tell me you'll never run from me again. Tell me you are mine."

Her eyes flutter open, the flush of pink across her cheeks making her even more beautiful. "Please, fuck me. Please let me come, Eros. *Please.*"

"What else. Say it."

She trembles harder, her bound hands clenching and unclenching against her stomach. She gnaws on her lip, and the hesitation has me shifting my hips, dragging my cock against her clit once more. "Fuck," she says, tipping her head back and exposing that gorgeous expanse of neck to me. "I—I won't run from you," she whispers. "I'm yours."

Her eyes dart to me when I pull back and grip my cock, giving it a few firm pumps as I stare down her perfect body. Pressing the head of my cock to her, her entire body stills, even her breath seeming non-existent in the wake of anticipation.

The second I slam into her she screams, her core fluttering and clenching, unraveling around me. My hands launch out, fingers curling harshly into her skin at how hard she just came from me entering her. Fuck, she was beyond close. A glass on the verge of overflowing with the smallest of movement. Grunting, I try to breathe through her orgasm tightening around me and start to move.

Her cunt is like a vice, gripping into me hard enough that it's difficult for me to move without the fear of tearing her from the inside. She moans, writhing under me as I push it further, not allowing her to come down from the orgasm ravaging her body.

This is the other punishment, one that is both devious and satisfying. I won't let her come down from this high until I'm good and ready, and even then, I won't stop until her body is completely spent. Maybe then I can quiet her mind and stop her from running. You can't exactly run away when you're incapacitated. She can hate me later for it.

"Eros!"

I thrust into her, pushing past the tightness clenching around my length. My fingers dig in harshly on her hips, yanking her into me with each pump of my hips. Her breathes wheeze out of her, her bound hands launching out to grip into one of my wrists. It's like she can't decide whether to pull me closer or push me away, her body reacting completely out of her control.

My teeth grit together when she comes again on a broken scream, my name falling from her lips over and over again. I breathe through it once more, throttling into her harder. Her eyes meet mine, widening at whatever she sees there. It could be my lust-filled gaze, the savagery of my thrusts, the way my muscles tense and flex, proving how much of a struggle it is to control myself around her.

"Again," I growl. She shakes her head, her grip on my wrist tightening. I lean forward, curling my fingers around her throat and squeezing enough to make her eyes flutter. I kiss her, willing her to take all of me and feeling the subtle pull of her power against mine. "Again," I snarl. "Come for me again, Venessa."

"I can't," she chokes out, but I silence her, smashing my mouth against hers until all she tastes and breathes is me. She comes, a muffled cry and tears streaming down her cheeks. I did what I set out to do. I broke her perfectly, and soon she'll be ready to be put back together.

CHAPTER FIFTY-THREE

EROS

I watch as the numbers on the elevator tick down, feeling a bit bad with what I just did. Not the fact I fucked her until she was a barely moving puddle, passing out after I cleaned her up and put her back in bed. No, the reason I feel like a traitor is the fact I lied to her in telling her I wasn't keeping her prisoner.

Pulling out my phone, I open the security app that allows me to control most things within my building remotely. A heavy breath rattles out of me the moment I hit the office floor, pushing the button on the security system that prevents the elevator from reaching the top floor.

She's definitely going to hate me when she finds out. I pause when the door opens, Ikelos leaning against the wall with his foot propped up against it. His arms are crossed and I'm not a fan of the frown that's marring his features.

"What is it?" He jerks his chin towards my office, and I sigh, following him quietly.

"We have a bit of a problem," he says the moment I step through the door. Jackson is still on the computer, leaning towards the screen in heavy concentration.

"What's the problem?"

"Leon is here."

"What? What do you mean he's here?" Jackson lifts his hand, calling me over to him. Leaning down, I watch as he zooms in on the footage. On *my* footage. "He's in the fucking building?"

"Eating like he doesn't have a care in the world."

Anger rips through me, a snarling breath slipping through my lips. I jerk up, my muscles going taught at the thought that he's this close to Venessa. I should have put out his info right away to my staff, but I wanted Jackson to get all the information he could on him before I did that. He's been watching the CCTV footage this whole time so how did he miss him coming this way?

"Can you explain to me how this happened? I thought you were keeping an eye out for him?" I ask, trying to tamper down my anger. It's not his fault that this happened, but I can't just let this go either.

"I tried. I had the program running this whole time, but it kept coming back empty. I didn't get a hit until it was too late. He's been here for about ten minutes."

"We should have shared his photo to the staff. Fuck, I'm such an idiot."

"You were busy. How is she by the way?"

"Sleeping." He quirks a brow, his lips twitching as he fights back a smile. "I didn't drug her."

He laughs. "What did you do? Fuck her until she passed out?" He snorts. Well, this is awkward. I can't help but divert my gaze, which just makes him laugh harder. "Holy shit, you did!"

"It wasn't my intention."

It was one hundred percent my intention, but I'm not admitting to them how fucked up I am. The sight of her weak and satiated in burned into my memory. The way her skin glistened with a thin sheen of sweat. The way my cum oozed out of her once I pulled out. The way her full chest heaved with every harsh breath until it steady in the tub.

She was so docile once I got her into the bathroom, her eyes drifting closed with each pass of the washcloth against her skin. I couldn't help but pepper her with kisses as I took care of her, loving the small hums that greeted my ears.

"Do you want me to send security into the restaurant to take care of it?" Ikelos asks, his own smirk of amusement painting his lips.

"No. I want to speak to him myself. He is not welcome here at all, and I want him to know that Venessa is under my protection."

"He's basically mafia, Eros. You're going to end up pissing him off."

"Do you think I give a fuck? He can't do anything to me. He can't fucking hurt me, and as long as I can keep an eye on him, Venessa is safe."

"She might be safe here, but she's not going to be able to handle being locked up, and as long as he's out there, she'll always be in danger. She's survived this long because she's stayed a few steps ahead of him, staying on the run. Now? Now, she's been caught and she's trapped. She can't run without him knowing, and living in this level of fear isn't a life," Ikelos murmurs.

I hate that he's right. I know she can't live this way and she won't. She might be trying right now, but how long can she handle being completely collared. Even *I* can't keep her contained for the rest of her life. I couldn't do that to her and I won't.

"Jackson, you stay here with the girls. I'm going to go with Eros to the restaurant."

"Why do you get to go?" He grumbles.

"I'm scarier than you," he chirps with a grin. He shoves his hand through his hair, disheveling it to the point he literally looks like a villain. I quirk a brow. "What? I am."

"I'm not denying it," I snort.

"We're going to go pick up some dinner to eat after you're done. We can chill for a few hours before the club opens again tonight," Mckenna says, standing from the couch to straighten her clothes. She gives me a warm smile and grips her sister's hand.

"I'll come with you. I need to grab some air and stretch my legs anyways," Jackson sighs.

We go our separate ways, Ikelos trailing me as I head towards the elevator to access the restaurant the next floor up. We stand in silence, the music filtering through quietly.

"Elevator music is so bad," Ikelos groans, leaning his back against the side wall to face me.

"What would you prefer?"

"Anything but this shit."

"It's not like you're in here for very long," I say, motioning to the door as we hit the floor.

"Still not the point. Every second should be enjoyable, including elevator rides."

"You're acting like a spoiled brat," I chuckle.

"It's your building. You should be able to pick the tunes we ride to."

"If it'll make you happy, I'll change the music." He grins, a new pep in his step as he matches my pace.

"Mr. Knight," Jolene says, eyes wide and darting to the shadow behind me. "I—I didn't expect you. Uh." She glances down at the sheet in front of her, frantically flipping through the pages. "Did we miss an order for you? Did you have a reservation? Not that you *need* a reservation, but you usually make one to give us time to prepare. I'm—"

"Relax, Jolene. We're not here for dinner. There's a guest that's currently dining that needs to be removed from the premises."

Her mouth pops open in shock. "Do you need me to call security?"

Ikelos pops his head around me, a maniacal grin spreading across his face. "I'm all the security he needs," he purrs.

I roll my eyes at his psycho behaviour, but I can't help chuckling when Jolene squeaks in surprise. "He's harmless."

"Hey!"

"Okay, mostly harmless. At least in regard to you. He's here to help escort Mr. Volkov out. Can you tell me what table he's seated at?"

"Oh." She flips through the pages again, stopping on the third sheet. "He's in a party with three others at table twelve. The one right by the south bathrooms."

"Let's go," I say to Ikelos, jerking my head for him to move ahead of me.

"Should we be concerned?"

"Everything is fine," I say, plastering my best smile, even though I don't feel good about this. I feel as though something is wrong, my skin itching like I'm missing something vitally important about this entire situation.

Ikelos is halfway across the restaurant by the time I catch up to him, his eyes narrowed and locked on Leon at the back table. Thankfully this table is more secluded with barely anyone around them. I'm hoping we can get him out of here with barely any trouble or making a scene.

"Leon Volkov," Ikelos says, his voice deadly calm. The asshole glances up, barely acknowledging him and showing no emotion on his face. His eyes are truly soulless, void of any life or kindness. "We're here to escort you from the building. You are not welcome anywhere near this property."

"And who are you to tell me where I can be?" He asks, leaning back in his chair with a look of disgust on his face. His goons shift as well, their hands shifting to their hips subtly.

"I'm asking you to kindly leave before I turn into your worst fucking nightmare."

I step in next to him, Leon's eyes shifting towards me. I catch a hint of acknowledgment, and that's enough for me to realize that he's probably done some research on me as well. I mean, why wouldn't he. He would have to know what he's getting into and who he's dealing with if he has any chance in getting to Venessa. He did, and that failure on my part will be something I hang onto for the rest of my life.

"This is my establishment, and you've been asked to leave. You will not be welcome within the building, and you will not be receiving any form of subscription that you've applied for. We check our applicants thoroughly Mr. Volkov, and we know why you're here."

He smiles at that, and it's so sinister in nature I actually feel a chill radiating up my spine. This man is evil through and through. I don't know what he's gone through in his past, but I sense no true human emotions from him. He's after Venessa and I just wont stand for that. I want him out of my building. I want him out of my fucking city, but that might be too much to ask for.

"Ah, so you're the illustrious Mr. Knight," he says in a mocking tone.

"If you know who I am then why are you still seated?" I growl, struggling to keep my growing anger tampered down.

"We're still eating."

"I don't give a fuck. Get up, get out, and I never want to see you again."

His features turn even more sinister, something I didn't think was possible. "Where is Venessa? I know she's here, and I know she's working for you."

His men scramble back, drawing their guns the second I wrap my hand around the fucker's throat and lift him from his seat. "You will not go near her. You will not look at her. You will not even say her fucking name." I draw him in closer to me, lowering my voice to a deadly level. "You touch her and I'll fucking kill you."

The asshole actually laughs, the sound ringing out loudly and making the other patrons within range turn their attention to us. Some begin to lift from their seats, noticing the growing tension in the room.

"You clearly don't know who I am," he cackles. "You won't touch me because if you do, we don't just come after you, we come after your entire family, friends, even your fucking pets. We'll wipe your entire lineage and associates from this planet."

The room gets plunged into a sudden darkness, three strangled grunts ringing out through the blackness. My eyes try to adjust, but this isn't a normal darkness, and I feel my skin prickle at the feel of magic in the air. The other patrons cry out and scream, the sound of scrambling feet greeting my ears. Slowly, the lights begin to flicker on, Ikelos looming over the three guards lying on the floor, their guns all gripped in his hands. Fragments of shadow cradle the dark metal and caress his fingers.

Leon stares in shock, a hint of fear finally creeping into his face. He grips at my wrist, trying to pry me off him, but I squeeze into his throat harder. "You were saying?" I sneer. "Try to come after me, my family, or what belongs to me, and we will obliterate you from existence. I don't give a fuck who you think you are, asshole, and your biggest mistake will be underestimating me and my power." I lift him off the ground, tossing him towards his minions. He slams into the one trying to get up, letting out an unnatural grunt. "Get out. I won't say it again."

"You're going to regret this," he snarls, lifting to his feet and desperately trying to compose himself.

We follow them out, making sure to escort them right to the door and out onto the sidewalk. The restaurant was practically bare, the commotion of removing the dick causing the patrons to run in fear. I'm going to have so much crowd control to deal with when everything is said and done. Between what happened last night and what happened today, the reputation of the club could very well be at stake.

Jackson and the girls are heading back, the two with their snow-white hair too hard to miss. Jackson frowns, eyes drifting to the delinquents in front of us. I stop just outside the doors, Ikelos following them enough to prove a point. I tilt my head in confusion when Leon turns suddenly, his phone gripped in his hand. He grins, barely glancing down at the screen before swiping his thumb across it.

CHAPTER FIFTY-FOUR

EROS

I can't hear anything but an incessant ringing in my ears. Everything hurts, my eyes trying to blink away the darkness clouding my retinas. Wet heat creeps down my brow and I blink again. Screaming filters through the ringing and I struggle to pull myself from the ground.

What the fuck happened? How the fuck did I get here? "Eros!" Disoriented, I glance up, seeing Ikelos running towards me with panic written all over his face. Sirens wail in the distance, and the screams get louder as he begins to come into focus. He crouches down, ducking under my arm to help me to my feet. He turns his head quickly, fury overtaking his features. "Mckenna!" He roars.

I catch a dark blur in the distance, the girl darting through the crowd forming on the sidewalk as she chases after something or is it *someone*. "Is he okay?" Jackson asks.

Who is he talking about? Is someone hurt? What the fuck happened? I still can't gain my bearings, relying heavily on Ikelos supporting my weakened and sluggish body. Addison runs up to us, touching her fingers gently to my scalp. She frowns, glancing at Jackson.

"Why would she take off like that?" Ikelos asks, and I can feel his body vibrating with rage and panic.

"She went after Leon. He took off as soon as he triggered the explosion. He got a little cut up, but nothing compared to some of the people within range." She grimaces, her eyes trailing across my face. "You look like shit."

"Explosion?" I ask, my tongue feeling thick in my mouth.

Her frown deepens, Ikelos' hold on me shifting so Jackson can take hold of me instead. He takes off running, moving through the crowd like a liquid being as he hunts down Mckenna. No doubt he's tracking her with his connection to her nightmare self, but his panic for her was palpable.

"The fucker blew up your building, man. I don't know if everyone is going to get out, and the emergency units are still a few blocks away. There's so much fucking damage. Hey!" He screams when I rip away from him and stumble to the side, crashing into one of the light posts on the edge of the street. "What the fuck are you doing?"

"Venessa," I croak out, trying to get my footing and hating the way the world spins around me. I was close enough to the building that I got a shit ton of the shock from the explosion and I'm paying for it now. My healing time feels sluggish, but I need to move. I need to get to her. "She's—she's still in there."

"The alarm system should have gone off. She should be able to still get out, Eros. Wait for the emergency crews to get here. She's safe on the upper floor for a little while, and if she's lucky, she should be able to still access the elevator and get out. I'm going to assume he set something up in the restaurant somewhere, so it's far enough away from your side of the tower to the upper levels."

I shake my head. "I disabled the elevator. It can't get to her floor."

He frowns, his eyes flashing brightly for a moment. "What? Why the fuck did you do that?"

"I didn't want her tempted to run," I admit, feeling guilt wash through me at the fact I just possibly signed her death certificate with that stunt. I never expected Leon to do something so reckless—something to put so many lives in danger, and for what? Senseless revenge over a girl that had no recollection or knowledge of what happened to his brother. She didn't kill him on purpose, but this fucker doesn't even care.

Jackson tries to grip into me to stop me, but I shove him off. "Eros, you're fucking injured. You're not healing right, and if you go in there like that, you might not come back out."

"I don't fucking care!" I roar. "She's in this situation because of me and I am not abandoning her. She's had no one her entire life give a shit about her, but that ends today."

"What if you can't get her out?" He says, shifting awkwardly as his eyes drift to the building behind me.

"One way or another *she* will make it out of there."

I push his away, motioning for him to get back as the emergency crews pull up along the curb. Someone else is yelling at me to stop, but I ignore them, making my way towards the now shattered doors on unsteady legs. The heat is suffocating the closer I get, half my building up in flames already and quickly spreading. My home is destroyed, but all I care about right now is *her*.

"Sir, you can't go in there!" A hand grips my arm, trying desperately to stop me, but the poor sap is getting dragged along while my body is fueled by desperation. He's trying so hard to stop me and pull me back from the flaming building. The heat bites into my skin enough that I feel it burning away with each step, but I don't care. "Sir—"

"She's still in there!" I roar, ripping out of his hold and running into the flames licking across the now shattered doors.

I can barely breathe or see, but I know this building in my sleep. Pushing through the flames, I have no choice but to ignore the fact my skin is burning away with each touch of heat. It hurts, but not nearly as much as the pain I feel in knowing I trapped Venessa in an inferno with no way out.

I practically sob in relief when I notice the flames haven't reached the elevator, quickly slamming the button over and over, cursing for it to open faster. Once inside I bypass the security clearance and stare at the numbers as they ascend.

The upper floor is free of flames, but the smoke is starting to whisp its way through the elevator shaft onto the floor. I need to get to her quickly and get her out of here before the entire place goes up in flames. I'm surprised she's not already out in the hallway trying to get out of here since the blaring of the alarm is loud enough to scrape against my skull.

"Venessa!" I call out, the apartment door slamming against the wall as I rush into the space. "Venessa!" I run towards the bedroom, panicked when I see her lying there, still as death, exactly where I left her. "Venessa, you have to wake up!"

She groans, her brows pinching in irritation while her arm flails to try and shoo me away. "Five more minutes," she grumbles. "Turn off the alarm."

Fuck, she's out of it. I quickly move to her dresser, pulling out a pair of sweatpants and a t-shirt before grabbing a sweater from her closet. I hate that I don't have time to salvage her things, the small number of belongings she's been carting around for who knows how long. Material things can be replaced. Her life on the other hand, cannot.

"Come on, we have to go. There's a fire."

She rouses from her sleep enough to blink up at me; my hand gripped around her wrist as I try to pull her up into a sitting position. She seems disoriented and confused, frowning as I tug the shirt on over her head.

"Fire?" She mumbles. "What are you talking about?"

"I'll explain later, but we need to leave before the entire place gets burned to the ground with us in it." She blinks, eyes going wide as my words finally register in her sleep-hazed brain. I cup her cheeks, pressing my lips gently against hers. "You'll be okay. I'll get you out of here."

"What happened?"

My lungs seize at the panic on her face. "Leon was here. We escorted him out, but he must have set something up before we got to him."

"Oh my god," she gasps, bouncing to her feet and grabbing the pants from me to quickly slip them on. She slides her feet into some ballet shoes and tosses the sweater over her head. "I—everything I own is in this building."

I hate the way her voice trembles, the sadness in it gripping at my heart. "I know, love, but your life is more important than the things that can be replace. Let's go."

Her hand vibrates in mine as I pull her along behind me, back into the hallway. I'm hoping the elevator is still functioning and not compromised due to the fire, but when I push the button, the normally green light turns red.

"What..." I quickly pull out my phone, bringing up the security program to see if I only temporarily reset the function. Confusion hits me when flashing text covers my screen.

Access Denied.

Access denied? It's *my* fucking system, and my staff would never lock me out of it. The failsafe on the building wouldn't lock down the elevator either, something I had to fight to keep active. I made sure that everything was reenforced steal and fire resistant so that the elevator itself would stay intact in case of a situation like this. I had to do it because I don't have any emergency exits, no stairwell to allow us to descend the building on foot.

"Jackson," I say, pressing the phone to my ear.

"Did you get her?"

"I did, but we're trapped on the upper level. Someone pushed an override on my code and locked me out of the system. They removed the permissions to the elevator to open on this floor."

"But the elevator should already be up there."

"I know that! It won't fucking open because of the security. Can you get in and hack the system?"

A beat of silence stretches through the line before his voice comes through deathly quiet. "My computer is in your office, Eros. I—I can't do much with out access to one, and I don't think I have enough time to find one before…" His voice trails off, but I don't miss the rattling breath he lets out before continuing again. "The building is coming down fast. The fire department is here, but they're struggling to contain the flames. I think Leon used some type of accelerant to prevent anyone from trying to put it out before its run its course. They've…shifted their attention to protecting the surrounding buildings at this point."

"But we're still in here!"

"I know. I don't know what to do. Me and Addison could try using our powers but—"

"That'll draw too much attention to you, and it'll expose you to the mortals," I murmur. Their hands are tied, but I can hear the pain in his voice—the need within him to help me any way that he can. "We're getting out of here," I say, pulling Venessa back towards her apartment.

"How do you plan to do that?"

"We're going to jump."

"Eros, you're immortal but you can be hurt. You might not be able to survive that fall, and Venessa probably will die on impact. We don't know if she can heal."

"I don't have a choice. I'm not just going to sit here and do nothing." I can't risk waiting out the flames because he's right, we don't know what'll happen to Venessa if we bide our time and wait this out. The only real chance for her to survive is to jump from the balcony and cushion her fall.

"I'll try and slow down your decent as subtly as I can, but you're going to have eyes on you." He's panting now, more than likely shifting himself to be positioned near Venessa's balcony window.

"Eros, what are you doing?" Venessa asks as she tries to rip from my grip. I hold onto her harder and drag her towards the balcony doors, ripping it open and shoving her outside.

"We're outside."

"We see you," Jackson says, and I glance over the edge to see him in the distance, unable to get closer due to the caution tape set out to prevent the pedestrians from crossing into the danger zone.

"Jackson," I whisper. "If—if I don't make it, can you promise me something?"

"We'll take care of her," he says, emotion clear in his voice.

I swallow the lump forming in my throat, closing my eyes. "Thank you." I hang up and turn Venessa towards me. Sadness grips at me at the fear and panic on her face. "Venessa—"

"No, I'm not jumping!"

"We don't have a choice. I'm going to hold you and brace your fall." She shakes her head, trying to step back from me, but I yank on her arm until she slams against my chest. "Please, just trust me."

She's shaking like a leaf in my arms, but she's no longer fighting me, she's gripping into my shirt hard enough to turn her knuckles white. "Please don't do this," she whispers.

"I have no choice."

She shakes her head and tips it back to look up at me, tears streaming down her cheeks. "I don't want you to die," she sobs. "I—I don't want you doing this because I don't want you dying, Eros. It's too high."

I glance over the railing, my vision tunneling at the deep drop to the ground below. It's definitely not a short distance, and normally I think I *would* survive it. It takes a lot to kill a god, but I'm not who I was when I first met her. I bleed and feel true pain, but it's worth it if I can save her.

"You won't survive the fire, Venessa."

"But *you* will!"

Cupping the back of her head, I slam my lips to hers, relishing in the taste and feel of her mouth on mine. I can feel her warm, wet tears, against my own skin, mingling now with my own that have broken through. I pull away enough to rest my forehead against hers, my words falling from my lips on their own. "I think...I love you," I whisper, before tipping us over the edge.

CHAPTER FIFTY-FIVE

VENESSA

A flood of emotions rip through me as we drop over the edge. His arms tighten around me and his body twists, so his back is to the ground. I scream when I see the ground coming up fast, but he grips the back of my neck and buries my face against his chest, completely cocooning me in his embrace.

I can't stop the erratic rhythm of my heart, knowing that this could be the end for the both of us. His final words to me before he launched off the side keep repeating in my head. He loves me. How is that possible when he said he couldn't feel the emotion? I had hopes that eventually he may learn to love me, but how does he know? What did I do to make him feel this way?

A cold wind caresses our bodies making me shiver and curl in further against him. I bury my face into his neck, breathing in the smell of him. I don't want to think about the fact this might be the last time I get to smell him, or the last time I'll be held in his strong arms. The drop is insane, and a normal human would be nothing but blood and gore on the pavement below.

We jerk slightly in the air, as though some phantom wind is trying to slow our fall, but it's not nearly enough to save us. We slam down, Eros letting out a cry of pain while the sound of metal crumpling and glass shattering rings out around us. Screams erupt, my head pounding and pain lancing through my entire body.

My head spins as I try to lift myself up, Eros' arms falling limply away from me. There's so much blood. It's pooling under Eros and pouring out in rivulets across the car we crushed from our impact. His clothes are ripped, the skin visible covered in cuts and blood. A slow stream of it flows from his mouth and nose, and the worst part is that his eyes are closed.

He doesn't move. Fuck, I don't even think he's breathing, and I'm quickly losing control of my own body. White sparks cross across my vision before a weird dark haze settles in, clouding my vision and robbing me of Eros in front of me.

"Eros," I croak out, tasting the thick tang of metal against my tongue. My body sways, and I think I hear Jackson and Addison screaming out, but their words are distant and distorted. I can't hold myself up any longer, my arms giving out from under me, forcing me to slam back into Eros' already broken body. He doesn't make a sound. The only sound I hear is the cracking of my broken heart.

CHAPTER FIFTY-SIX

EROS

Fuck, I'm in so much pain. The sound of beeping rings through my head, and what sounds like dripping. Everything seems so loud, and I'm struggling to open my eyes. I pry them open, regretting it instantly when the lights of the room around me burn into my retinas. I groan, trying to touch my aching head and feeling resistance on my arm. It sends a sharp pain through me, tugging at the skin.

"What the fuck," I mumble, struggling to form the words.

"Fuck, you're awake." My eyes focus enough to see Jackson pop up from a chair in the corner, his face contorted in a mixture of pain and fear. "I didn't think you would."

"Venessa?" His body stills, his eyes darting to the door for a second before glancing back at me. "Did—did she make it?" He nods. "How bad is it?"

"She's in pretty rough shape, but the doctor said she should pull through." He steps closer, close enough for me to see the bags forming under his eyes. “You on the other hand, we didn’t think you would make it. It was bad, Eros, and your healing seems slower than it did the last time.”

“You try falling from one hundred feet and tell me how well you’d fair.”

“The doctors are already in shock at the fact you’re even breathing. A normal human would have died on impact, especially the way you fell.”

“I felt your cushion. I think it would have been a lot worse if you hadn’t been there to help us.” I swallow, trying to sit myself up in the tiny ass bed. Jackson moves closer, helping me and tucking the pillow a bit more under my back. “How’s the building?”

“It’s pretty much a write-off.”

“Fuck. I hate that all the work you guys put into it literally went up in flames.”

“It was your home, Eros. I’m sorry that you lost everything because of that prick.”

“Not everything. As long as Venessa pulls through, I have what I need.” I glance down at the gown covering my frame, small cuts and bruises still clearly visible on my skin. He’s right, my healing isn’t where it was, and that’s a bit concerning in this situation. “I think I did something stupid,” I whisper.

“Just add it to the list, but what happened now?”

"I told Venessa...I said that I think I love her before I pulled us over the ledge."

He hums low in his throat, the sound pulling my attention towards him again. "You thought you were going to die, didn't you?" I nod. "Did you mean it?"

"I think so. In that moment, nothing else mattered to me but her. I needed to save her. I needed to show her that someone in this world cares about her life. I didn't care if I didn't survive as long as she made it out alive."

"Well, that's something the both of you are going to have to talk about once you get out of here."

"Where are the others?"

"Mckenna and Addison are out hunting down Leon. She caught his scent and has been scouring the city, but no luck so far."

"What about Ikelos?"

"He's keeping guard over Venessa." My eyes widen at that, and he gives me a sad smile. "You don't give him enough credit, Eros. He cares about you, and in turn, about Venessa. He won't go down without a fight, and I would hope Leon wouldn't try to blow up a hospital with innocent people inside."

"It didn't stop him from blowing up my club."

"Thankfully, there were no casualties. The building only had your staff since most of the restaurant escaped when you and Nic started fighting with Leon and his guys, and it was early enough that the club wasn't open yet."

"I need to see her."

"You need to rest."

"I need to fucking see her, Jackson. I need to see with my own eyes that she's okay."

He sighs but nods his head, steadying me as I swing my legs off the side of the mattress. "The nurses are going to be pissed," he murmurs, glaring at me when I pull the I.V. out of my hand and take the monitors off. The steady buzz of coding rings out and the door opens within seconds.

What are you doing?" The nurse says, her eyes darting from Jackson to me leaning heavily against him. "You shouldn't be moving around. You're severely injured."

"I'm fine," I cough, covering my mouth and pulling it away to see blood coating my hand. Fuck, I have internal bleeding. Jackson is right, I should be dead, but I'm still here and I refuse to just sit here when Venessa is so close to me.

"He wants to see Venessa Daye."

The nurse huffs, folding her arms across her chest in defiance as she blocks the doorway. "She's resting and already has a visitor. You need to rest, Mr. Knight."

"Move out of my way before you're the one who ends up in that hospital bed," I growl, my tone menacing. Her eyes widen and her body stiffens at the threat. "Please," I add through gritted teeth.

"You shouldn't be moving," she says again, but she's more reluctant in her words, feeling my threat. "You get five minutes. If you're not back in your bed by then, I'm calling security and having you tied down to it."

I grin, leaning in closer to her. "Careful, nurse, I like the kink."

Her mouth pops open and her eyes widen, a blush of pink creeping up her cheeks. We leave her standing there, gawking at us as we squeeze by her. Jackson leads me down the hallway, where we're greeted with looks of surprise and shock. A few of the nurses shake their heads and roll their eyes, clearly remembering me from the last time I was here. I'm becoming a frequent guest at this point, something I never would have believed in the past.

Jackson opens the door to the room and instantly Ikelos is on his feet, storming towards us. "What the fuck are you doing walking around?"

"It's nice to see you, too," I grumble, trying to slip past him but he grips my arm. "Let me see her. I only get five minutes before the nurses have me chained down."

"You could have died today."

"You say that as though I should care. I don't care what happens to me as long as *she's* okay. Now, let me go to her." Reluctantly, he releases me, but he follows me into the room while Jackson closes the door and moves to sit on the small chair Ikelos was occupying. "Hey, love," I whisper, brushing her hair back from her face.

Her skin is littered with cuts and bruises as well, a bandage covering her temple. She looks so vulnerable and weak, and I just want to take away her pain. I lean over her, pressing my lips gently against hers, willing her internal creature to take from me in the hopes that my energy can help her heal quicker.

Her lashes flutter on her cheeks, a small frown forming between her brows. Slowly, she opens her eyes, their light slightly dimmed and unfocused. "Eros?" She croaks, blinking rapidly and tipping her head to get a better look at me. Tears brim her lashes and her chin trembles. "You're alive."

"As are you," I whisper, kissing her lips softly again. "I'm so happy you made it."

"I thought I lost you. There was so much blood, and you weren't moving. I—"

"I'm okay."

She lifts a trembling hand to touch my cheek, like the touch is what she needs to believe that this is real and I'm here with her. "You're okay?" I nod. "Did you mean it?" I frown at the tears now streaming down her cheeks. "What you said to me on the balcony. Was it real?"

My heart clenches painfully in my chest. A mix of emotions washes over her, from pain and sadness, to hope and joy. I never thought those emotions could paint such a heartbreaking picture on her features. Was it real? I think it was. From how Ikelos and Jackson described the emotions they experience around their other halves; I feel that I might be feeling that, too. I can't picture my life without her any longer, the thought alone painfully devastating.

"I think so."

She settles her other hand on my chest, my heart thumping against her palm. "What do you feel in here?"

I cup her cheeks in my palms, willing her to stop crying for me. I don't want to see her cry at all, least of all because of me. "In my heart, I feel that I would be nothing without you, Venessa. You're beautiful and kind and broken and full of life and love yourself. I just hope that I'm enough for you. I want to be enough because..." Pulling in a rattling breath to settle my nerves, I lock my eyes on hers. "I feel that this is what it's supposed to be like."

I can't say the words. They get tangled on my tongue as though they're a lie, even if I believe it to be true. Disappointment flashes across her face for a fraction of a second, but it's long enough for me to know I fucked up.

She turns away from me, her throat bobbing visibly. "I'm tired," she says quietly, pulling away from me.

"Okay. I couldn't stay for long anyways. I'm under strict orders and I wasn't even supposed to come visit you." She nods, ignoring my fingers brushing down her cheek. "I'll visit again when I'm allowed," I sigh. Jackson gives me a pitying look, gripping into my elbow when I sway in front of Ikelos. "Please, keep her safe," I say quietly.

His brows furrow and his jaw twitches. "Get some rest," he says, patting me on the shoulder before settling himself back into the chair. I give Venessa one final look over my shoulder, but she's not looking at me. Her back is to me, and her shoulders shake slightly as she sniffles. I know I said the wrong thing, but all that matters is that she's safe. I'll have to try and fix the issue I've created between us because my mouth moved before I could think better of it.

"Are you okay?" Jackson asks the moment he closes the door behind us.

"I couldn't say it. I couldn't say the words to her again." I'm fighting back my emotions, but I can't quell the burn of tears building at the back of my throat. "What's wrong with me? It felt so easy to say earlier, but now, with her right in front of me, I couldn't say it to her face."

"It's okay. We'll get all this under control and then you guys will have time to figure it out. I'm proud of you for admitting that you felt that way towards her after everything you were made to believe."

"It doesn't make sense. Why now? Why *her?* All this time I've been alone—for fucking centuries—and now I feel this way about someone?"

"The only explanation is that she's your soulmate—your other half. Trust me, I know the feeling, Eros. I was alone for a long time, too. Not as long as you since I began my life as a human and loved then, but the years I spent wandering were very lonely."

The nurse from earlier is standing by my open doorway, tapping her foot impatiently. "I said five minutes."

"Does it look like I have a watch on me?" I snap back. She rolls her eyes, motioning me back into the room. I settle myself back into the bed, wincing in pain. I feel awful, but I glare at her when she grabs a new I.V. catheter. "No."

"Excuse me?"

"I'm fine. I don't need that fucking thing stabbed back into me." She just stands there and gawks, her eyebrow twitching in irritation. "You can go now."

"We have protocols."

"Fuck your protocols. I'm capable of walking out of these doors if I want to right now. I'm sitting here as a curtesy, not because I actually listen to the likes of *you*."

"Mr. Knight—"

"Enough. Let me rest."

"At least let me give you something for the pain."

I shake my head, but Jackson clears his throat. "Come on, Eros. Stop being stubborn. The pain meds will just take the edge off and help you heal. You're too stressed out and worried which is going to slow down your shit." He gives me a look, not wanting to go into details in front of the nurse.

"Fine," I say through gritted teeth. She grabs a needle and bottle from a locked cart and turns to me, but I'm eyeing that fucking needle. Why is it so big? "I hate needles."

"Do you want me to hold your hand, big guy?" Jackson snorts.

"Yes." His brows go up in surprise, and his steps are slow as he walks towards me. I hate the fact the nurse stifles a giggle when Jackson reaches out his hand to me, and I take it with no hesitation. "Thanks," I mumble.

"You really don't like them, eh?" I shake my head. He pats the back of my hand with his other one and grips mine in both of his. "Look at me," he whispers. I turn away from the nurse, flinching at the prick of pain in my arm. "It's okay."

"All done. Try and get some rest," she says, patting me on the shoulder before heading out. My hand is shaking by the time I release Jackson from my death grip. "I'm going to grab myself a coffee, but I'll be back."

He heads towards the door, my mouth opening before I can stop myself. "Jackson?" He pauses in the doorway as he looks back at me. "Thank you for everything."

"Of course," he grins. "We're family."

CHAPTER FIFTY-SEVEN

VENESSA

"Are you okay?" Ikelos is quiet, almost tentative of the question.

"Fine," I grumble, curling further on my side away from him.

"I don't think you are. You're upset, but I can't quite figure out why."

"It's fine, Nic. *I'm* fine."

"You know you can talk to me, too, right? I may not be as approachable as Mckenna or Addison, and obviously you don't hold the same affection towards me as you do Eros, but I'm still here if you want to talk. Talking can help you work through things, like your emotions and thoughts."

I know I don't have to be so hesitant in talking to him, but it's still weird for me. How am I supposed to talk through what I'm feeling when I don't *know* what I'm feeling. I sigh, rolling over in the bed to face him. He's still sitting in the little chair; his forearms braced on his thighs with his hands hanging loosely between them. His face is neutral but pensive, welcoming me to open up to him.

"I just—I don't know how to react to his response."

"What did you expect him to say?"

"Before we went over the ledge, he told me he thinks that he loves me. It wasn't a full declaration, but it felt like it. I thought he would say it again—I *hoped* he would say it again. Now I just feel like he said that in the heat of the moment because he thought he would die."

"Do you want to know what I think?" I nod, shifting the pillow under my head a bit to get more comfortable. "I think Eros doesn't understand what he's feeling. He's lived his entire life never knowing what it's like to love anyone. He's never let anyone close enough to show that emotion towards him either and you giving him real attention—genuine attention—has made him feel things he's never had the chance to feel before. Now, I can't say he truly loves you, but if he's gotten to the point that he feels that way, it's because he's feeling an emotion that's foreign to him."

"Then how would he know that's what it is though? What if it's just infatuation or obsession and not genuine love?"

"Give him time. You need to be a bit more understanding with him, Venessa. Take yourself for example. Have you ever really loved anyone? Do you know what that truly feels like in your own heart? Have you ever had anyone in your life love you unconditionally and without question?"

"No. I thought that I loved my boyfriend, but what I feel for Eros is different. I don't know what I'm doing," I admit.

"Neither does he. You'll both figure it out in time, you just need to give yourself a bit of grace."

"Thank you, Nic."

He gives me a warm smile that changes his features complete, dimples popping in his cheeks. "Of course. Get some rest, I'm going to grab some coffee, but I won't be long."

I nod my head, rolling onto my back to stare up at the bare ceiling. I thought my life was complicated before, but this is beyond anything I would have expected. It's a weird feeling, having people who care about me and my wellbeing. They've accepted me into their lives, and I don't really know how to react to that.

My instincts have always told me to run before allowing anyone to get close to me. That's one of the main reasons I never made friends. I didn't want to form any attachments, especially emotional and meaningful ones because it would hurt so much more when I left them behind.

Touching my fingers to my lips brings back the phantom sensation of Eros' lips against mine. He didn't hesitate to share his energy with me, even though he looked about ready to pass out. His injuries were extensive, and it was stupid of him to walk around, but it warms my heart that he wanted to see me. I can only imagine how much pain he's in and how long it might take him to heal from this. The fact his healing has slowed so significantly sends a pang of worry through my chest.

I don't want him to get hurt anymore, least of all because of me. How is it possible that I've become his weakness. I'm no one. A fractured soul trying to survive, but he sees me and wants to help me. I think I love him, too, and if he would have said the words, I think I would have said them back.

Now? Now, I don't know what to do. I don't want to say the words and put that pressure on him, especially if he still believes he's incapable of the emotion. I didn't think I would be able to feel love either, but Eros has definitely changed that.

The click of the door rips me out of my thoughts. I thought Nic would be gone longer than that, but maybe the cafeteria is closer than I remember. I tip my head towards the door and freeze, my blood turning into ice in my veins.

CHAPTER FIFTY-EIGHT

VENESSA

"No." My voice barely comes out, a plea into the ether. My eyes widen as he steps into the room, and I frantically claw at the bed in search of the emergency call button. He's beside me in a second, gripping my wrist painfully and forcing the device to drop uselessly to the bed.

"I've finally found you," Leon grins, his eyes void of anything but malice. "You've found yourself some interesting friends. It's unfortunate since I'll end up killing them because of you."

"Please," I beg, trying uselessly to pull my arm out of his hold.

"Shhh, none of that. Begging won't get you anywhere. You have a debt to pay, and I plan to collect. You've run for a long time, Venessa, but it's over."

"You're going to kill me." My voice chokes out on a broken sob, and I can't control it. I can't stop the panic and fear ripping through me.

"Eventually, yes, but I plan to make you suffer just like you made my entire family suffer. You took my brother from me. Do you know what that did to my father and mother? Do you have any idea the fucking pain you caused us? You ran instead of taking responsibility for your actions. He liked you and you fucking killed him." His hand grips my throat suddenly, robbing me of precious air. "Tell me why. Tell me what you fucking did to him," he growls viciously.

I claw at his arm, trying and failing to loosen his grip enough to take a proper breath. How is he here? Did he hurt Mckenna and Addison? I know Nic mentioned earlier that they were out hunting for him, following his trail with Mckenna's abilities, but he's *here*.

"I—I'm...sorry."

"Sorry won't bring him back. Sorry won't bring *anyone* back."

My eyes widen when he pulls a gun from his back, pressing the muzzle of the silencer to my temple. Tears break through my lashes, streaming down my cheeks in hot waves. This is it. This is where I die. I thought I would at least have time to tell Eros how I really feel about him, but now it's too late.

My eyes drift to the door at the sound of it opening, Nic's wide eyes morphing into black pits when he sees Leon. His coffee cup drops to the floor as he launches himself towards us, dark shadows erupting from the corners of the room.

Bang.

I blink, watching as Nic's frozen body stands there for a second, blood oozing out of the hole in his skull before he crumples to the ground. No. No! This can't be happening.

"Nic!" I try to scream, but Leon's grip is harsh, tightening further as I thrash under him. Fury overtakes me and I grit my teeth, clamping my hand around his wrist harder. I will my power to the surface, beg for it, plead for it to do what it's done all this time and end this man in front of me. Nic can't be dead. He *can't*.

Heat spreads through my body, an electric current rippling through my skin. Leon sways and blinks harshly before turning to me with fury in his eyes. I didn't think it were possible, but his eyes darken further, mimicking the dark abyss that coils in wait in the great beyond. I pull harder, but my power feels muted and heavy. I watch in horror as he raises his gun before slamming the butt of it against my temple.

Darkness settles across my vision, and I lose all control of my body as his blow pulls me into oblivion. I tried. I really did try to fight and be strong, but the one time I wanted my power to work, it failed me. It's fitting really. I turned away from what was natural for me, pushing it and crushing it down into my subconscious until there was nothing left but a broken soul and the death echo of my past.

CHAPTER FIFTY-NINE

EROS

I jolt awake at the sound of the door bursting open and smashing against the wall. I'm disoriented, blinking rapidly to try and clear my mind of the haze from the drugs they gave me. Addison is panting, eyes wide and glowing as Jackson rushes over to her.

"What's wrong?" He says, her panic causing his powers to slip out, shifting his hair into icy blades and his eyes to lighten to white orbs.

"We fucked up," she pants. "We tracked Leon, but when we realized he shifted his movements, it was too late." Her eyes drift to me, her head shaking back and forth. "I'm so sorry, Eros."

I rip the sheet off my body, sluggishly moving towards my clothes. "Ikelos was protecting her."

"He's—he's been shot. Mckenna is with him now, but he hasn't woken up. She's not in a good headspace at the moment. She's fighting with herself—the need to stay with him and the desire to go after Leon and kill him is causing her power to go out of whack."

"Ikelos isn't dead then." She shakes her head. "I don't understand. He should be able to handle a bullet."

"The fucker shot him in the head. Thankfully the wound healed before the nurses showed up, so Mckenna is playing it off like he was just knocked out. A bit hard to explain all the blood, but she's trying her best to tamper down their panic."

"...and Venessa?" My chest tightens asking what I *need* to know. Did he kill her? Is she lying on that bed, unmoving and no longer filled with life?"

"He took her."

Those words ring through my head like a banshee screaming that the end is near, my own heart tightening painfully at her words. My body sways. My hand launching out to brace myself, stopping me from crumpling to the ground. He took her. He *took* her. He took my girl from me and who knows what he plans to do with her. He didn't kill her here, and a new fear blooms in my chest. He's going to torture her. He's going to torment her and punish her for what she did in the past.

"I need to go." I don't care that they're both in the room, quickly ripping off the gown and tugging on the clean clothes that Jackson went out and bought for me. This is literally all I have—all that I own since my entire life went up in flames.

"You're not at full strength. We can handle this, Eros," he says, moving towards me to try to stop me.

"She is mine! She's mine to fucking protect, Jackson, and I'm failing her at every turn! I don't care if I'm weakened. I don't fucking care if every bone in my body gets shattered beyond repair, I *will* save her."

"What are you going to do?"

"I'm going to kill them all. Every. Last. One of them." I'll find a way, even if I have to do it with my bare hands. Leon Volkov is dead.

CHAPTER SIXTY

VENESSA

"Fuck," I groan. My head is throbbing painfully, crusted blood coating my skin and hair. Chains clank and snap against my wrist when I try to tentatively check the damage done to me. Taking in my surroundings, panic hits me. Where the fuck am I?

The room is cold and dark. A basement perhaps? It's dilapidated and smells of moisture and mold. The walls are uneven, broken stone mixed with concrete, the floors, stained and cracked cement. I really don't want to know what the dark patches are caused from, but the scent lingering in the air reminds me of death. There is no light. Not a flicker of sunlight or spark of electricity in sight, my eyes adjusting to the darkness like a natural aura.

My breaths are short and sharp, a struggle to keep myself calm as I take in all the details around me. How long have I been here? Oh, god, Nic. He shot Nic in the head and took me. Sadness grips me at the pain Mckenna will feel at finding him like that. He tried to protect me, but even a god of nightmares didn't stand a chance against a mortal weapon that is forged to do one thing. To kill.

Clanking and the heavy groan of a door greets me, my eyes drifting to one side of the room. My eyes slam shut at the sudden light burning through my retinas and the sound of dark laughter rings through my ears.

"Finally awake. Excellent. We can get started then." He pulls a lever, and I cry out when my body gets ripped up by my arms. My feet barely touch the ground, my toes skimming the cold floor as my body swings above it. Absolute fear hits me when he walks towards me with a large knife in his hand. A wicked grin spreads across his lips, and I try to jerk away from him, but he's quick, grabbing my throat viciously. "Let's see how you bleed."

The knife trails down my body, cutting away the thin gown still clinging to my frame. I can't stop my body from shaking as he exposes my entire body to the open, chilled air. He hums low in his throat, dragging the knife across my collarbone and down the center of my body.

"No wonder my brother liked you. You have a beautiful body and it's a shame I'll have to ruin it. Not like anyone will get to see it ever again once I'm done with you," he chuckles. "You can scream as much as you like, no one will hear you. This is one of the properties my family owns—nice and secluded from the outside world. I'd prefer it if you scream." He leans in close to my ear, my stomach roiling in disgust when his hot breath cradles against my skin. "I like begging, too," he sighs.

Why won't my powers activate? He's touching me, even if just barely, but yet, my body isn't doing what it normally does. Has my contact with Eros weakened my abilities or is it just a lack of control? Has the fact that he's been keeping me well fed stabilized me enough that I no longer draw on energy on a whim? Fuck, this is the worst timing for me to *not* be the monster I was born as.

I can't break. I can't give him the satisfaction, but when the knife digs into my skin, I have to bite my tongue to stop myself from screaming. It burns through my body, and my breath rattles out of me when he pulls the knife away.

"Hmm, looks like you're a strong little thing. I mean, it makes sense. You've survived this long, running and evading all my sentries to live a life you don't deserve. Was it nice to con that fool Eros? I should get an award from him for saving his life from the likes of you. You'd end up killing him anyways." He drags the blade against my skin again, cutting me deeper than before. "I know about your other boyfriend from when you were younger. You're like a death omen, and everything you touch, dies."

I can't stop the tears from streaming down my cheeks, but it's not from the pain, it's from the truth of those words. He's right. Of course he's right, I'm a cancer on this world and have been for most of my life. I tried so hard but only got so far with my constant running and checking over my shoulder for the looming threat that is this cruel man. I deserve this. I deserve all the pain he's giving me because he's right, I shouldn't exist after what I've done.

"How does it feel seeing the life bleed out of you. I'm going to cut you apart, piece by piece. You might not be screaming now, but you will be when I'm done with you."

He cuts me again and again, and each time I struggle to keep my heart beating. It hurts so fucking much. Each cut deeper and more brutal until I finally break. I scream when he stabs the knife into my side, missing the vital organs to drag out my torment for his sick pleasure. I wish I could say the worst mistake in my life was falling for his brother, but the worst mistake was ever being born. I should have died along with my parents, saving myself of this pain and misery and the heartache I've created for Eros. He would be happy and safe right now if I never came into his life.

"What the fuck?" I pry my open to see Leon frowning, his eyes focused on the handiwork he's done to me. "What the fuck are you?" He says, reaching out to touch my skin. My head shakes as I glance down, my eyes widening at the skin knitting itself back together right in front of him. A cruel smile pulls his lips, and a wicked gleam settles into his dead eyes. "Oh, this is great. You're a plaything that I can keep torturing over and over again. A fucking blank canvas that I can keep painting red until I'm satisfied." He laughs again. "Can you die?"

"Yes," I pant, not knowing if I can at this point, but I would assume so. Just because I can heal doesn't mean I can't die.

"At least I still get the satisfaction of ending you once I'm done destroying you."

"Please," I whimper. "Please, just let me go."

"Why would I do that?"

"I'm sorry," I sob. "I'm sorry about your brother. I—I didn't mean to. I didn't mean to kill him."

"At least you can admit that you did it. How did you do it? What the fuck did you do to my brother?"

"I don't know. I don't know how to explain any of this." It's true. I don't know what to say to him because how do I explain to a human what I am? I don't know if there are rules to that sort of thing, but I would assume so.

I could get killed just for speaking to him, and I hate that I can't defend myself and tell him it was out of my control. I could really use that lack of control right about now. I don't think there's any way out of this, and honestly, I don't want to hold out hope that the others will come for me. Eros was in no condition to be hunting down Leon, and I doubt Mckenna and the others hold any loyalty towards me.

"You're a murderer, that's the reason. You're a piece of shit human that needs to be put down before you hurt anyone else."

"You're one to talk! You're going to kill *me*!"

"I'm doing this world a justice by removing you. I'm not the bad guy here, Venessa. You are." He backs away, his eyes locked on the blood dripping from his knife. He smiles again, bringing it to his mouth and licking the metal like a fucking psychopath. "We'll pick up again in a bit. I have a wonderful dinner waiting for me upstairs."

He turns from me and panic hits me at the fact he's leaving me strung up like a pig. "Leon!" I scream, but my desperate plea falls on deaf ears. My arms are screaming in pain from the weight of my own body, and the damp chill quickly settles into my bones. My head falls forward in defeat, wishing it would all just be over already.

CHAPTER SIXTY-ONE

EROS

My leg is bouncing obnoxiously and I know it. I don't need Jackson glaring at me because his own leg is shaking *because* of my leg against his. "Turn there," Mckenna says, pointing down a side street I don't recognize.

How the fuck did he get so far out so fast? I mean, it took us a bit to even get a proper trace on the fucker, but for them to be this far out of the city, he must have been flooring it the whole way.

"Where the fuck are we going?" I grumble.

"I'm not sure. We're getting close to the Kolby Cliffs, but there isn't much out here for residential properties."

"Can this thing not go any faster?"

Ikelos turns his head to look at me, making Mckenna panic. "Nic! Eyes on the road." He doesn't look away, accelerating the car faster while his eyes stay locked on mine. "Nic!"

"Go ahead and crash it. It won't stop me from fucking finding her," I whisper harshly.

He rolls his eyes, finally looking away. Poor Mckenna is breathing harshly and she's pissed, smacking him hard on the shoulder. "Don't fucking do that shit," she snarls.

"Did I crash?" She huffs, turning away from him. "You know me better than that, Mckenna. I'm very capable."

"Don't do it again."

He grabs her hand and brings it to his lips, kissing her knuckles gently. "As you wish, my queen."

A pang of jealousy hits me at their relationship dynamics—the clear love in their eyes and aura. It brings me joy to see it, but at the same time, I'm envious. I've always been envious of the budding connections that are made naturally and the ones I've had my hands in as well. It's one of the most beautiful things to witness on this planet. Seeing two people completely entwined in each others' beings and no longer living just for themselves but for their other half.

A sudden grip on my thigh has me twisting my head to the side, Jackson's worried gaze locked on mine. "You need to stay calm," he says, steadying my bouncing knee. "Trust me when I say this, reacting emotionally is going to end up making things worse. We need to try and go into this with level heads, so we don't make any mistakes."

"You all could level their entire home to the ground without a second thought. I vote we go in guns blazing, I don't fucking care about the casualties."

"And in the process, we could end up hurting Venessa. We also can't forget the fact we have laws, Eros. We can't kill humans."

"The laws have changed slightly because of you and Ikelos."

"Sure, but they're not non-existent. We can't kill for shits and giggles. We're allowed to defend ourselves and those we claim as our own, but what about everyone else?"

Icy rage skitters up my spine. "They're all dead. All of them had a hand in taking her from me and tormenting her for half her life. I will not allow anyone to escape, Jackson."

The sigh he lets loose is filled with exasperation. I know my words are harsh, but none of them deserve to live after what they've done. They've destroyed my home, put so many people in danger with their mindless vendetta, and they've tormented a girl to the point of fleeing and fearing for her life. Fuck, she was willing to end it all just to have that taste of freedom she's longed for.

Mckenna leans towards the windshield, eyes narrowed and glowing fiercely. "This is it." Her lips curl back, showing teeth that are sharpening into dangerous points. Her hair lifts, shadows weaving through the strands with her growing agitation. "I can smell her. She's here."

Ikelos drives past the property, pulling the vehicle into a section of bush that hides the car from view. The sun is slowly setting in the distance, visible through the treeline into the field behind the house. It's a monstrous mansion, shooting into the sky with a dominating presence. The gothic flare with dark pillars and ominous aura sends a chill up my spine. I never would have thought a building could feel evil, but this home holds no warmth or light. Not when it's filled with pure evil that wants nothing more than to destroy the only thing good to me in this world.

I can't admit to them that I still feel like shit, the only thing I can do is put on the persona that I am. Everything hurts internally, like my body was crushed from the inside. The wounds that littered my skin have healed at least, so on the outside I can fake it with them. My limbs feel heavy, my feet dragging slightly as I follow them up to the house.

Mckenna and Ikelos move ahead of us, hiding our movements within their shadows. I watch in awe as Jackson shifts forms, his hair sharpening, and claws growing from his fingertips. Addison's form isn't as jarring, but her skin pales further as well as her hair, flickers of frost licking the ends.

"Easy," Ikelos croons, brushing his hand down Mckenna's hair and across her back. "Don't react until we're ready."

"I smell blood," she hisses, a low growl slowly rumbling in her throat. "It smells like *her*."

Panic careens through my body, sending a jolt of electricity through every nerve. I need to get to her. Fuck, what has he done to her? We took too long to get here and the fear that we're too late keeps pounding away in my mind. What am I supposed to do if we're too late? I shake my head, trying my best to rid myself of that thought, but it's already there, festering and gnawing at all the good memories I have of her.

CHAPTER SIXTY-TWO

VENESSA

My body is frozen, and my limbs are numb. I don't know how long I've been hanging here, naked and alone, but it feels like an eternity. The shaking in my body has gotten worse, no longer in my control. I've cried so much that my tears have gone dry and everything hurts. I feel weak—useless—and fucking broken.

I just want it to end, but Leon isn't done with me, not even close. He still hasn't come back, enjoying his dinner with his minions and leaving me here to starve and suffer. It's getting harder and harder to breathe in this position, my own weight suffocating me with each passing second. My shoulders scream in protest as I try to adjust myself, gripping into the chains to try and give myself some form of reprieve. It's useless though. I'm too weak and numb to get any traction and my toes are barely touching the ground.

My head bobbles on my neck when I finally hear the door open and I weakly look up. New fear overtakes me at the fury on Leon's face as he comes down the stairs, stomping his way towards me. I frown when I see clothes in his hand, confusion washing over me. He flips the switch to the pully system so fast that I don't have time to registered what is happening. Not like it matters. My legs are too weak for me to catch myself and my body crumples to the ground in a heap. The first real breath burns in my lungs, shaking and stuttering desperately.

He throws the clothes down, hitting me in the head with them before he crouches down in front of me and grips my jaw harshly. He pulls my face up, forcing me to look up into his hollow eyes filled with fury. "How did they find you?" The venom in his tone sends a chill right down to the marrow of my bones. "Tell me," he grits out.

I'm shaking. I can't *stop* shaking. *They*? Does he mean Eros and the other? They came for me. My relief is quickly squashed though. New fear blooms in my chest because for all I know, Leon has an army with him. They're all gods and have powers that can do catastrophic damage, but I still don't want them getting hurt. Is Nic with them? Did he survive being shot in the fucking head?

Leon quickly unlocks my cuffs, shoving me back as he gets up. "Hurry up and get dressed. I'm planning to use you as a shield if I have to."

Of course he is because why *wouldn't* he use me. They won't attack me if I'm within range of their power. Unless it's Mckenna attacking and Nic is actually dead. If that's the case, she'll take down anyone in her way to get to Leon for revenge. I wouldn't blame her if she ended my life in order to kill him. I would do the same thing if I were in her position and felt the pain of losing someone I love with my whole heart.

His anger grows when I struggle to pull on the clothes he's provided, my hands still numb from lack of circulation and the biting cold of the basement. I've barely finished pulling the sweater on when he grips my hair harshly, yanking me to my feet.

I cry out, clawing at his hand and pleading for him to let me go, but there's no point. This is what he wants—what he's *always* wanted. My suffering gives him joy, and he laughs as he drags me across the floor, my feet scrambling to try and slow him down. My back slams against each step painfully, jolts of electricity ripping up my spine in an excruciating wave.

And then I feel it. It's barely there—a small whisp of smoke and ember glowing in my mind. I reach for it weakly, trying to grip into the heat of my power that's begging me to let it loose. Leon grunts and stumbles, falling to his knees and letting me go. He blinks; his face filled with confusion and exhaustion. It wasn't much but it's enough. My power bought me those few precious seconds that I needed, and I force myself to me feet by sheer will alone.

He swings out his arm, trying to reach for me, but I kick back, nailing him in the face as I hurry up the stairs on all fours. I have no idea where to go or how to get out of here, but that doesn't matter because the moment I rip the door open, I'm faced with multiple guards.

They all stare at me, dumbstruck and confused before scrambling to try and grab me. I run. I run as hard as I can, dodging body after body as they reach and claw for me as I scurry past them. My legs feel like lead, a sob of relief slipping out when I see the door to the entrance.

My eyes widen, my feet coming to screeching halt when one of them plants himself in front of the door with an evil sneer on his face. "Where do you think you're going?" He laughs, moving to pull out his gun. I dodge him, beelining if for the darkened staircase in the corridor to the side. "Hey!" He screams, calling out to me. Multiple sets of feet pound against the wood floor below, but I keep running and running, cursing the angle of the stairs and the never-ending elevation.

Where the fuck does this lead? I hit a door at the top, but I don't question it, gripping the handle and ripping it open. Cold wind greets me, taking away the last remnants of breath in my lungs at the sudden frigid slap to my face. "What..."

I take a second to let it sink in that I'm trapped. Who the fuck has a staircase leading up to the roof of the house? It's something I've never seen before, and if I wasn't in the situation I'm in I would take the time to appreciate it. It's gorgeous with lounge chairs and tresses for plants in the summer months. There's a barbeque set off to the side, covered now for the winter.

Yelling pulls me from my admiration and I quickly turn, slamming the door behind me and pushing one of the heavy pots in front. I back away slowly, a sob slipping through at the aggressive banging and shoving coming from the other end. I'm trapped with no where left to run. I could try hiding, but how long would that last? I run to the edge of the roof, my stomach churning at the massive drop below.

It's like déjà vu, the distance beneath nearly as high as the jump Eros and I survived a short time ago. Panic locks my limbs, my arms shaking on the ledge. I know I should jump. It could either save me or kill me, but either way is better than staying here and letting Leon get his hands on me again. I can't go through another minute of the torment he has planned for me, and the thought of never seeing Eros again has tears pooling in my eyes.

Those tear break when the door smashes back, the pounding feet behind me matching my own erratic heartbeat. "You can't run, Venessa," Leon laughs, but his voice sounds strained with panting breaths.

"I know I can't," I whisper, closing my eyes and picturing Eros' face in front of me. His beautiful eyes and kind smile. The flickers of joy on his face when he looked at me. The way the hardness in his features would ease when I showed him kindness. I think I'll miss him the most, even though I didn't know him for very long. He's permanently burned his presence into my heart, and I'll never forget him. Not in this life, or the next.

CHAPTER SIXTY-THREE

EROS

The front door blasts of its hinges, the three of them ready for a fight the second they step through the door, only to stop frozen in their tracks. “Where is everyone?” Jackson murmurs, glancing around the empty entrance and open living space in front of us.

Mckenna’s head snaps to the left, shadows pulsing out of her body before she takes off running. “For fuck’s sake, Mckenna,” Ikelos grumbles, taking off after her and leavings us with no choice but to follow.

She’s like a bloodhound, tracking both Leon and Venessa with precision and lethal grace. Ikelos truly created a beautiful nightmare that holds both emotion and compassion with her deadly honed skills and bloodlust. She’s perfect and somehow still holds her human soul.

We hear yelling from up the stairs and quickly follow Ikelos and Mckenna, bursting through an open door to a decorated rooftop. Mckenna and Ikelos are ripping through Leon’s men like deadly honed weapons, Jackson and Addison quickly jumping into the fray. Me? My body is frozen; eyes fixed on the gut-wrenching scene in the distance. Venessa is trying to climb over the edge of the roof while Leon grips into the large sweater around her frame, trying to drag her back to the ground. She's screaming at him and trying to kick him but quickly stops moving when he pulls a gun and points it at her.

"Fucking do it!" She screams. "Fucking shoot me, you piece of shit!"

No. What the fuck is she doing? She's not fighting him to get him off her, she's fighting him so she can jump off the edge. We're high enough up that she won't survive that fall, and yet, she's clawing to try and pull away so she can do just that.

A loud bang rips through the air and Venessa cries out in pain, gripping her thigh quickly. The moment she releases the edge he takes advantage of her distraction, ripping her down to fall heavily against the ground.

"Stop whining. We both know you'll heal from that."

What?

What the fuck does he mean? She heals? The bigger question is *why* he knows that she can heal. What the fuck has he done to my girl?

"I told you I'm not done with you, and I need you as insurance to get out of this mess." He points the hand holding the gun towards me and the chaotic melee happening in front of me. Venessa's eyes widen when they meet mine, her head shaking back and forth in horror.

"Run!" She screams, kicking the back of Leon's knees and dropping him to the ground. He turns quickly, the back of his hand making contact with her face in a sickening slap. She cries out, her body reeling back from the blow and all I see is fucking red.

"Don't touch her!" I roar out, shoving one of the guards running towards me. Another tries to punch me, quickly panicking when my hand collides with his face. I grip into him with all my strength, shattering his skull in my palm. Thick red heat trickles down my hand, but I pay no attention to the blood now coating me. "Get the *fuck* away from her!"

Leon recovers quickly, scrambling to his feet and gripping into her hair harshly when I get close. "Stay back or I kill her."

"Why don't we test who's got the quicker reflexes then?" It's a bluff at this point because I can't risk moving or attacking him and him deciding to shoot her out of panic or spite.

Venessa tries to grab at his arm, but he slams the butt of his gun against her forearm, forcing her to recoil. "Don't touch me. You're not pulling the same shit you did before, freak."

If Venessa hit him with her power already, how is he still standing? Understanding dawns on me when I meet her panicked gaze. Fuck, it's because of me. Her starving succubus has been satiated with my energy and doesn't feel the need to consume everything it comes in contact with. She doesn't know how to control that side of herself yet, so anything she's been able to drag to the surface must be weak and muted. This is what our goal was, but now it's backfiring on us at the worst possible moment.

"You should have heard the way she screamed. It took a bit for that to happen, I think because she has no real emotions, but I got it out of her. One thing I will say is she never called out for you." A wicked grin pulls at his lips, and he drags her to her feet, pinning her against the edge of the roof. "She did beg though. She begged me to stop, and she begged me to end it. She must not care about you enough because she lost her will to fight to survive pretty quickly."

I can't keep the pain off my face when her eyes meet mine. Her beautiful eyes swirl with emotion, but she shows no fear, only resolve. No. I know that look and I fucking hate it.

"I do wonder if you're like her. It seems like your friends are all freaks as well." He aims his gun at Ikelos and fires without hesitation, the bullet slamming into his back. He lets out a roar and turns quickly, eyes blazing with fury as he glares at Leon. "I shot that fucker in the head, but he's still standing. Hmm, maybe I'll use your little plaything as leverage to control you. Do as I say and I won't hurt her," he grins.

"I'll fucking murder you," Ikelos snarls. Mckenna moves towards Leon as well, but Ikelos stops her when he shoves her partially over the edge.

"Don't!" I cry out.

"Stand down." Ikelos and Jackson glance towards me and I give then a shake of my head. "This is too easy," he laughs. "On your knees." My body is shaking with rage, but I do as he asks, slowly lowering myself down to my knees. I can't risk him hurting Venessa. The others may be able to reach him in time, but if they can't...

"Eros," Venessa whimpers, tears now freefalling down her cheeks. A sad smile pulls at her lips as she shakes her head. "I never wanted this."

"Sucks for you then, doesn't it?" Leon snarls. "You did this. Everything that's happened is because of you. Don't you get it? Their lives would have been better if you would have just stayed away. Better yet, the world would have been better if you were the one that died, not my brother." His grip on her tightens and he shakes her, pulling another cry of pain from her. "You're the problem here, you fucking murderer."

"Stop! Stop hurting her!" I can't take my eyes off her and the pain on her face buries deep into my soul.

"Eros," she sobs, slowly lifting her hand up towards Leon's hip. He doesn't notice it, his eyes locked on me with pure, venomous rage. "I love you."

The words hit me like a slap in the face, freezing my body like stone. It all happens so fast—too fast. She grabs a blade from his hip, kicking out at him at the same moment she slashes through her hair, cutting away the only hold he had on her. 'The serene look on her face is the same one she wore when she welcomed death in front of that car, and she's falling, slipping over the edge faster than any of us can react, including Leon.

CHAPTER SIXTY-FOUR

VENESSA

Everything Leon said was true and I couldn't let my existence be the reason they all became a slave to him. Eros didn't even hesitate to drop to his knees for him, his mind only focused on saving me. There is no saving me. The idea of it was only a flimsy hope, a whisp of smoke in the distance that quickly dissolved the more time passed. There was never a chance of touching it because it was a tease of a brighter future.

The words fall from my lips but they're true. I *do* love him. I feel like I've loved him for all my life, but I just didn't know it. He's been a beacon of light, drawing me to him across time and space, and I hate that our time together was so fleeting. He showed me kindness and happiness, two things I never got to experience in this world. He showed me acceptance, too. Never turning away from me when he knew what I was.

I do love him, and I'll love him until my heart stops. No. I'll love him even after. I'll love him into the next life, where me might be able to finally be together under different and better circumstances. He called me a butterfly, and in this moment, I feel like I am. I felt the change in myself, turning into the thing he expected me to be. Something beautiful and full of life and light, and now I'm flying. Well, falling, but as the air cradles my body I feel at peace.

My eyes widen at the visceral scream from above. "No!" I scream when I see him launch himself over the edge, piercing through the air towards me. It's like time slows, his hand reaching towards me and gripping my arm. He yanks me into him, just like he did before and presses his lips to my forehead. "Why?"

"Until the end, Venessa. I love you, too."

I gasp when our bodies suddenly stop midair, the sudden stop in movement jolting me. Slowly I open my eyes, my mouth dropping open in shock at the gleaming wings blasting from his back. The look of surprise on his face tells me he had no idea he had these locked away within himself.

His arms tighten around me, and his face settles into one of pure fury. He launches back into the air, hovering above the roof where everyone who is still standing stares up at us in shock. The others are fighting the grunts again, shots ringing out left and right. It's like the god don't give a shit that they're being flayed and littered with bullets, tearing through each human like they're blades of grass in the wind.

Leon glares up at us, pulling another gun out from behind him and pointing both of them up at us. He shoots, the projectiles piercing into Eros' flesh. He grunts in pain but doesn't waver, shielding me from the attack. The hair on the back of my neck begins to rise, a prickle of electricity creeping up my spine.

"Enough!" He roars, and actual sparks of electricity rip out of him, slamming down into the ground and the roof. That gets everyone's attention, freezing them in their tracks. The wind shifts around us, and the sky darkens further as ominous clouds begin to form above us. "You dare harm what is mine!" He snarls, shifting my body to one side as he lifts his hand towards Leon down below. "You dare challenge a god?" Lightning licks his skin and the clouds above snap with power. Lightning strikes all around us, and for the first time around him, I feel true fear.

A wave of darkness shrouds Ikelos and the others, swirling and shifting into a sphere of protection, as though anticipating what is about to happen. The darkness of his orb gleams, glittering and solidifying as ice skitters around the undulating waves.

Eros screams out into the night, and I swear I feel space itself shift as this lesser god comes into his power. Blinding light erupts, forks of lightning slamming into the roof and homing in on Leon's stupefied form like an arrow of pure destruction. His body jerks and convulses, electricity skating across his skin, cradling his teeth and plunging into his wide eyes.

The rooftop explodes, screams erupting all around us as the fire licks and burns the flesh of everyone standing within range. Nic's sphere gets launched off the rooftop from the force of the blast, tumbling off the side to slam into the ground. The darkness swirls and recedes, showing three very terrified gods within. This is raw power—pure and undiluted in its form.

Eros' grip on my hip tightens and his chest heaves against my palm. I glance up at him, my throat tightening at the ethereal glow in his eyes. His blonde hair shifts in the wind, sparking with flashes of electricity as the power around him cradles him lovingly. He *is* this power. It's not about control and manipulation; it's untethered and a part of him. Who would have thought the simply known god of love was so terrifying and wielded so much power?

"Eros?" I whisper, reaching my hand up to cup his jaw. His rips his gaze from the destruction, his eyes softening when they lock on mine. "It's over."

"He hurt you," he whispers harshly.

Nodding, I brush my thumb against his lips. He parts them and his warm breath caresses my skin. Bits of electricity slide against my skin, but there is no pain from it, just heat and a feeling of familiarity. "You didn't have to come for me."

He frowns. "Of course I did. I wasn't letting him take you from me, Venessa. I—" His throat bobs on a heavy swallow and he dips his head down, resting his forehead against mine. "I love you."

"Do you?" I whisper, feeling the heat of his breath brushing against my lips.

"Yes. The thought of losing you tore at my heart. I was desperate and delirious to get to you—to save you." He pulls back enough to stare at me, cupping my cheek in his palm. "You can heal."

"Yeah. Leon realized it when he cut me. He was thrilled that he could keep tormenting me over and over." His jaw clenches and pulses, his hand ripping away from me and shooting out behind me. I sigh at the loud explosion behind me and glance back to see the building blown into something completely unrecognizable. "Was that necessary?" I sigh.

"I wish the stupid fuck would come back to life so I could kill him again for hurting you."

I smile, my chest swelling at how deranged but adorable he's being. This beautiful god is mine and he came for me. He protected me and saved me, no matter how much I tried to push him away. My fingers trail back, gripping into his nape to bring him closer to me. I nip at his lip, darting my tongue out to taste him and he groans, parting his mouth as he slams it against mine.

The kiss is feral and all consuming, the electric current rippling off of him, seeping into my body and warming me from the inside out. I moan into his mouth tugging and pulling at his hair while he shifts his arm back around me, squeezing me to him.

"You guys okay?!"

Eros growls against my mouth, diving his tongue in, plunging it so deep I feel like he's literally devouring me. The peanut gallery down below starts hooting and hollering, and I can't help but smile against Eros' lips as his kiss becomes more aggressive.

He rips away from me, glaring down at them all smiling up at us. "Will you shut up!"

"Get a room!" Jackson laughs.

"I swear I'm going to murder them," he grumbles.

"No, you won't," I laugh. "They're your family and they love you."

"You're my family, too," he says quickly, hugging me tightly against his chest while he begins his decent.

CHAPTER SIXTY-FIVE

EROS

I'm still trying to wrap my head around what happened. She's here. She's safely tucked away in my arms, but it feels like a fever dream. I only had one thought running through my mind when I launched myself off that roof—save her.

I didn't care what happened to me or what awaited me at the bottom, all I cared about was protecting her at all costs. I don't know what was different this time around, both times following the same pattern, but each having completely different results. I never knew I had this much power at my disposal, but I've never been pushed to the breaking point emotionally and mentally.

My feet hit the ground, but I don't release Venessa, much to her dismay. The others rush towards us, their eyes wide and enamoured by the monstrous wings flexing behind me.

"Damn, that's fucking cool!" Jackson laughs, darting in behind me to get a better look.

"You've been holding out on us," Ikelos grins.

I shake my head. "I swear I had no idea this was even a possibility. I've never felt this kind of power before." I hold up my hand, staring at the flickers of electricity moving across my skin as I flex and curl my fingers. "I don't know what happened."

Ikelos smacks my shoulder hard enough that I stumble sideways, barely holding onto Venessa. I glare at him, but the fucker just smiles wider. "You're in love." I blink, tilting my head in confusion. "This is what the gods have been trying to figure out. My brother doesn't believe it, and they're all still digging into other possibilities. My powers increased exponentially because of my connection to Mckenna."

"More like obsession," she mumbles, earning a glare and an eye roll from him.

"Whatever you want to call it," he huffs. "You're like us," he says, holding his arms out wide with his chest up, as though filled with pride. "Welcome to the family."

"Wait...I thought I already *was* part of your family."

"I mean, you were...are...fuck. Okay. I just mean you're *more* like us because you understand the feelings inside of you now and you've allowed them to take root. You're stronger now, Eros. Even if your body is weakened and you can blead, your abilities are more than you could ever dream of. This is your true self, not the watered-down version you were before. Your belief in the fact you couldn't feel love is what weakened you and kept you stagnant in your abilities."

I look past him to the burning mansion smelling of cedar, flesh, and blood. None of this would have happened if that stupid fuck would have just left her alone. We wouldn't have been hurt, and I wouldn't have lost my home, but I also wouldn't have found *her*. If Venessa weren't on the run, she would have never sought out the position I was offering, and I wouldn't have found my other half. I know it in my heart, she's mine. She's always been mine. Like a spirit that has wandered the ether until finally finding its one true home.

Her small hand rubs against my chest, drawing my attention down to her. She looks exhausted, her beautiful face covered in dirt and remnants of blood. We've both been through too much these last few days, and I hope that we can finally rest and just enjoy our time together. The light tingling of her power seeps into my skin when she shifts her hand up to cup my cheek.

Who would have known that the beast inside of her would become docile enough to be dormant when she needed it the most. That's one of my goals after everything; to teach her how to control it and draw on that power when it's needed. It could have saved her today, but it at least bought her enough time for me to get to her.

"How are you feeling?" I ask her, hating how tired my own voice sounds.

"Happy." That surprises me enough that she smiles at my expression. "I mean, I'm sore and tired and a bit depressed, but I'm happy you're here. I'm happy you came for me."

"You were going to sacrifice yourself again," I say, running my hand through her ruined hair.

She touches it self-consciously, dropping her eyes to my chest. "I didn't want you throwing your freedom away because of me. I figured if I were no longer in the picture, you could fight your way out of it and finally end Leon and escape."

"I wasn't leaving you, Venessa. No matter what would have happened, I wouldn't have left you. I would have fallen once more with you because I only wish to be by your side. I would have cradled your fall and risked every bone in my body being shatter if it meant you were safe."

I wish she would finally realize what she means to me and how much her existence has threaded itself into my own. The thought of her no longer existing is painful and nothing but a dark void in my bleak life. She's brought light into my life with her resilience and sassy attitude, and I wouldn't have it any other way.

"What now? You've lost everything because of me," she whispers.

I hug her to me, letting my warmth seep into her chilled body. "I didn't lose everything. The one thing that was the most important to me is in my arms and safe. Everything else is material things, Venessa. Things that can be bought and rebuilt, but a life is precious and irreplaceable." I pull back to look down at her, hating that she just continues to stare at my chest. She gasps when I grip her jaw and force her gaze up to meet mine. "Will you stay with me? Will you live your life now? Live it free and without fear? Will you allow me to be a part of that life?"

Tears well in her eyes, brimming her lashes until they fall through and cascade down her cheeks. "You still want me after everything?"

"I do…because I love you."

EPILOGUE

VENESSA

"Mrs. Knight?" I glance up from my desk, lifting a brow at how nervous my assistant is in the doorway. "Uh, we have a bit of a situation on the club floor."

"What kind of situation?"

"There are a few guests that are refusing to leave."

I sigh, pushing back from my desk and carefully smoothing my shirt back down over my pants. "Where's Eros?"

"He's on the main floor trying to deal with it but he asked me to come and get you."

We slide into the elevator, and her nervousness seems to be getting worse as the floors tick by. "I'm not sure what he expects me to do in this situation. He's more capable than I am, and he can call security."

"I'm just following orders," she murmurs.

It's been a year since the building burned down, but with Mckenna's connections and Eros' money, they were able to rebuild Cupid's Hollow quick enough. In that time, things have been a whirlwind of emotions, tears, and joy. He proposed to me a few months into our official relationship, not wanting to go another day without officially calling me his. Not that a ring is necessary for that. I've been his since the first day he claimed me, but he's a hopeless romantic and still completely new to love and everything that goes along with it.

It's amazing to see how much his personality has changed, the way the hardness in his features softened over time. More so when he looks at me, and that makes me unbelievably happy. Even now, I still get butterflies in my stomach with the way he looks at me. Like I'm the best thing in the world.

The door to the elevator opens and I freeze, confusion washing over me when dead silence greets me. "Holly, what—"

"Surprise!"

I jolt back when a horde of people jump out from every nook and cranny, the lights flaring to life to reveal a full house filled with people I know and people I don't. Mckenna and Addison rush towards me, huge smiles on their faces.

"Happy birthday!" They say in unison.

I blink, staring at them in shock. "How did you—"

"Jackson dug into your personal info since you didn't include it in your application. Why didn't you tell us?"

"I—" How the fuck do I explain to them that I never make it a point of telling anyone my birthday for the simple reason I was never in one place long enough for anyone to care. I've never had a real birthday party, let alone anyone who remembered or got me gifts, but here they are, each holding out bags to me. "I've never celebrated," I whisper, hating to admit that to them.

They both frown, glancing at each other before shoving the bags towards me. "Come on," Mckenna says, looping her arm through mine and leading me through the crowd. They part, letting us pass with kind smiles and small waves. We stop a few feet away from Jackson and Nic who are holding a massive cake between them. Their smiles are blinding as the set it down on the table behind them. "Go on," Mckenna urges, giving me a light shove towards them.

I can't help but glance around, subtly trying to see the one person I expected to be here but isn't. I'm trying not to cry, both with the overwhelming emotions at the fact they threw me a birthday party, and the feeling of disappointment settling into my gut.

"Happy birthday, Venessa," Nic smiles.

"Thank you."

"Make a wish and blow out your candles," Jackson adds, practically bouncing with excitement. "The cake is really good." I quirk a brow. "...not that I tasted it or anything."

I laugh at his antics, appreciating the way he easily cheers me up with his natural personality. Closing my eyes, I try to think of something I could possibly want when I already have everything I need. Anything I would have wished for in the past has come true, like my silent prayers had finally been answered because of an actual god. That's all I want. Him. Forever.

Everyone claps and cheers when the flames go out, a smile plastered to my face while Jackson and Nic get to work cutting and handing out the cake. Nic slides a plate in front of me and crouches down, tilting his head curiously. "What did you wish for?"

"If I tell you, it won't come true."

His eyes drift behind me and light up. I startle when warms presses against my scalp and lean back the second it pulls away. My heart stops for a second, my eyes transfixed on the man leaning over me with nothing but love and kindness in his amber eyes.

"Hello, beautiful. Happy birthday."

"You're here."

He leans down again to kiss my forehead. God, I love it when he does that. It's something so simple, but it makes me feel special and seen. "I wouldn't miss it for the world," he whispers, kissing my nose. He comes around the side of the couch and sits down next to me, setting a box in my lap. It's beautifully wrapped, the black paper gleaming in the light. "I wish you would have told me yourself, but I understand why you didn't."

I move to open it, but Addison clears her throat. "Open mine and Jackson's first." I narrow my eyes, but she just laughs, leaning into Jackson's side with a smile on her face. I pull out the tissue paper. Okay, this is getting weird.

"A bathing suit?" I ask carefully, pulling out a cute two-piece suit. It's cute, but a strange gift from the couple. A few more things are hidden beneath it. A pair of sunglasses and flip flops. "Thank you?"

"Open ours next," Mckenna says, sitting on the arm of the couch with Nic hovering behind her. He settles his hand on her shoulder, and she glances up at him lovingly.

I cautiously pull out the tissue paper in this one, anticipating something even weirder, like lingerie or something, and sure enough. "Seriously?" I sigh. "I'm not pulling this out."

Mckenna giggles and Nic rolls his eyes before snapping his attention to Eros beside me. "What? I had nothing to do with picking that out," he snorts. I pull out a bottle of lube and handcuffs, making him laugh. "Now, that was me."

"Seriously, I'm going to kill you," Eros grumbles.

"You'll thank me later," he chuckles.

"Now mine," he whispers against my cheek. A shiver slips up my spine, and the gentle caress of his words has me leaning into him as I unwrap his gift. I freeze, my hands trembling over the picture frame nestled in between the tissue paper.

"I—I don't understand."

"I had Jackson dig as deep as he could and we found this. It's your parents, Venessa, and that's you." I carefully pull it out, lifting it closer to my face and studying the photo. "You were about two there. Your father was a doctor, and your mother was a humanitarian. She helped people all over the world. Once he dug far enough, a bunch of information popped up. Jeremy and Harper Scott."

"I don't know what to say." I brush my fingertips against the glass, taking in my mother's features, which are a lot like mine. "Thank you for this." Tears fall onto the glass, and I quickly wipe them from my eyes, hating how easily I broke at seeing something so simple but so meaningful.

"I wanted you to see this because you can clearly see how much they loved you. You were *loved*, Venessa. From the moment you were born, your parents adored you. You were everything to them and they took you everywhere with them. There are news articles on them up until their passing. They lost track of you once you were put into the system, but this is who you are."

My parents loved me. I had hoped and dreamed of knowing about them—of the people they were before they died. I still dream of what my life would have been like if they were still here in my life. I can't be upset with the way things turned out, even if I wish they were here. If things didn't happen the way they did, I may have never met Eros. I would have known what I was from the beginning and I would have had control, but would I have found happiness in the end?

"This is more than I could have ever asked for," I say quietly, gently placing the picture frame back in the box.

"When you're ready, I can show you everything we found on them and their life up until their passing." He cradles my head, pulling me towards him to kiss my temple. "There's one more thing in there."

I was too focused on the photo to even check if he put anything else in there, but now that I look, I see the edge of an envelope tucked under everything. He takes the box from me, setting it on the table while I open the envelope. I blink, frowning. "I don't understand."

"We never got a proper honeymoon. With everything going on and the rush to get the club up and running again, I sort of allowed it to be put on the backburner."

"I told you I didn't need anything extravagant." This explains the random gifts from the others. The little fuckers knew the entire time and kept it hidden from me. They kept *everything* hidden from me, including this surprise party.

"I know you did, and this is one of the many reasons I love you so much. It doesn't take much to make you happy, but I want to take you away for a little while so we can enjoy ourselves, alone." He emphasizes the last word, glaring towards Nic and Jackson.

"Don't start with the attitude or we'll rescind our offer to hold the fort while you're gone."

"I'm beginning to regret agreeing to it for the simple fact you'll treat it like a party house."

Nic grins, brushing his disheveled hair back from his face. “Who are you kidding?” He snorts. “We both know we already treat it that way. We should go to Vegas at some point, too. All of us. We can all party all night long.”

Eros shakes his head, draping his arm across my shoulders. “What do you say, my little butterfly? Are you ready to spread your wings?”

“Paris?”

“The city of love. I think it’s quite fitting, don’t you?”

I smile, cupping his cheek in my palm. “City of love with the god of love. I can’t think of anything more perfect.” I press my lips to his, feeling my heart swell with immeasurable joy at the life I get to live now, in peace thanks to him and the family that I’ve fallen into. Everything happens for a reason, and you have to be strong enough to endure the hardships in order to find the joy and light at the edge of that darkness. Eros is my light, my home, and my future.

The next book in the series is available now for pre-order. A new god, a new life, a whole new set of problems, but you haven't seen the last of Ikelos, Mckenna, Addison, and Jackson.

Releasing April 17th.

TIME

A PARANORMAL DARK ROMANCE

BOOK 4 IN THE FORGOTTEN GODS SERIES.

www.ingramcontent.com/pod-product-compliance
Lightning Source LLC
LaVergne TN
LVHW041054080826
845145LV00007B/1576